Jayne Denker's books:

"Love the story! Five stars!" **WITHDRAWN**
—*Sandra's Book Club*

"Definitely a light read that is great for summer! There were some scenes that made me laugh, some that made me swoon, and a few that made me want to cry – the author did a great job of giving me feels ;)"
—*The Slanted Bookshelf*

"I would recommend...to romance readers who want to be entertained enormously, and feel that heart squeeze only great main characters can give you. Four stars!"
—*Harlequin Junkie Reviews*

BOOKS BY JAYNE DENKER

Your New Best Friend

Marsden Novels:
Down On Love
Picture This
Lucky For You

Other works:
Unscripted
By Design

YOUR NEW BEST FRIEND

Jayne Denker

For my son—all the love now, all the royalties later

ACKNOWLEDGMENTS

Where would I be without these rock stars? Not here, that's for sure.

Super-duper agent Jordy Albert, for hooking me up with...

Gemma Halliday Publishing, for taking a chance on an up-and-coming five-year veteran of the chick lit writing world, and for hooking me up with...

Editor Gwen Hayes, for her oh-so-wise and insightful advice.

Viola Estrella of Estrella Designs, for the cover art I've always dreamed of.

Chick lit authors Glynis Astie, Tracie Banister, and Tracy Krimmer (and Jordy again!) for reading early drafts of *Your New Best Friend,* even though they weren't anywhere near mean enough with their critiques. Love these ladies!

Tracie Banister (again), because she demanded a beach scene with a "wet, shirtless Conn," and I could not refuse.

My mother, who can't manage to wrap her mind around the publishing process but fakes it really well.

Mike Decker, for generously allowing me to use the details of his Appendix Saga. By including him in this list, I can say, "Look! You're in another one of my books!" (Happy now?)

CHAPTER ONE

———

"Melanie Abbott is in the house!"

"I'll alert the media. And don't say you're 'in the house' ever again. It's just wrong."

Ooh, somebody sounds cranky. I let the door to the coffeehouse swing shut behind me. The place immediately reverts to its standard half-gloom, an arty kind of light, and a relief from the bright May sunshine outside. I cross the wide, pegged planks of the two-hundred-year-old floor, familiar with every odd dip and rise, and push against the wooden counter.

"It's three o'clock," I say lightly.

As if my friend Conn, the owner, needs reminding that I show up at this time every day. He barely glances up from the papers spread in front of him, and I twist the upper half of my body to get a peek. All I can tell is they look financial before he sweeps everything up into a neat stack.

"Get away. Nosy."

I've seen that expression before, many times. It's a cross between a can't-you-see-I'm-busy scowl and a half grin that assures me he's not actually in a bad mood. Okay, if he wants to be all secretive, that's fine. I'll get it out of him later. For now, I strike a pose, a bright smile on my face. My arrival, after all, is the highlight of his day.

Or not.

He ignores me.

At least he pretends to. Then, not missing a beat, he puts down his pen, stuffs the papers under the bar, and reaches for a small white cup to make my usual triple espresso.

"Aw, you do love me."

He shoots me a glare from under the ledge of his eyebrows but says nothing, then focuses on skillfully and smoothly grinding the beans, packing the grounds, and finessing the temperamental machine that's held pride of place behind the counter since Deep Brew C opened three years ago.

"Haven't you heard that bartenders are supposed to be chatty?"

Deep Brew C is also a bar and restaurant with an environmentally conscious bent, so Conn wears several hats: manager, barista, bartender, host, herb garden pruner, rainwater collector, compost turner, and recycler. I don't know a whole lot about organic, locally sourced, farm-to-table (and ocean-to-table) practices, but there must be something to it because the food is phenomenal, at least in my opinion. DBC has everything I need—coffee, food, and drink—which makes it my second-favorite place in the world. My own home comes in first, and that's only because I can wear pajamas and ditch my bra there. If I didn't care about proper dining attire, I'd live here instead.

Still Conn says nothing, just to be contrary. I know darn right well he can talk up a storm when he feels like it. I fill the gap, shouting over the gurgling sound of the espresso maker. "Hey, I had the weirdest dream last night." I wait. The noise dies away, but he doesn't ask for details. I end up watching the broad expanse of his back as he pares a bit of lemon rind. I clear my throat, subtly. Nothing. I clear my throat a little less subtly.

"Coming down with a cold?" How the guy's voice can be smooth and rumbly all at the same time is a mystery, but there it is.

"Oh, good. You're still able to talk. I thought maybe Harvey had taken the whole cat-got-your-tongue thing literally."

"Harvey's too old to make that kind of an effort, and you know it." He turns around with a genuine smile. Even a mention of his geriatric feline best bud gets him all mushy. The softie.

"Do you want to hear about my dream or not?"

"Not."

"So okay," I charge on. I knew he'd say no. I was going to tell him anyway. "I was late getting to this party, right?"

"Accurate so far."

"Quit it. It was at my dad's house, but it didn't look like my dad's house." I pause as Conn's head drops to his shoulder, his eyes close, and he starts snoring. "Are you going to listen to this or not?"

"I already said not. Nobody wants to hear somebody else's dream. They're always boring, and they never make any sense."

Mine is no exception, I realize. At least I'm not going to be able to explain it easily—how the party was crowded with everyone in town (a couple thousand, many of whom I actually know, at least by sight), but I couldn't manage to engage anyone in conversation. How bereft I felt when people started leaving but I had to stay. How I got lost in the dozens of rooms I didn't recognize. It wasn't the events, but the weird feeling the dream gave me, the mood it put me in that lingered even after I woke and put in most of a full day's work, that's still compelling me to decipher it. I know Conn could offer some insight…if he were interested.

"Would you change your mind if I said you were in it?"

Conn raises one eyebrow as he slides the espresso toward me, a curlicue of bright yellow lemon rind standing out against the white of the cup. "Depends on what I was doing in this dream of yours."

I make a face at the innuendo. "You were there at the party. And so was George the mail carrier, and Chelsea who runs the daycare, and—"

"Okay, Dorothy, I get the idea."

"Oh—and there was a creepy doll room. I mean wall-to-wall, floor-to-ceiling bug-eyed antique dolls."

"You do know the connection between dreams and the dreamer's mental state, right?"

I adjust my bag on my shoulder and pick up my drink. Conn holds out one large hand, palm up, and flicks his fingertips in an expectant gesture.

"Put it on my tab."

"Your tab rivals the national debt."

"You know I'm good for it." His hand is still out. "What?"

"Tip?"

"Use SPF 45 or higher."

I head for my usual seat, a wingback chair by the hearth. Then I hear it: a voice. Coming from my chair. *My* chair. A woman, on the phone. Well, I hope she's on the phone, because there's nobody else in the place. Then we'd have more of an issue than the fact that she doesn't know enough *not to sit in my chair.*

Really, this is unheard of. I gawp at Conn, shocked. He just grins, the bastard, and shrugs. As if this were no big deal. But it so clearly is.

Do something! I mouth to him.

"Hey, it isn't the *Friends* couch. It's not automatically reserved for you."

"Yes it is," I say, incredulous, then add belatedly, "unofficially." Sure, when the summer people get here in a few weeks, all bets are off. The place will be packed with pie-eyed tourists who don't know the rules, habits, traditions of our Massachusetts seaside town. But till then, that's my seat.

"Too bad. She's a paying customer. You, on the other hand…" he says, glancing significantly at the espresso-on-credit I'm holding.

"You could have *steered her* to another seat," I hiss.

Conn snorts and starts wiping down the bar. "Sit someplace else, blondie. It won't kill you."

I can't even fathom this. "What? Where?"

"The other chair?"

There is indeed a second wingback chair opposite mine. But it won't do. It faces the large, sixteen-paned mullioned window looking out on the main road. "The sun gets in my eyes."

"Oh, for God's sake. Here," he says, gesturing to one of the bar stools. "Sit, and I will admire your beautiful face."

It's my turn to snort. "Don't get all sentimental on me, now." Guess it's up to me to right this ship. I come up on the woman quietly and peek around the wing of the chair, a painfully fake-feeling smile plastered on my face. "Excuse me."

She jumps a mile, turning to me with a shocked look, and I immediately feel terrible. Almost terrible enough to let her stay there, but not quite.

"Yes?" she whispers.

She's about my age, maybe a little younger, but dressed older, in tan pants and a beige and pink striped tailored shirt. Everything about her, from her wardrobe choice to her freckles to her skin to her hair that extends out from her hair band in every direction, is some variation of light brown. She does have a phone tucked under her curls, held up to her left ear. Thank goodness. Not crazy.

"Sorry to disturb you, but...I'm afraid you're in my seat."

Her (tan) eyebrows converge above her thin nose. Her eyes are also light brown. I want to buy her turquoise contacts to break up the monotony. "What?"

"My seat," I repeat. "You're in it."

After staring at me for a second, frozen, she bursts into a flurry of motion, putting her phone away and frantically gathering up her things scattered at her feet—(brown) purse, some sort of (tan) messenger bag, short (beige) trench coat. She stands and stares forlornly at her mug and small plate, unsure how to bus her dishes.

Now I feel like a complete turd.

"Oh, hey, no," I backpedal. "No, don't get upset. I'm sorry. You stay right where you are—"

Her eyes brimming with tears, she stumbles out the door and rushes past the window, possessions clutched to her chest and head bowed.

I'm not sure what just happened.

"Way to run off my customers, Abbott."

Conn's close behind me, his substantial arms crossed, a dishcloth dangling from one hand.

"I didn't mean to," I protest. "She was *not* exactly normal."

"And you weren't exactly the epitome of graciousness." He glances at my espresso, still in my hand, now uselessly tepid. "New one?"

Handing over the cup, I mutter, "I don't feel like it."

Then I'm out of the shop as well, heading in the opposite direction from Miss Beige.

CHAPTER TWO

———

"Stupid Garvey," I mutter as I fling myself onto my couch, my phone clamped to my ear. I've already changed into flannel pajama bottoms, fuzzy socks, and a cami. I'm in for the night, even though it's only late afternoon.

"Connacht Garvey is a lot of things, but he's not stupid," says the familiar voice of my bestie, Taylor.

I sit up straighter, surprised to get the real Taylor and not her voicemail. "Oh! You're there!"

"I'm always there for you, babe."

"Give or take a hundred and fifty miles."

"Don't be picky."

She's right. I'm thrilled Taylor is so busy—and happy—with her new broker's job in Provincetown, which she started a couple of months ago. It was a great opportunity, and there was no question she should take it, but it isn't the same around here without her, especially at the real estate office. It's tough to go from seeing her almost 24/7 to hoping to catch her by phone or text a couple of times a week.

"What did he do this time?" she demands, prepared for another round of my favorite pastime, complaining about Conn.

"Nothing," I answer with a sigh. I can't bad-mouth Conn—not this time, anyway. I was a jerk to that poor girl this afternoon. His witnessing it, however, made it so much worse. "He was just...*there*, doing his judgy thing. I hate it when I screw up in front of him and he looks at me with his disappointed-parent face."

"Tell him to stuff it. He's not your parent."

Not even close. Conn is only a little older than I am—five years and four months, to be precise—yet he's got that older-and-wiser thing down to a science. "Yeah, well, he acts old enough to be my grandfather."

"Your grandfather was never judgy. Neither is your dad, for that matter."

True. My father is much more forgiving...too much, sometimes. He probably wouldn't have batted an eyelash at my behavior today. He probably would have blamed Miss Beige for the whole thing.

He'd have been wrong.

I'm not proud of the way I acted. I've been brought up quite properly, and I have a reputation to uphold. My family, the Abbotts, own this town, and that's not just a figure of speech. It is called Abbott's Bay, after all, thanks to some Puritan ancestor whose first order of business in the New World was to stake claims all over a prime piece of the future Commonwealth of Massachusetts. We own far less of the town these days, but our chunk is still significant, and our history gives me a certain standing in the community.

"Conn is the antidote to my indulgent relatives. Always has been."

The Garveys have lived in Abbott's Bay for ages—not nearly as long as the Abbotts, but then again not many families have—and our lives have always been entwined. In other words, Connacht Garvey, all-around good guy and pride of Abbott's Bay, has plagued my existence for almost the entirety of my nearly thirty years.

The years Abbott's Bay was Connacht-free, first when he was at Harvard getting his BA and MBA then when he spent several years in Seattle, were the most peaceful of my life. Also the most boring, if I'm going to be honest, but if anyone asks, I'll deny it.

Taylor laughs. "Hey, he hasn't had to do any Melanie-shaming in quite a while. You're great."

I flinch. That's not entirely true—as illustrated by today's little adventure—but I don't want to discuss it. "Tell me about all the sales you're making on the Cape."

Taylor takes the bait. We spend the next several hours talking shop, and it's almost like she's back in Abbott's Bay.

* * *

Right. New day, better Melanie. I have resolved to get back in my groove and not let Conn get me down. In fact, I've decided to get some DBC coffee on the way to work. It's a beautiful day, the town is already bustling, and I've managed to get out the door early enough.

I've greeted half a dozen people on the street, including police officer Pauline who's already writing a ticket—what with all the tiny, twisting lanes of our historic district, parking violations are a goldmine—and gourmet grocery owner Henry, who's prettying up the fresh fruit displays on the sidewalk, when I spot Miss Beige headed straight for me. What a perfect opportunity to redeem myself.

She draws closer, and I try to smile in an encouraging, friendly way. *I'm really an all-right person! Let me prove it to you!* When she spots me, her eyes widen in alarm. She drops her gaze to the pavement, rocks back and forth a little as though she can't decide which way to turn, and spins around to go back the way she came. She's not getting away that easily though. I have amends to make, dammit, and I'm going to make them. I lunge forward and grab her elbow.

"Hey! Hi!" Whoa, *way* too high-pitched and perky. I dial it back. "Um, I guess you remember me. Deep Brew C yesterday afternoon?" Still saucer-eyed, she nods. I take a breath. "Look, I'm sorry about…you know. I was totally out of line, and I didn't mean to upset you. Forgive me?" I beg with my best smile.

I feel her arm relax in my grip—oh God, I'm still clutching her elbow. That won't help matters. When I let go of her, she finally smiles back.

"I'm not a loony tune. I promise. I mean, Conn can vouch for me." We're standing near the coffeehouse, and fortunately he opens the door at just this moment, broom in hand. He really does sweep the sidewalk each morning, like a character in a Disney movie. All he needs is the full-length white apron. "Right, Conn? I'm completely normal. Tell the girl."

"Good morning to you too." He leans on his broom, studying me as though he's never really thought about my state of mind before, then declares to the woman, quite definitively, "Melanie here is completely unhinged."

"Thanks a bunch."

He grins and starts sweeping. "I'm kidding. She's fine. A little high strung at times…"

"Could have stopped a few words back."

"Are you here for coffee or to jack up my stress level as early as possible?"

"I have to choose?"

He lets out the agonized sigh of a long-suffering martyr and jerks his chin at the interior as he goes back to sweeping. "Beebs can help you out."

The line is fairly long, but everyone in the restaurant at this time of day is on his or her way to somewhere else, getting their coffee and pastries to go, so by the time Conn's deputy barista hands over our orders, the place is mostly empty. I gesture to the wingback chairs.

Miss Beige seems hesitant to sit in the seat I scared her out of yesterday, but I pointedly take the other one, so she finally settles in. When Conn comes back inside, I tilt my head toward my coffee companion. *See? Making friends!* He rolls his eyes, and his casually dismissive wave labels me as irresistibly incorrigible. I can work with irresistibly incorrigible. I'd add adorable to it, but it's enough for now.

Amends made all the way around. Good.

I turn to the woman opposite me. First order of business: name. I can't keep thinking of her as Miss Beige.

"I'm Melanie Abbott, by the way."

"Hannah Clement."

"It's nice to meet you." I give her yet another encouraging smile, determined to put her at ease, but she's still fidgeting, breaking crumbly pieces off her vanilla almond scone. I try again. "You're not from around here, are you? I mean, Abbott's Bay isn't all that big. I can always spot a newcomer. Are you here for the summer?"

And all of a sudden Hannah's eyes are brimming with tears again. What the…?

I put my coffee cup on the small table between the chairs before I drop it. "Did I say something—?"

"No, no." She fumbles around in her bag for a tissue, finds one, and dabs under her eyes. "I'm sorry. It's just…I'm going through…something."

"I'd never have guessed."

She puffs out a wry laugh and wipes at her tears more vigorously. "I'm sorry," she says again.

"Honey? Stop apologizing." She looks up at me, startled. "If you're going through something, then own it. Let me guess: you…broke up with your boyfriend, and you're hiding from the world for the summer, licking your wounds, regrouping, reassessing."

My apparent accuracy startles her enough that she stops crying. "S-sort of," she stammers.

"Which part did I get wrong? Boyfriend? Hiding out for the summer? Reassessing?"

"Well…"

Her chirping cell phone interrupts, and she scrambles for it immediately. The ex? A broken engagement, even? Hannah looks like a textbook example of a woman who's had the rug pulled out from under her—she's even kind of dust bunny/lint-y, if you know what I mean, like everything in her life exploded around her and she's still walking around in a daze, trying to figure out what happened.

"Sorry, I—" She blushes a little at my silent reprimand delivered by raised eyebrow. "I need to take this."

Deciding to give her some space, I drain my cup and go back to the counter for a refill, where Conn's filling some large carafes with different blends to last the rest of the morning.

"How's it going over there?" he asks while he works. "Making a new friend?"

"Please."

"What's the problem?"

Leaning in, I whisper, "She's kind of weird."

Conn gives me a loaded look, communicating something to do with a pot and a kettle.

"I refuse to be judged by a guy in a leather vest."

"What's wrong with my vest?" He looks down, fingering the edging by the buttonholes lovingly.

"Are you kidding? You look like you skipped out on your shift at the Salem pirate museum."

"Talk about judgy."

"Hey, fashion says a lot. She's all beige, and I'm getting the distinct impression she's the same on the inside."

"You've talked to her for all of five minutes. Why don't you go back over there and find out more about her before you write her off?" At my skeptical look, he adds, "You were the one who said I need to make bartender-type conversation."

"I didn't mean psychoanalyze *me*. Just...coffee me. It's all you're allowed to do."

"Yeah, yeah..." he mutters, pulling my cup toward him.

I glance over my shoulder. Hannah is still on the phone, and she seems more agitated than ever. I drink my second cup at the bar and venture back over.

"Why can't you...I know, but..." I shouldn't be listening, I know, but I can't help it. She sounds so upset. "I need...I understand. I do. But isn't it your *job* to...?" Muffled talk drifts from her phone. "Okay. Okay, I get it."

When Hannah notices me picking up my things, I say softly, "I have to go."

"Thank you for the coffee," she whispers back, teary again.

"Are you okay? Is that the boyfriend?"

She shakes her head. "It's..." Then her attention is captured by the person on the phone. "I understand your point," she says. "I don't happen to *like* it."

I'm impressed with that little bit of fire there. Happy that she seems to be more contentious and less soppy, I leave the coffeehouse and walk to work, only a little bit late.

CHAPTER THREE

"Abbott! Get in here!"

That familiar bellow doesn't make me move any faster. Sauntering through the office, I nod at one of my fellow agents, the birdlike, skittish Laura, who's flinching at every shout from the inner office and flapping at me frantically, urging me to obey my summons. At the risk of giving her a heart attack, I stop by my desk first, drop my bags, and turn on my computer. I catch a baleful glare from another agent, gorgon Maude, but I'm used to it. She hates me just because I'm...well, me. Because I have the mixed privilege/curse of calling the boss...

"Daddy. Good morning," I say cheerfully when I lean in his office doorway a minute or two later.

"You're late."

"You know I'm always working, even when I'm not in the office."

"Close the door."

"Charles, are you firing me?"

My father is standing behind his desk. He hardly ever sits. Hitching up his pants over his slight potbelly and smoothing down his silver hair, he mutters distractedly, "Funny. Anybody ever tell you you're funny? Come here a second."

Oh God, not this again. I sigh and round the desk. He's tipping his neck at a weird angle and pulling down his shirt collar at the back.

"See that?"

"What am I looking at?" I'm up on my toes and squinting, even though I know I'm not going to actually see anything.

"Does it look strange to you?"

"What, an elderly man—"

"Watch it."

"A *mature* man asking his daughter to diagnose some strange mark on his neck?"

"So you do see it!"

I don't, actually. "All I see is a mole that's been there as far back as I can remember."

"It feels lumpy now. Does it look lumpy? Does it look different?"

I poke at it halfheartedly. The tiny, pale thing looks absolutely no different, and feels no different, than it ever has. "It's fine, Dad. I swear."

"I don't like it."

"You're not dying. But if it bothers you so much, call your doctor."

"That quack."

"She is *not* a quack," I say patiently. "And you're going to have to see her eventually."

Dr. Graeling is a highly skilled professional with a degree from Columbia. However, she's also new in town and pretty young. Add in the fact that she took over the practice from Roger, my dad's golfing buddy who retired and moved to Key West, and my father's firmly in the NMWMB camp: Not Messing With My Body.

"I'm not letting some...*child*...poke at my body and give me candy pills for some life-threatening illness. I'm not having it."

"You're a pain in my neck, Daddy."

"Like this tumor!"

At the risk of sounding way too Schwarzenegger-like, I sigh, "It's *not* a tumor, and you're *not* dying, but you *are* driving me nuts. Now, did you just call me in here to conduct a spot check on your nonexistent moles?"

"Of course not. It's that time of year. Gotta get cracking."

I groan and drop into the chair in front of his desk. "Come on, Charles—"

"We've only got a few months till the election."

"You're the incumbent."

"Even so."

"And you're running unopposed."

"Makes no difference. I still want this town to know who I am."

"They *do* know who you are. Your name is on the *Welcome to* sign and the *Now leaving, come again* sign and almost every sign in between. If they don't know who you are after you've been an assemblyman for four—"

"Six."

"Six years, then there's no hope for them."

"We have to schedule some appearances."

I sigh heavily. My dad doesn't take no for an answer. No need to wonder where I get the trait. "Why me?"

"Because. You're my girl."

Oh, not fair, playing the "dearest daughter" card this early in our semi-yearly tussle over his political ambitions and my role in them. At least the town's election season tends to be shorter than most, and we've navigated it so frequently that his campaign practically runs itself. This year should be no different from two years ago: I make a few calls, I schedule some appearances, I get his butt on a Fourth of July parade float, and bam, he's back in office.

"Besides," he adds, with the winning smile that's gotten him elected to three terms already, "you do this so well."

I sigh again, stand up, and head for the door. "I've got work to do."

"I knew you'd do it for your old dad."

"I mean houses to sell, places to rent. You know—the moneymakers?"

"Buyers and renters will always be there. The campaign season is now!"

"But I have bills to pay. Since you're still aboveground, I can't tap my inheritance just yet."

"Cruel girl."

"Love you, Daddy."

I'm not making an excuse to leave his office—I do have work to do. I'm a damn good real estate agent, and I never coast because my father owns the place, no matter what Maude thinks. Although I'm a little behind on my commissions, my slump won't last long. The summer season's about to start—if you listen closely, you can hear the Porsches and Audis in the distance, revving their engines, waiting for the signal to invade our gorgeous North Shore town.

Abbott's Bay really is beautiful, and I'm not just saying that because the place bears my family's name. It has oceanfront, bayside, fishing, farmland, shopping, the arts, and a picturesque historic town center that's crazy-popular with the tourists. The super-wealthy think nothing of dropping obscene amounts of money to get a little piece of heaven for the entire summer, and I'm the perfect agent to find them the perfect place.

When the summer people come calling, it's a frenzied rush for a while, and then, once everyone who's in need of a dwelling for the season gets four walls and a roof, things slow *way* down. Giving me plenty of time to work on my father's campaign. Of course I will, because no matter how much I gripe about it, he's still my dad.

Right now though, I need more clients. As if on cue, someone enters the office. Maude's head snaps up at the sound of the door opening, but she's going to be denied this prospective client, not only because I need one, but because of who, exactly, just walked in.

"Hannah!" I exclaim, charging the length of the office before Maude's even out of her chair. "What brings you here?"

As usual Hannah gets her deer-in-the-headlights look and shrinks back a little as she glances from me to Laura to Maude, becomes alarmed at Maude's feral we-got-a-live-one look (she really needs to tone that down), and looks back to me. It's obvious she sees me as the least offensive choice, if not the least predatory.

"Well," she says softly, "I'm looking for a place in Abbott's Bay."

"You are? Why didn't you say so earlier?" I put my arm around her to lead her toward my desk.

"I didn't know you were a real estate agent. The nice man at the coffeehouse told me you could help."

"Conn?" As I get Hannah settled in my guest chair and move my phone aside, I notice there's a text from him: *Incoming. Sending you a client. BE NICE!* "He's right—I can find you the perfect place. Now, what are we talking? Purchase? Rental? A few weeks? All summer? Longer?"

Hannah's expression starts to show little flickers of her recurring panic. "I'm…not sure."

"Oh?" I've had plenty of indecisive clients, but their indecision tends to run more along the lines of oceanfront or bayside, number of bedrooms, whether they need a place that comes with a gardener and housekeeper/cook, and what's more important: walk-in closets or deluge showerheads or maybe they should hold out till they find a place with both. I don't understand why she doesn't know what she needs for the foreseeable future, but I can talk her through it. "Okay," I say slowly. "Tell me what's going on in your life, and we'll figure it out together."

* * *

"…I just don't know what to *do*. What do you think?"

You know the saying "opening the floodgates"? I thought I understood what it meant, and I even thought I'd experienced it many times. That was before I asked Hannah what's going on in her life.

Yikes.

The bad news: girl's had a lot of drama recently—so much that it made my head spin—and it's amazing she's still standing. The good news: she's actually an okay person. Nice. I think she's best experienced in small doses, mind, yet she's still here an hour later, staring at me with an earnest look on her face, as though I've got the answers to all her problems but I'm holding out on her.

I am now well acquainted with the following Hannah Clement-related information:

—She decided to come to Abbott's Bay because she has some hazy memory of vacationing here when she was little. Apparently it's a fond memory, even if she can't recall specific details.

—She has come into a bit of money but for a heartbreaking reason—she recently lost her mother. Her father died when she was a teenager, so now she's an orphan, she says, because even if you're twenty-six, you're still an orphan when both your parents are dead. I can't really argue.

—She recently broke up with her boyfriend. I wanted to high-five myself for guessing it early on, but she was so upset I sat on my hands instead. I'm not really sure who broke up with whom or why, because whatever she said was garbled by strangled hiccupping sobs. I'll get the details later.

—She has decided to take the summer to "find herself," whatever that means. She admitted she doesn't quite know what it entails either. So she wasn't being coy—she really has no idea how long she's staying.

All I wanted to know was what type of property she's interested in.

"So? What should I do?"

Hannah is asking me for life advice? When we just met? Crazy. Plus she told me the stressed phone conversations I witnessed yesterday and this morning weren't with her ex but her therapist. She shouldn't need *me* to dispense some heavy dose of wisdom. Then again, she did express a certain amount of…*unhappiness* with her chosen professional. I believe she called her a "waste of money," which surprised me. It was the first time I've seen her get really irate, besides the time she snapped at the woman on the phone.

"Do?" I stammer. "Do about what?"

"Everything! I need to get my head on straight, don't I?" she asks, then answers her own question. "I do."

"Okay, hold on. I'm a real estate agent," I say slowly and clearly, making sure she's paying attention. "I can help you find a darling rental that'll be the perfect home base for you to conduct your soul searching. I might even be able to find you something right on the beach…er, maybe beach access. But I'll get you close to the water so you can take long walks by the ocean, watch the sunrise, whatever you need to, um, get your head on straight, like you said. After that, it's all up to you."

"But—"

My text alert pings, and I lunge for my phone. "I'm sorry, honey. I have to take care of this," I say after I read my message. "How about if we meet up later, and I can show you some houses? Sound good?"

She agrees, and I hustle her out of the office with the suggestion that she visit the cute boutiques nearby. I give her a minute to get down the block and around the corner then head out of the town center, down the beach road.

CHAPTER FOUR

"What's going on? What do you need?"

"What are you doing here?" Conn asks, baffled, as I let myself into his house and close the door behind me.

"You texted me."

"I asked if we could meet *sometime*. I didn't say right now."

"No time like the present."

"Uh-huh. How did you know I was home?"

As if I don't know his schedule. "The breakfast crowd has died down, the lunch rush hasn't started, and because it's Wednesday, you're here to give Harvey his every-other-day potassium supplements with his second breakfast. Obviously." I toss my purse and my portfolio onto the couch and look around. "I see things haven't changed around here. Pity."

"I *know*," he says. "You've been telling me that for years."

"It's been true for years. And what's that smell?"

"There is no smell, and you know it. I clean."

He's right. There is no smell. But it stinks in here all the same—of wasted potential. A property worth millions, and he's bringing down the value by keeping the shag carpeting, the cheesy plywood paneling, and that nasty-ass plaid couch. The marketer in me is weeping salty tears of frustration. "Do you realize how great this house could look with a little bit of updating?"

"It was good enough for my parents."

"This was all new when they moved in. In *1978*. Now it's not even retro kitsch trendy. It's just *tired*. And way, *way* too plaid. Oh, the things I would do to this place…"

Crossing to me and leaning in like he's got the best

secret in the world, he says, "Well, maybe now's your chance."

"What do you mean?" I squint at him suspiciously. He's way too close. Not that it's a bad thing. Conn Garvey is a six-foot-two hunk of he-man whose looks can knock women over at twenty paces. He's always had that effect. Not on *me*, you understand, but others. Lots and lots of others. Still, I can appreciate his attractiveness in a detached way, the same way I can admire a painting in a museum without wanting to run off with it and hang it in my living room.

He purses his lips, and I'm distracted by trying to figure out whether or not I like his new scruff. Honey-colored, with a hint of copper glinting on his chin, dusting his jawline and circling his lips. I wouldn't call it a beard quite yet, but it's getting there. I wonder how long he's going to let it go, and what it'll look like when...oh. He's said something.

"Sorry...can you repeat that?"

Conn draws back and shoots me an amused smirk. "Pay attention, Abbott. This is your big chance."

"For...?"

He drops into the leather recliner near the picture window. Mid to late twentieth century décor might be back in style lately, but not all the trends from the era were exactly wonderful. I put picture windows in that category. Why anyone would have a giant window that doesn't open looking out over the ocean is beyond me.

Conn's cat Harvey appears from out of nowhere and leaps onto his lap. He pets the geriatric longhair gray feline absently as he says, "I officially give you permission to get this place in shape. So you can list it."

"What?"

"I want you to sell the house."

I sink onto the couch. The coarse plaid fabric tickles the back of my knees. "Conn, no!" I whisper, horrified.

"Melanie, yes! You sell houses, so...make it happen."

"But...it's your home!"

"Come on. It's just a house."

"It is not *just* a house!" I can hear my voice getting more strident, but I can't manage to tone it down. "It's...it's...been your family's home for years!" Unmoved, he just looks at me, a small patient smile on his lips. I try a different tack. "It's beachfront in Abbott's Bay! You don't throw a place like this away!"

"I'm not. I'm asking you to sell it. Usually that means I get cash, and—may I remind you—so do you."

This is unheard of. Conn is breaking the unwritten code of Abbott's Bay lifers. Generations-old Abbott's Bay families know the value of their properties and would sooner die than give up their homes and land. I've seen residents with family histories that go back centuries flat-out refuse to sell to high-powered millionaires waving obscene amounts of cash in their faces, because you can't put a price on heritage.

Conn takes a breath and tries again, leaning forward while taking care not to displace the cat, as though he can get through to me if he gets a few inches closer. "It's okay, M," he says, using the intimate abbreviation of my name only he can get away with. "It's no big deal. My parents gave me this house and trust me to do what's best. I've decided selling is best."

I hesitate. Conn isn't an impulsive guy. He must have a plan, a reason for selling the house. Maybe he's going to use the money to buy—or possibly build—a nicer one. After all, this place *is* pretty damn ugly, outside as well as in. A squatty, angular, unpleasant-looking thing, its value comes from, as that hoary old real estate meme goes, "location, location, location." I wouldn't be surprised if whoever eventually buys it knocks it down and builds something better in its place.

But I don't *want* anyone else to buy it, whether they knock it down or not. Homely as the place is, it figured prominently in our childhood, with birthday parties and barbecues and other get-togethers here as far back as I can remember. I don't want Conn to sell those memories. I can't for the life of me understand what could be more important than keeping his family's house.

"Melanie," he says, "you're the best agent in town."

He's blatantly trying to butter me up. I'll let him, for now. "Damn right I am."

"We've known each other forever. I know I can trust you."

"Of course—always."

"So you'll do it?"

Reluctantly I whisper, "No."

I know what's coming next. Conn will either argue with me until the fishing boats come in for the night, or he'll turn on the charm. I can argue back, no problem—I've done it a million times before, from fighting over whether I was safe or out in a game of kickball to whether I've had too much caffeine (just the other day, in fact), and I can do it again. As for his charms, I'm immune. Comes from knowing pretty much everything there is to know about him...not to mention having seen him with chicken pox. That mental image neutralizes charm—let me assure you.

He sits back again, watching me thoughtfully while absently stroking his proto-beard. I'm fascinated by the movement of his hand. It's soothing. Like watching a cobra sway.

Finally he strikes. "Never mind. It's okay. I mean, I figured you'd be better than Eric—"

"Eric the Red?" I snap. He's pitting me against my coworker—the company's most cutthroat, albeit most unreliable, agent—and I'm falling for it. Dammit. "He'd set a ridiculous asking price and run off every potential buyer who made an offer even a hair under it."

"He does play hardball. Laura, then?"

"Our little weirdo who hasn't sold a house in three years? You do realize my father keeps her on staff with a base salary out of pity, right?"

"Then I'll call Maude."

A bridge too far. "Don't you dare."

"Well, who else am I going to go with? That's everybody in the office, unless I can talk your dad into taking listings again, which he won't. Should I go to Prime One?"

Ugh, the real estate agency with the stupid redundant name. He can't be serious. Everybody knows they survive on our castoffs. Abbott Realty is the only real game in town.

"Look," he continues, obviously struggling to remain patient, "I'm selling the house whether you're in or not. What's it going to take to convince you?"

I check my watch. "Buy me lunch." At the sight of his

triumphant grin, I add, "That is *not* a yes. I'm just hungry."

Conn doesn't actually join me for lunch, of course. He's much too busy. The only time I'll see him is when he brings my food to my table. While I wait for my order, I bookmark different properties I think Hannah would like. Then I text her to let her know I'm ready when she is.

Deep Brew C is hopping for a weekday. Another group of people come in, blinking with the change of light from the bright sunshine outside, and Conn directs them to an empty table. He gathers up some menus for them as I see Ornette, the cook, put my food on the counter. I decide to help Conn out—mainly because I'm too famished to wait—and I get it myself.

"Hey!" Conn appears beside me and slaps my hand as I reach for a few extra napkins. "Quit that."

"Quit what?"

"The giant clump of napkins. Do you plan on bathing in the salad dressing or what?"

"What's the big deal?"

"Napkins don't grow on trees, you know."

"They kinda do, actually."

"You know what I mean. Put 'em back."

"Okay, okay. Sheesh."

I do as I'm told, but as soon as his back is turned, I sneak two or three and carry them back to the table under my plate. I realize paying attention to the number of napkins handed out is all part of DBC's sustainability practices, but come on. Whoever heard of a restaurant owner denying his customers napkins? Good thing he doesn't serve barbecue.

There's a text from Hannah waiting for me. I stuff a piece of lemon-and-herb grilled chicken into my mouth as I unlock my phone with my other hand. She's eager to look at houses too. Good. I tell her to meet me here in half an hour.

She's staying at The Windward B&B, which is practically on top of Deep Brew C, so I'm not surprised when she shows up twenty-eight minutes and fifteen seconds later. I'm still rooting around in my salad for the last bits of chicken and slivered almonds, so I gesture for her to have a seat while I finish.

"Conn has the best food. Have you had anything here

besides his coffee? Because if you haven't, you should."

"Not yet," she says, slipping into the chair opposite mine. "This place looks really popular though."

"Oh, you have no idea. Wait till you see it during the tourist season. Crazy. You'll have to do at least three different wrestling takedowns to get to the counter for coffee in the morning."

"Well, if you find me a place with a good kitchen, I'll be making my own."

"I like your optimism. I promise the place you rent will have a good kitchen. Maybe even a gourmet kitchen."

I fire up my tablet and show her the different properties I have in mind, getting *oohs* for some and uncertain pinchy-face reactions for others. Fair enough. I can filter. I am here to serve. Just like the big guy over there.

"Hey, garçon? Refill?" I waggle my empty iced-tea glass at him. Conn nods and scoops ice cubes into a new glass. "So I'm thinking we start at the top of the list, high-end first..."

Hannah's not listening. Instead, she's resting her chin on her hand, staring at the bar. Or, rather, the figure coming around the end of the bar. "Must be nice to have a hot guy wait on you hand and foot," she murmurs in a dreamy voice.

I snort. "Oh, I pay. I pay dearly."

Just in time for Conn to hear me as he delivers my iced tea. "Funny, I have a running tab that says otherwise."

"Will you get off the tab thing? That's the second time you've mentioned it in two days."

"Because it's still there."

His deadpan game is strong. I can't tell whether he's teasing or actually wants me to pay my bill. I decide to ignore it altogether. "Conn, have you met Hannah Clement? Hannah, this is Conn Garvey."

"We have met," he says, "but not formally." Now he brings out his best, brightest smile for Hannah. "Welcome to Abbott's Bay."

"Conn short for Connor?" she asks, shaking the hand he extends, her cheeks going pink.

"Connacht, actually. Family name."

"That's very different."

"Just like its owner," I mutter.

"That's enough out of you, before I throw an apron on you and make you work off your outstanding balance. Don't think I won't do it."

Hannah and I watch him walk away. I'm rolling my eyes while Hannah barely blinks, she's so captivated by his backside. I scoop up my belongings and push my chair back.

"What do you say we find you a house?"

CHAPTER FIVE

"Ugh. Beer me."

Conn laughs and continues to rinse out some glasses. "Since when do you self-medicate with alcohol?"

"Since I started taking Hannah house hunting."

"Find anything?"

"If we did, would I be begging you for booze in the middle of the afternoon?"

"You seriously want a beer?"

I actually consider it. But then I deflate, collapse onto the nearest bar stool, and sigh, "No, not really."

"Triple espresso then."

"It is that time of day."

After Conn makes my coffee, he rests his elbows on the bar and studies me for a moment. In a somber tone, he asks, "Do you want to talk about it?"

He sounds so serious that for a second I almost buy it. I squeeze the lemon rind over the cup, watching the spritz zing the tan foam, and mutter with a smile, "Shut up."

"No, no—I really want to hear all about it."

"You do, do you?" I take a sip of my espresso and contemplate which story I should regale him with. Maybe I should give him the entire rundown so he can get the full House Hunting with Hannah experience.

The problem isn't that she's super picky, which is too bad—I can handle super picky. When you cater to millionaires, you learn how to field some crazy demands. You know—they'd *love* to rent the beach house for six weeks, if only they could move a wall or two, rip up the entire lawn, and put in fresh sod…and a pool. I can make it happen, can't I? Or they want the refrigerator restocked by invisible elves every day. For free, of course.

That isn't what I'm faced with this time. Hannah is the opposite of super picky. She wanted to take *all* the houses I showed her. Like Dory, she was newly delighted every time we walked through the door of another one. Each house was "it"...until she saw the next place. Rinse, repeat. All day.

Eventually I suggested, if she liked them all, it was simply a matter of...oh, I don't know...*picking one.* Any one. Eenie meenie miney mo. She'd decide on one and would be ready to sign, but then she'd think back to a previous house. Maybe it was better. One house had the best views. Oh, but the first one was so charming. Wait. What about the place that looked like it belonged in *Architectural Digest*? No, maybe that one was too fancy...

On and on. And on. And on.

"I showed her the Miller place."

"Ooh, that's a stunner," Conn says.

Bless him. He gets me. "Right? But she wouldn't even consider it. 'Belongs to a family,' she said."

"Well, yeah, but they're selling it."

"Hannah got all sentimental and said it looked like the kind of place where children should be running around. And...and grandparents should be chastely embracing by the fire pit while Mom and Dad serve up s'mores. Whatever tourism ad started running in her head."

"Okay, she didn't feel at home there. No big deal. Did you show her the A-frame on the spit?"

"Ski resort."

"Huh?"

"She says it belongs in the mountains, not on the beach. Out of the running."

"Cripes, sell her mine."

"Stop it."

"I'm serious. Rent to own. If she wants it after the summer's up, she can keep it. Everybody wins."

"I told you, I'm not selling your house."

Conn holds an invisible phone up to his ear. "Hi, Maude? Got some business for you."

I slap his hand away. He grins at me and starts fitting

printouts of the dinner specials into the menus.

"Anything good tonight?"

"Please. I've got something good *every* night."

"Okay, whoever told you that? She lied." Conn snorts as I pick up one of the small squares of paper from the stack. There are noticeably fewer options and no dessert specials at all. "Going a little short lately?"

He shrugs. "I don't want to overwork Ornette, you know?"

"Ornette likes coming up with the specials. He lives for it."

"Yeah, but there's such a thing as too many choices. Why do you care, anyway? You'll still get your meatloaf."

"You know I always order the scallops," I fire back lightly, even as my stomach twists.

I don't know why this change in routine bothers me, but it does. Like something's off-kilter. I just can't put my finger on what, exactly. And then it hits me.

"The napkins!"

Bugging his eyes at me in a *spot the loony* sort of way, he whispers, "What about the napkins? Are they talking to you again?"

Conn tried to keep me from taking what he suddenly considered to be too many. Now he's cutting corners on the menu and nagging me about my outstanding bill and even wants to sell his house…

"Are you in trouble?" I blurt out.

I've always assumed Deep Brew C is making a nice profit because it has a steady stream of customers, but it could be going under for all I know. Conn's behavior certainly makes it look like that's the case.

"What?" Even though he punctuates his question with an astounded laugh, I'm still suspicious.

"If this place is…I mean, if you're having trouble, just say so. Do you need money?"

Uh-oh. His brow lowers like a storm cloud, darkening his blue-green eyes. I've overstepped. But I can't seem to stop talking. It happens sometimes.

"Not…not charity or anything," I stammer. "A loan. Do

you need a...a little bit to get you over the hump? Till the summer people get here? Is that what's going on?"

And the giant, foot-thick, studded-metal, bulletproof door of Conn's private affairs slams shut in my face. He looks down and stuffs another specials list into another menu. "Everything's fine, Melanie."

His voice is hard. If I know what's good for me, I'll back away now. But so very often, even when I do know what's good for me, I choose to ignore it. This is one of those times. Unfortunately. "I'm just saying..."

"*Stop* saying. Okay? Mind your own business."

Ouch.

Annoyance radiating from him, Conn doesn't look up again. That gets me to stop talking, finally, and I back away a couple of steps. Keeping one eye on him, I scoop up my purse from the floor, root around in it, find a pen, scribble out a check, and gingerly slide it across the bar. I feel like I'm feeding the lions at the zoo, and my hand could be bitten off at any second.

"Paying my tab," I whisper.

As I turn away, I catch a glimpse of a smile—a tiny one—as Conn shakes his head disbelievingly.

* * *

"'Lo."

The cell phone slides off my head and hits me on the side of my nose, waking me up a little bit more. I have no idea what time it is. Dark o'clock. I fumble with the thing, cursing its slipperiness, while a muffled voice says something unintelligible.

"Wait, wait," I say a little more clearly. "Hannah? What's going on? Has the B&B burned down?"

There's a pause on the other end of the line. "No," she says, sounding puzzled. "Why?"

"Because you're calling me in the middle of the night."

"It's 11:30."

"Like I said."

"I'm sorry! I thought you'd be up."

Her voice is throaty, and her nose sounds plugged. She

may have caught a cold since I saw her several hours ago, but I doubt it. Those are tears. I push myself up a little, stuffing one of my pillows behind my shoulders. "What's going on?"

"You know what? It's nothing. Go back to sleep."

"Hannah, I'm awake now. Don't waste my good will."

"Can we go for a walk?"

"I beg your pardon?"

"A walk. Can we?"

"*No*, we can't go for a walk. It's the middle of the—"

"I just got off the phone with Marty."

Oh. Her ex. I swipe my hand across my bleary eyes and groan. "Give me five minutes. I'll meet you out front of the B&B."

Five and a half minutes later, we're walking the nearly deserted streets of the town center. I've always loved the cramped, uneven, brick-paved historic district, with its gas streetlamps and tiny shops all crowded in on one another, like a little American Hogsmeade. I feel like we should be wearing black robes instead of yoga pants and hoodies.

"He wanted to see if I was okay," Hannah murmurs.

"He *wanted*," I correct her, "to check up on you."

"That's what I said."

"There's a difference. He was checking to make sure you're still devastated and not, you know, dating someone else already."

"Oh, Marty wouldn't do that. He still loves me."

I can't stifle the indelicate snort that bursts out of me. "Sure. Okay."

"You think he doesn't?"

"I'm sure he cares, in his way. But men are territorial by nature. If he's finished with you, it doesn't mean he's okay with somebody else having you."

"You make me sound like leftover Chinese food."

I shrug. If the cardboard carton fits…

"Marty's not like that."

"So he broke up with you…why? Wanted to 'take a break'? Get some space? Do his own thing because he's 'too young to be tied down yet but let's revisit this in a few months or a year'?"

Hannah stops walking and stares at me, wide-eyed. "No! He asked me to marry him!"

I did not see that coming. "Well, what happened?"

Her head droops, and she starts shuffling forward again. "I...couldn't decide."

Shocker.

"Okay then," I say, catching up to her with one long stride. "If you had any doubts, you were right to not say yes."

"But I *wanted* to marry him!" she wails.

"Then why *didn't* you?" I wail back.

All I get is a shrug. We turn a corner by the darkened candy shop, and I suddenly wish I had a glass cutter with me—one pane of the window removed, silently and stealthily, with minimal damage, and I could reach in and grab the multicolored lollipop that's calling to me from the lower shelf of Macomb's display.

Eventually Hannah whispers, "I wish I were more like you."

Dragging my attention away from the siren song of the lollipop, I laugh and say, "The only person you should want to be is you."

"But you always know what to do! You never hesitate. About anything. Ever!"

"That's not entirely true." But it isn't entirely *untrue* either. What can I say? I always know what I want. Like the lollipop. Which I'll probably buy tomorrow when I don't need to worry about where to find a glass cutter.

"I'll bet when you get proposed to, you won't have even one doubt."

"Probably not, but since nothing like that is happening in the near future, I don't have to worry about it."

"Oh, I don't know." She flashes me a small smile and starts walking again. "I figured Conn would be getting around to it pretty soon."

I'm rooted in place, flabbergasted. "What in the world are you *talking* about?"

"You. And Conn. Perfect proposal, perfect wedding, perfect marriage. It's so obvious."

I close the gap between us, grasp her by the upper arms,

and look her in the eye to make sure she absorbs what I'm about to say next. "Hannah. Conn and I are *not* together."

Her pale eyebrows come together in a peak over her nose. "Sure you are."

"I swear to you, we're not. He's just an old family friend. He always has been."

Hannah chews on this for a moment, mutters, "Huh," and wanders off.

"Hey—"

"Where does this go?" she asks suddenly.

I want her to repeat back to me that she understands the situation between me and Conn—or rather, that there isn't one— but she's come upon one of the most picturesque streets in Abbott's Bay, a narrow lane that's barely a legitimate street by modern standards.

"Down to the beach, eventually."

"It's cute."

That's an understatement. South End Close is lined with tall, narrow houses butted right up against the sidewalks, giving the impression they're leaning over to gossip with the ones on the opposite side of the road. Some sport artfully-weather-beaten-to-dove-gray clapboards. The rest are painted dark brown or a muted blue or even, in some cases, the near black you can only seem to get away with in old seaside towns like this one. Almost all of them have bright flowers in their window boxes and in large, painted ceramic pots on their front stoops.

She's already halfway down the sidewalk, looking from one side of the street to the other, eventually stopping in front of a familiar dwelling. "Melanie, this house is for rent. There's a sign in the window."

"I know."

"Why didn't you show it to me before? It's adorable."

"No, it isn't. It's small. And it backs up to the shopping district. Believe me, once the tourists got here, you wouldn't be able to hear yourself think."

"I don't know. This street seems pretty peaceful to me."

"But the house isn't big and airy and on the beach, like you want."

"Who said I want big and airy and on the beach?"

"Everybody wants big and airy and on the beach!"

"Beach air makes my hair frizzy. Can you get us in to look at it first thing tomorrow? I really want to, Melanie. Please."

Wow, she expressed herself decisively. I can't shoot her down now. "What time is it?"

She checks her phone. "Midnight."

"Really?"

"One minute past, to be exact. Why does it matter?"

With a sigh, I climb the front steps. "Because it's apparently first thing in the morning, now."

Hannah gapes as I punch in the code on the lock box hanging on the door and pull out a key. "How did you…? Are you psychic?"

Dear God. I should be in bed—asleep, comfortable, oblivious. Instead I'm showing houses in downtown Abbott's Bay at midnight. "No, crazy person. My dad owns the house."

"Why didn't you show it to me before?"

"My dad owns the house," I repeat. That *is* the explanation. Hannah doesn't get it, so I add, "I love my dad, but you don't want him as your landlord. Trust me."

"Is it the money—?"

"No, it's…you know what? Never mind. Let's take a look around."

I push open the front door and step inside to turn on the lights. Hannah walks past me into the narrow entryway, taking in the ornate ceiling, hardwood floors, plaster walls, and elaborate trim around the doorways. I've seen that look before: she's a goner. Totally hooked. The place could have four feet of water in the basement and a colony of fruit bats living in the bedroom closet, and she'd take it. For the record, this house has neither. It's actually quite nice, if you like small spaces. Hannah apparently does. She dashes through the rest of the rooms, upstairs, downstairs. When she returns to me, the look on her face only confirms what I already know.

"You want it, don't you?"

Hannah nods eagerly, eyes shining.

"Well when it's right, it's right. Congratulations on knowing what you want."

"In houses, anyway."

"You mean 'if only you applied this kind of decisiveness to the Marty situation'?"

Hannah nods again, her eagerness subsiding. She stares at the blank fireplace, saying nothing.

"Oh, come on." I try desperately to jolly her out of her sudden funk. "Today a rental, tomorrow the world! Get yourself a backbone, woman—I know it's in there somewhere."

"I know. But...I screwed up things with Marty, maybe for good. I feel like I'm...hopeless. Am I hopeless, Melanie? What should I do?"

"You have *got* to stop asking me that."

"I *really* need advice."

"Not from me, you don't."

"But...you're so...put together! And confident! And...I don't know...you seem to know what to do in any situation."

"Well," I demur, "that may be true, but all this is your business! Well, yours and your therapist's. Why don't you give her a call in the morning?"

"I think I'm going to fire Dr. McCrory. She never actually gives me advice. She says all she should do is help me come to my own conclusions. I get that, but don't we all need someone to point us in the right direction sometimes? I know a lot of people who would pay good money for *that*." She slumps against the wall and heaves a sigh. "I wish I had someone to tell me the *truth*, even if it's ugly. Like...'Hannah. Babe. That color does *not* work with your complexion.' Or 'Nut up and leave that no-good idiot in your past.' You know, like you do."

"Hannah. Babe. What you're describing is called a *friend*."

She smiles warmly. "That's what I need."

I smile back in spite of myself. "Okay. You've got one of those." Over her chipper little "yay," I add, "And if you want frank talk about colors and complexions, I can tell you right now you have *way* too much beige in your wardrobe. It washes you right out."

"Oh." I'm afraid she's going to be upset, but she just nods. "It's my funky skin tone. When you have parents of different races, sometimes you have a gorgeous, rich color, but mine ended up kind of...weak."

"I think you should stop calling yourself weak anything. Your skin tone is unique, not funky. Wearing the right colors will make all the difference in the world, so when it's daylight, we're going shopping."

"Oh, shopping! That's the perfect friend thing. What's your hourly rate?"

"A professional friend? Interesting business prospect. I'm not sure about fees yet. I'll have to assess the market."

CHAPTER SIX

————

I slap down the rental agreement on my father's desk the next morning, drawing his attention away from his WebMD research on suspicious rashes. "South End Close, rented."

He glances at the paper then goes back to Hypochondriacs "R" Us. "I don't see a signature."

"Hannah's coming in later to sign and get the keys. Then I'm going to help her move in."

"I didn't know we were such a full-service agency."

"She's a friend of mine."

Dad looks at me curiously. "Hannah? Am I supposed to know you know a Hannah?"

"She's new in town."

"Well, then I'm looking forward to meeting her. She'll make a good tenant?"

"A very good tenant. Don't terrorize her."

"Me?" My dad draws back, shocked—shocked!—that I would dare suggest such a thing.

"You can be a little…particular."

"Don't stereotype."

"It's got nothing to do with your sexual orientation, old man, and you know it. I'm talking about you being type A. Just leave the poor girl alone. Trust her to keep her bathtub scrubbed, her front stoop clear, and the backyard tidy, and don't…do what you did last time."

"I was perfectly within my rights. I didn't enter the home without prior permission from the tenant."

"Peering in the window was not a fair tradeoff."

"How was I supposed to know the woman had a tendency to do nude yoga in her living room?" he roars.

"Well, she did. One downward dog later, and you were practically a resident of the Graybar Hotel."

"I was more traumatized than she was," he sniffs.

"*Trust*," I admonish him. "Stop worrying about your precious properties. Focus on your reelection campaign. Or try to reconcile with Jerome."

"I'm not interested," Dad says, entirely unconvincingly. "I have you," he adds, patting my hand affectionately.

Great. He and his boyfriend have been broken up for three months, leaving Dad with *way* too much time on his hands, which makes him do suspect things like stalk tenants and google his latest imaginary affliction. I refrain from rolling my eyes as I take the contract off his desk.

"Reelection campaign," I repeat, not sure he heard me the first time, because he hasn't looked up from his computer. "Focus."

"I could say the same to you. How about my platform?"

"'Chickens reclining in a sunbeam on a gleaming oak floor and a kitten in every pot.' There."

"Will you take this seriously, please?"

"You first." He waves me away, but I hang back in the doorway. "Um, Dad?"

"Hm?"

"Did you know Conn wants to sell his house?"

"Mm."

"Is that a yes?"

"He may have mentioned something about it when I ran into him the other day. Says you won't list it."

"Of course not! It's the Garvey homestead!"

"What have I always told you? There's no room for sentimentality in real estate."

"I'm not being sentimental." ...Much. "I just think he's making a mistake."

Finally my dad looks at me over his monitor. "Do what the client says. Ignore your history with him."

"What's that supposed to mean?"

"Touchy. It means you two pretty much grew up together, so you have...*feelings*."

"Dad!"

"What? I *meant* you have feelings for the house. Conn too, eh?"

"Okay, I think we're done here."

"You were the one who brought it up."

"And I deeply regret it."

While I wait for Hannah, I work on my dad's campaign schedule. It's not too hard: I check his agenda from two years ago and update it with the new dates and times for the same old functions—the Memorial Day parade, the Fourth of July parade, the Labor Day parade. In between we've got the town carnival, the arts and crafts festival, the Symphony on the Pier, the town-wide flea market, and the Up All Night festival where all the businesses in the historic district stay open, well, all night. With the summer portion of the schedule filled, I relax. It'll tide Dad over for a while.

When Hannah arrives, I introduce her to Laura, expecting afraid-of-her-shadow Bates to barely make a peep, but within minutes they're gabbing away like old friends who haven't seen one another in a year. I don't think Laura said that much to me in the first six months of her employment with Abbott Realty. I have to admit there is something about Hannah that makes you want to open up. She even snookered me, and here I am, her new best friend.

After a while I break up their bonding session and have Hannah sign the lease so we can move her in. She only has some essentials—pretty much whatever would fit in her car—so it doesn't take long to unload her stuff at her new house. Abbott Realty has a storage space full of staging items we use to make a vacant house more appealing. We could spare a sofa and a couple of tables—and certainly a bed—for a few months, so I've arranged to have them delivered. Some suitcases and a few boxes later we're done, with enough time left over to put Hannah's clothes away in the wardrobe. Yep, all beige. Shopping will definitely be on the agenda soon.

First I take Hannah on a walking tour of Abbott's Bay, pointing out the landmarks, best places to eat, and best places to shop. Hannah stops at a lot of gallery windows—we're heavy on the arts and crafts around here—to admire the work on display.

"Do you create or just appreciate?" I ask her, seeing a particular light in her eye that denotes more than a passing interest in the visual arts.

"Oh, I don't know," she says shyly. "I've taken some classes, and my teachers have said I have talent. I was thinking maybe I could work on my painting this summer."

"So I was right? You *are* going to hunker down and lick your wounds, and you need something to focus on, so you don't spend all your time sleeping and eating ice cream by the pint?"

"Is that what I'm supposed to do to get over Marty?" she asks with a laugh. "Become a cliché?"

"I heartily discourage clichés of any kind."

"I'll skip the ice cream binges, then."

"Good choice."

"Wait. Does that mean MooMoo's is out?"

"MooMoo's is never out," I assure her.

On the way to the ice cream stand on the pier, I point out the marina and the glut of houses clustered around the bay to the south, then the landmark lighthouse to the north. In between, on a shallow crescent of beach, lie the most majestic houses in town (and, admittedly, some old crapholes like Conn's), several of which Hannah rejected in favor of an old, narrow townhome built in 1830. Go figure.

Hannah's certainly a puzzle, but as we walk back up toward town, giant ice creams in hand, I sneak a peek at my new friend and note that for the first time since I've met her, she seems genuinely happy—or at least at ease. There's still a bit of sadness in her eyes, but when she's out in the sun, catching drips down the side of her cone, a bit of gravitas works to her advantage. I decide then and there that I enjoyed being roped into being her friend.

Okay, I walked into it willingly. I admit it.

* * *

"I am *never* going to remember all that."

Hannah and I collapse into the wingback chairs at Deep Brew C late in the afternoon, too walked-out and shopped-out to even stop at the counter for a drinks order.

"It's easy," I answer, slipping off my shoes and wiggling my toes. "Always be nice to Pauline so you'll have a better chance of getting out of a parking ticket later. And *never* call her a meter maid. The Little Brown Jug is the best package store in the area. Tell Natasha I sent you, and she'll hook you up with some great wine. Only shop at Henry's Grocery for essentials. Filling your fridge there will require a bank loan. Make the trip to a supermarket outside of town instead. I hear we might be getting a Wegmans soon, but don't mention it to Henry or you'll make him cry. It's his worst nightmare. No, seriously—he actually dreams that a Wegmans comes to town and he's forced to close up shop because they have a better cheese selection than he does. Oh—and speaking of large chains, never, *ever* mention the double-D in this place."

"How dare you."

I knew even a shorthand reference to Dunkin' Donuts would bring Conn around. I beam up at him from my unladylike slouch and flutter my eyelashes. "Sorry, darling."

Before he can read me the riot act, Hannah says in a winsome voice, "Melanie was giving me a list of dos and don'ts for living in Abbott's Bay. Dunkin' Donuts was on the 'don't' list."

Conn's expression clears. "So you're living here now?"

Hannah tells him about her new residence and what we've been up to all day, and he responds enthusiastically. Now that the bear has been sedated, I reach out and touch his wrist.

"Conn, honey, would you be a doll and bring us some coffee? We've been on our feet all day, and we're pooped."

"Really? You're that helpless?" He knows he doesn't have to turn on the charm with me. He's also not falling for my Southern belle impersonation. He doesn't say no, however.

"Please?"

"Good grief."

"Love you!" I call after him sweetly. I turn back to Hannah, only to find her studying me closely.

"Are you *sure* you two—?"

"Completely."

"Not even—?"

"Not even anything. Not a past relationship, not a one-night stand, not an unrequited thingamabob. Nada."

My protests fall on deaf ears, as Hannah's attention is focused on the beautiful ballet Conn performs behind the bar when he's making up drinks. I don't blame her. Stronger women than Hannah have succumbed to the Power of the Conn. I've seen fiercely independent females swoon at the mere sight of his muscular forearms. But if she's still moping about that Marty guy, she doesn't need to complicate matters with a crush.

I drag her attention back by snapping my fingers at her. "Hey now, woman."

"What?"

"Not for you, do you hear me?"

"He's gay, isn't he? The perfect ones always are."

"No, he's not gay. He's broken."

"I am *not* broken!" Conn bellows from across the room. "Stop telling people that!"

I swear he's part bat. The things that man can hear from an alarming distance…it's not natural.

"Mind your own business, Garvey."

He stalks over carrying two cappuccinos. In his hands the enormous mugs look like teacups. He places them on the table between our chairs and grumbles, "How is this not my business when you're gossiping about my private life?"

"I wasn't going to tell her anything everyone doesn't already know," I murmur, picking up my mug and taking a sip.

"You know, not everybody needs to know my personal…"

"Heartbreak?"

"Quit it," he growls.

"Fine." I sigh, rolling my eyes. When his back is turned, I mouth silently to Hannah, *Later.*

"Okay then," Hannah ventures when we're alone once more, "if not Conn, is there some other special someone?"

I raise one eyebrow at her, but I can't maintain the illusion of mystery for long. I answer honestly, "Nope. Nobody."

"Huh." She props one elbow on each armrest, holding her mug under her chin. "That's really surprising."

"Why?"

"You've got everything else in your life. Why not a guy? Or…girl?"

"Your inclusiveness is admirable, but I'm not gay either. Dad's got that covered."

"Wow. Do you have two dads, like Heather's two mommies?"

I know which kids' book she's talking about, but that wasn't my childhood experience. "No. Just one. Mom's not in the picture anymore."

I don't want to get into the drama of my thirteenth year, which was filled with declarations and turmoil and confrontations and tears…and all those were from me. Just kidding. I was a typical freshly minted teenager, at my most self-involved that year, but the drama was coming from all three of us in the house. Once the dust settled, there was me (sad and stunned) and Dad (also sad but relieved) and a big vacant space where Mom had been.

Hannah's waiting quietly for more information, so I give her the executive summary. "Dad's happy. He now has Jerome, an art dealer. Very nice guy. Travels a lot, but he brings great souvenirs when he comes back. Well, they're having a little bit of a rough patch, but I'm sure they'll get through it. Mom's in the Berkshires, working as a stage manager for a theater company. She's happy too."

"What about you?"

"I," I declare with finality, "am fabulous. Simply too busy for a man in my life right now." I decide to turn this into a teaching moment. "Hannah, you're making the mistake of assuming 'having everything' has to include a 'special someone.' When you have a full life, you don't have time to go sniffing around for a guy, trying to shoehorn in someone just because it's expected. That's what this summer should be all about for you." I lean forward, warming to my subject. "Go ahead and wallow and reassess for a while, but by the end of the season, I want to see you independent with a full life all on your own. I want you to be able to stand tall and tell the world you don't *need* a man—not Marty or anybody else. It's not necessary. I mean, look at me! I don't have a man, and I'm fine."

Hannah is less enthusiastic about all this. "Well, sure, but…"

"But nothing! Be independent!" She gets that timid, skittish look, so I dial it back. "But what?"

"Don't you kind of *want* a special someone?"

"Listen to me." I shift in my seat and put on my game face. "You said you admired me. Did you mean that?"

"Yes."

"Then try it my way for a while. Take a break from men. Live your life for you and you alone. Can you do that?"

"I guess."

"A little stronger there, Clement."

"Yes!" she yips. "I can."

"And you will?"

"I…I'll try."

It's a start.

CHAPTER SEVEN

———

Hannah, my new best friend, is a darling, and I love being her mentor as well as her friend. She acts like a sponge, taking in everything I say, which is flattering and a little disconcerting at the same time.

I got my mitts on her wardrobe and finally broke up all the beige with colorful tops and shorts and dresses from the town's trendy boutiques. She even was willing to buy scarves and try a bright peachy-pink straw hat I picked out for her, which looks fabulous with her skin tone. We also revamped her makeup—well, added makeup, as she tended not to wear any at all. More defined eyebrows and some mascara is making all the difference in the world.

I'm sure she's going to turn plenty of heads, but she's obviously still not over Marty. I keep telling her to forget him and not let him keep her on a leash with his periodic calls "just to say hi and see how she's doing." When I lecture her about her ex, Hannah gets kind of quiet, and I can tell she'd rather not be having the conversation. Fine—she doesn't have to agree yet, but she'll see I was right soon enough.

Conn is the first individual with a Y chromosome who goes out of his way to compliment Hannah, which is perfect. She needs acknowledgment that the changes she's making are noticeable and positive, and Conn is the master of being friendly and flirty without tipping into creeper territory. A few days after Hannah has perfected her new look, Conn does an exaggerated double take and looks her up and down.

"Wow, Ms. Clement, I almost didn't recognize you there. You look great!"

Hannah blushes to the roots of her hair but manages to reply pretty smoothly, "It's all thanks to Melanie!"

"You don't say."

When Conn glances over at me, I wave a self-deprecating hand, but I don't deny it. Project Hannah has been sort of time consuming, but it's been rewarding in the long run.

"Going into the personal stylist business on the side, M?"

He doesn't sound too impressed.

"Just helping out a friend," I say with a tight smile.

"Right."

With that one skeptical utterance, he's planted a tiny, niggling seed of doubt, making me wonder if I'm really not that generous. Conn has that effect on me—like he can reach down to the bottom of my soul, find unpleasant traits I turn a blind eye to, pluck them out, and hold them up to the light with a triumphant look on his handsome face. Which I now want to punch. I help plenty of people. I'm known for donating to charities and doing fun runs and organizing…well, all sorts of things. How is this any different?

I'll ignore it. Prove I'm the bigger person. I won't poke the bear. I won't. Must…not…poke…oh, forget it.

"Is there a problem?" I challenge him. "Do you think I *wouldn't* help Hannah?"

"No, no," he protests, hands up in surrender. "Of course you would." Hannah excuses herself to go to the restroom, and as she walks away, he leans down and whispers, "The thing is, I can't help wondering…what's in it for you?"

"Nothing!" I exclaim, drawing back from his warm breath on my ear. "She's my friend. Friends help friends. That's all."

He studies me a moment then mutters, "Okay," before walking away.

When Hannah returns, I drain the last of my coffee and stand up. "Come on," I say, shouldering my purse. Conn is still watching me from across the room as he works, and I'm suddenly ready to go somewhere else—anywhere else, as long as it's away from Connacht Garvey's judgmental eyes. "Let's get your painting supplies."

On the way out I swing closer to the counter, where he's restocking to-go cups, while Hannah goes on ahead. I can't let him have the last word.

"Just what is your problem, exactly?"

"I have no 'problem,'" he answers smoothly. "I do, however, wonder why you're trying to turn Hannah into your Mini-Me. Mini-Mel."

There's no point in his trying to be funny. He's infuriated me too much. In the back of my mind, I know I'm overreacting, but I also know why. Today is not the day to provoke me. It's the worst of the 365 options, to be honest.

"I am not—!"

He braces the heels of his hands on the edge of the bar. "Oh, so it's a coincidence you've been telling her how to act, what to think, and what to wear? I see the difference."

"I'm trying to impart a little class, a little style on the poor girl. And for your information, nimrod, any changes we've been making have been *good*. Haven't you noticed she's stopped crying at the drop of a hat?"

"You're taking credit for that? Impressive. What I want to know is why she's suddenly adopted your style. Hell, the pair of pants she's wearing—"

"Capris," I correct him.

"Whatever. They look exactly like a pair you own, if I'm not mistaken."

"Okay, first of all," I splutter, "you know specific pieces in my *wardrobe*?" He doesn't answer, so I continue brusquely, "And they are absolutely not the same. I tailor my recommendations to what would work for *Hannah*. She could never pull off my look. She's from *Dayton, Ohio*, for God's sake."

"What does *that* have to do with anything?"

"Nothing," I backpedal, realizing I'm sounding like the world's biggest jerk. "I'm sure it's a lovely place. Look…you stick to coffee and leave fashion to me."

"And you," he says, eyeing me significantly, "don't mess with that sweet girl. She's fine the way she is."

"I'm not *messing* with her. She asked me for help, and I'm giving it to her. What's the harm in that? And another thing: where do you get off asking if there's something in it for me? I help plenty of people without expecting anything in return."

"Yeah, but I've never known you to go so far as to hang

out with the peasants."

"How dare you?" My voice is low and heated, fueled by the sudden red-hot lump of rage in my belly. "I am *not* a snob. I'm friendly with all sorts of people. I even joined the library's old fossil book club, for God's sake!"

"So everyone could bask in your astute interpretations and inspired readings of the latest accessible commercial literature…and admire you even more."

"You suck."

"I'm just observing," he says mildly.

"You're judging. And assuming. Like you always do."

"There's precedence, so I'm *pretty* sure my opinion is valid."

"You've got nothing."

"Oh? Remember, I was around when you and Taylor were waging your reign of terror around here."

My mouth falls open in what I'm sure is an unflattering manner. "What 'reign of terror'? There was no—"

"Okay."

"And stop using one-word sentences to shut down a conversation!"

Conn starts to respond when Hannah pokes her head back into the coffeehouse. "Melanie? Are you coming? I got two blocks away before I realized I was talking to myself!"

"Sorry, honey," I say as cheerfully as possible then cut Conn a scathing look. "We're going to buy Hannah some art supplies, if it's all right with you. She needs to do something creative to achieve some peace of mind."

"Is it her idea or yours?"

"Why do you think I always push people into things?"

Conn raises one eyebrow and lets me fill in the blanks. *God*, he's irritating.

"Don't spend too much of her money."

"She's got plenty," I hiss.

"Not as much as you think. Not as much as you. Be careful."

"Didn't we already talk about how you have to start minding your own business and not be judgy?"

"Melanie—"

"Nope." I hold up my hand. "I think you've done enough talking for one day. Stop now, because you're really pissing me off."

When I meet Hannah on the sidewalk, I'm still livid. I'm not out to ruin her or turn her into a "Mini-Mel." Where does Conn come up with this stuff? I'm trying to help her get over a rough patch in her life. I'm sensitive to how it feels to lose a mother. Okay, not to death, but at least when she's removed from your life. I'll do whatever it takes to help her.

"Melanie! Slow down!"

I'm stomping across a side street, my fury at Conn propelling me, and poor Hannah is tottering along behind me, her new wedges not playing nice with the cobbles.

"What's happened? You're upset. Did I say something—?"

"What? No! God, no!" When she catches up to me, I give her a little side-hug as we continue toward the art store. "I'm fine."

"You and Conn were arguing, weren't you?"

"Don't worry about it," I answer breezily. "Happens all the time. He'll get over himself someday."

"But—"

"No, really. I have survived Hurricane Conn many times, honey. This is a mere squall."

Speaking of squalls, I don't know what's gotten into the weather today. It started out promisingly enough, even warm for late May, but by the time we buy Hannah paints and brushes and pads of paper and all the other stuff she needs, clouds have rolled in. Because she and I are relentlessly optimistic, we go to the beach anyway, and she sets up her new easel, cheerfully noting the suddenly blustery weather will make dramatic waves and interesting light.

I settle on a rock nearby and pull out my phone to check my work email. As the wind picks up even more, Hannah stands at her easel defiantly, like a captain at the prow of her ship in a storm. She's really going to make a go of this, I think, while psychically sending a raspberry to Conn. She's trying out her pastels, defining the horizon on her canvas. She looks darn good behind that easel.

And then the easel blows away.

Hannah chases the runaway frame as it tumbles down the beach, and I tackle the rest of her supplies before they make a break for it as well. So it's a bad day for painting a landscape. Big deal. It's a false start, a little bit of bad luck. She can try again tomorrow. Am I mentally arguing with Conn, who I'm now picturing smirking at me with an I-told-you-so look? I certainly hope not. He's not worth it.

We collect all her things just in time. Fat droplets of rain start to fall, punctuated by some unseasonal flashes of lighting. It'll take too long to get back to my house or hers without getting soaked, so I lead her on a new route diagonally across the beach, slogging through the soft sand that's quickly getting saturated with rain.

"Where are we going?" Hannah calls from behind me. "Shouldn't we get away from the water? It's dangerous to be on a beach during a thunderstorm, isn't it?"

It is indeed, but we're almost there. I lead her up some steep wooden steps to a house's wraparound deck. At the side door I tip over an ugly ceramic statue of a frog clutching a flower pot, grope for the hidden key up the amphibian's butt, and unlock the door.

"Oh, this is nice," Hannah exclaims as she drops her easel and tote bag on the kitchen floor.

"You don't have to be polite. It's not mine."

"But I like it! It's homey."

"Homey, homely. Potato, bit of roadkill."

"You don't like it," she says, swiping wet tendrils of hair off her face.

Shrugging, I make my way down the hall to the linen closet and pull out two big beach towels. "It's all right. Could be nicer." I meet Hannah in the living room and toss her one of the towels.

"It 'has potential.' Isn't that what you real estate folks say?"

"There's plenty of potential, absolutely," I agree from under my towel as I try to dry my hair a bit. I pull it down onto my shoulders and look around. "Gut the place to the studs and start over, and you could have something."

"Don't tell me this is a client's house you're selling."

"No. I don't walk right into any of those. I knock first. Usually," I add with a wink.

While Hannah peers out the living room picture window at the storm, I raid the kitchen. The rain is impressive, and I'm not inclined to go anywhere until it passes.

"Snack?" I exit the avocado-countertop, harvest-gold-appliance, walnut-cabinet kitchen of my darkest nightmares carrying a package of Oreos and a bottle of vodka fresh from Conn's freezer.

She's scandalized. "Melanie! It's not even lunchtime!"

"Fine," I groan, putting the vodka on the coffee table and going back into the kitchen for some orange juice and two glasses. "We'll pretend they're mimosas and call the Oreos brunch. Conn will never miss them."

"This is Conn's house?" Hannah frowns as she watches me mix some very pale screwdrivers. I fear she's going to express her disapproval about semi-breaking and entering the Garvey manse, but instead she says, "I don't think Oreos go with orange juice."

"Take it or leave it. I'd suggest keeping the Oreos and drinking the vodka straight, but noooo. You have to mask our sins with orange juice."

Finally she smiles and relaxes. "I'll take my chances." It only takes one bite of an Oreo followed by a sip of screwdriver for her to make a face and give up her cookie. She keeps her drink, however, and stares out the window again. "Wow, look at the sky. I should paint that."

"Or you could finish your drink."

"You corrupt me."

"Good. You could do with some corruption."

Hannah settles into Conn's favorite recliner while I stretch out on the couch. The minute the springs creak in the old chair, a giant gray puffball lands in Hannah's lap.

"Oh! Kitty!" she coos, setting her glass down and going full-on petting machine which, of course, Harvey loves. "She's so fluffy!"

"She's a he. Meet Harvey Garvey."

"Are you named Harvey Garvey?" she asks the cat in a

goofy voice, her newly manicured nails the perfect instruments to tickle his cheeks, which he loves. "Are you? You're so handsome. Yes, you are." Harvey immediately starts purring and leaning in to get more of those good pettings. "So," she ventures, once she's bonded with Harvey, "you feel perfectly comfortable letting yourself into Conn's house and drinking his booze, huh? Does this happen often?"

"Pretty much. This is where Conn grew up, and I've been coming here ever since I was little. Our parents were friends."

"You two were friends as kids? That's so cute."

"Not exactly. When we were young, our five-year age gap felt more like a twenty-year chasm. *Now* we're friends, of course. But back then? It was more like we grew up in the general vicinity of one another."

"What was Conn like as a kid?"

The eager look on her face makes me laugh. "Exactly like he is now, with less facial hair. Too cool for his own good."

"Was he cute?" Hannah leans forward, elbows on her knees, and Harvey, realizing he's lost the new human's attention, jumps down and marches off. Faint crunching sounds come from the kitchen as he has his own midmorning snack.

"See for yourself."

I wave my glass at the hallway that leads to the bedrooms. Hannah jumps up, taking her drink with her. I don't follow her. I know what's on those walls—Conn Garvey's Life in Photos. Her giggle means she's discovered his third-grade picture, when he had more gaps than teeth and a ridiculous bowl-shaped haircut. Then she *oohs*, and I know she's gotten to his football photo. A squeal means she's reached his prom picture with Autumn Rufino, the little tramp. He was too good for her.

"Hey, Melanie?"

"Yep?"

"Why is this space empty?"

"Ah."

I pour myself another drink, and she comes back into the living room, ready for another as well.

Refilling her empty glass, I observe sagely, "You found the Picture Hook of Doom."

"The what?" She laughs as she takes a slug of her fresh

drink, wincing at the strength.

I widen my eyes and do my best horror-movie-narrator voice. "Where the wedding photo used to hang. It is no more."

"He was married?" she squeaks.

"*Was* is definitely the operative word."

"Ohhh," she breathes. "So that's it. What you promised to tell me."

"The saga of What Broke Conn? I suppose you're ready."

The story of Conn's early adult life is simple and complicated at the same time. I make an effort to keep it simple for Hannah, only hitting the highlights: he went off to Harvard for his undergraduate degree and came back with a diploma (simple), an eye for a business career (also simple), and a fiancée. Sasha. Guess what part's complicated.

Hannah's hooked, of course. "Ooh, what was she like?"

I take another large swallow of my drink and study the ugly acoustic-tile drop ceiling. "She was…perfect."

"Looks, or personality, or spirit, or what?"

"All of the above."

"Was she nice?"

Aw, trust Hannah to ask the important question. I try to explain how Sasha was grace personified—impeccable manners, a generous personality—but terrifying. She intimidated the hell out of teenage me. Despite my years of etiquette and comportment classes, I felt like a drunk moose around her. She was a whole different level of aristocracy. Plus she was ridiculously beautiful.

"She was like…this movie star or something. She didn't seem real. All blonde and flawless skin and white teeth and perfect."

"You're blonde with flawless skin and white teeth and perfect."

"No, I'm not," I protest, wondering vaguely if my words are starting to slur. Nah. I finish my second drink and reach for the vodka bottle again, skipping the orange juice this time. It gives me canker sores anyway.

"Have you looked in the mirror lately?" Okay, *Hannah's* words are definitely slurring. I pour her another drink anyway.

"While my hair may be some shade of yellow, it's not enough to make me comparable to Sasha Carlisle. I mean, this girl was tall and willowy and unreal...Grace Kelly. Like that."

"You're—"

"Don't even. I'm solid." There's no denying it. Nobody is ever going to mistake me for a supermodel. Not with my below-average height, not to mention my thighs, souvenirs from my high school and college track team days. Which, by the way, I know better than to try to whittle down to the circumference of my neck, no matter what the latest fashion trend. "Anyway, nobody could compete with Sasha. She always...blew everyone away."

"Including Conn."

"Including Conn. For a while, anyway."

Conn and Sasha only stayed in Abbott's Bay for a short time before going off to spend a year abroad. The naysayers tutted that too much togetherness in foreign places would kill their relationship, but they came back as solid as ever and ready to get married.

After Conn completed his MBA, they set a date for the wedding. Then he and Sasha dropped the biggest bombshell, at least in the eyes of Abbott's Bay residents: they were moving to Seattle after the wedding. Our neighbors couldn't imagine wanting to live anywhere else but Abbott's Bay. But this was Conn and Sasha, so they just nodded, talked about the job market and opportunities in the Pacific Northwest, and didn't question. When Conn and Sasha left, we all waved our hankies, dabbed away proud tears, and said nothing but good things about them after they were gone.

The marriage lasted about six years. When it was over, Conn moved back to Abbott's Bay, disillusioned and bitter. That was his dark period, but after a while, he rose from his own ashes, dusted himself off, and opened the restaurant. I'm really happy for him. Not that he isn't still a little bitter—okay, a lot bitter—about his failed marriage, but it's obvious he's a survivor.

"Huh," is all Hannah says then falls silent, staring off into the distance as the rain hammers the roof and the deck. After a moment she states definitively, "Sorry, I need visuals."

"What?"

"I'm a visual person, so I want to see Sasha."

"You want to go to Zimbabwe? Because I heard that's where she is now. Doctors Without Borders."

"She's a *doctor*? Doing third-world charity work? Jesus."

"Told you. Perfect."

"Social media?"

"She doesn't believe in it."

"She *is* perfect," Hannah breathes. She thinks a moment then declares, "Picture Hook of Doom."

"What about it?"

"Their wedding picture—what did Conn do with it?"

I shrug. "No idea. When Broken Conn moved back in, down came the photo. His parents argued with him because they loved it so much—and they loved Sasha, no matter what happened between her and Conn—but he insisted. He might have had his dad toss it off the deck while he tried his hand at skeet shooting with his old BB gun. Who knows?"

"Conn didn't skeet shoot his wedding picture. He's too nice."

"He's not that nice," I snort into my glass.

"I still think it's around here somewhere. Let's find it."

"You mean go through his stuff?" I'm not necessarily against this. I'm just surprised Hannah is suggesting it.

She's already on her feet, looking around the room, wondering where to start. She also might be hesitating a bit, because helping ourselves to Conn's Oreos is one thing; poking through his stuff is quite another. Looks like I'll have to get the ball rolling.

"You look in the piano bench. I'll take the sideboard."

As Hannah lifts the lid of the seat and sifts through tattered sheet music, she calls, "Does Conn have a girlfriend now?"

"Nope. I told you—he's broken."

"He said he's not."

"He's a guy. What do they know about their own feelings?"

I root through the top drawer of the sideboard and come up with vintage tat: a wall hanging (a macramé owl clutching a real twig in its yarn claws), a bunch of dish towels, and some dusty, abandoned glass ashtrays because hardly anybody smokes anymore, but you can't just throw them away, right? But no wedding photo. I pull open another drawer and shift the neatly folded tablecloths. No photo there. Hannah doesn't have any luck either.

Where else would he hide a framed photo? Kitchen? Doubtful. Well, depending on Conn's mood, maybe the broiler...nah. Not even he would do that. Which only leaves...

We look down the hall toward the shadowy bedrooms then look at each other.

"We can't go through Conn's drawers," Hannah whispers.

"Why not? Plenty of women have tried."

She giggles. "But it sounds like none have succeeded."

"Not since Sasha. Broken, I tell you. Even if the man denies it."

"Do we dare?"

"Hannah, if we do not dare, we have not lived."

CHAPTER EIGHT

———

There's a gap. In my memory. I'm pretty sure certain events have been squeezed out by the vise that is currently shaping my head into a close approximation of a banana. Fortunately the excruciating pain is offset by a wonderful feeling of floating. I'm warm too. I wasn't, but now I am. Plus there are nice smells. Coffee, mostly. Rain. Soap.

I turn my head and press my nose into the fabric of Conn's shirt. He's carrying me. I like it. I'm safe.

I may or may not take a deep breath to smell those wonderful smells again, which prompts him to whisper, "Melanie? You awake?"

I don't want to answer. I just want to be carried, cradled. And do some more sniffing.

Then, "Bitch, you drank all my vodka." His voice is still soft though, and affectionate, and it makes my heart bloom in my chest.

He places me gently on his bed. Starts to back away. Although I've been pretty much limp in his arms up to this moment, suddenly I move like a ninja, despite what it does to my head-vise, which tightens even more, and I grasp his shirt.

"Don't leave me," I whisper.

He hesitates, and I freeze. I can't believe I said that. He kneels down in front of me, smoothing my hair back from my forehead.

"I'm sorry," I mumble. "About earlier."

"Don't apologize. *I'm* sorry. I didn't notice the date."

I don't say anything for a moment. He remembered. I don't think even my father remembered or, if he did, he chose not mention it.

"Did you call her?"

I nod. It makes my head swim. "Got voicemail."

"She'll call you back."

"No."

She hardly ever does. I wonder what my mom's doing on her birthday. Is she sitting home alone, avoiding the world, reflecting on her life? Or is she out with friends, having too much fun to notice her only daughter called? Most likely she's working. It's Saturday—there'll be a show today. Probably two. Yes, I decide, she's so busy working she hasn't had time to call me back.

A realization hits me. "Where's Hannah? She drank your vodka too, you know."

"She's in way better shape. She asked me to check on you—said she tried to move you, but you whacked her."

"I did not." But I may have. Those gaps in my memory.

"Sleep it off, Abbott."

"That was good vodka."

He kisses my forehead and brushes my cheek before rising, and I close my eyes with a small smile. I have my friend back.

*   *   *

I wake up, who knows how much later, and get up slowly, testing my basic motor skills. I'm far more functional than I was before my nap. My stomach is rumbling. I'm not sure if it wants food or is in the first stages of shriveling up and dying.

The rain has stopped, and through a crack in the curtains I can see that the sky is golden behind the last lingering clouds. The ocean, still riled by the weather, slams against the shore. I pull aside the heavy drapes at the sliding door and watch the whitecaps for a few minutes until I hear noises coming from the main part of the house.

Conn is sitting on the couch, Harvey draped over one thigh. He doesn't look at me, but he knows I'm in the doorway. "You sure had to dig deep to get to these," he says, referring to the photos he's studying.

"You really need to throw out some of those old, ripped T-shirts—they take up too much drawer space."

"Apparently they're a lousy barricade too."

"Yeah well, we were pretty determined."

I sit down next to him. He's not looking at the formal wedding portrait in the frame, the one that had hung on the Picture Hook of Doom. It's tossed aside. I have a vague recollection of going through every drawer in his bedroom then triumphantly unearthing it from under that pile of faded T-shirts while Hannah did an end-zone victory dance. I remember lying down in the living room, staring at it until I pushed it under the couch, turned my head away, and fell asleep.

Conn is looking at a different picture from the stack we found with the formal portrait: an unframed eight-by-ten of the entire wedding party acting goofy on the photographer's orders. Except for Sasha. She's the sole composed, dignified person in the photo, though she's smiling delightedly at the rest of us. Conn, on the other hand, is reaching over the top of his head from behind and hooking his fingers in his nostrils.

Now he rests the tip of his finger on the picture, at the very edge—on the shortest, youngest bridesmaid out of Sasha's lineup of nine, all in strapless periwinkle chiffon gowns with crystal waistbands.

"What in the world was I doing there?" I laugh softly, not entirely comfortable looking at my seventeen-year-old self. God, was my face ever that round?

"Saving my ass."

"There was no ass-saving done that day. You're imagining things."

Conn turns to me, those unusual eyes—the ones that I never know are going to be green or blue on any given day, any hour, in any mood, in whatever light—meeting mine. "I don't think I am," he says evenly.

I stand up in a rush, my disturbed innards suddenly clamoring, *Slow it down there, missy!* "Sorry Hannah and I broke into your house. We needed to get out of the rain. I've…got to go. You probably do too." It's the dinner hour, and I've kept him here longer than I should have by stupidly begging not to be alone. I'll never live it down, but damned if I'll ever acknowledge I said it out loud.

"Melanie—"

"Thanks for…everything, Conn. Really."

"Let me drive you home."

"No!" I snap, racing for the door. "I mean…I want to walk. It'll…clear my head. Have a good night, okay?"

* * *

What the hell. We've never talked about his wedding. Never. Not when it happened. Not after. Not before Conn and Sasha moved away, not when Conn came back alone. Never.

I wonder if he knows the truth or if he's just guessing.

God, when did the walk up from the beach get so steep? I stop halfway home to catch my breath. Stupid vodka. A few people I know pass me, and I straighten up and put on a smile to make sure nobody stops to ask if I'm all right. If I breathed within a foot of them, one exhalation would melt their faces off like in *Raiders of the Lost Ark*.

I round the corner into the commercial district…and smack into a wall of people. It happens like that, every year. I should be used to it. The majority of the summer people seem to arrive simultaneously, like an airborne division of the military parachuting from the same plane. One minute there's nobody but the locals, the very next…*boom*.

The shops and restaurants are lit up, ready for night to descend. I can't believe this day is over already. I can't believe I drank to hide from it. It shouldn't matter that it's my mother's birthday. I'll be thirty years old soon. I don't need my mommy. My father has been both mom and dad for me since I was thirteen, and he's done a fine job. Yet something deep inside me keeps reaching out, reaching for her. Of course, if she showed up, arms outstretched, eager for a hug, I'd probably run the other way. No, I *know* I would. I wouldn't know what to do with a mother at this point in my life. Not after living without one for this long.

Still, I check my phone one more time, sort of hoping for voicemail, a text, or even a "missed call" alert. There's nothing.

I work my way through town, across the streaming current of tourists, and come up on the office just as Laura is turning off the lights. For an agent with no clients, she sure does spend a lot of time here. She spots me as she pulls the door shut and turns her key to lock it, so I can't even dodge her.

"Hey, Laura," I mumble, eager to get home.

She looks me up and down, eyes wide under her bangs and a ridiculous, what I presume to be hand-knit hat, which is more than a little incongruous, considering it's almost June. The bright green and white stripes and amateurish, irregular stitch don't capture my attention—and horror—as much as the flaps hanging down on either side. It might be my midday hangover talking, but I'm pretty sure they're dog ears. When she turns to me fully, I know they're not a hallucination because they go with the pair of half-dollar-size googly eyes glued to the front of the hat.

"Melanie. Wait."

Her usual ghost of a whisper is so faint it takes me just about as long to decipher what she just said as it does for her to go back inside, grab something, and hand it to me. It's a bottle of water. Girl's pretty perceptive—I have to admit.

"I look that bad, huh?"

She doesn't answer, just reaches into her purse and thrusts a fistful of loose Twizzlers at me. I muster up a smile, reject that offer as politely as possible, and go on my way. I trudge up another incline into the residential streets, going slower with every step. By the time I enter my carriage house apartment I want to collapse just inside the door, but I force myself to put my purse down, set my keys in the basket on the table in the foyer, finish Laura's bottle of water—the first of what will be several tonight—and get another from the fridge. I cross the room and look out over the town before I draw the blinds. The trees are almost fully leafed out, but I can still see all the way down to the shopping district from my upper-floor apartment. All of this is my domain, I jokingly tell myself. But really, it is my home. I belong here. Other people—my mom, Taylor, eventually Hannah—leave all the time, and I'm still here. Which is fine. It's the way it's supposed to be. I have my dad, and Conn, and…other people. Friends, neighbors, coworkers. I'm not lonely…I don't think.

But once I shower, put on my pajamas, and get my third bottle of water, I find myself reaching for my phone. Not to call my mom again. I have a rule: one attempt at communication per birthday. I refuse to look desperate. This time I call Taylor.

"Happy mom's birthday, darling," is the way she answers. "How are you holding up?"

"I'm okay." To avoid any in-depth discussion of my motherlessness, I tell her all about my Laura sighting. When Taylor worked at Abbott Realty, she and I used to dish about Laura's eccentricities all the time. Now that she lives in Provincetown, Taylor relies on me to keep her up to date. She laughs uproariously as I describe my coworker's hat and Twizzler bouquet, which makes me feel a little better...until our conversation and her reaction reminds me of Conn's accusation. I almost don't want to ask, but I have to know. "Hey, Taylor? Did you and I wage a 'reign of terror' when we were teenagers?"

"Of course we did!" she exclaims immediately.

I groan. "I was hoping you'd say no."

"I detect a hint of Eau de Connacht. He never did approve of us."

"He doesn't approve of anything."

"Nothing fun, no. My question is, why do you care?"

"I don't!"

"Good," she replies. "Don't. Nothing good can come of it."

"Connacht Garvey is a judgy-pants. There's no way I can get on his good side, and I'm not interested anyway."

"He does have a lot of good sides though."

"Don't you growl with lust, woman. It's...icky."

"What are you, nine? You still prefer horsies?"

"*Boys* aren't icky. I'm saying you making lustful noises over Conn turns my stomach." The lingering effects of day drinking don't help, I neglect to add.

"So why are you and Conn reminiscing about our reign of terror, anyway?"

"I have no idea. He got a bug up his butt about it this morning. Don't you growl again," I warn her.

"Mmmm...Conn Garvey's butt..."

I crawl into bed and cradle my water bottle like a teddy bear. "Will you focus, please?"

"Oh, I *am* focusing."

"Quit that. Tell me you and I weren't that bad when we were together."

"Honey, we were *terrible*. Remember when we flashed the sailors' retirement home?"

"Oh God..." It's occurring to me that maybe I've blocked a lot of memories I'd rather not recall.

"Or when we used to crash the middle school dances and demand the seventh grade boys dance with us?"

"Thank goodness we were only fifteen at the time. We could have gotten in real legal trouble."

"Oh, we didn't do anything filthy with them." Taylor pauses. "Wait. Did we?"

I can't believe Taylor's got me laughing, today of all days. Now I don't feel the need to go to sleep right away. Instead, we spend an hour trading memories of our adventures growing up in Abbott's Bay: hacking the school computer before the first day of school and changing everyone's schedule around...hiding in the woods at the country club and replacing golf balls that landed nearby with impossible-to-see green ones from the miniature golf course...sending love letters from one random townsperson to another (that effort actually resulted in a couple of real relationships, come to think of it, although the married and otherwise attached subjects of our pranks ended up in hot water)...on and on. By the time we ran out of memories, I realized we weren't *bad*, exactly. I'd call us mischievous. Most of the time anyway.

"It just goes to show Conn has no sense of humor," Taylor concludes, "if he considers our epic adventures a form of terrorism."

"Oh, he's all right. He does, however, need to get that stick out of his butt."

"Mmmm..."

"Do *not*!" I cut myself off with a huge yawn.

"Sounds like you've had a day."

"You have no idea."

CHAPTER NINE

I'm almost back to normal the next morning. To be on the safe side though, I stay within my own four walls for a while. The slightly stale granola I have for breakfast is a small price to pay to avoid Deep Brew C...and Conn. I consider it my penance.

Before I give my apartment a long-overdue cleaning, I go through yesterday's mail and open up the weekly edition of the *Abbott's Bay Bugle*. Yes, it's a *paper* newspaper. Because the *Bugle* staff members' average age is about ninety-two and a half, digital is not really their thing, yet they never seem to get around to asking their great-grandchildren to help them out. The *Bugle's* website is cutting edge—for 1998—and the "latest news" posted there is almost as old, so paper it is.

It takes less than five minutes to skim the entire thing, and the general news (articles on the beginning of the summer season, planned construction zones, and the recently completed lighthouse renovations) and sports stories are minor impediments on the way to the juicy yin and yang of Abbott's Bay gossip: the police beat and the "Bugle Bites" social column. Unlike inclusion in the police beat, being mentioned as a Bite is something every resident *wants*. Except for the blind gossip items at the end of the column, Bites on the Bottom.

I read the Bites carefully but don't see any mention of Dad, and that's my fault. It's my job as campaign manager to get the town residents talking about him. I make a mental note to drop by the *Bugle* office soon. With cookies.

There are only two blind items this week, neither of which I'm really interested in deciphering. One is a comment about an older gentleman doing some not-too-secretive early morning skinny-dipping. Obviously he's not interested in shocking people if he's daring the frigid ocean this early in the season, in the early morning, to reveal not a whole heck of a lot after all that cold. The other is about a "familiar young Henrietta Higgins" taking a "suddenly lovely, freckled Eliza Doolittle" under her wing.

…Wait.

*   *   *

I thought the population of Abbott's Bay had increased at the end of last week, but that's nothing compared to Memorial Day. Those extra people I spotted on Saturday evening when I walked home from Conn's have multiplied exponentially almost overnight and are now absolutely everywhere—clogging the roads, filling the pier, and making the sidewalks along the parade route entirely impassable.

After excuse-me-pardon-me-ing for about a block, I want to give up, but I have to get to the start of the parade route to check on my dad who's driving one of the vintage convertibles—not behind the mounted police this year, I hope— ostensibly to chauffeur some of the local veterans who'll be waving to the crowd, but also to remind the residents he's up for reelection to the town assembly.

Somehow Hannah finds me in the crowd. I get a tap on the shoulder and turn around to find her smiling merrily. "I'm so glad you're still alive."

"Are you kidding? It takes more vodka than that to kill me." I give her a hug and then pull back to survey her outfit. Rose-colored linen skirt, crisp sleeveless blouse…I approve. Except…I pull her yellow-and-pink cabbage-rose-printed scarf from her neck, duck behind her, and wrap it around her head, tying it under her hair instead. "There you go. Now you look perfect."

"You have good taste."

"I'm glad you trust me."

"Melanie!"

An arm snakes around my waist and pulls me sideways. I turn to find Joann Forrester, Henry the grocer's wife, smiling at me delightedly.

Before I can greet her properly, she exclaims, "I had no idea! Congratulations! Fame suits you."

"…Thanks?" My eyebrows creep toward my hairline. "I'm sorry, Joann, what are we talking about, exactly?"

"Henrietta Higgins!"

Oh. The blind item in the paper. "That's hardly fame. Infamy, perhaps."

"Don't be so modest."

"Let's say the Bites on the Bottom writers are a little desperate for gossip…" I drift off, distracted by a woman standing nearby, staring at me with a hawk-like gaze. I have no idea who she is. I'm not one to blush and run, so I stand my ground and nod in greeting. She nods back. Okay then. Apparently we've passed muster with each other.

Still, she's weirding me out a bit, so I say goodbye to Joann with a promise to get together for coffee soon, grab Hannah's hand, and tug her farther down the block toward the start of the parade route. "Come on," I say over my shoulder. "My dad's been asking about you. I want you to meet him so he can calm down about who's in his rental."

I face forward again and walk right into the same woman who was watching me a few seconds ago. How she got from behind Hannah to in front of me in a blink, I'll never know. It's freaky. But all I say is, "Oh, I beg your pardon."

I try to navigate around her, but she blocks my path, demanding bluntly, "You're Henrietta?"

Rude. "No, I'm Melanie. Can I help you?"

"Henrietta Higgins," she says, eyeing me up and down. "Everyone's talking about you."

I don't have time to reflect on the implications of that, because with one wiry arm, the woman reaches out sideways into the crowd and hauls in a girl the way one of our fishermen would land a giant cod. The young teen is obviously her daughter. Although it's hard to see her face because she's staring at the sidewalk, she has the same coloring as her mother—black hair, pale skin, and a slight build with narrow shoulders and hips. I look back at the mother who's staring at me expectantly.

"Yes?" I prompt.

"What's wrong with my daughter?"

Hannah and I exchange stunned looks. Neither of us manages an answer.

In the silence the woman demands, "According to the newspaper, you fixed her." She points casually at Hannah with her free hand, her other still gripping her daughter's arm. "So tell me what's wrong with my daughter." She gives the girl a little shake to make me look in her direction.

The woman's manhandling of her daughter makes me furious. I have to find my voice before she shakes the poor girl again, but nothing comes out.

"Look," she says, "I buy her the best clothes. Designer all the way. Tailored. I make sure she's clean and neat. But she always ends up looking like she just got out of bed. It's a nightmare. What's wrong with her?"

"Don't ask me!" I blurt out, interrupting what seems to be turning into an endless rant. I know these kinds of moneyed women. They'll keep carping until they get results. Obviously this issue has been eating at this one for a long time, probably the girl's entire life. I don't even know the kid, and my heart breaks for her. She's radiating defeat already. It's clear from her…"Posture."

"What?" the mother snaps.

I take a breath and start again. "There's nothing whatsoever 'wrong' with your daughter."

"But—"

I hold up a hand to stop her. "It's not the clothes or how clean she is. It's her posture." Reaching out carefully, I detach the mother's claw-like grip from her daughter's arm and turn the girl toward me. "What's your name, sweetie?"

She lifts huge brown eyes to glance at me for a split second. "Zoë."

"Okay, Zoë. I want you to do me a favor, all right? Just relax." I gently push her shoulders back and down, since she's kind of hunched. Then I straighten her hips, push in her torso a bit, and generally make sure she's standing up straight and her body is aligned. The last thing I do is put a finger under her chin and lift it up so she's looking me straight in the eye.

"That's different," the mother murmurs. "That's better!"

She looks impressed, but I'm not feeling it, because she starts berating her daughter.

"I've been telling you to stand up straight for years!

Look how different you look!"

Oh, I have to stop this, or I'm going to start swinging. "Zoë, are you here for the summer?"

"Yes."

"Well, welcome to Abbott's Bay." I brush her hair out of her eyes, and give her a reassuring smile. "I want you to have the *best* time this summer. There's so much to do and see, so get out there and have fun." Although I'm still talking to the girl, I direct a veiled threat at the mother: "I'm positive I'll be running into you all over the place, and I want to see you happy, okay?"

I try to move past them, but the mother grabs my arm—damn, I don't know how her daughter puts up with it—and stuffs something into my hand.

"You're good," she says. Which is not a thank you, but it is in keeping with what I've seen of her personality so far.

When they're gone, I open up my hand. There's a fifty-dollar bill in it.

"Wow," Hannah says over my shoulder.

"Ew!" I don't want her money. "I'm seriously questioning the quality of people visiting Abbott's Bay these days."

"What about me?"

That isn't Hannah's voice. I look around, hoping Zoë and her mom are back so I can return this blood money, but instead I'm face to face with a petite, slim blonde—also probably a summer person, as I've never seen her before either. "I'm sorry?"

"You fix people?" she asks eagerly. "Can you do your fixing thing on me? Tell me what's wrong with me?"

My God. What's gotten into these people? Are they serious? Do they *actually* think there's something wrong with them? This young woman is perfect. She's beautiful, in a Barbie-doll kind of way, with a size 2 body, blue eyes, expensive highlights, and fancy manicure. She can't be questioning her looks. She also seems to be well-mannered—more than Zoë's mom, that's for sure—so what could she be asking for?

And since when do so many people pay attention to and discuss the Bites, anyway?

"Go on," Hannah urges me. "Do your thing."

"I don't have a 'thing,'" I hiss at her.

"These folks think otherwise. Might as well." To the young woman, she says, "Melanie's been *so* great with me."

"You're not helping, Hannah!"

"Melanie?" the stranger repeats, blinking. "I thought her name was Henrietta."

"It's a joke…never mind." I sigh and look her up and down. I can't critique this girl. It's not polite. But she's standing there, eyes alight, waiting. "Uh…too much spray tan? You might want to, er, back off on that a bit?"

Her mouth falls open, and I expect her to storm off, offended, but instead she exclaims, "For serious?" then rummages around in her purse.

Coming up with a fairly large compact, she flips it open and stares at herself in the round mirror for a long time. I mean, a *long* time. I exchange glances with Hannah, who shrugs.

I'm about ready to slink off when the girl whispers, "Wow. Nobody has *ever* told me that before. Not anybody in my family, or any of my friends, or my boyfriend. Do I look, you know, ridiculous?" All I can do is shake my head dazedly. The girl grabs my arm—people have *got* to stop clutching at me today—and cries, "You're right. You're absolutely right. I do look ridiculous."

"No!" I yelp. "I never said that. I mean a lighter shade, maybe not so…you know what? This is crazy. You don't need to change one bit—"

"I've been walking around looking like a freak, and nobody I trusted even told me."

"Freak? I never said you looked like a freak!" But she kisses me on the cheek—what!—and hands me a twenty before stepping off the curb and crossing the street, still studying her reflection.

The thuds of the bass drums sound in the distance as the high school marching band starts its first tune. The parade may have begun, but I appear to be a bigger spectacle. I feel eyes on me. Lots of eyes. And there are whispers. I catch snatches of "Bugle Bites" and "Henrietta—you know, like Henry Higgins in *My Fair Lady*?" I want to correct them that it was *Pygmalion* first, but I want to avoid engaging, so I don't bother. There are also various comments about Hannah's "transformation," which is crazy. I helped her get a few new outfits. Big deal.

"Let's go," I say to Hannah, who's somehow ended up with a paper poppy and a small flag in one hand and a red, white, and blue sno-cone in the other.

"But—"

"Wait. What am I saying? I order you around way too much. Stay and watch the parade. You don't have to follow me everywhere. I'm sorry I even suggested it."

I start to walk away. Hannah's right there beside me. "Melanie?"

"What?"

"What if I *want* to hang out with you?"

I glance over skeptically but say nothing.

"Come on. Who cares what the Bugle Bite said?" Over my dismayed groan she adds, "It was cute. People have been stopping me ever since the paper came out, asking me what you did for me. And you know what? I tell them."

"I didn't do anything for you."

"You did *so* much for me."

My slightly queasy stomach quiets down a bit. "You don't think of it as…" I wave the dirty money in front of her. "A business transaction?"

She grins. "Maybe charity, since I didn't pay you."

"Hey, Melanie!" someone shouts. It's one of the young landscapers my dad uses to take care of his properties. I wave, and he calls, "How much for you to fix my sister? Might take a whole day. Hell, might take a whole month!"

I never did like that guy.

My wave turns into a different gesture entirely before I manage to disappear into the crowd.

CHAPTER TEN

———

Now I can't go anywhere without people approaching me, exclaiming "Do me next!" It's unnerving. I want no part of this…this…Miss Melanie's Finishing School for the Awkward and Clueless or whatever you want to call it. Granted, I might be a little free and easy with my advice, but I don't market myself as a professional…anything. I'm not a fixer, not a beauty consultant, not a shrink. Not a "Henrietta Higgins." (Oh sure, the first time in recent memory the fossils at the *Bugle* get clever, and I happen to be the target. Thanks a bunch.)

Today it's a relief to be sitting in my usual seat at DBC, drinking my usual triple espresso, with Conn in his usual spot behind the bar, everything perfectly normal, nobody bothering me. Deep Brew C is more crowded lately, but that's also normal with the summer adjustment in population. I'm glad to see the number of customers is up, even though it means I might have to fight harder for my favorite chair, because I've seen Conn with a pile of official-looking documents in front of him more than once since the time I stepped in it asking if he was in financial trouble. It upsets me to see him hunched over the far end of the bar, fingers clenching his short, light brown curls as he studies whatever is on those papers. I can practically feel the tension radiating off him. There's irony for you: I *want* to help *him*, and he's the only person who would never ask me.

I stand and stretch, ready to meet some incoming renters to hand over the house keys, when I feel something poke the middle of my back.

"Don't move another inch," a voice growls. "You are so busted."

I freeze for a moment then raise my arms in surrender. Some tourists sitting nearby stare openmouthed, and I wink at them before spinning around and pulling Taylor's finger backward toward her wrist. "Amateur. You think you can take me without a fight?"

"Ow! Ow, ow, ow! Okay, I give up!"

I look over my shoulder and raise one eyebrow at the tourists, who are still frozen in their shocked pose. "Nothing to see here, folks. Move along. If you know what's good for you."

It looks like they're actually about to scramble when I realize what sort of a display we're putting on. Are we thirty years old or a third that? I start to straighten my clothes, but Taylor derails my attempt to regain my dignity by grabbing me in a headlock. Now all I can see is the floor and her fashionable heels.

"What are you doing here? When did you get in? Why didn't you tell me you were coming?" I fire off in the general vicinity of her left boob.

My friend frizzes my hair with a vigorous noogie before releasing me. "Maybe I didn't want to give you any advance warning."

"It can't be because you don't want me to throw you a party. We all know you're an attention whore."

"True. But the whole thing about an intervention is you *don't* give any advance warning."

I have no idea what she's talking about. "Who needs an intervention?"

Taylor doesn't answer. Instead, she saunters over to the bar and roots around in her enormous purse until she comes up with a newspaper.

"Hot off the presses," she declares, snapping it open and folding the page back. "'Local Socialite Is Your New Best Friend,'" she announces in a loud, clear voice.

"Local socialite is what, now?" The words stick in my suddenly tight throat.

I march over to grab the paper—this week's edition of the *Abbott's Bay Bugle*—but she takes a step away from me, tosses back her sheet of dark hair, holds the *Bugle* high, and keeps reading.

"'Melanie Abbott, daughter of real estate mogul and Assemblyman Charles Abbott and employee of Abbott Realty, is on a mission: to improve people's lives, one new best friend at a time.'"

"Me?" There's an article about me in the paper? And…wait. "That's how I'm described?" I squeak. "As my father's daughter?" I know it's not the question I should be asking first, but it comes out anyway. "Which nineteenth-century time traveler wrote this bilge? Who's got the byline? It's Aurelia Hoffstader, isn't it? Isn't it? And why is she writing about me anyway?"

Taylor flicks an eyebrow coyly and continues reading in a sing-song voice reminiscent of a school educational video about the Grand Canyon or puberty, "'And the best part: all you have to do is ask. Drawing on the wisdom accrued in her scant twenty-nine years—'"

"Oh now, that was a dig."

"'—In her scant twenty-nine years,'" Taylor repeats, "'she'll dispense frank advice to improve the lives of others. It's a unique business venture, and it suits Miss Abbott to a *T*, as her regal bearing and impeccable taste have made her a star in the crown of North Shore society.'"

"Dear God," I groan, rubbing my temples.

"That's a compliment."

My head snaps up at the sound of Conn's voice.

"How long have you been standing there?" The last thing I need is Conn getting in on this. Taylor's bad enough.

He doesn't answer my question. Instead, eyes alight, he peeks over Taylor's shoulder at the article. "And it's a mixed metaphor," he adds.

Taylor doesn't get it. I can tell from her bewildered expression.

"A star is in the firmament; a jewel is in a crown." I don't even know why I bother to explain—maybe to avoid having to think about the implications of whatever else she just read aloud. "'A star in the crown' sounds like the title of a fantasy novel."

"And a crown in the star sounds like some celebrity's dental records."

"Hush, you," I snipe at Conn.

"He's right though—it's high praise," Taylor says.

"Aurelia's always liked me. Which is why I want to know what's up with this hit piece."

"It's not a hit piece. It's…informational. And I, for one, want more information. Let's read on, shall we?"

Before Taylor can continue, Conn picks up the narration. ""She's helped me so much," says Miss Abbott's first client, Miss Hannah Clement, a summer visitor hailing from Dayton, Ohio. "She's been a true friend and has given me such great advice. I don't know what I'd do without her." According to Miss Clement, the idea for the consulting business came about when she and Miss Abbott determined people would "pay good money" for the practical advice Miss Abbott dispenses every day.'"

"Do *not* tell me that's not a hit piece."

"Sounds pretty neutral to me. Should I continue?" Conn asks.

"No. Yes. No! Wait. How much more is there?"

Conn takes the paper from Taylor and scans the rest of the article. "Um…blah blah blah 'helpful,' blah blah blah 'genius idea,' blah blah blah 'available for consultations immediately…' You are?"

"Well, if Aurelia says so, it must be true." I slide onto the nearest bar stool and bury my head in my hands. "Oh God, why?"

"Who's this Hannah Clement person?" Taylor asks.

"I told you about her. She's here for the summer." Trust Taylor to forget.

"Why's she so willing to blab about you to Aurelia for the paper? Is she some sort of viper, or is she stupid?"

"She probably thought she was doing Melanie a favor," Conn counters. "She's far from a viper. Or stupid."

Grateful that he's defending Hannah, I give Conn a tight smile. "It's all a big misunderstanding. I'm going to call Aurelia right now and get her to issue a retraction."

"A retraction will run next week," Conn says. "What are you going to do in the meantime?"

I have no idea, to be honest. How in the world did the *Bugle* staff expand one measly Bite on the Bottom like this? Why did they think it was worth writing an entire article about a "business venture" of mine that doesn't really exist? And why, for the love of William Randolph Hearst's ghost, didn't Aurelia

Hoffstader approach *me* before writing this ridiculous article?

Well. I know why. Because the *Bugle* staff members wouldn't know real journalism if it met them in a dark alley at midnight and clubbed them with a lead pipe. Aurelia is a retired hairdresser, for God's sake. I shouldn't expect *Boston Globe*–quality reporting.

Of course, after the Memorial Day debacle, I stopped answering my phone because of all the people trying to contact me for their own personal revamping, so Aurelia *may* have tried to find me. But I opt for a dollop of righteous indignation instead. It'll help fuel my efforts to get out of this. Not only am I completely uninterested in dispensing advice to strangers, I *definitely* don't want anyone to think I'm taking money for it. Très gauche, as this alleged "socialite" would say.

Socialite. Humph. If I didn't have to meet some clients, I'd hunt Aurelia down and make her print a new edition of the paper this very minute. Using the old letterpress in the Abbott's Bay Museum if necessary.

I look over at Taylor who's concentrating on applying a fresh coat of lipstick. I'm about to ask her how she thinks I should get this all straightened out when I realize something. "You didn't come here for an intervention."

She smacks her lips together and says distractedly, "Hm?" as she continues to study her reflection in her mirror.

"You didn't come here because of this article. This edition published today. You must have picked it up when you got here."

"So?" With a nonchalant shrug, she makes a business of putting her cosmetics back in her purse.

"*So*...why are you really here?"

She straightens her tunic tank top, pulling the asymmetrical hem down and plucking at the neckline to get it to fall properly, and says absently, "I've got a business meeting."

"You're working on a deal? Here?" If it has to do with real estate, I'd have heard about it, and I haven't.

"Mm, sort of." Before I can ask for the details, she leans across the bar toward Conn. "So I was thinking, since it's kind of early, what do you say we drive down to Boston for dinner?"

Wait. Taylor...and Conn? What sorcery is this? Conn

doesn't even *like* Taylor. Before I even know what I'm doing, I round the bar and take Conn by his elbow.

"Can I talk to you for a minute?"

Without waiting for an answer, I drag him bodily into the narrow back hallway. I know full well if he didn't want to be dragged, I wouldn't have been able to budge the mountain of a man half an inch, so it's a good sign that he's followed me. It gives me the courage to ask the questions I need to ask.

"So, Conn," I start then hesitate.

"Melanie." He raises one eyebrow at me.

"Going to Boston for dinner with Taylor? Do you think that's wise?"

"No," he snorts, crossing his arms and resting his shoulder against the wall. "I mean, I'm not going to Boston with Taylor."

"But obviously you two have made plans. Going to tell me what this is all about?"

"If I say no, are you going to let it go?"

"Of course not."

"Didn't think so."

I wait. He says nothing, just grins at me. "What?" I demand. I cross my arms as well, realize I'm mirroring him, and hastily uncross them.

"Melanie," he says again, his voice warm and intimate, and that tone does something to my insides. Before I can figure out what exactly is going on in my stomach, he ducks his head toward me and murmurs, "Are you jealous?"

"What?" I exclaim. "Absolutely n—I mean, how could—wha—?"

"It's not so farfetched. I know you and Taylor have always been a closed party of two."

Oh.

Jealous of *him* infringing on my friendship with *Taylor*. For a minute there I thought…but no. He's still entirely wrong though, no matter what kind of jealousy he's talking about. I take a deep breath and regroup. "I'm…*concerned.* That sounded an awful lot like a date."

"And?"

"Yeah well, she's more fond of you than you are of her,

okay?"

"Is she, now?"

"So you might want to be, you know, a little careful there...stop looking so smug!"

He turns his grin into a glower, heavy eyebrows dipping so low they obscure his eyes completely. He adds an exaggerated frown. He's probably trying to get me to laugh, but it's not going to work.

"Just tell me you're not listing your house with her because I turned you down."

"Oh, is that what you think?" His expression clears again, and he rolls his eyes. He has no right to be so amused by me at this moment.

"Well, you want to sell your house. Taylor's an agent."

"And you think I'd drag Taylor all the way back from Provincetown to list my house? You know that doesn't even make sense."

"Well what am I supposed to think?"

"Nothing," he says, his voice soothing. "I can promise it's got nothing to do with you. Not everything does, you know."

"That's all I'm going to get out of you, isn't it?"

"Yep."

He turns away, ready to go back out to the main part of the restaurant, but I stop him, this time with a gentle hand on his arm. At first I'm not sure what else I want to say, so when the words, "Conn, *is* it a date?" come out of my mouth, I cringe. He's going to laugh at me again—I know it—and it's going to be humiliating.

Then he surprises me by smiling—a soft, caring smile. He puts his arm around my waist, pulls me in for a half-hug, and kisses my temple. "I swear," he whispers into my hair, "it's not a date."

I let out a breath, too relieved to really examine why I even care. But Conn isn't finished. He hasn't let me go yet.

"Now...someday soon," he continues in his rumbly, rough voice, "I'm going to ask you why the thought of me going out with Taylor upsets you so much. I'm going to be really interested in your answer."

Yeah, so am I.

CHAPTER ELEVEN

I spend all weekend trying to track down someone from the newspaper so I can get my retraction, but I fail utterly. I should know better—nobody mans the news desk at a small-town weekly on Saturday or Sunday. On Monday morning, however, my call to Editor-in-Chief Randall Bell nets me many obsequious and apologetic comments of the "goodness gracious…no idea" variety, plus a promise of a personal visit right away. I inform Randall I'll be at Deep Brew C awaiting my Very Special Apology and Retraction.

When I enter the restaurant, Beebs is behind the counter, Ornette in the kitchen. They call to one another, cracking jokes, and I get a feeling about those two that I've had before. Despite the fact that I want no part of this imaginary business the *Bugle* says I've started, I admit I do have a certain instinct about people, which I've acted on in the past. But not Beebs and Ornette. Not yet anyway. I don't know if they're dating, but if they aren't, they should be. I could help.

While Beebs warms up a blueberry muffin for me, I peruse a flyer taped to a pillar: *Boat for Sale.* My heart twists. It's Conn's boat in the photo—well the family boat, which he inherited along with the house when his parents decamped to hot, sunny Arizona for their retirement years. It's nothing fancy, just a clunky old thing good for carrying a pile of hyper kids and several gin-and-tonic-swilling adults up the coast and back again on a Sunday afternoon, but like Conn's house, it's familiar and constant.

And now he's selling it.

What if he's trying to sell off everything he owns to pay his bills? Even though I don't actually have proof that he's in financial trouble, it seems to make sense. Before I can decide what to do about it, there's a tap on my shoulder. I turn around with a beatific smile plastered on my face, the one I've been perfecting all weekend as I've put off strangers and random acquaintances yelping, "I need a friend!"

Nobody yelps this time though. Okay, I do. Because suddenly I'm nose to nose with my silent, moon-faced coworker Laura. Who has no concept of personal space.

"Ack! Laura!" I struggle to recover my cool as I stumble back a step. "I mean, good morning." As casually as possible, I collect my order from the counter. "What's going on? Does my dad need me?"

Her eyes widen behind her glasses, and she shakes her head. She follows me to my usual spot by the hearth, which is blessedly free of invading summer people this morning.

"Oh, are the Utkins arriving this morning? I thought they were coming in this afternoon. Can you let them into the house and show them how to work the water heater? I've got…a thing." I have no idea why I don't come right out and tell Laura I have an interview with a *Bugle* reporter. What's the big deal? They screwed up, and now they're going to make it right.

She shakes her head again and gnaws on the coils of a stenographer's notebook she has clutched in her hands, looking for all the world like a squirrel breaking into a walnut. No, wait—she did say something. I just couldn't hear her.

"Sorry, Laura—can you repeat that?"

Son of a gun. I could have sworn she said, "I'm here to interview you."

"You?" I gape. *Terrible manners,* my inner Emily Post scolds. "I'm sorry, you…really caught me off guard."

That's an understatement. I didn't even know Laura works for the *Bugle*. Okay, I don't know a whole lot about her in general, even though we've worked together for years, but that's beside the point right now. The only thing I can focus on at the moment is I'm sitting across from one of the most uncommunicative people I've ever known, and she's going to be the one responsible for the retraction and apology. I'd better take charge of the situation, or we're going to be here all day.

"Okay, Madame Reporter," I say with a wink, trying to get her to relax. "Let's talk about this retraction."

She blinks back at me and is silent for a few moments.

Finally she manages to peep, "Retraction? I...I wasn't told anything about a retraction."

"I talked with Randall an hour ago. The article about me was completely false. I'm not starting a new business. You need to print a retraction and set everyone straight before all these people drive me crazy asking for help."

"I was told..." She clamps her rainbow-striped pencil between her teeth and starts flipping through the pages of her notebook. "...To interview you and get more details about how you're offering to be people's New Best Friend." She looks up at me and removes the tooth-marked pencil. "Randall says there's a feature story in this. Could be front page."

"Laura," I say patiently, "there isn't going to be a feature story. Because there is no New Best Friend business. Understand?"

"How much are you charging? Is it a flat fee or an hourly rate?"

Apparently she does not understand. She's sitting forward, her pencil poised over her notebook, and I resist the urge to yank both from her hands and fling them into the cold fireplace.

"Oh...I guess that's the wrong question to start with. Wait..."

She starts flipping pages again, locates her list of questions, and fires one at me, sounding almost authoritative. Whatever she asks doesn't sink in, however, because my attention is drawn to a familiar figure blocking the sunlight as the front door opens. Conn enters Deep Brew C, ushering in another man who's dressed in a well-tailored suit and carrying a briefcase. He's looking around at the coffeehouse in an assessing kind of way, and I'd bet my broker's license I know what he's here for. Those mannerisms scream "banker." And the suit? It screams "not from around here."

I catch snatches of what Conn is saying to him—things to do with "seating capacity" and "revenue"—as the banker nods, looking appreciative. While I'm trying to eavesdrop, my brain dimly acknowledges that Laura is repeating the question I didn't hear the first time (or this time, for that matter), following it up with, "Melanie? Melanie?"

Conn leads the important banker toward his office but is waylaid by local retiree and fishing aficionado Frank Comey. Never very good with timing, Frank marches right up to Conn and starts asking him about his boat. Conn claps him on the shoulder with a promise to discuss it with him later, and then he and the other man disappear into his office.

Once Conn and the banker are gone, Frank turns to some of his cronies at the bar, jerks his thumb toward the flyer, and declares quite clearly, "Had my eye on that baby for a while. Gonna get a good price for her."

Cheapskate, I think bitterly. Trust Frank to try to take advantage of Conn when the poor guy needs all the money he can get. What if Conn lets the boat go for the buck fifty Frank is sure to offer him? I can't let that happen. Hell, *I'll* buy the boat if I have to. I'll outbid him. I'll overpay—I don't care. Then I have an even better idea.

"Laura!" I exclaim, and she jumps. "Let's talk details about my very, *very* special service. You will have room for a list of fees, right?"

*   *   *

"Have you lost your *mind*?"

The best description I can come up with for Conn's expression is "incredulously perplexed." Or "perplexedly incredulous." I'm not sure which, and I'm not sure it matters. All I know is his facial muscles obviously don't know whether to frown or laugh, so they're doing both simultaneously, which makes me fear his face is going to seize up at any moment.

"Relax." I try to make my voice as soothing, and as confident, as possible. In all honesty I kind of wonder if I *have* lost my mind. This morning I sent Laura back to the *Bugle* offices to write her feature, her steno notebook bulging with juicy quotes and incredible detail about Your New Best Friend...all of which I made up on the spot. "I've got it all under control," I lie.

"I think it's a great plan, Melanie." Hannah, my most loyal supporter and true friend—take *that*, Connacht Garvey— blinks furiously at my side, her red-rimmed eyes brimming with tears.

"Thank you."

"It doesn't quite warrant tears of joy," Conn says, studying her with concern.

"Oh, I'm not crying. Not that your plan doesn't deserve happy tears," she rushes to assure me. "I'm just getting used to these."

She dabs at the corners of her eyes, which are now, as I'd always wished for her, turquoise. The contacts completely transform her face and look fabulous—or, rather, they will, once the inflammation dies down and she stops looking like a demon bunny—and I've told her so several times today so she'll keep them in and tough out the adjustment period.

"That right there," Conn snaps. "Your advice, I presume? And look at the poor girl. She can barely see."

"She'll get used to the contacts. Come on. Don't they look amazing?"

"Very zombie chic. No offense," he rushes to qualify, in case Hannah starts crying for real.

"And what does Hannah adjusting to her contacts have to do with it?"

"Everything." He plants his elbows on the bar, clasping his hands, and leans toward us. "Melanie Abbott, you know I love you, but I'm saying this for your own good: sometimes you give lousy advice."

I draw back, shocked. "I beg your pardon! I have impeccable taste and remarkable instincts."

Conn clamps his lips tight, likely to make sure nothing flies out that he'll regret later, then sighs in resignation. "Fine. Have it your way. You always do."

"Yes, I do. And with good reason." Maybe it's the second beer I've nearly finished, but I'm feeling pretty darn good about my plans. "It shouldn't bother you, anyway. All you have to do is make up a *Reserved* sign—which I've been expecting for years, by the way—and put it on my chair. Keep the food and drink orders filled for my many clients, and everybody wins. If it bugs you that much, I'll even give you a cut of my proceeds. Consider it chair rental."

I'm going to get money into Conn's pockets one way or

another. The less he knows, the better, of course, because if he found out I was doing this for his benefit, he'd have my head. If he'd accept a cash gift to help him through whatever financial difficulty he's having, I wouldn't have to jump through these hoops. Damn his pride.

"What can I do?" Hannah pipes up. "I want to help."

"Honey, you can't even see," Conn says, not unkindly.

"I'll get used to them."

"No," I sigh. "I don't think you will. Go on. Take them out, Hannah."

"Oh thank God," she breathes, making a mad dash for the ladies' room.

Conn moves down the bar, serving the usual drafts to the usual local patrons, who now have to share their space with knots of vacationers sucking down mojitos. Conn hates to make those, but he doesn't bat an eyelash—just nods and smiles and reaches for some more mint fresh from the restaurant herb garden out back. I watch him work, the muscles of his forearm flexing as he conducts the dreaded muddling while he laughs with the regulars and makes small talk with the summer people.

He catches me staring and gives me one of his bright smiles. I knew he wouldn't stay mad at me for long. He never does. When he comes back over with a glass of seltzer with a lime wedge (he knows I always take a break after two beers), he says, "You realize I'm going to be keeping an eye on you while you conduct this ridiculous business of yours, right?"

"Wouldn't have it any other way." I take a sip of my drink. "Not that there's anything to protect me from, of course."

"You need protecting from yourself."

I just smirk. Whatever he needs to think.

With another resigned sigh, he says, "Potato skins?"

"You have to ask?"

CHAPTER TWELVE

My feature runs in the Friday edition of the *Bugle*, and by Saturday I have three appointments set up. By Monday I have twelve. I should have known people in Abbott's Bay were eager for this. And why not? I've got skills, and the residents of Abbott's Bay respect me.

I've already made good on my promise to get more money into Conn's pocket. I always meet every prospective client in Deep Brew C, where I point out to them that if one has a meeting in a food service establishment, one should purchase something, not sit there taking up valuable space like a lump. This should net him a nice little profit because every waking moment I'm not at the Abbott Realty office, I'm at the restaurant, meeting with my new best friends.

It's exciting…and exhausting.

After I see the last of my appointments for the day, I ease onto one of the barstools, prop my head on the heels of my hands, and close my eyes. Conn slides a triple espresso in front of me, but I push it away. I've had way too much coffee today— almost one with each appointment. I make a mental note to switch to water, or I'm never going to get through this with my nerves intact.

"Do I want to ask how it's going?" he murmurs in a low voice, one that practically vibrates in my bones. "What's on tap with all those best friends?"

"Oh, you have no idea." I smile wanly at him.

The requests that came in today alone: throwing a baby shower, helping someone move, being someone else's euchre partner. Nothing massive. Small favors. Friend for hire, that's me. It's not quite what I expected. I thought I'd be doling out advice—helping people improve their wardrobes, directing their love lives, teaching them what all those forks and spoons are for in a fancy place setting. This is all...*active*. And tiring. I close my eyes for a moment. When I open them, I find Conn watching me closely.

"What?" I ask suspiciously.

"You sure this is a good idea?"

That's something I've asked myself several times since I started getting calls, but I will not admit defeat so soon, especially not to him. I straighten up and brush my hair back. "Of course it is. I love helping people."

I brace myself, waiting for a snide comment, but he just smiles gently. "Yeah, you do." Then he falls silent.

"That's it?"

"What were you expecting?"

"Oh, some reference to 'hanging out with the peasants,' perhaps?"

He winces. "You know I didn't mean that."

"I know."

We're both silent for a moment. He reaches out and gently straightens a lock of my hair by my cheek. "It seems like a lot of work though."

"Careful—you might be admitting Your New Best Friend is an out-of-the-gate success," I murmur, while Conn smirks.

"Are you going to be able to handle all these requests by yourself?"

"You offering to help?" It comes out on a sigh as I gratefully lean into his hand. His caring touch is a comfort right about now.

"Me?" he says, pulling his hand away abruptly and stepping back, breaking the peaceful little spell between us. "I'm too busy with the restaurant."

He busies himself with things behind the bar and won't look at me. He doesn't really think I expect him to help, does he?

"Don't forget Hannah offered though," he adds.

"Mm." I demur without actually saying no. I can't really picture Hannah doing what I do.

"Think about it. If this is going to take off like you predict, you might need the support."

* * *

Support? Hogwash. I'm fine. I'm better than fine. It's hardly painful to make people happy. Helping Crystal and Floyd Phelps go through all the video footage of their wedding to choose what to include in the final version? Cakewalk. Even if "*all* the footage" meant eighteen hours' worth. It's what a friend does. And I was very forthright when they asked my opinion, because a friend would tell them they might want to leave out shots of the bride in pin curls, not to mention the close-up of Cousin Ralph's wide, dimply, alarmingly white backside when he decided to give the happy couple a special (inebriated) salute. Things like that. It was fun. Plus we ate defrosted wedding cake.

And who would mind playing board games with the residents of the sailors' retirement home? It was kind of surreal to be playing checkers with the same old guys Taylor and I might have flashed fifteen years ago, but I wasn't going to bring it up if they weren't. Fortunately no one did.

Going to the movies with Amy Aarons? Hardly a chore. How could I turn down a single mother who'd just watched her last child (of four) leave the nest? The poor woman was going stir-crazy, what with the sudden, overwhelming silence in her house. Of *course* a friend would take her out. Even if her movie of choice was a very loud, colorful animated flick. One that might have been prone to inducing seizures in the susceptible. (I think Amy was reliving her early days of motherhood or something.)

Choice of movie notwithstanding, I enjoyed getting to know Amy better. In fact, getting to know all my clients has been a high point of this venture. I'm sure they appreciate the chance to become better acquainted with me as well.

Not to say this project hasn't had its drawbacks. I was sort of hoping to get more clients like the first two who started this thing, back on Memorial Day: the summer people. The well-connected. The secretly needy and inherently insecure. The ones with the most important feature: deep pockets. If this thing is going to work, I'm going to need more cash than what the permanent residents of Abbott's Bay can offer. I've been scaling my fees according to everyone's financial situation, but I can't save Deep Brew C if I keep getting paid in sponge cake and lobster bisque.

The latest food payment, in the form of an apple kuchen, came from Jewel Loftus. I certainly couldn't turn her down when she asked me to help her plan a farewell for her beloved Reginald, including the wake, the ceremony, and the buffet lunch reception afterward. It's not appropriate to say it was enjoyable, of course, but I was happy to use my party planning and social skills to take some of the pressure off Jewel.

Now here it is a week later, and she's asked me to pick up Reginald, because he's "ready."

So I do…and before I deliver Reginald to Jewel, I take him to Deep Brew C for a drink. Okay, I'm the one who needs a drink, but it's the thought that counts. I'll put one in front of him as well, and we'll toast Jewel.

"What the hell is *that*?"

I love it when Conn gets all wild-eyed.

"Glass of pinot grigio please, darling? Oh, and one for my friend, here. It's downright balmy outside, so something chilled would be wonderful right about now."

Conn doesn't get my drink order. He does, however, loom over me, bracing his hands on the edge of the counter until the muscles stand out on his arms. I'm so busy staring at those I almost miss his snarled words, "Get that thing off my bar."

"I thought you were more egalitarian than that, Mr. Garvey."

He looks closer at my companion. "…Reginald?"

"Dear departed Reginald Loftus—yes indeed. He's visiting before settling into his final resting place, most likely Jewel's mantel. Or maybe her grand piano. We're going to try him out in a few different places to see what he prefers."

"Why don't you go do that right now?"

"I beg your pardon?"

"Move along. Reginald is scaring off my customers."

I glance around. There are individuals on both sides of me looking askance at my drinking companion, but no one has set their glass down and retreated.

"It's not like he's going to go for their jugular." To emphasize my point I pick up Reginald and bob him toward

Conn, adding a little *raarr* for effect.

Not like ferrets ever say *raarr*, even when they're alive and not stuffed with sawdust as Reginald, poor thing, is now and forever shall be. Long may his glass eyes glitter as he holds what I can only assume is a typical ferret-y pose, long and lean on his wooden base, one front paw raised yet curled, as though he were about to knock on your door and ask if you happened to have any spare rodents he could snack on.

Conn stares me down, so I sigh and stuff Reginald unceremoniously into my handbag. I leave his little nose sticking out so he can get some fresh air though.

"I think this side business of yours is getting to you," Conn says as he finally pours my glass of wine.

"We've had this conversation already. I told you, I'm fine." Never mind that I contradict my words by grabbing the wine he hands me and chugging it like it's Gatorade.

"You're toting around a taxidermied, recently deceased ferret."

"*Shhh.* Reginald is very sensitive about his current state. And where's his glass of wine?"

"We don't serve his kind here. If *you* want two drinks, say so."

"And risk you labeling me as an alcoholic?"

"Not an alcoholic. A self-medicater, maybe."

"Gimme."

"How's your dad's campaign coming along?"

I watch him pour, and I wiggle my fingers, urging him to get that blessed liquid sunshine a little closer to the rim. "Dad's campaign can run itself." At my friend's inevitable skeptical look, I wave my hand dismissively and say, "We talked about it on Sunday when we went for a nice drive and Father's Day dinner. We're good."

"And Hannah?"

I raise my eyebrows. "What about Hannah?"

"Have you seen her lately?"

When *was* the last time I'd hung out with Hannah? Long enough that I have to stop and think about it.

"You are one of her only friends here," he reminds me.

"I'll call her," I promise. I take one more swig of wine

and stand up, only a touch lightheaded, and swing my bag onto my shoulder. Reginald's nose nudges my armpit. "Better get going. I don't want Jewel to think Reginald and I have run off together."

Conn nods and pats the bar in a goodbye gesture on his way to the kitchen.

"You don't have to be anywhere right this minute, do you?" I ask my companion once we're on the sidewalk. Reginald grins up at me, which I assume means he's flexible—well, as flexible as you can be when you're nailed to a board—so I take a little walk to Hannah's place.

The rental looks nice and neat from the outside, with a pot of purple lobelia and hot pink dahlias on the clean stoop. I'm glad my father won't have anything to complain about if he ever stops by to check on things. I think I've scared him off sufficiently enough that he won't be peeking in any windows anytime soon, but with him you never know. I use the brass knocker to rap on the red lacquered front door, but Hannah doesn't open up. She must be out. Maybe she's painting a lovely landscape somewhere.

I don't have time to check the beach or call her to see if she's nearby, because I have to deliver Reginald before it's time to meet another client for dinner. I check my phone and find four missed calls, three voicemails, and seven texts. And Conn thought this was a dumb idea. He still might be right, but it's definitely a *popular* dumb idea. I add two items to my to-do list: check on Dad and connect with Hannah. Now I have to find the time to squeeze it all in.

CHAPTER THIRTEEN

———

Next up on the campaign trail, one of the summer's most important events: an afternoon party at the Abbott's Bay Yacht Club on July 3. The actual Fourth might be all about cookouts and fireworks, but on the third, all that hominess is counterbalanced by a healthy dose of high living.

I arrive to find my dad already making the rounds, chatting up all the residents. He doesn't leave out any of the summer folk either, because he knows most of them from his real estate business, and he's a social kind of guy. There's a good turnout, and the place looks fabulous.

"This sure is the way to picnic." Hannah, sounding awestruck, sticks close to my side.

"See why I vetoed the denim shorts you were going to wear?"

"Well, you *said* barbecue."

"There's barbecue, and then there's barbecue."

The scene in the country club could be considered ridiculous if it wasn't so impressive. The patriotic decorations are festive yet tasteful. The red and white checked tablecloths are cute and as homey as the yacht club gets. The food supposedly pays homage to American summer traditions, but there are no hot dogs or hamburgers here. Servers circulate with trays of small grilled lobster halves on skewers, two different kinds of sliders (lobster roll and pulled pork), short corn on the cob smeared with herb butter and sprinkled with grated cheese, baby back ribs with some kind of heavenly-smelling glaze, and the requisite oysters. More food fills a couple of buffet tables decorated with elaborate ice sculptures and flower arrangements.

While the patio and deck are open, pretty much everyone's in the air-conditioned dining room, because sweating is unacceptable outside the confines of one's gym, especially when one is wearing designer clothing.

These are the people I'm looking for.

"Now remember—this is business," I remind my friend.

Conn's guilt trip worked. I asked Hannah to be my assistant, fielding calls and setting up appointments, and she couldn't have said yes any faster. Although I worry this is taking her away from her "me time" and her painting, she insists she was getting bored and this is far more interesting.

Speaking of friends, Taylor also got in on the New Best Friend action. Out of the blue she texted me some links and demanded I check all of them out immediately. Naturally I suspected she'd found some new sources of porn (let's just say it wouldn't be the first time), but they turned out to be social media accounts she'd set up for me—something she's especially good at—because, she said, if I'm going to do this, I'd better "do it right."

Now I need to pull this all together and get it to work in my favor. The yacht club party is the perfect opportunity to expand my client base. I'm in an enclosed space with a fair number of wealthy folks. I'm going to land some big fish choking with cash for Your New Best Friend or die trying, all for…well, that individual walking through the door, in fact.

Conn pauses at the entrance, hands in his pockets, looking like he's stopped for a red carpet photo. Hannah claps eyes on Conn as well, and she lets out a small, involuntary squeak. Really, who could blame her, in the face of the magnificent sight that is Connacht Garvey all cleaned up? Hair brushed, scruff trimmed. Open-collared white shirt, pegged pants, polished shoes. Plus the indigo color of his nicely tailored suit jacket insists his eyes make up their mind and be blue today. A few of the Ms. Moneybags start circling him like sharks, which I find hilarious. Should not tease…should not…and yet I'm crossing the room almost immediately, Hannah trailing after me.

"Well," I say, sidling up to him, "I'm shocked."

"Why? I have an invitation."

"Don't be so defensive. Of course you have every right to be here. I mean…this." I wave my hand up and down, indicating his outfit. "Very stylish. Honestly, you're behind the bar so much lately I forget you have a lower half to your body. It looks good. You should show it off more often."

"Cut it out."

"I'm not sure I can. I'm so in awe of your Garveyness I can't seem to control myself." I move to poke him in the ribs. He manages to block me without even looking my way. It doesn't matter because it was merely a feint. While he's busy deflecting my right hand, I pinch his ass with my left. Hannah gasps then giggles as a mini wrestling match breaks out. It's nothing to draw the attention of the yacht club members—just one of our usual subtle slapfests Conn always wins.

Except today, when he suddenly steps away from me, the tips of his ears turning pink. Have I gone too far? Hardly. I've said and done way worse in my day, and frequently in such tony surroundings as this. I follow his gaze and spot an older, slightly stooped gentleman and a woman in a wheelchair. Ah, that explains it.

"Mr. and Mrs. Garvey! How nice to see you!"

He and I approach his parents and, while Conn takes over wheelchair duties from his father, I hug Conn's mom. From what I've heard from my dad, her hip replacement surgery went well, but she's been relying on her wheelchair a little too long. She looks good though, as does her husband, and I tell them so.

"You're too sweet," Mrs. Garvey says, but the grim expression on her face contradicts her words. She's never liked me—I have no idea why—and she's tough as an old boot, so her small polite statement is like gushing praise. I take it as permission to continue chatting with her.

"Are you here for the rest of the summer?" I ask, cursing the chipper squeak of my voice.

"Absolutely," Bruce confirms, raking his fingers through his thatch of blindingly white hair, made even whiter by the contrast with his deep lots-of-golf tan. "Phoenix is broiling, and we miss this old town. Besides, gotta check in on the boy once in a while."

"You know I've got that covered for you."

"Yes," Constance says, drawing it out in her best Snape impersonation.

Before I can figure out what she's implying, Bruce asks,

"I trust he's taking good care of the house?"

"It's fine, Dad," Conn says, cutting me off.

When I bug my eyes at him, he gives me a barely perceptible shake of his head. He hasn't told them he's planning to sell? I turn back to his parents and opt for *a* truth, if not the *whole* truth. "It's exactly as you left it."

"That's a relief," Bruce says.

That's a matter of opinion. "Are you staying with Conn?"

"Oh, no, no," Constance replies. "We're staying with the Davises—in their guest house. The beach house isn't ours anymore—"

"Mom, I told you, it's no problem—"

"Well, maybe we don't want to see so much of *you*, have you thought about that?" His mom's sharp words would be startling if not for the twinkle in her eye that contradicts her tone. She can be fierce with everyone else, but not Conn. She adores her boy.

"Impossible," he mutters, but he's smiling.

Conn introduces his parents to Hannah, gets them settled at a table by the windows overlooking the harbor, then fetches them some food from the buffet. I leave Hannah chatting with the Garveys and follow him.

"You're going to sell the house without telling your parents?"

"I'll tell them. Eventually."

"Really? When? When they decide to stop by for a visit and the new owners call the police to report an elderly couple attempting to break in?"

"I'll tell them when I sign a contract with a real estate agent. That is, once somebody *gives* me a contract to sign."

"You mean Taylor?"

"Stop fishing. I already told you she's not selling my house. If you recall, I'm still waiting for *you* to get it in gear."

"And *I* told *you* there's no way I'm listing it. Besides," I can't resist adding, "maybe something good will happen soon and you won't have to sell."

He stops foraging for food to stare at me, eyebrows furrowed in confusion. "'*Have* to'?"

"Melanie Abbott! I always knew you were destined for

great things!"

Evidently Rose Perdue, yacht club board president, has heard about Your New Best Friend, which is exciting—she's so well connected, she could help get me some new business.

"Oh, Rose, it's going to be a while before I hit the Fortune 500 list."

She rests her hand on my arm and laughs merrily at this. "I think you're well on your way. So tell me. How did you do it?"

"Do…? Oh, I don't know. The usual way—I came up with the idea and ran with it."

"No, I mean the press coverage!"

"Oh, of course—the *Bugle* has been instrumental in getting the word out."

She clutches my arm tighter. "The *Bugle*? Darling, I'm talking about the big time—your article in the *Huffington Post*!"

"The…what, now?"

Then I remember the last thing Taylor said after she talked to me about my social media setups—that she had one more surprise in the works. And here it is. It has to be her—no one else I know has the connections to get me mentioned in *HuffPo*. I have no idea how she managed it, but I'm immensely grateful for the exposure. It'll give me legitimacy that even multiple features in the *Bugle* and a whole roster of Abbott's Bay locals couldn't manage in a million years.

* * *

After Rose spreads the word that Your New Best Friend is featured on the famous news site, I start getting calls from cash cows. I'm thrilled the next part of my plan is coming together, but I won't abandon my low-rent customers now that the moneyed folks are calling. They need best friends too.

Right now I'm juggling planning a 25th anniversary celebration, coaching a couple of senior citizens on how to operate their smartphones, and my personal favorite, taking (very slow) walks in the park with old Mrs. McCluskey and her yippy dogs. Even though one of them tends to pee on my shoes when he gets excited at the sight of his leash, I enjoy the leisurely time with her. It's a nice break from the mounting chaos. Hannah, however, manages my calendar like a pro, and I start getting into a pretty good groove with my clients.

And then I get my first wakeup call.

Most of the people I work with are women. I don't try to speculate as to why that is, but if pressed I'd say it's because more women than men are on the lookout for best friends. My theory about this is men get by just fine with a handful of casual buddies, but women need at least one intimate, heart-to-heart-type bestie. That need is what most of my business is based on, to be honest.

Then I get a client like Petey Fagle, and I wonder why I didn't stipulate, in the *Bugle* article Laura wrote, that I would *only* work with women. Or would it have been discriminatory?

Doesn't matter. Right now I have to focus on Petey sitting across from me at Deep Brew C, perspiring profusely and fidgeting. I'm grateful we're meeting in a public place. Oh, Petey's not dangerous, but he is a little eccentric, not very socially adept (hence the sweating and twitching), and…okay, he makes me uncomfortable. He makes a lot of people uncomfortable.

Still, a client is a client. Even better, he's a highly desirable unicorn—a wealthy local—so I smile gamely, take a sip of espresso (for this meeting, I've decided, I need the loving support of caffeine), and begin.

"Petey, it's good to see—"

"I need a friend." His knee is jiggling, and I'm captivated by its motion while put off by the high percentage of polyester in his trouser fabric.

"That is the line," I agree with a smile. "So what can I do for you?"

Petey reaches for his extra large mocha whip frozen drink. I watch in fascination as his tongue sneaks out like a reddish snake from a gap in a wall and flails about, seeking the straw. Eventually they connect. He clamps his lips around it and slurps for a few seconds. Finally he says, "Would you like to have coffee with me sometime?"

"We're having coffee now," I reply patiently.

"So…now?"

"Petey, do you think this is a date?"

"I *am* paying." he blurts out, pushing up his glasses, which have slid down his nose, accelerated by a sheen of sweat. The seeking tongue starts its dance again as it goes for the straw once more.

Out of the corner of my eye I see Conn drift closer, ostensibly to clear a nearby table, but I can tell he's keeping an eye on me. Although I can handle Petey on my own, it gives me a warm feeling to know Conn has my back.

"That's not how this works, you know," I say, keeping my voice congenial and my expression neutral.

"But I paid you."

"Not yet. And I wouldn't take money to go out with you. That's a different kind of business altogether, and you know it. Let's not get them confused, okay?"

"But—"

"Nope." Time to shut this down, not debate it. "I'm here to be a friend, not a date." Petey looks crestfallen. "Hey, how come you've never asked me out on a date before?"

"I did."

"No, you didn't."

He nods emphatically, the sudden burst of energy inspiring him to grab his drink's straw with his other hand and actually put it between his lips instead of employing the usual halfhearted tongue flailing. I'm glad I don't have to see the snake tongue again. After more slurps he says, "When we were in high school. I asked you to go to the Founder's Day Ball with me. The ball, remember? Founder's Day?"

He's slipping into a loop, so I cut him off quickly with, "Founder's Day. Yep. Go on," to get him out of it.

"And you said no. Your friend was there. You both thought it was really funny. I didn't think it was so funny."

I have no memory of any of this, but I have a sneaking suspicion the incident may have occurred during Taylor's and my dreaded reign of terror. I'm getting tired of that clever term, darn Conn anyway. But that's not the point right now. Petey's pride is.

"Did you really like me back then?" I ask in a softer voice.

He nods, head bowed. Considering how obnoxious Taylor and I were at the time, I'm not surprised I didn't let him down gently.

"Do you still like me now?" He shakes his head vigorously. "Oh, thanks very much, Petey." He looks up finally, and I smile at him. "Then why are you asking me out?"

"Because I thought this time you wouldn't be able to say no."

"Because you paid."

"Not yet."

"Touché. I'll bet you like somebody else by now anyway, right?"

At this the color rises in his cheeks, and he rolls his eyes awkwardly. This guy is twenty-seven going on twelve. And it can only mean one thing: he needs my help.

"Would you like to talk about it? Maybe I can give you some advice on how to ask *her* out instead?"

He nods so enthusiastically I think his glasses are going to fly off. I settle in for an interesting and, I hope, informative talk with Petey. Conn comes up on my right and picks up my empty cup. I catch his eye, and he winks, the ghost of a smile on his lips.

* * *

I'd like to say my adventure with Petey was the only time a guy tried to finagle a date with me through the business, but I'd be lying. Petey was a prince compared to the douchewaffles who hit on me. They got past Hannah, normally a great gatekeeper, with some fake issue. Then once I was sitting across from them, they started propositioning me.

To Abbott's Bay's credit, they were all summer people. And if I thought Petey was stubborn, these guys were far worse, because...well, because douchewaffliness knows no bounds. They acted as though they were doing *me* a favor, offering to take me out. Or—you know—stay in. Wink, wink. Sure thing, studmuffins. I'm desperate, and you're the answers to my prayers. As if.

It's not like I don't think about meeting someone. I meant it when I told Hannah I don't need a man in my life, but it'd be nice all the same. I dated one or two guys from town back in the mists of time, but I've always assumed I'd end up with someone from away, mainly because I know all the residents of Abbott's Bay a little *too* well at this point in my life. My flirtations with summer people have been fruitless so far though. I've met some nice enough men, but the summer's too short a time to determine whether we're serious enough about one another to begin a long-distance relationship when the season is over, and it simply doesn't happen.

So I stick with my friends, my family, and now my business, hoping for the best while not holding my breath. Fortunately, I'm able to stay optimistic, even when the *Abbott's Bay Bugle* publishes another one of their sneaky little Bites on the Bottom, this time about a "budding matchmaker who, curiously enough, can't match herself."

Gee, I wonder who they're talking about.

CHAPTER FOURTEEN

———

"Can you believe that? I've been rejected!" I punctuate my heated words with a powerful swing of my golf club. I intend to send a ball soaring majestically through the air, but actually I just chuck a divot. It lands several feet in front of me, the dull *thud* of its impact nearly drowned out by Conn's snickering. "What's so funny? It's true." But it's not what you think.

"Rejected by a backwater local TV station—this bothers you why, exactly?"

At Taylor's urging I pitched Your New Best Friend for a spot on a local morning show, hoping to get some traction from my *Huffington Post* mention, but they turned me down flat, saying it was too close to an advertisement to be acceptable as a human interest story.

I should have known I wouldn't get any sympathy from Conn. Bristling, I snipe, "Why are you here, anyway?"

"Conn graciously stepped in," my dad declares, joining us on the country club's practice green, "when Bruce had to cancel."

Dear God, Dad's wearing his favorite golf pants. Red and blue stripes with huge white stars. I kid you not. They're from the bicentennial era, and they look the same as they probably did back then, because heavyweight seventies polyester never dies, although he's had them altered several times over the years so he could keep wearing them even as his build changed from twenty-something gangly to his more robust physique of today. He loves them *that* much. I've been trying to get rid of those pants for years, but somehow he always catches me sneaking them into the trash. He's got some sort of inhuman bond with them. Once I donated them to a church rummage sale where he found them, repurchased them, and brought them back home. The prodigal pants.

He sets his golf bag down and pulls something from a side pocket. With most golfers, it would be a flask. With my father, however..."Sunscreen?" he offers, holding the tube out to me.

I rub some lotion on my nose and cheekbones and pass it to Conn as I address my dad. "You do know Conn's a lousy golfer, right?"

"I am not."

"I'm better," I say smugly.

My father nods. "She's got you there, boy."

I puff up with pride and make a so-there face at Conn. Without missing a beat, he silently points at my fresh divot.

"I was getting out my aggressions."

"I like you anyway, Garvey," Dad continues. "You're like the son I never had and all that. Wear sunscreen. I want you around for many years to come." He gestures to the tube, and Conn pops the cap.

"Who's our fourth, Charles?" I ask, looking around as my father puts away the sunscreen and pulls out some hand sanitizer. "One of your drinking buddies from the nineteenth hole, or what?"

"'Or what' indeed."

I'd know that lazy voice anywhere. "Jack!"

Jack Rossiter the Ridiculously Good Looking strides up to our group, simultaneously pinching the back of my neck affectionately with one hand while reaching out to Conn for a bro-hug with the other. After they've back-thumped each other nearly senseless, Jack turns to my father with a more sedate handshake.

"Mr. Abbott, sir. Good to see you looking so well. Excellent golfing togs."

He looks my dad up and down, and I wince, but Jack seems completely sincere, even as he's taking in the glory of those Old Glory pants.

I haven't seen Jack in quite a while. He used to be a fixture in Abbott's Bay back when he and Conn were in college together. Jack spent almost every summer and holiday here, even though his family was based in New York City in the winter and the Hamptons in the summer. He always said he preferred

Conn's family to his. From what I'd heard about the Rossiter clan, I didn't blame him. Jack is an American Brahmin with scads of money, houses all over the world...and almost no relationship with his parents. Poor little rich boy, but so darned privileged, confident, and pretty it just doesn't matter.

I'm not exaggerating. He's like a Ken doll come to life— perfect, yet without Ken's blank-eyed, psychotic expression. Scratch that. He's like a Disney prince. Exquisitely styled brown hair, smiling brown eyes, blinding-white teeth, slightly tanned skin, classically stylish—and clearly very expensive—clothes. And he'll charm your socks off too.

If you like that kind of thing, of course.

Okay, there *was* a time when even a tiny bit of attention from Jack would send me into a fit of giggles and uncontrollable blushing, but that was ages ago, when I was young and impressionable (read: stupid). The guy does nothing for me now. I put away my Ken dolls and Disney videos years ago, and—

"Miss Melanie. Don't you look ravishing today."

I did *not* giggle. I didn't. And my face is warm from the sun—that's all. "It's good to see you, Mr. Rossiter. What brings you to Abbott's Bay?"

"Oh, this and that," he says as he pulls on a leather golf glove. "Some business deals. You know how it is."

I don't actually, because I find it hard to picture Jack actually working. His family owns a huge number of companies, and I'm aware he's been "gifted" with at least one of them— probably more by now—to run as he sees fit, but he still gives off the air of a responsibility-free frat boy living off the endless stash of family money.

"Of course," he adds, "since I'm in the area, I can't resist sticking around for this month's main event."

"My ribbon cutting for the remodeled community center?" my dad asks hopefully.

"Ah, Mr. Abbott, it is at the top of my list. But I was talking about our boy, here."

Of course. Conn's birthday is coming up. What with all the New Best Friend craziness, I'd nearly forgotten. Nearly.

"I don't want to make a big deal about it."

"And yet we will," Jack intones ominously, putting his

arm around Conn's shoulders and squeezing his clavicle until he winces.

Conn's eyes meet mine, and I know we're sharing the same disconcerting premonition of an evening in his near future: Boston or New York, strippers, bottle service, illegal substances, and quite possibly time in a holding cell until Jack name-drops to get them released and all charges dropped. And Conn's got the nerve to criticize Taylor's sketchy friendship qualities. Honestly.

It looks like Jack's plans for Conn's birthday are going to overshadow what I usually do to mark the occasion. Actually any other type of commemoration would kill mine dead. Not that I wouldn't go all out if Conn let me, but he's always too busy working. Plus he never likes to make himself the center of attention. No matter what his schedule though, he always spends a few minutes with me at closing time when I bring him a cupcake with a candle in it. The idea that this year our tradition is going to be preempted by events that will embarrass the hell out of him amuses me greatly.

"Have fun with that," I murmur, entirely unable to hide my ear-to-ear grin.

"Tee time," my father announces, shouldering his clubs. "Let's get going. I had to make an appointment to see my own damn daughter, and I'm not going to waste it."

"Charles!" I gasp, affronted. "You know I'm at your disposal whenever you need me."

"Oh, that sounds impressive, but in reality you're too busy, aren't you?"

"Never too busy for you, Daddy."

"Really? Coming with me to the Up All Night festival?"

"I'll have Hannah clear my schedule. I swear."

"Did the Abbott's Bay real estate business pick up that much?" Jack asks.

"Oh, it's…" Do I really want to talk about Your New Best Friend? Suddenly I'm feeling modest, possibly because Jack has a tendency to mock people's ideas a little too much. He always means to be funny, but funny often veers into cruel before he even recognizes it.

"You haven't heard about her new enterprise?"

Dad proudly tells Jack all about Your New Best Friend

as we make our way to the first tee. Out of the corner of my eye, I catch Jack looking at me, impressed, and I feel my cheeks grow warm for the second time.

"Our Miss Melanie is famous?" he asks eagerly, and I can't tell if he's making fun of me or not.

"Don't get all excited. It's just a local thing."

"Ladies first," he says, gesturing to the tee. "So why the long face?"

I focus my attention on teeing up and make sure I sound casual when I answer. "I pitched a spot on the North Shore News morning show, but they passed."

"Their mistake."

"You're nice." I plant my feet and position my driver. "It's no big deal though."

"Well, of course not. North Shore News is small potatoes. If you're going to be on television, it should be worth your while—something national."

I laugh a little and take a swing. No divots this time. The ball lands a respectable distance away.

When I pass Jack on his way to the tee, he stops me and says quite seriously, "I can make it happen. All it'd take is a phone call."

If that comment came from any other person, I'd never take it seriously. But this is Jack Rossiter. With his connections? I know he could do it. He balances his ball on a tee, glances over, catches me staring, and winks at me.

I'm not sure how to answer. My father is busy scribbling our names on the scorecard—no modern score-tracking apps for him—and seems not to have heard. Conn, however, is watching me, his face inscrutable. He doesn't give me a clue as to how to proceed with his old frat brother.

I decide to laugh it off. "Golf, Mr. Rossiter," I order him lightly. "And don't worry about me. I can take care of myself."

By the eighth hole—we're only playing nine today—I'm in second place, Jack's in third, and Conn's last as usual. He has many talents, but golf definitely isn't one of them. I'm sure Jack is usually way better than this, but he's the type to chivalrously let me get ahead. And we all play a game of "let the Wookiee win" when it comes to Dad.

I line up my putt on the green, feeling all eyes on me. Normally this doesn't faze me, but as I stand over my ball, getting a secure grip on my putter, I make the mistake of looking up to find Jack watching attentively. It's a little unnerving, which is silly. What's sillier is how my insides surge in response to the sight of Conn watching Jack like a hawk. A suspicious hawk.

No, not suspicious. Jack must have been talking, and Conn was simply paying attention. That's all. That reasoning is enough to help me refocus on the game, and I sink my putt in one stroke.

Jack's up, so I take his place next to Conn at the edge of the green.

"Nice shot," Conn says grimly.

I can tell he's censoring himself. "But...?"

"Just a little..."

"Go on."

"Ah, nothing."

Jack looks up at me and grins while he clears away some detritus, likely imaginary, between his ball and the cup. I smile back as I say out of the side of my mouth to Conn, "No, go on, please."

"A little...you know...hippy."

"Excuse me?"

Jack misses the putt.

"Sorry! Mulligan?" I call and then glare at Conn. *"Hippy?"* I hiss.

"Not like that." He's not the least bit penitent. "I'm not calling you fat."

"You'd better not be."

"You did have a little extra *swing* going on there though."

"Oh *really*."

"It could affect your game."

"I sank the putt."

Two thoughts are careening around in my head right now. First, Conn was watching my hips. Which were *not*, in fact, swinging. Were they? Of course not. I know how to stay still and putt. Second, the last thing in the world Conn should be doing is critiquing anyone's golf game, least of all mine.

...Conn was watching my hips.

Had Conn been glaring at Jack for checking me out?

...Conn was watching my hips.

I'm not sure how that makes me feel, to be honest, but I'm extremely glad I don't have to spend much more time as part of this golf foursome, because now all I can think about is how my hips are moving, and suddenly every step feels awkward. Jack pulls ahead of me with a birdie on the ninth hole. It bothers me less than it usually does because I'm preoccupied with what happened on the eighth hole. My dad wins, as usual, and Conn loses, as usual. I don't even bother mocking Conn's score. It's no fun, since he doesn't care about his golf game.

The men see me off at the clubhouse where they'll retire to the restaurant—or more realistically, the bar—for another couple of hours. I, on the other hand, have another New Best Friend appointment, so I take my leave of them at the valet stand. I give my dad a quick kiss, hug Jack and promise to see him again before he leaves town, and then stand in front of Conn, contemplating my goodbye for him. I opt for a featherlight swipe at his cheek.

"Don't call me hippy again."

"I didn't. I said your *moves* were hippy."

"There's a difference? Don't answer. I don't want to know. Stop talking about it."

"You brought it up."

"It was good to see you out in the fresh air today. You should do more of that before you turn into Gollum, clutching a bagel in the middle of the restaurant and hissing 'my precious.'"

"Ah, you wouldn't mind seeing me in a loincloth."

I can't argue that point, so I just give him an affectionate shove before turning to the parking attendant as the men walk away. A few minutes later, as my car is being brought around, someone grabs my elbow.

"What are you doing later?"

The warm breath on my ear startles me. Its intimacy makes my stomach leap, despite who's doing the whispering. "What are you up to, Jack?"

"I want to hear more about this new business of yours."

"Oh, you find my little enterprise that fascinating?"

"Maybe I do." At my skeptical look he wheedles with his winning smile, "Come on. I can't spend my entire time in Abbott's Bay looking at Garvey's ugly mug."

He still hasn't let go of my arm. I'm keenly aware of that. But I'm not sure how to reply.

"Come on, Miss Melanie," he says again. "You, me, the beach—it'll be relaxing. Humor me?"

CHAPTER FIFTEEN

———

"Melanie Abbott. I always knew you'd turn out smokin'."

"Say one more thing like that, Rossiter, and I'm burying you in the sand and leaving you for dead."

"And feisty as always. I like it."

"Stop. You're turning into a walking cliché."

I'm used to Jack's flirtatiousness, and I never take anything he says seriously, but I am enjoying having a good-looking man stare appreciatively as I take off my beach cover-up. I'm in my best vintage-style, halter-top two-piece in a shade of turquoise that sets off my blonde hair nicely. I settle onto my blanket and tilt my face up to the sun.

"I'm wounded," he whines.

"Doubtful."

"All right. I know the way to your heart—tell me all the details about this new racket of yours. You really hang out with people for a price? And they fall for it?"

Indignant, I turn to him and lift my sunglasses so I can look him squarely in the eye. "What do you mean, 'fall for' it? I take this very seriously."

"I'm sure you do. But you've got to admit, it sounds a little ridiculous."

"I help a lot of people."

"Like…?"

Jack's smirking at me as only Jack can. He doesn't want genuine examples of how I've improved people's lives. So instead of talking about acts of kindness, I regale him with tales of Mrs. McCluskey's yippy, bladder-control-impaired dogs. And Petey Fagle. And Reginald the Ferret. Once he's gotten his "ridiculous" fix, I segue into more serious clients, like Amy Aarons and her empty-nest syndrome. I think her transition in life is poignant but hopeful, and I've been proud to help nudge her into her new phase. But Jack laughs at that too, and now I'm annoyed.

"What's so funny?" I demand.

"This woman is still watching kids' movies so she can relive their childhood without them around? And she wants you to join her? That is so pathetically sad."

I shrug. I don't think he's ever going to understand. So many people can be helped in so many different ways. Much of the time, I've found, it all boils down to simply *being* there for a client—sometimes as a sounding board when they need to talk or merely sitting with them when they don't.

A little farther up the beach, past Jack, a young, dark-haired girl in a white one-piece waves in my direction. It takes me a second to focus. Then I recognize her: it's Zoë from Memorial Day weekend. Her mother's on a lounge chair behind her in a seriously age-inappropriate bikini. She speaks to Zoë—sharply, it seems, because the girl immediately pulls herself back into her shell. Apparently her daughter was a little too emotive for her taste. I wave back enthusiastically, and Zoë brightens.

"More clients?" Jack asks, tipping up his sunglasses and squinting in their direction.

I nod and reposition myself on my stomach, resting my cheek on my forearm. "Good ones."

"What's their story? Did you hook Mom up with a billionaire? Give the girl comportment classes? She looks a little on the awkward side."

I'm not giving him the satisfaction of ripping on them. Especially not Zoë. I don't want to amuse Jack anymore—not at my clients' expense. I shrug again, trying to act noncommittal.

"So what's the attraction in all this, Miss Melanie? Why do it?"

"I like to help people."

"Okay, Mother Theresa."

"And the money doesn't hurt," I add, because it's something he can relate to.

"Like you need it."

"No, but it could go to a good cause." I hesitate then say, "The birthday boy, for example." Jack is the best resource I have to get to the bottom of Conn's financial issues. Why not work it till I get Garvey's secrets?

Jack barks a laugh. "What are you talking about?"

Hm. It's possible Conn hasn't told his best friend about his money issues. Connacht Garvey is nothing if not a ridiculously proud person after all.

I need to know, so I go for broke. "You have to swear not to tell him I talked to you about this."

"Mm, you want me to keep a secret? That's going to cost you."

"Oh, for God's sake." I sigh, impatient. "What do you want?"

He rolls onto his side, facing me and. Propping his head on the heel of his hand, actually leers at me over the top of his sunglasses. "Oh, I'm sure I can think of something."

"Don't be gross."

"Don't be a tease, Miss Melanie. I'd reveal all of Conn's dark deeds for a little alone time with you."

"Will you focus, please? I need some answers." He waves at me to go ahead, so I clumsily blurt out, "Has Conn said anything to you about his…financial status?"

Jack doesn't answer right away. I'd swear he knows something. But he remains cagey, turning away from me again, looking out at the ocean, and asking casually, "In what way?"

"What way? Come on. Is he broke or not? He's got me worried, selling his house and his boat like he needs cash. So I've decided he's getting all the profits from Your New Best Friend. All I have to do is figure out how to convince him to take the money."

Drip.

The single icy drop on the small of my back should have been a clue. And the shadow that's suddenly blotting out the sun. But it's Conn's distinctive baritone amusedly asking, "What's this, now?" that finally gets me to realize the last person I want to hear me asking about his money issues is standing over me.

I roll over and go up on my elbows just in time to get dripped on twice more, once on my stomach, once at the top of my cleavage. "Where did you come from?" I squeak, feeling the cold droplet slide down between my breasts.

Conn raises an eyebrow. It *is* a stupid question,

considering he's wearing a red swimsuit and is soaked from head to foot, sporting a layer of wet sand from his calves to his toes. I should change the conversation, but honestly, now that I'm looking up at him, I can't even make a sound, let alone form words. I've seen Conn in a swimsuit plenty of times before, of course, what with the whole living on the ocean thing, but he's spent so much time holed up in his restaurant lately I've forgotten what's hiding under his jeans and work shirts. Yes, I'm staring. At his matted curls, darkened from the water, at his ledge of a brow as he squints in the sun, at his strong jaw dusted with whiskers.

When my eyes drop to his muscled shoulders and broad expanse of chest and my gaze follows the smattering of chest hairs down between his pecs, over his belly, into his navel…and out again…and notice his shorts have been dragged down on one side, just enough to reveal his hip bone, I can't even remember my own name.

Conn doesn't even notice me derping all over the place, and for that I'm immensely grateful. But then he makes it worse. He slings his towel around his neck and drops down next to me.

"Shove over, Abbott."

There's not much of anywhere to shove over *to*. I'm paralyzed anyway, so I remain immobile in the middle of my towel, hoping my mouth isn't hanging open, while Conn settles on the scrap remaining, his chest against my arm, one prodigious thigh grazing my ass. I should move away. Shove over, like he said. Run for the hills before I do something stupid.

Like, oh, I don't know…lean against him. Which is what I absolutely do—to cool my own suddenly blistering skin against his, icy from the Atlantic, to feel that hardness up close like I'm hardly ever allowed.

I relax against Conn and practically melt. God, he feels good. Too good. I know I've been denied male contact for a while now, and I'm probably overreacting because of it. Then again, I've spent an hour next to tanned, lean, waxed, six-pack Jack, the best-looking guy on our crescent of a beach—quite possibly the entire North Shore—and never felt a flutter.

This however…this…this…can't continue. I have to move—*now*. But if I do, it might imply Conn repulses me, which couldn't be further from the truth. Or that I've been enjoying myself a little too much, which would be worse. If I *don't* move, it's going to get awkward. My only option is to overdo it.

"Yeah, baby. You know what I like," I purr, nestling into Conn's chest with an exaggerated wriggle of my shoulders. "How about a little backrub, since you're there anyway?" I expect Conn to either comply or knock me over jokingly, but he does neither. He doesn't move an inch, in fact.

He only seems to come to life when Jack says pointedly, "I sure could go for a beer right now."

"Well, make like a commoner and get 'em from the fridge."

"Ah, I'd rather have my manservant do it."

"You left Jeeves back at your mansion, so it's you or nobody."

I look up at the underside of Conn's chin while he watches Jack jog back to the house. "Is he staying with you?"

"No. At the inn." Conn's voice vibrates against my back, and I have to work hard to stifle a hungry groan.

"How..." I clear my throat and try again. "How did he get a room in the middle of summer?" When locals say "the inn," they're referring to the venerable Bay Inn up on the bluffs outside of town, close to the lighthouse. It's always booked solid from early May through mid-September.

"He's Jack Rossiter," he says with a shrug, as if that explanation is sufficient. And it is. Some people lead a charmed life. Obscene amounts of money help generate the magic, of course. I wouldn't put it past Jack to slip the owners enough to make them "accidentally" cancel someone else's reservation and give the room to him. "Hey," Conn rumbles, but doesn't follow it up with anything. I look up again. A few strands of my hair are caught in his short beard. "Watch yourself with him, okay?"

This leaves me stunned. "Are you kidding? It's just Jack." Conn doesn't answer. "Is that why you appeared out of nowhere?" I laugh. "You rose out of the ocean like a Greek god to cockblock Jack?" When Conn still says nothing, I add, "He's your closest friend."

"Exactly. I know him too well."

"And I'm a big girl."

"I'm well aware."

"This had better not be another comment about me being fat."

"How many times do I have to tell you? I never—!" He checks himself and sighs. "Look, just...be careful, all right?"

He runs his hand over the top of my head to dislodge my hair from his whiskers. It's an intimate gesture, and it makes my heart race. Then his eyes lock onto mine, and my capacity for breathing abandons me. I can't keep staring at him, but I can't manage to look away either. I'm frozen again, even though the chill is gone from Conn's body and there's nothing but heat and a slight slick of sweat between us. I absolutely cannot move, but suddenly I wouldn't have it any other way.

So of course, at that very moment, Conn's gone in a flash. One blink, and he's on Jack's towel, leaving me with an empty space behind me and a knot in my stomach. I'm not sure what just happened.

Before I can even take the time to figure it out, Conn says gruffly, "Now, let's talk about this money thing."

Dammit. He did hear me talking to Jack about Your New Best Friend's profits. Time slows down, and I find myself thinking through my possible responses quite methodically, even as I feel a stir of panic. Denial isn't an option—not with him looking at me like that.

"What, uh, what did you hear?"

Glowery Conn surfaces. "Do you really think you're giving me all the money from your business? I hope I heard wrong."

"Oh, please. You know *I* don't need it, and I *certainly* had no intention of even starting a side business. But there it is, and it's doing well, so every penny from Your New Best Friend, of which there are now quite a few, is going to you, whether you like it or not. Don't sell your house, or your boat, or your...soul, or whatever you're doing for cash."

I watch his jaw working as he mulls this over. "Melanie, I don't know why you're doing this. What in the world makes you think I need cash?"

"Selling your house and your boat isn't a dead giveaway? Not to mention bugging me about paying my tab."

"Teasing you, you little drama queen."

"Lecturing me about taking too many napkins."

"Trying to be environmentally responsible. Do you know nothing about my restaurant? Also? Teasing."

"Then how in the world are you going to keep Deep Brew C from closing?"

"Wh—closing? It isn't closing!"

I stop to regroup then fire off, "The guy who came in, checking the place out. Banker, right? Assessing the value of the place?"

"Yes."

"Ah-*ha*!"

"To determine the risk factors of funding a *second* location."

You know how sometimes, when you're fairly fluent in a foreign language, like Spanish, and then someone says something in a similar language, like Italian, and you can almost but not quite understand them? This is one of those times. It's like Conn is speaking not-quite-English. I stop to parse his words, translate them into something I understand. "A...second location?"

"Expanding," he confirms quietly, leaning toward me, the ghost of a smile appearing behind his scruff. "Not closing."

I don't trust myself to speak yet. I have to think for a moment. Then I put everything together. "Provincetown?"

"I hear it's a happening place."

"Taylor..."

He nods encouragingly.

"...Is helping you look for a space there."

He nods again. Then he tips his head, studying me. "You were really going to give me all the money you made from Your New Best Friend? Just like that?"

"Well, you wouldn't straight up take any cash from me as a gift or a loan. What was I supposed to do?"

Now he's grinning. "I don't know. Talk to me about it, maybe?"

"Oh, because you're so approachable." I drop my vocal register and try to strike a manly pose, patented Conn frown and all. "'I'm fine, Melanie. Mind your own business, Melanie.'"

"I do *not* sound like Snuffleupagus." He shakes his head, disbelieving. "You'd really do that for me?" he asks again.

"Rethinking my priorities as we speak, so maybe you can just forget about it."

CHAPTER SIXTEEN

———

I'm grateful for this New Best Friend appointment tonight. I need to get my mind off my afternoon at the beach with Jack and Conn yesterday. It's turned me into a complete wreck. First I had to process the information that Conn's restaurant isn't in trouble. Then I had to figure out why I'm still doing Your New Best Friend if not to get money into his pockets. After much soul searching I determine my business will continue because I have a great capacity for helping people, and I like doing it. I'll set aside the money in case Conn needs it in the future.

And the other stuff that happened, namely my drooling over Conn like an idiot? As far as I'm concerned, it didn't happen. Yes, he's gorgeous. I'm well aware of that. I've always been aware of that. It's kind of hard not to be. But he's my *friend*, and I refuse to think of him any other way. He's a fixture in my everyday life. Like the ocean. Or the sky. Or wallpaper. One does not suddenly wake up one morning and decide to start licking the wallpaper, no matter how enticing. Unless one is visiting Willy Wonka's chocolate factory.

Okay, stopping that train of thought right there. Never again am I going to consider Connacht Garvey a sexual being. He's just Conn. Unlickable wallpaper. And I will find myself a decent guy to date to make sure I don't get distracted again.

Because I don't have any dating options at the moment, however, I'm focusing on work instead. Tonight's appointment: Louise Westwood, a summer person I've never met before…and still haven't, not yet. Claiming she was too busy to meet me at DBC or even talk on the phone, she scheduled our first meeting at her house by text. I'm not surprised she didn't have the time to chat; some quick googling has shown Mrs. Westwood is quite the prominent socialite from Chicago with an important, wealthy financier husband. As long as I have a minimal sense of what type of person I'll be dealing with and the basics of her request, which is to utilize my organizational talents and local connections to help plan a cocktail party for more than a hundred guests, I can kick some Best Friend ass.

I ring the doorbell and take in my surroundings. The Westwoods' place is ultra modern, gray angles of concrete backlit by small spotlights in the purple twilight, punctuated here and there with strange greenery forced to sprout tall and narrow from stone pots. No blow-up rafts, plastic sand pails, water shoes, or boogie boards by the heavy mahogany double front doors, no sir.

So I'm a little surprised when a kid answers the door.

I recover pretty quickly and say cheerfully, "Hi there. I'm Melanie Abbott. I have an appointment with your mom."

The dark-haired boy, who seems to be on the pre-growth-spurt side of thirteen, stares at me for a moment, his eyes serious behind trendy glasses perched on his freckled nose. Finally he backs into the house, opening the door wider. "Come in. You're expected."

That was sort of oddly worded for a kid, but all right. I walk into a tiled foyer with artfully placed track lighting, more potted plants, and very, *very* expensive yet spartan furniture. Classical music wafts from unseen speakers.

"So..." I venture, when the boy makes absolutely no move to get his mother. "I gave you my name—?"

"It's a pleasure to meet you, Ms. Abbott. My name is..." He swallows and then says, almost defiantly, "Vernon Westwood."

Ouch. That is one cruel set of parents. I can tell he's bracing himself for the laugh he's expecting to burst out of me, but that's not my style. Nodding, I ask, as casually as possible, "Family name?"

"Of course."

"Great grandfather? Great-great—?"

He stifles a sigh. "All of them."

"Of course."

"Please come in." He gestures almost robotically, ushering me farther into the house. "Perhaps you'd like to get some fresh air on the balcony."

I look out the French doors at the large slab of concrete overlooking the ocean. There's no one out there. And the house is suspiciously quiet. "Vernon—"

"Please." He gestures again. "There's a lovely breeze."

Okay, this kid is as odd as they come. I humor him for now and leave the air-conditioned comfort of the living room for the humid air outside. He doesn't follow me. I assume he's going to find his mother—I hope so anyway—so I have a seat at the table. More plants, more indirect lighting, a couple of redwood chaises, and a telescope in the corner. I wait a few minutes, impatiently tapping my fingers on the glass tabletop. It doesn't take long before I give up my pose and start to pace.

Vernon doesn't come back, and his mother doesn't show up either. Did Louisa forget about our appointment? Did she change her mind? Did Vernon kill her and is right now stuffing body parts into the subzero freezer?

Okay, he's not *that* weird. But this whole thing is kind of off, even without the psycho-killer angle. I lean on the balcony wall and tell myself to wait a few more minutes. The beach is beautiful this evening. The lights of the pier flash on the water, adults stroll along the shore, children shriek as they play Ghost in the Graveyard nearby, close to the pilings of the houses, just like Conn and I and the rest of our friends used to do years ago.

"Some refreshments." Vernon comes onto the patio carrying a tray loaded with cheese, crackers, fruit, and a pitcher of what looks like sangria.

"Vernon…"

Once he puts the tray on the table, he turns to me and fidgets nervously. "I—I have to apologize, Ms. Abbott. I'm afraid I brought you here under false pretenses."

"*You* brought me here?"

He nods, not meeting my eyes. "My mom doesn't need your help. I do."

"I don't accept underage clients, Vernon."

"That's why I used my mother's name."

"So there's no cocktail party?"

"Oh, there is, but my mother never needs any help with party planning."

I return to the table but only to pick up my things. "I don't like it when people waste my time." I look down at the spread he brought out. "And I told you I didn't want any refreshments." Hoisting my bag with one hand, I snag a cluster of grapes with the other. To tell the truth I'm starving, but I'm still out of here.

"I'm sorry!" the kid bursts out. "I…need…"

"A friend," I finish for him. "I know. Don't we all."

"No, I mean…" He sighs and plops into the seat I'd vacated before, resting his elbow on the table and rubbing his forehead while shielding his eyes. He sounds teary when he says, "I need several friends, actually. Because I don't have any."

Crap.

My bag slides off my shoulder and hits the deck with a thud as I slip into the chair closest to him. "Where are your parents, honey?"

"Out. Having dinner with friends."

"Do they know—?"

"They don't know anything. They don't know I asked you to come here or how. Or why."

"Maybe you should talk to them about this."

"No." He says this so emphatically it's obvious he's been dealing with this issue on his own for a long time.

"I'm sure they'd understand."

"It's not that. I don't want them to know I've…"

"What?"

"Failed. At anything. Even this. Especially this."

"So you're seeing the whole 'friendship' thing as something to pass or fail? Like a…science project?"

"Of course not!" he bursts out. "It's not the same at all—I know that."

"But you've done the research, observed your peers interacting in the wild, employed all friend-making recommendations, and none of it seems to be working?"

I know I've read him right when he doesn't answer. His silence says everything. The poor kid is approaching this from the head, not the heart.

Sitting back in my chair and crossing my arms, I do my best to sound stern. "I don't usually work with people who lie to me, Vernon."

As I expect, he seizes on the pivotal word *usually*. He brightens a little. "But—?"

"I *might* make an exception, just because you're breaking my heart."

"I'm okay with that."

"Honey, you are a hot mess."

"I know. It's why I'm asking you for help. I have the cash." He reaches into his pocket and comes up with an impressively fat wad of bills.

I don't hesitate for a minute. "Keep your money. Sometimes I work *pro bono*."

"I'm not a charity case. We either do this the right way, or the deal's off."

"Hey, that's *my* line." I study him for a moment. There's a little light in his eye that wasn't there before. He's hopeful. Can I help him? Without a doubt. Do I want to? More than anything. Way more than I'm letting on. "Okay," I say with a sigh, "here's the deal. I'm not meeting with you alone for one more minute. Liabilities and all that. First I talk to your parents, and *if* they give their permission, I'll help you. Got it?" He nods but with a concerned frown. "Don't worry. I can be very convincing. Once they say they're okay with this, I'll get your social skills up to snuff." I look him up and down. "And we're going to get you some decent clothes."

At the moment he's dressed in pressed khakis, a short-sleeved button-down shirt, socks, and soft-soled lace-up shoes. Not even nerd-chic. Just straight-up nerd.

Suddenly he's on his feet. "Wait. Please. I've got an idea."

I wander back to the balcony wall while Vernon's in the house. I can't believe Hannah and I fell for this. I'm glad we did, though. Vernon's problem is more interesting than all the adult clients' issues I've handled. Put together. If I help this kid now, it could affect the rest of his life. What could be more worthwhile?

"How about this?" Vernon is standing by the doors, dressed in a short-sleeved polo shirt and madras shorts. "My cousin left these behind over the Fourth of July holiday. They're a little big…" he says uncertainly, plucking at the shirt, which is indeed roomy but in a stylish way. His mother wouldn't agree, I'd bet, judging by his previous outfit, which was more along the lines of a prepubescent Bill Gates.

"They're perfect. You look cool."

"I do?"

"You do. Also cool: deck shoes *without* the dark socks. Make a note of it for later."

He joins me at the wall. "You really think you can help me?" he asks eagerly.

"I can help anyone. But I've got to warn you. I tend to be pretty blunt when I'm giving advice. Can you handle it?"

"Indubitably."

"Totally," I correct him.

"Sorry?"

"Say 'totally.'"

Now he's grinning from ear to ear. "Totally." He even puts a little dudebro-type spin on it, which impresses me. He'll take direction well.

"There you go. Is this your telescope?"

"Yes. You can use it if you like."

"Totally." I lean over and peer into the eyepiece on top. "You're an astronomer? Or do you peek into people's houses with this thing?"

"Ms. Abbott!"

I laugh softly at his pearl-clutching and wait.

Finally he confesses, "I'm not looking for...you know. *Naked women*," he whispers. "I just like being able to see what other people's lives are like. It's...interesting."

"You're a trip, Vernon." I look up at him. "Hey, what's your middle name?"

"Abraham."

"Ooh, maybe you should try going by your middle name from now on: Bram. Sounds tough, right?"

Vernon—Bram—finds this hilarious. I'm glad he's feeling more at ease. I return my attention to the telescope and don't even pretend I'm not swinging it toward Conn's house. My new friend doesn't ask any questions, bless him—he just shows me how to focus the thing. It takes me a few seconds to get a bead on the side window. Conn's not alone. I focus a little more and see it's not Jack. It's a woman. My stomach surging, I step back from the telescope. I don't know why I'm shocked to find out he might be spending time with someone I don't know about. What did I expect to see, a domestic portrait of Conn and Harvey sharing shot glasses of milk while watching Animal Planet? I feel my face heat up. I shouldn't be spying on him. But there's no question I'm going to take another look.

The woman is wandering around the living room with a glass in her hand. Tall, willowy, her blonde hair scraped back into a tight knot. Very Gwynnie. She's dressed all in white: slinky yet classy walking shorts, silk tank, open-weave cardigan. Oozing money. She's got to be a summer person, which isn't surprising. If Conn kept all the napkins with phone numbers scribbled on them that his vacationing customers nudged across the bar, he'd…well, he'd stop criticizing me for taking too many when I have a meal at DBC—that's for sure.

Shaking my head, I try to look away, but I'm drawn back the instant the woman walks up to him, throws back her head, and laughs, trailing her hand along his shoulder. Normally I'm not awed by wealthy summer people, but I have to admire this woman's style. The last time I was so bowled over by someone's vibe like this was…

Oh no.

It's Sasha.

CHAPTER SEVENTEEN

"This isn't working."

"*Shh.* He'll hear you."

"I doubt it."

Hannah's right. There's no way Vernon—er, Bram—is going to catch our conversation over the noise on the street. The Up All Night festival, one of Abbott's Bay's big summer events, is in full swing, and hundreds of people are clogging the historic district. All the shops, art galleries, and restaurants are open, small bands and solo musicians are strategically placed throughout the town so their sounds won't overlap, clowns are making balloon animals. Quite a few partygoers will indeed manage to stay up all night, wrapping up the festivities by the town-sanctioned beach bonfires as the sun rises.

I'm enjoying the festivities, not only because it's the perfect setting for Bram to find a batch of friends, but also because it helps me keep my mind off what I saw last night. And what *did* I see, exactly? Sasha being back in town after all these years was enough of a shock, but what was she doing cozying up to Conn? He's always been quite clear about his post-divorce feelings for his ex. His favorite epithets, in fact, have included "harpy," "ice queen," and variations on "manipulative, stone-hearted, selfish super-bitch." That scene at Conn's, however briefly I spied on it, seemed to contradict everything Conn's expressed over the past five years.

I'm proud of the fact that I didn't spend every moment last night and today trying to figure it out. I'm also proud that I decided not to share the news with Hannah till I know exactly what I'm—er, what *Conn* is dealing with. Of course, it helped that I had to work on Bram's situation. First I got in touch with his parents and, as it turned out, I didn't even have to try to get their blessing. Mr. and Mrs. Westwood have been secretly worried about their son's social status, or lack thereof, for a while now, but they've been at a loss as to how to get him to connect with his peers.

Lucky for them, I've come up with plenty of ideas. Bram has been renamed, reclothed, and coached on how to be friendly and approachable yet be himself. Hannah and I canvassed the festival to locate some likely potential friends, and when Bram arrived we sent him over to approach the group. At the moment, however, he's hanging back uncertainly, keeping us in his sights through the crowd.

"The poor guy," Hannah coos.

"He's doing great," I insist while making an odd woop-woop fist-pumping gesture to show my support. He frowns, confused. I give him a *never mind* wave, directing his attention back toward his targets.

The kids we chose seem friendly and cool but not too racy—they're hanging out by Macomb's candy shop instead of under the pier smoking weed. Hey, I did my homework. I don't take this assignment lightly.

Hannah's wringing her hands. "Should we help him?"

"He's got to do this on his own." We're here to rescue Bram if necessary, but adults can't push teens together. It would have the opposite effect. I smile at my friend and drape my arm over her shoulders. "You are a bleeding heart, Clement, and I love you for it. I'm so glad you're here."

For some reason that makes her squirm uncomfortably. Then she manages to say, "I—I meant to tell you. I'm…going out of town for a little while."

I'm more alarmed at her news than I'd expect. "What? Where? Why?"

"I thought I'd go home for a couple of weeks, see what everybody's up to."

Everybody as in Marty. Now I know why she was squirming. Of course she has other friends in Ohio, but from the way she's avoiding looking at me, I know he's definitely on her agenda, and she knows I don't approve. The worst thing she can do is see him—she'll get all confused about her feelings, and all the progress she's made this summer will go right down the drain. Good grief, why do people ask for my advice if they're only going to ignore it?

Before I end up saying just that to her—and thank goodness because it wouldn't come out nicely—I feel a...*presence* beside me.

"What are we watching? Is this street theater?"

At least I think that's what Laura just said. Considering the level of noise overwhelming her tiny voice, she could just as well have said, "Come see my pet lemur." Which, come to think of it, wouldn't surprise me. I glance over at her. Then I do a double take. Laura looks completely ordinary—no funny hats tonight. However, hovering above and slightly behind her is a bright pink and yellow Chinese dragon. It's a kite.

The thing is, there's no wind tonight.

It takes me a minute to realize there's a stiff wire attached to it instead of a string. Good grief, can't this woman act normal for just five minutes?

"If this is street theater, it's kind of boring."

"Laura," I try to explain, sounding exasperated, "it's not...never mind." I don't have time for this. "You know what? I hear the food truck by Dipsy Doodle's, the kids' clothing store, is offering to deep fry anything you bring them."

"Ooh, I have my backup pencil sharpener in my pocket."

Of course she does. I wave as she scoots away, her pink and yellow dragon bobbing along energetically over the crowd.

When I turn back to Bram, I feel a little surge of panic in my belly. Hannah was right: it's not going well. Bram's shoulders are hunching, and he's fading into the background instead of engaging the other kids. Operation New Friends is starting to head south at an alarming rate.

"He's in trouble. I'm going in."

"Let me."

Let...what? Hannah? Do what? As I'm puzzling this out, she walks up to Bram and says in a loud, clear voice, "Aren't you Bram Westwood?" She ignores the boy's stunned look and adds, "The winner of the Golden Key Award in Orga—"

Tweaking to what she's up to, I mutter worriedly, "Don't say that part." Golden Key Award sounds cool and mysterious; Golden Key Award in Organic Chemistry is a bit too geeky for this crowd.

"Golden Key Award?" she repeats and ends there. I let out a little breath, suddenly a believer in telepathy.

Bram is only sweating a little bit. "I...uh, yes?"

The other kids are looking at him, curious. I hold my breath. Hannah's ploy might work.

"Do you mind?"

Hannah whips out her phone for a selfie, and I'm captivated by her impressive acting ability. She's all sincerity as she holds it at arm's length, putting her head close to Bram's. He shifts from stunned to only semi-stunned, plus a touch flattered. I can see his chest puffing up from here. The other kids watch as Hannah takes the photo, squeals her thanks like she's just met a member of the hottest boy band, and heads back over to me.

"Genius," I whisper, truly impressed.

"I know!"

Where did this unexpected, outspoken Hannah come from? She's grinning from ear to ear, and the whole situation is so ridiculous that I start laughing as Bram runs up to us.

"They're talking to me! They're talking to me! They invited me down to the beach. What do I do now?"

"You go, obviously!"

"But they said something about playing Frisbee. I don't know how to play Frisbee!"

"Fake. It."

After a few moments to give them a head start, Hannah and I follow the group down to the beach to make sure they really are playing Frisbee and it wasn't code for smoking weed under the pier. It doesn't take long before we find out that Bram isn't kidding about his lack of Frisbee skills. We arrive just in time to see him get clocked in the nose by a particularly fast-moving disc.

*   *   *

"Okay, so maybe they weren't the best kids to approach," I say as I blot some blood from under his nose.

"You think?"

"Well, it's not like they took you out on purpose."

"They didn't stick around once I was out of the game either."

He's right—they weren't very gracious. I sit back on my heels with a sigh. This is my fault. An error in judgment. It doesn't happen often, but once in a while I might—*might*—drop the ball. Or, in this case, the Frisbee.

"I should have known this would never work," he mutters, his voice thick from the tissues stuffed up his nostrils. "I guess I don't have what it takes."

"Come on, Bram. You're immensely likeable."

"I think you're great," Hannah offers.

Bram just shrugs and looks more dejected than ever. A couple of old ladies' good opinions carry no currency in the teen years. I whisper to Hannah to get some ice. She nods and dashes off with her flip-flops in her hand, her bare feet flinging puffs of sand behind her. I peer down the beach, trying to locate the kids Bram had been talking to. There's no sign of them. No matter. I can find him other friends. What's more important is getting him motivated again.

"Am I going to have a black eye?"

"Maybe two. But they'll make you look like a badass."

"I don't want to look like a badass," he groans, struggling to his feet. "I want to go home."

"Are you kidding? The night's barely started! You've got to get out there and—"

"Ms. Abbott? If it's all the same to you, I think I'd like to give it up. For now, anyway."

I start to protest, but he looks so defeated I don't have the heart to argue with him. This might be the very first failure I've had with Your New Best Friend. Even Petey Fagle managed to ask out his crush, the young woman who works at the bait shop on the pier, after a few sessions with me. I saw them together earlier tonight, which means they've been dating for two whole weeks now.

Bram is heading up the beach toward home, already far enough away that he's fading into the darkness. I can't let this happen. I trip to my feet and take off after him, veering onto the packed, wet sand close to the water so I can move faster. My phone pings with a text. It's either Hannah asking where she can get some ice without battling the crowds, or it's my dad, who I last saw handing out campaign buttons by the food trucks. I wrestle the phone out of my purse without slowing down and hold it up to see the screen—and then my shoulder smacks hard into someone else's arm. My phone is pitched out of my grip and flies backward several feet, as though someone's hooked it with a fishing line. It lands on the sand with a plop.

"I've got it!" A woman in a pale dress scoops my phone up before a lapping wave reaches it.

"Oh God, thank you so—" Then she stands up, smiles, and holds the phone out to me. "Sasha. Hi." Yeah, my voice isn't stilted. Much. Suddenly I sound about as wooden as I feel.

Sasha, however, lights up in recognition, crying, "Oh my goodness—Melanie!"

She grabs me in a tight hug that I try to return enthusiastically, even though I've been totally blindsided, and I'm not talking about having physically collided with someone on the beach. Sasha lets me out of the hug but keeps a grip on me as she studies me at arm's length.

"Look at you," she practically sings. "So beautiful. It's such a shock seeing you all grown up. I can't help but think of you as a teenager even after all these years!"

I'll return the compliment as soon as I find my voice. There's plenty to praise. She's still gorgeous and perfect. Even in the dark I can tell she's tanned—but not too much—by the contrast of her skin against her white, gauzy dress. Her fine blonde hair is pulled back into a tight bun again, which emphasizes her sharp cheekbones and pronounced jawline. Her whippet-thin, muscular arms only remind me how fleshy mine are.

She hasn't changed—still ageless and perfect, the queen of everything and the only person who can render me speechless. She continues smiling down at me from her several-inch height advantage. I'd better say something. Something clever, preferably. Or, you know, anything at all, because this silence has gone on a few seconds too—

"Hey, Abbott, nice linebacker move."

OhthankGod. I've never been so happy to see Conn in my life...even if his proximity means he was with Sasha. On the beach. In the moonlight.

He comes up to us, rubbing his arm. I was so fixated on catching up with Bram, I didn't even notice it was him I ran into. He stands with his back to the water, the three of us forming a neat little triangle.

"I've been asking Conn where you were! I wanted to see you," Sasha says, glancing from Conn to me and back again.

"Guess now you have," I say lamely, holding my hands out and then letting them drop in a weak *ta-da* gesture.

"I'm *so* glad. We *have* to take some time to catch up while I'm here. How long has it been?"

Five years plus however many months since the last holiday Conn and Sasha spent together in Abbott's Bay before the divorce, I think. But I just say, "*Too* long." Ugh, her cadence is contagious.

"Abso*lute*ly!"

"What…uh, what are you doing in town, anyway?" I ask, wincing at my own bluntness.

Sasha is too classy to call me on it. She half smiles as she glances at Conn. "Well…" she begins uncertainly, but Conn answers for her.

"Visiting. You know. Vacation. Where were you off to so fast that you had to knock me over?"

Nothing knocks him over, least of all five-foot-three me. I smirk at his hyperbole. "Business," is all I say.

"You have a client? Tonight?"

"I can mix business with pleasure. Happy birthday, by the way." It comes out coldly, and I'm not sure if I mean it to or not. I texted him first thing this morning with a birthday greeting like I do every year. And every year he replies with the rudest emoji he can find. He didn't text me back this morning though, and now I know why. I still play dumb, however. "I thought you'd be knee deep in New York strippers and blow by now."

Sasha laughs musically. "I love the way you talk, Melanie. You're so cute and funny, and you don't care *what* you sound like."

Before I can ask what that's supposed to mean, Conn makes a face and says, "I'm a little too old for that, don't you think?"

"You let Jack down? I've got to admit, I'm shocked."

"An early dinner in Boston was good enough. I wanted to get back to keep an eye on the restaurant during the festival."

Sasha clucks adorably and latches onto Conn's arm, pressing her cheek to his shoulder. "He did. I managed to pry him loose from the place eventually. It's such a beautiful night. I couldn't let him hole up in there."

Vaguely I realize it's my turn to say something, but I'm stuck staring at the tableau in front of me: Sasha all clingy, and Conn standing there, not really minding.

Conn fills the silence by circling back to my earlier comment. "So…you had a client?"

"Yes—"

"Ooh, Conn was telling me about your new business! Congratulations!"

"I kind of lost him though. Did you see a kid go by? About thirteen but looks younger, kind of skinny, dark hair?"

"You're advising *kids* now?"

Uh-oh. Is Conn doing warmup stretches for a "scold Melanie" rant? I don't need that right now.

"It's a special case," I explain. "A one-time thing. Don't worry."

"No, no—I was going to say kids need help too. I mean, Hannah said you changed that Zoë kid's life with a two-minute consultation. It could be a genius move. As long as you handle it right."

Well, that's a surprise. I try not to think he's sounding noble and supportive because Sasha's standing here.

"Of *course* I'm handing it right."

"Except you lost him?"

I knew he wouldn't be able to keep Judgy Conn buried for long. "We had a minor setback, and he headed home. It's not like he's lost at sea. He lives right over there." I point at the bank of houses looming over the thin strip of sand.

"The kid there? In the plaid shorts?"

I squint in the direction Conn is indicating, and sure enough I can see a familiar figure in the light of the nearest bonfire. Hands in his pockets, he's fidgeting exactly the way I coached him not to, but he's also talking to a girl.

A familiar-looking girl.

"Bram!" I wave energetically until he spots me and runs over.

"Ms. Abbott! It worked! Everything you told me? It worked."

"Of course it did," I say. "But that's not someone from the group you were talking to earlier."

"No. Is that okay?"

"It's fine. I know Zoë. She's great. I wholeheartedly approve."

Why didn't I think of Zoë in the first place? This is *perfect*. They're perfect together. Both a little shy and awkward, both in need of a friend—what could be better?

"There's only one problem," Bram says. "I told her about my telescope."

"And?"

"She wants to try it out. But I can't bring it down to the beach. It's delicate equipment. I don't want any sand getting into it."

"Then invite her to your house. Your parents are home, right?"

"Yes."

"All right then. Have Zoë call her mother and tell her where she is. Or better yet, have your parents call her. They might even know one another already. A little stargazing, some refreshments—how could she refuse? You're a magnificent host, Bram. She'll love it."

"Uh, Ms. Abbott?"

"Yes?"

"Can you call me Vernon again? 'Bram' is different and all, but I don't think it's exactly…"

"You?"

"Totally."

"Gotcha."

"Thanks." He fidgets again, drawn by the pull of his new friend but politely staying with me to wrap up our conversation properly. I decide to cut him loose before he spontaneously combusts.

"Go on then…Vernon."

He grins, nods at Conn and Sasha like the well-bred kid he is, then takes off again. I raise my eyebrow at Conn, silently daring him to argue against any of this.

"Nice," is all he says.

"I know," I reply, more than a little smug. Out of the corner of my eye I see even Sasha is looking impressed, which is just gravy.

CHAPTER EIGHTEEN

Then again, any advantage I think I've gained—hey look, I'm a grownup! I have my own successful business! so stop calling me cute!—is ripped away on the brisk night breeze only minutes later. I text a reply to Hannah and she meets us on the beach, clutching a baggie of ice for Bram's—er, Vernon's—nose. Her arrival should give me the perfect excuse to take my leave of these possible lovebirds (urk), but Hannah's natural sweetness charms Sasha, and pretty soon they're deep in an animated chat. Every once in a while Hannah glances over at me guiltily, aware that Sasha is supposed to be the enemy, but then Sasha draws her back in with another question about Hannah's life, and they continue their bonding session.

Which leaves me with Conn. He and I make small talk: what Sasha gave him for his birthday (a book), where he and Jack went for dinner (a Summerville bar they frequented when they attended Harvard, for nostalgia, chicken wings, and beer), even a little bit about how my dad's campaign is going. Nothing of substance. A good thing too, because I'm terribly distracted, wondering what Sasha's presence means. Is she visiting for his birthday? She hasn't come to Abbott's Bay once since their divorce. Have they gotten over their differences—or rather, has Conn gotten over his bitterness toward her? Most important, does he see Sasha's blatant attempt to cozy up to him again, both figuratively and (shudder) literally? Because it's crystal clear from where I'm standing.

"Conn, sweetie?" Sasha calls from a few feet away, where she and Hannah have drifted. "I'm chilly."

"Pick a bonfire," I suggest. "It's what they're there for."

"Let's go back to the house instead," she says to Conn, crossing her arms and hunching delicately. "We still have to talk—don't forget."

"Sure," Conn concedes without hesitation, and we all start trudging back down the beach.

Talk? About what? I'm dying to ask. I can't ask. It can't be anything good. My stomach churns as I get more and more riled up at this whole situation. It took years for Conn to get over his ex. I should know—I witnessed it. Hell, I helped him through it. And now that he's back on an even keel, here comes Sasha to knock him askew again.

Sasha and Hannah walk ahead of Conn and me. From the snatches of conversation that come back to me on the wind, I can tell Hannah is in the middle of relating the saga of her and Marty. Sasha is hanging on every word, which makes Hannah glow.

As I'm trying to decide whether to jump in to try to diffuse the glamour fogging Hannah's brain, Conn says, "Thanks for the birthday text. Where'd you find an emoji of a unicorn jumping out of a cake?"

"I never reveal my sources."

"I don't suppose I get a cupcake this year, huh?" He stops walking and gives me an endearing grin, but I'm feeling a little too salty to succumb to his charms.

"Looks like you've already got all the cupcake you can handle, mister."

"What?" he drawls, smiling wider and stuffing his hands into his pockets.

Connacht Garvey does many things very well, but pulling off "disingenuous" isn't one of them. It's unnerving—he's always such a straight shooter that when he decides to skirt an issue, especially one involving a skirt, he's about as smooth as Vernon.

"Don't even try it," I hiss. "What do you take me for?"

"You're going to have to be more specific, Abbott. Use your words, now."

"Stop it. You know what I'm talking about. What's with all the kissy-face with Sasha? It wasn't too long ago you described her as…what was it…a 'frozen-hearted harpy'? And now you're besties?"

"Oh, come on. There was no 'kissy-face.' And may I

point out using that term is trivializing your argument."

"I know what I just saw."

"You're exaggerating."

"And you're playing dumb. A romantic stroll on the beach? Your fifth wheel nowhere to be found?"

"You're right here."

That stings. *"Jack!"*

"Oh, right. We left him several tequila shots deep in a political argument with some of the gang at DBC. What's the big deal?"

"Cut the crap, Conn. What's her agenda? What's she doing here? Are you sleeping with her again or not?"

Conn's jaw drops, and I fall silent. Over the shush of the waves, quieter now that we're farther away from the water line, comes the sound of Sasha's uncharacteristically strident voice shouting from Conn's deck.

"Hurry up, you two! We're going to light the chiminea. Conn, do you have any marshmallows?"

Like Sasha eats marshmallows.

His eyes stay locked on mine as he calls back brusquely, "We'll be there in a minute."

I wait. After a moment or two he looks off and up, at the sparks spitting from the bonfire in the distance, at the dim stars in the dark sky, anywhere as long as it isn't at me.

"Conn..." I begin uncertainly, while at the same time he mutters, "Wow."

"I know. I'm sorry—"

"See, that's the thing. You're not."

"No, really, I—"

"You just asked for—no, *demanded*—details of my *sex life*, and you actually expect an answer." He laughs a little, but there's no humor in it.

"I don't."

He doesn't hear me. "What is *with* you lately? It's like a theme: 'Melanie Takes an Unnatural Interest in Conn's Love Life.' I mean, first you make a *very* big point of telling Hannah I'm not available—"

"For her own protection. She's still recovering from her breakup, and I didn't want her to mistake a crush for—"

"Come on. Why would you take it seriously? *Hannah* doesn't even take it seriously."

He's right. Hannah admires Conn because he's a smart, friendly, good-looking guy, but it's obvious her heart is still with Marty (I'm no dummy). I don't bother telling Conn any of that. He's not waiting for me to respond anyway.

"*Then* you warn me Taylor is after me, which is completely *insane*, and now Sasha?"

"I—"

"What I want to know is…why? Really. What makes you think you have the *right* to tell me who I can and can't spend time with?"

"Because we're friends! And…and friends look out for one another."

"Seriously? *That's* your reason?"

"Okay, maybe all the stuff with Hannah and Taylor was…misguided. But Sasha? After she broke your heart, you're going to let her waltz back in here and—"

"I think that's my business, don't you?"

"Oh, here we go again. *Your* business. In case you've forgotten, I was right here when you moved back home. I saw what was left of you when she got through with you. I saw you at your worst—because of her—and I helped you put your life back together…"

I don't need to say this. Conn knows. He still gives me grief about it, teasing me about how I kept bothering him, being obnoxiously cheerful, invading his personal space when all he wanted to do was sulk in his house with only his equally grumpy cat for company. I saw him through his darkest moods. I have a right to express an opinion about this.

"Why would you think I wouldn't have something to say when she turns up out of the blue with that…that *look* in her eye?"

"Oh, you always have something to say," he snaps. "But for your information she didn't 'turn up out of the blue.' I invited her."

I can feel my mouth working, but nothing's coming out. Finally I manage a few weak words. "You…you *want* her here?" Now it's my turn to look away. I cast my eyes down at the sand, clumped in little hills from the many feet that have kicked through it today. I focus on a bent cigarette butt poking out of a nearby mini-dune. "Well then." I take a deep, slow breath. "You're right. I overstepped. Forget I said anything."

I turn to go, but Conn reaches out to stop me. "Hey. It's not like that."

Flinching, I pull away so he doesn't actually touch me. "Don't. You're right—you don't owe me any explanation. It's my own fault that I think you do."

"But you're upset that she's here."

"Of course I am!" I erupt. "I know how this goes. She's going to do it again."

"Do what again?"

"Dazzle you, blind you…what she always does. And then…" The tendons in my neck ache from the strain of trying not to shout, trying to hold it together, the pressure on my heart so intense I think it's going to burst. "Take you away. I couldn't stand that because you wouldn't be…" I stop again, choking on unshed tears, horrified at the thought that's surfaced.

"What?" he demands. "Wouldn't be what?"

Mine.

"Around anymore," I say instead. "And it wouldn't…be the same. It wouldn't be right. Conn, I…I need you here."

"You need me here? For what?"

Everything. I don't dare answer. I don't know what to say that won't sound presumptuous, stupid, proprietary—everything I have no right to feel, but I'm feeling anyway. I need him here because…

"Melanie?"

Conn's voice sounds distant, muffled. It's drowned out by the thundering of my heart, the roiling of my insides, and the chaos of my own thoughts. I need to respond. I have to acknowledge Conn is talking to me.

"I'm so sorry," I fight out, with effort. "Really. Please believe me."

"Okay. It's okay. I get it. You're looking out for me, like you said."

No. I'm not. I'm looking out for *me*, trying to catch the pieces of my shattered heart that are falling through my fingers as I realize. This isn't about Sasha, not really. It's about *any* woman coming between me and Conn. He really has been everything to me, for a long time. Once he was the cool kid I idolized. Then he was the young man I admired. But recently? So much more. A really good friend…at the very least. Normally I don't let myself think any further than that.

Now he's looking at me fondly, a warm light in his eyes as he shakes his head in wonder. "Yeah, that's us: I pull you back from whatever virtual cliff you're about to wander off of, and you keep my head on straight. I'm glad you care about me." Then he winks. "You, er, *do* care, don't you? That's what you were going for, right?"

I start nodding, almost violently, like I can't control my body. "I…I love you."

Apparently, I can't control my thoughts either, because that one actually comes out.

My eyes are wide when I look at him, stinging when they're hit by a salt-laden breeze. The lobster roll I had for dinner is threatening to make a grand reappearance on my shoes. For quite possibly the first time in my life, I'm terrified. I didn't tack on "you doofus" like I usually do. Because this time…I mean it. I mean *really* mean it.

Conn is smiling, genuinely and almost bashfully. I don't move—I can't—so he reaches out and pulls me into a hug. I'm stiff as a board, not even able to raise my arms to hug him back, because now it's not just Conn holding me. It's *Conn*. The man I…love?

Ho-ly…this is bad. This is really bad.

One ear is mushed into his chest, and he's covering the other as he cradles my head with his hand, but I'm still able to hear what he says next: "And I love you right back. We…" He hesitates long enough to make me wonder what he's trying to say. "We make a…a good team, don't we?"

Maybe not anymore, because the way he loves me and the way I love him…for the first time in our lives, they're not the same.

I squeak something unintelligible into his shirt, all the while trying to ignore his familiar scent, the hard muscles beneath the fabric, the way he holds me.

Then his arms tighten around me, and I feel the vibration of his voice all the way to my core as he says, "Melanie..."

"Hey, you two!" Whatever he's going to say is interrupted by the arrival of a painfully chipper Sasha. "What's going on?"

I stiffen all over again, but she's not suspicious, not even when she finds us locked in an embrace on the beach. Of course she isn't. I'm only little Melanie, after all. Hardly a threat to her and Conn.

As if to confirm that, Conn answers cheerfully, "Our usual little lovefest."

"Oh? I hope I wasn't interrupting." Pleasantly teasing, not even a hint of jealousy. I'm insulted.

Conn releases me from his hug and, with one friendly, brisk rub between my shoulder blades, says, "You know me and Melanie. We fight, we make up. She loves me, really."

"Of course she does!" Sasha drapes an arm over my shoulders and turns me toward Conn's house. "It's been that way for as long as you've known each other. Hasn't it, sweetie?"

Damn, the woman has pincers for hands. She squeezes my arm like she's trying to snap it off just below the shoulder socket. Maybe there's some jealousy there after all? But her expression is mild and neutral. Conn doesn't follow us. I don't dare look back. I can't look at him now.

I'm not sure I'm ever going to be able to look at him the same way again.

CHAPTER NINETEEN

———

"Melanie!"

For a moment I think it's Conn calling to me from down on the sand, and I tense up. Sasha's gone into the house with Hannah. I'm still on the deck, trying—and failing—to draw air into my lungs. I'm afraid he's going to come up the stairs and confront me about my feelings for him...even though he has no idea what those feelings really are. My brain is hash. I'm not used to being this out of control, and it's wrecking me.

But the voice calling my name is coming from in front of me, not behind me. Jack lurches down the steps from the road, looking like a marionette whose operator has gotten its strings tangled. His knees buckle, his legs bow, his arms flail before they catch hold of the railing. Several tequila shots? Is there a word for *many severals*?

He hugs me, leaning heavily until I feel my knees start to give. "Hey, beautiful. I've been looking for you all night."

Where? At the bottom of a shot glass? How flattering. I start to peel him off me while trying to make sure he stays upright, when I suddenly have help.

"Oookay, let's get you level, big boy."

Jack's face lights up again. "Sasha! Hey, beautiful. I've been looking for you all night."

Nice.

"It looks like your night's over. Let's get you back to the inn, all right?"

I seize on this opportunity to get away from the Garvey home—and its owner—as quickly as possible. "I can drive him, Sasha. No need for you to go out of your way." We can dump Jack in the back seat, where he'll likely pass out. Then all I'll have to do is find someone at the inn strong enough to haul his ass out of the car and up to his room.

"Thanks, sweetie, but I'm going there myself."

"You're staying at the inn too?"

Huh. Jack managing to get a room during peak season is surprising; Sasha getting one as well is...waaaait a minute.

Sasha nods, preoccupied with guiding Jack through the door, which Hannah holds open from inside. Sasha thanks Hannah, but Jack doesn't even notice she's there, mainly because, aside from the amount of alcohol coursing through his veins, Jack's hanging on Sasha completely, acting more than a little familiar, with his nose buried in Sasha's neck and his hand in the vicinity of her navel. She's propping him up and nudging his lips away from her ear as she tries to guide him into the house. Almost like she's used to it.

The minute Sasha and Jack are in Conn's house, I pull Hannah out of it.

"We've got to go. *Now*."

"You want to go back through the festival? I'd love to see more of it now that we don't have to watch over Bram. Where is he, anyway? Did he find the kids again?"

Dear, sweet Hannah. The poor girl has no idea why I'm dragging her up the road from the beach house. I'm on sensory overload. I need to sort out all this out. And for that, I need...

"Snacks," I demand, as we enter the barricaded area filled with festivalgoers. "No, wine first. I need wine for this."

"Melanie, what in the world is going on? You've been weird ever since we finished up with Bram."

"I know. I'm sorry. He's fine. He met Zoë. They're stargazing as we speak, and everything's perfect with them. He prefers to go by Vernon again, by the way. Now...wine. Need." Then I add, belatedly, "Please."

I push through a group of people milling around in front of a winery's tasting table, Hannah close behind. The pourer perks up at the two new arrivals. "Can I interest you in white or red tonight?"

"Yes," I answer distractedly, and grab two already full plastic cups lined up behind a little tented card reading *Chardonnay*. I push one into Hannah's hand and chug the other.

"Okay, wait," my friend says. "Something's going on."

I slam another white. Gewürztraminer, I think. I don't really care, to be honest.

"Uh, miss? Would you like to know a little bit more about—"

"We're fine. Citrusy notes. Vanilla. Starburst…pink, if I'm not mistaken." Who cares what it really tastes like? I feel bad about torpedoing the girl's perkiness, impressively still in play this many hours into the festival, but hey, I'm having a crisis. "What's over here?" I ask, moving on to the reds.

"Melanie." Hannah follows me but only to tug me away from the wine.

"Is it time for snacks? I think it's time for snacks."

Cradling several plastic cups in the crook of my arm and hooking a few more with my fingers, I push back out into the crowd, ignoring a plaintive voice behind me calling, "Um, miss?" What? I didn't take an entire bottle. She should admire my restraint.

"Okay, stop." Hannah takes a few samples away from me and dumps them into a nearby trash can.

"Hey!"

"Sit! Stay!"

I obey, dropping onto a nearby bench.

"Tell me what's going on. Right now."

"I need a gyro."

Hannah never loses it, but I can tell she's reaching the limits of her patience now. Sighing, she says, "I will get you a gyro. Then we're going to talk. Understand?"

I nod, and she crosses the street to Zelda the Greek's food truck. The owner is neither named Zelda nor is she Greek, but her tzatziki sauce is to die for, so nobody questions. They just eat. By the time Hannah comes back with a drippy gyro wrapped in foil, I've polished off the wine she didn't take from me. The gyro is as big as my head. I will eat all of it, I've decided.

"Let's walk," I say, picking pieces off the pita. "I need to get out of this crowd." As we head for the pier, I decide to tell Hannah my suspicions about Sasha but nothing else. "Okay. I know you think I don't like Sasha because I'm jealous of her."

"Are you?"

"No." *Yes.* "Not really." *Yes, really.* I can't start off with wall-to-wall lies, so I amend my answer. "Maybe a little. But that's beside the point. What's more important is I don't trust her." I fill Hannah in on how overly familiar Sasha behaved toward Conn on the beach before Hannah arrived, and share my theory that she's trying to get something out of him or is even trying to get him back. "I know," I say quickly. "It's none of my business. Conn certainly would be the first person to tell me so. But Sasha's not good for him. You'd know what I mean if you saw Broken Conn after they divorced. But it started long before that, and I knew it. I knew all of it. They had a mess of a marriage and an awful divorce…because of me."

Hannah throws me a puzzled half smile. "You think an awful lot of yourself sometimes, don't you?"

"Hannah, listen. They never should have gotten married in the first place. It's my fault they went through with it, and I've regretted it ever since."

I feel funny saying all this. It's been twelve years, and I haven't told a soul—not even Taylor, and she knows more of my dirty secrets than anyone else on the planet. Should I let this one out now? Well, if it saves Conn from another round of misery with Sasha, it's worth every ounce of my discomfort. I dive in.

I'm not a big fan of revisiting my teen years, what with the whole parents-divorcing-and-mom-leaving kickoff in my thirteenth year, followed by the "reign of terror" era with Taylor. It was only natural that I gravitated toward Taylor's strong personality because she helped me forget about life at home, but for the amount of trouble we got into, it definitely wasn't worth it. Fortunately, it only took a couple of years for me to realize that kind of behavior really wasn't "me," and by the time I was closing in on my seventeenth birthday, I had calmed down quite a bit. I was starting my junior year in high school, focusing on getting my grades up, when Conn and Sasha set the date for their wedding, scheduling it for the following summer.

I was in awe of Sasha, and I was so excited when she asked me to be a bridesmaid. Although I was outnumbered and intimidated by the others—her wealthy, beautiful, sophisticated cousins, childhood friends, and sorority sisters—Sasha was really kind to me. She made sure I never felt marginalized at any bridal event and included me in everything, except for the bachelorette weekend in New York. I was allowed to take the train down for the day, but I had to get out of town before sundown when the real partying began. I still got a thrill when Sasha snuck me a mimosa at brunch.

The wedding was held halfway between Abbott's Bay and Sasha's Connecticut hometown, in one of our venerable, classic New England churches. Everybody knows the type—white, minimalist, with a tall, thin spire and lots of echo-y sunlit space for declaring vows punctuated by elderly aunts' sobs. The bride and her attendants were sequestered in a side room off the foyer before the ceremony. It was loaded with flowers—white roses, of course. And champagne. Lots of champagne.

When the male half of the wedding party arrived, they milled around outside in front of the church, tweaking one another's bow ties or trying to figure out how keep their boutonnieres from going cockeyed. Jack, Conn's best man, was the best-looking of the bunch. I overheard at least three bridesmaids arguing over who was going to hook up with him. In my eyes, though, he was no match for Conn. Jack had clean-cut good looks and charm for days (and some women found his millions gave both a turbo boost), but Conn was the whole package.

I never admitted it then, but I guess I can be honest now: when I first caught sight of Conn in his tuxedo, brushed and groomed and polished, it was as though he were the first real man I'd ever laid eyes on. I couldn't stop staring. Sasha even teased me about it later that night at the reception. Come to think of it, she teased me about my relationship with Conn pretty frequently over the years, pointing out whenever I was overly attentive when he was talking or when I stared at him a little too long from across a room. After a while Sasha's gentle ribbing made me self-conscious about how I behaved around him, but I was grateful. It corrected my behavior and kept me from looking foolish.

On their wedding day, however, I couldn't keep myself in check no matter how hard I tried. Conn was *that* incredible. And not only handsome. He seemed to be the epitome of what every woman should want in a man—cool, poised, kind, friendly, funny, gentle, and so loving toward his bride. I mean, he always was all of those things, but it was like he had a spotlight shining on him that day to show that *here* was a man among men.

The sheer magnitude of the high-society, money-is-no-object wedding production was overwhelming. I decided I wanted my wedding to be just as grand one day, so I took photos with my tiny digital camera whenever I could, practically putting the official wedding photographer to shame, to remember every glorious detail.

I was especially proud of my stealth tactics that allowed me to get plenty of candids from around a corner or behind a tree. Did I pull a *Love Actually* and get nothing but footage of Conn for some private mooning sessions later? Not at all. After listening to the other bridesmaids talk about Jack, I was looking at him in a new light as well, the way I'd never really considered men up to that point. As the slightly older, vastly more experienced women put it, he was "sex on a stick." I couldn't deny it. Mostly though, I focused on all the men interacting with one another. I felt like I was on safari documenting a new species, and it was fascinating.

I was pulled away from my photojournaling project fairly frequently. As a bottom-rung junior bridesmaid, I was assigned the emergency repair kit—needle and thread, safety pins, bobby pins, sticky tape, antacids, bandages. I took the task so seriously you'd have thought the little plastic box was the president's nuclear football. I was also the designated gofer. We'd forgotten the baby wipes, but Sasha's aunt had some in the car. One of the men dropped his watch, and I went hunting for it. Find this, get that, fetch something else. I had no idea nineteen other people could need—or lose—so much stuff.

Then, as the first of the guests started arriving, the matron of honor pulled me aside, looked me straight in the eye, and gave me the most startling, daunting assignment of all.

"Find the bride."

CHAPTER TWENTY

———

Hannah actually screams at this point in my story, startling me so much I nearly fling my MooMoo's cone—we've moved on to dessert, or at least I have—over the pier railing into the water.

"What is *wrong* with you?" I blot a few drops of ice cream off my shoulder before it seeps into the weave of my summer sweater.

"She didn't run."

"Oh, she most certainly did."

"Did it involve a horse?"

"Like Julia Roberts' escape? No. Maybe only because no horses were in the vicinity."

"They didn't have a horse-drawn carriage?"

"Way too tacky."

"It was good enough for Princess Diana," Hannah sniffs. "Well, where did she go? What happened?"

Ah, what happened. I snuck out a back door of the church and, once out of anyone's view, took off at a run. There were very few cars in the parking lot—the attendants had arrived in two limousines, Sasha in a white Rolls-Royce—and none seemed to be missing, so Sasha couldn't have gotten far. Finding a statuesque blonde in a huge ivory dress was harder than you'd think though.

Eventually I caught a glimpse of tulle in the distance, among the heavily leafed-out trees on the border of the property near some neighboring houses. I found Sasha on a rustic swing made out of a single board suspended by some coarse ropes knotted under the seat. It would have made a great photo if she didn't look so glum. She wasn't so much swinging as she was listlessly twisting…and eating a Big Mac.

She didn't even look up when I approached her, just stared at her hamburger and said, "You know, I've been craving one of these for almost a year."

"I didn't know you ate McDonald's at all," I whispered, wondering if she'd snapped.

"I don't. It's a side effect of all the dieting to fit into this dress. But now I have one." She didn't seem thrilled.

Not knowing what to say, and marveling at the dieting comment (nobody needed to diet less than Sasha), I asked blankly, "Um…where'd you get McDonald's, anyway?"

"Are you hungry?" Sasha held out the Big Mac to me, but nothing could have been less appealing. I shook my head. Shrugging, she took a bite, chewed for a moment, then murmured, "Goodness, this is foul. Oh—you asked me a question. I got it from a nice young man who lives in this house over here. He pulled up in the driveway and got out of his car with a bag. I asked him if I could sit on his swing for a little while, and when I said his food smelled good, he simply *gave* it to me. Can you imagine?"

I could. I suppose when a beautiful, sad woman in a giant wedding dress takes up residence in your yard, you don't deny her anything. Even your value meal.

"Hey, um, Sasha?"

"Mm?"

"Are you…are you going to come back to the church soon? The guests are starting to arrive."

"Oh, that." She looked off into the distance as though she was weighing her options then said, "I don't think so."

"*What?* Why?"

Sasha heaved a sigh and tucked the Big Mac back into its box. "I don't think it would work out."

"But…but…" This wasn't happening. It couldn't. Conn and Sasha! Sasha and Conn! The inevitable, enviable, perfect fairy tale couple!

"Melanie, you wouldn't understand. I know a lot more about relationships than you, and I know this one is…well…not a good idea."

I bristled at the thinly veiled implication that I was still a kid, but this was no time to worry about what anyone, even

Sasha, thought of me.

"Of course it is!" I burst out. "It's the best idea in the known universe! You and Conn are perfect together, and you know it. Where…where would you even find another guy who's so…nice and funny and smart and…great and…"

Although I could have pulled out two dozen more descriptors and not have been anywhere near finished praising Conn, Sasha was looking at me curiously—puzzled, exasperated, and impatient, but mostly really sad—and it made my campaign fizzle out as abruptly as it had begun. She knew how wonderful her fiancé was. I didn't need to tell her. What did I think was going to happen if I kept talking? She'd smack her forehead with the heel of her hand and say, "Good Lord, you're right, Melanie—I never thought of it that way"?

I decided to try another tack. I fumbled to turn my camera on. "Here. Look."

I scrolled through the photos I'd taken until I got to the pictures of Conn and his groomsmen. I stopped at a close-up of Conn, smiling and relaxed, the summer sun picking up the highlights in his hair, which was still rebelliously curling as much as it could, despite his fresh, close-cropped cut.

"That guy is standing outside the church right now, waiting for you. How could you walk away from a…a future with him? Look at him!"

I added that last admonition because she was staring at me instead of at the screen. When she obeyed, I scrolled through a few more photos, some of Conn alone, some with his friends. At one point she gripped my wrist, stopping me from advancing to the next photo. The picture on the screen was of Conn and Jack laughing uproariously at some joke Jack had made. She stared at it for a long time while I held my breath.

My argument was successful, obviously. Or Sasha came to her senses on her own. I'll never know for sure. But after a few moments she stood up without a word, neatly closed the food bag, said, "All right, let's go," and started walking back toward the church.

Halfway across the lawn, she stopped and grabbed my arm again. Her fingers were ice cold. "Melanie."

I forced myself to face her. Now that the crisis was

averted, I found myself furious that any of this had even come close to happening. "What?" I asked flatly. She kept looking away, not toward the church, but back toward the swing, so she wasn't even cowed by the powerful glare I was directing her way.

"Thank you for not saying anything about this."

Wow, she was good. She managed to order me to keep a secret and make it sound like I'd already agreed to it. "I—" What was I going to do? Run and tell Conn? I couldn't do that to him. If I did, even though Sasha was going to go through with the wedding, Conn would always have doubts. No, this was going to remain a secret. Like good New England stoics, neither Sasha nor I would speak of it ever again.

Nodding, I ushered her ahead of me, feeling like a guard escorting a prisoner. She looked the part too—pale, not her usual luminous self, and with her head bowed. As for me, I wasn't in awe of her anymore. I was disgusted. I reached out and took the McDonald's bag from her hand. She didn't even look at me, just went into the church through the back door while I made a small detour to throw out the food.

As I dumped the trash in a garbage can, letting the lid close with a bang, I smelled cigarette smoke on the breeze and saw a butt go flying into the yard. I peeked around the corner of the building in time to see a familiar figure in a tux hustling away.

"Jack?"

He spun on his heel, turning to me with a bright smile. "Miss Melanie." His expression flitted between placid and nervous as he ventured, "Everything okay?"

He'd been watching then, even if he hadn't been able to hear our conversation.

"Everything's fine," I answered evenly. "Sasha wanted some air."

There was a pause. It was obvious Jack wanted to ask a dozen questions, but he didn't dare. I decided to sweep them away with one simple statement. "The ceremony should be starting on time."

"Ah." His face fell, almost imperceptibly, and only for a split second. Then the regular cocky Jack Rossiter resurfaced.

"Have I mentioned you look lovely today?"

When I didn't answer, he came a step closer, turning up the wattage on his million-dollar smile. Still, there was pain in his eyes. Based on Sasha's reaction to that photo she'd just fixated on and his reaction now, it was clear what was going on. She hadn't been looking at Conn in that photo. She'd been staring at Jack. I didn't know if there was something real between them or an infatuation that was the inevitable result of him and Sasha spending so much time together because of Conn, and I didn't really care. I didn't feel sorry for either of them. And if nobody was going to come clean about any of this, I wasn't going to be the one to make them.

"You'd better save me more than one dance at the reception, understand? And I'm going to make sure you catch the bouquet."

I could see his persistent comments as harmlessly flirtatious, or offensive and inappropriate, but I certainly couldn't be charmed. Not knowing what I knew now.

Once Sasha was settled again and seemed to be back to normal, I slipped outside once more, weaving through the crush of guests in the foyer and out the front door. I needed to see Conn through Sasha's eyes. How did she view him, the bad as well as the good? What about him would make her question her decision to marry him even for a minute?

Maybe I should have let her run. Maybe everything would have turned out better, and they wouldn't have wasted six years. I know it's not possible to second-guess something like that so many years later, but even at that very moment, when I was a naïve seventeen, I knew she'd made the wrong choice by going through with it. It's why I blame myself for their misguided marriage. I talked her back into it. I never ratted them out. Because I couldn't bear to see Conn heartbroken on his wedding day. Was it better that he was heartbroken several years later? I don't know.

When Conn caught sight of me at the top of the steep steps at the front of the church, his eyes lit up, and he beckoned to me until I joined him on the lawn.

"Ready for this, kid?"

Oh God. He seemed so cheerful. Unable to look at him, I

focused on his lapel instead. His boutonniere was crooked. I busied myself repinning it.

"Hey. You okay?" Damn his perceptiveness. I nodded a little frantically, still messing with the straight pin. "Nervous?"

For him and his future, yes, but I wasn't about to say so. I shook my head, and a lock of hair dislodged from my braid and dangled in front of my eye, despite the fact that the hairstylist used what felt like an entire can of hairspray on me only hours before. Then Conn's fingers were in my hair, gently tucking the strand back in. My head buzzed with the contact, with worry for him, with his sheer proximity. I forced myself to look up into his eyes—a grayish blue that day.

He broke out that confident grin I knew so well. "You'll be fine. If you start freaking out, look at me when you come down the aisle. I can't promise I won't make a face at you though." He put his hands on my shoulders, leaned in, and kissed me on the forehead. "I'm glad you're here for this."

"I still don't know why I'm in your wedding," I whispered.

"Maybe because I asked Sasha to include you?" Conn smiled even brighter at my shocked look. "Melanie, you're important to me. I could have asked you to dress up in a tux and be a grooms...*person*, but I figured you'd rather wear a pretty dress."

He was wrong there. I would have worn a fuzzy fleece onesie with ice cream cones or pandas—or pandas eating ice cream cones—all over it if that's what he'd wanted. I felt myself blushing again and tried one more time to right his listing flowers. All I got for my trouble was a jab from the straight pin. I jerked back, and Conn grabbed my injured hand.

"Ouch," he said for me, examining the tiny bud of red blooming on the pad of my thumb.

"I have bandages inside." I tugged my hand out of his, which was surprisingly more difficult than I expected. I don't think he noticed how tight a hold he had. He was distracted, looking off to his left at the doors of the church, a somber expression on his handsome face.

Then he returned his attention to me and asked, "You sure you can take care of it?" At my hasty nod, he stepped back and stuffed his hands in his pockets. "Okay. Get out there and make me proud—you hear me?"

I was the first one down the aisle. I remembered to hold my head up as I'd been instructed. The clear view of the length of the church all the way to the altar made me a little dizzy, and I prayed fervently that I wouldn't stumble or, worse, faint dead away. That sort of indulgence was reserved for the bride, not the junior bridesmaid. I was aware of people—so many people—their faces all turned toward me expectantly, but they were all beige and brown blurs. Except for one. My view of Conn was crystal clear. He was staring me straight in the eye, and because the entire congregation was looking past me as they strained to get their first glimpse of Sasha, he was free to make good on his promise, firing off a series of goofy faces to get me to smile and relax.

It worked. Even with the memory of my conversation with Sasha rattling around in my head, my panic lessened, and I found it easier to breathe. I wanted to make faces back, but I knew my father was watching me, so I didn't dare.

The wedding went off without a hitch. Sasha didn't even hesitate when she had to recite her vows, say "I do," or kiss her new husband. Her hand didn't shake when they lit the unity candle together. Either she was a marvelous actor, or she'd rededicated herself to marrying Conn. I desperately hoped it was the latter. I really wanted them to be happy. I couldn't bear it if Conn was getting into something he'd regret.

Before I knew it, Conn and Sasha were husband and wife. The rest is history.

"Ohhh," Hannah sighs, completely transfixed.

"Please tell me you're not oohing and aahing over their picture-perfect wedding."

"No, of course not. Although I'm sure it was breathtaking."

With a weary sigh, I lean on the railing and stare out at the blackness of the ocean. "It was. Not to me though. It was like everyone was praising this expertly decorated dessert on display, and only I knew the frosting was covering up a cake filled with worms."

"Ew. Well, one thing's for sure..."

"You now understand Sasha is evil?"

"Not exactly. I mean, sure, she had her doubts, maybe a touch of cold feet, but she did the right thing in the end."

"It was *not* the right thing! She should have...I don't know...at least postponed the wedding until she was sure it was what she wanted. But she didn't, and they ended up wasting *how* many years? No. What she did was completely and utterly *wrong*."

Smiling slyly, Hannah murmurs, "Your bias is showing."

"Excuse me?"

"As I was saying...one thing's for sure: you've been in love with Conn for years."

If I had any more ice cream, I would have choked on it. "Hannah!" I exclaim in my best scandalized tone. "How many times have I told you? There's never been anything between—"

"And I haven't believed you. Not even once."

"I thought you were my friend."

"Friends call bull when it's warranted, and now is one of those times. What you say and the way you look at Conn...they don't match." Before I can argue further, she puts a reassuring hand on mine. "You keep forgetting I've been in love. I know what it looks like. I know what it feels like. And you, my friend, show all the telltale signs."

I could keep protesting. Or I could give up. Tears suddenly brimming in my eyes, I whisper, "I think I'm in way over my head, Hannah."

Hannah, ecstatic that she's able to comfort me for once instead of the other way around, pulls me into a hug. "I knew it! I knew it! Oh, darn—I shouldn't gloat, right?" She pats the back of my head like I'm a spaniel. "This is about you. You and Conn! It's so exciting!"

As she gleefully clutches me tighter, I manage to argue, "It's *not* exciting. It's the wedding all over again."

"Because you're crazy in love with him?"

"Because Sasha's cheating on him with Jack. Again. And I can't tell Conn. Again."

CHAPTER TWENTY-ONE

If this were a normal evening, Hannah and I would sort this mess out—what to do about my feelings for Conn, whether or not to share my suspicions about Sasha with him. But this, apparently, is no normal evening.

First Hannah's reply is drowned out by a *bloop, bleep,* and then a few buzzy honks from an emergency vehicle trying to work its way through the festival crowd. I don't have time to wonder what's going on before my phone starts ringing. I struggle to get it out of my purse.

Then the words in my ear don't make sense. I don't realize I'm frowning in confusion until Hannah asks, "What's wrong?"

"Uh…" It's as if I'm not sure. I should be, yet oddly enough I have to think about it.

"Melanie?"

"My…my dad," I finally manage to say. "It's Officer Pauline. She says he…I…um…have to go."

"Wait. What?"

I'm already making my way back up the pier toward town, Hannah scurrying to keep up with me.

"Melanie! What did she say?"

We're back at the food truck area quickly enough that I don't have to answer her. The scene speaks for itself.

"Dad!" I shout, pushing through the crowd that's gathered.

I can see his face twisted in pain as the paramedics lift the gurney into the back of the ambulance. He has a cannula for oxygen, and he's swathed in thin white blankets up to his neck.

"Wait!" I shout to the paramedics. "That's my dad. What's going on?"

There's a light touch on my shoulder, and I turn to find Sasha giving me her serious-doctor face. "Melanie. I need you to keep calm."

Which only makes me want to punch her. "Tell me what happened."

"Conn's parents called me. They were with your father. He wasn't feeling well. He collapsed just as I got here from the inn, and I called 9-1-1. He's in a lot of pain."

"Is it his heart?"

"I don't want to diagnose him without tests."

There's some confusion as to whether I can ride in the ambulance with him or not. Then I find myself being led to Hannah's car while the ambulance makes its way back out of the crowd, so agonizingly slowly I want to start pushing people out of the way myself. I keep glancing back as Hannah tugs me along.

*　*　*

"Melanie? He's fine." Hannah's voice sounds like it's coming from a mile away as she says in a soothing tone, "Okay? Your dad is fine."

Apparently this is true. The hospital employee told us so. I was so happy to hear it I didn't even care the person bringing the update was a bored-looking woman with a clipboard and a weary, impersonal demeanor instead of a hot *Grey's Anatomy* doctor with a colorful, perky scrub cap covering his magnificent hair (who then helped me celebrate the good news about my dad by spiriting me off to the on-call room).

My father is fine now that he's been divested of one rebellious appendix. The operation was a simple one that only took minutes, with no complications. My brain absorbed the words uttered by Definitely Not a *Grey's Anatomy* Hottie, but my nervous system hasn't caught up yet.

My dad is okay. It wasn't something serious. I repeat those words to myself, over and over. I'm embarrassed I spent even five minutes planning his funeral. (Come on. Everybody who's experienced a loved one's health scare has done it.) I feel drained yet wired at the same time. Suddenly the waiting room is too small and stuffy, and Hannah's back-patting is too irritating. I want to go for a run, feel a cool breeze on my prickling skin, get away from the worry and the tension and the peculiar hospital odors.

All I do, however, is take Hannah's free hand. "Thanks so much for staying with me. Now get out of here, okay?"

Hannah had intended to leave for Ohio early in the morning. Instead, she put off her trip to be here for me while Charles was in surgery.

Over her protests I insist, "Go home. You need some sleep before you start driving. I'm going up to the room to wait for my dad to come back from recovery anyway."

"I don't want to leave you alone."

"I'm not alone."

Not only has Hannah been waiting with me all night, so has Sasha…and Conn. Sasha followed the ambulance in her car, and Conn came rushing in after he heard the news from his parents. I'm grateful I have my good friends here with me…and, okay, Sasha too.

"You're sure about this?" Hannah asks me. Bless her loyalty—she's shed her fascination with the good doctor, even though she cuts Sasha more slack over what happened at the wedding than I do.

"I can handle it."

Hannah kisses my cheek and stands up as Conn and Sasha come over with coffee, including one for me. I can barely look at Conn. Not only because of how we left everything earlier—well, yesterday, as it's a new day now—but also because Hannah's right here, watching me. She's sworn to keep quiet about my feelings for Conn, and I trust her, but I'll rest easier when she's back in Ohio for a while. Without her around I'll be able to pretend nothing happened, convince myself that my feelings toward Conn haven't grown into something I can't handle, and get everything back on track. No matter what kind of mess is going on in my own head, it's imperative that it stay there. I can't have it spilling out and wrecking everything.

I have such high hopes for myself sometimes.

I'm an idiot sometimes.

"I'm going to get going too," Sasha says softly after

Hannah leaves. "Conn?" She addresses him expectantly, as though he's automatically going to go with her.

"I'll stick around for a while," he says which, judging by her perturbed expression, isn't what Sasha wants to hear. "I'll drive Melanie home."

"Why don't you leave Melanie your car? I thought we could chat on the way back to Abbott's Bay."

Oh boy.

"No," is Conn's abrupt answer. "I'll try to call you later in the week."

Is it my imagination, or does Sasha look almost angry? She doesn't say anything about it, however. Instead, she turns to me again. "Would you like me to talk to the doctor for you before I go?"

As if I couldn't possibly understand without her translating for me. I call my excellent manners into play and smile serenely. "That's sweet of you, Sasha, but I'll be fine."

Out of the corner of my eye I catch Conn watching me. I wonder if he thinks I'm a complete wreck under my placid exterior. I am, and not only because of my dad. Conn has changed his clothes; I fixate on his muscles defined by his uncharacteristically snug Henley paired with loose, weathered jeans, and it's suddenly hard to breathe.

"Would you both excuse me for a minute?"

I hightail it down the hall, but I have no idea where I'm headed. *Away from Conn* is the only motivation I've got right now. I blindly duck around a corner, trot several yards past a set of propped-open double doors. Leaning up against the wall, I close my eyes and try to quiet the jackhammer stuttering in my chest.

"M? You okay?" Conn has followed me. Of course. He's quite aware I am not, in fact, okay. "It *was* all good news about your dad, right?" he asks, stopping only inches away. "I didn't miss anything?"

I nod, unable to speak. I have to get hold of myself, and quickly. Unfortunately, my body decides it can't be in close proximity to this man any longer—not without my brain shutting down. Keeping my eyes down, I step to one side, muttering assurances that there was no bad news about my dad and I'm fine and…walk into a wall I didn't notice was there.

Then the wall speaks. "Okay. What the hell's going on?"

Dammit. I step back, away from the solid surface of his chest. "Nothi—"

"Yeah, yeah, 'nothing.' Right." I don't answer, so Conn prods a little more. "Is this about what happened earlier? I thought we were, you know, okay."

"We are," I answer a little too quickly. "We're fine. We're great."

"Then why can't you look at me?" he asks in a softer voice. It's the one that used to warm me down to my toes. Now it makes me come close to bursting into flames.

I force my eyes up from the three buttons on his shirt, past his whiskered chin, *quickly* past his lips (dear God), and to his eyes, greenish-gray right now, filled with concern. I have to reassure him and be convincing about it. Not that he'd ever drag the truth out of me—harness an entire whale pod and it wouldn't exert enough force for that—but I have to get him to stop staring at me before I lose it.

"Really, everything's fine." I force a smile—a weak one, but it's the best I can do right now. "I'm going up to my dad's room, like I said."

"Want me to come with you?"

God, he's not making this any easier. "No. Thanks though." I can't resist putting my hand on his arm as I add, "I want to stay a while. You should go home. I can get an Uber."

* * *

"Hey, Daddy."

"Mrf."

He looks better than I expected, albeit groggy. He raises his hand in greeting, as though the grunt might not be enough, while I drag a chair close to the side of the bed.

"You scared me there for a minute, old man." I'm not sure why I'm keeping my voice down, except it's three o'clock in the morning and, although there's plenty of activity at the nurses' station, the rooms are all dark, peppered with colored blinking lights—a hospital pretending to sleep in the wee hours, when it never really does.

My father mumbles something, and I lean closer. He repeats himself. "Told you I was sick."

"You've been waiting years to say that, haven't you? Well, you just used up your 'legitimate illness' allowance for the next decade."

"Party pooper. I hear I've got stitches."

"Congratulations."

Charles drifts off to sleep, and drained of adrenaline, I manage to drop off as well, despite sitting upright in an uncomfortable chair. I spend an unclear amount of time in some hazy twilight, dragged out of it at least once by the bustling arrival of a nurse checking on Dad and several times by my own half formed dreams that aren't soothing or otherworldly. What figures most prominently is the stuff I need to banish from my brain: Conn, Conn and Sasha, Conn and (I don't even want to think it) me. None of it is healthy, but apparently none of it is going away anytime soon either. Especially if my subconscious keeps fabricating scenes I won't let my conscious mind entertain. My whole body heats up at the thoughts that have drifted in as I dozed. The worst was an altered version of what happened between me and Conn before the wedding. Instead of his fond words, gentle touch to fix my hair, and a kiss on the forehead, he did a whole lot more. And I let him.

I never had those kinds of thoughts back then. Conn was an adult, untouchable, in love with Sasha. There was no fodder to spark a teenager's fantasies. My relationships consisted of unremarkable, age-appropriate high school and college boys.

When Conn returned to Abbott's Bay years later, alone and divorced and bitter, he was still just a family friend, now going through a rough patch, so I made sure I was there for him. Our age gap dissipated, and we grew closer based on our shared past and common interests. We saw each other every day at DBC, we hung out watching TV or playing video games a few times a week, and I let him vent about his divorce when he needed to.

Everything was fine, until last night when everything went kablooey. Now my feelings don't fit in the box labeled *Conn* anymore. Like grappling with an overpacked suitcase, I've figuratively sat on the lid and hopped up and down on it, but no luck.

I groan a little and rub my forehead. All my muscles ache, and it feels like sandpaper is tucked under my eyelids. Then there's a hand on my shoulder, heavy and warm, and I jump a mile.

"Come on," Conn whispers.

I stare at him, uncomprehending. He inclines his head toward the door and gently tugs me out of my chair.

"But..." I hang back, gesturing toward my still-sleeping father.

"You're exhausted. I'm taking you home."

"But..." My vocabulary certainly is suffering, that's clear.

"I told the nurses you'll be back to pick him up this afternoon. He's not going to be discharged any sooner. Okay? It's all under control."

Conn puts his arm around me and guides me toward the bank of elevators. While we stand in the cold, too-brightly-lit hallway, he gives my neck a gentle nudge, directing my head toward his chest. I let it fall there, and I close my eyes. Just for a moment.

Conn leads me through the parking garage and helps me into his vintage Mustang, first clearing a leather folder and some official-looking papers off the wide vinyl passenger seat. Expanding his business...of course he is. I should have known DBC isn't in financial trouble. Conn is practical, intelligent, and levelheaded, with a good business sense.

I shouldn't be too surprised Sasha's sniffing around him again. He's everything any woman could want: smart, ambitious, funny, clever, and gorgeous, but not obnoxious about any of it. She probably regrets letting him go, and she wants him back. The whole Jack thing though...I can't figure it out. Although lots of women find his, er, package attractive too. Swap ambition for status and millions in the bank, and wrap it up in a slick, polished appearance, and you've got a guy lots of women would consider a keeper as well.

I rest my head against the window and watch the Massachusetts landscape slip by, hazy and dim, as the sun rises pink through scattered, thin clouds. Conn doesn't try to engage me in conversation. He just drives. Someone else would have prattled on about how fortunate my dad was, would have told a story about their aunt's neighbor's brother-in-law who had major complications when his appendix burst. Conn, however, knows the value of silence, and I'm grateful for that. I'm also grateful he's taken so much time to look out for me and my father—time he doesn't have.

I break the silence with a tentative, "Hey, thanks for all this."

"Don't worry about it."

"Well, I feel bad. You're away from the restaurant and...everything." I don't mention Sasha specifically. I don't know if my theory is correct and she does want him back, but she really wanted some one-on-one time with him last night for something, which she missed out on solely because Conn was too nice to leave me alone at the hospital.

He shrugs as he takes a traffic circle at full speed, and I slide against the car door. "It's fine. Tommy's opening for me today."

"Not just the daily schedule. You have all the investment stuff to deal with, and finding a good location in Provincetown. You're extra busy."

"So are you, I hear. Hannah says your calendar is wall-to-wall appointments these days."

"Well, I'm good at what I do." I wink, hoping I look confident and cheerful.

Grinning ruefully, he snakes his car up the two-lane coastal road toward home. "Okay, you were right, I was wrong. I thought Your New Best Friend was a really dumb idea when you first told me about it, but you've made it into something special that helps a lot of people."

I decide to accept his praise graciously. He doesn't need to know one of the "helpful" appointments coming up is going out with Chelsea, the daycare owner, for a karaoke night because she can't convince any of her friends to go with her. Doing karaoke isn't only an excuse to drink and raise hell; it can increase someone's confidence and sense of adventure, so it is life-affirming. But I don't feel like sharing my justification for taking on the assignment.

Instead, because he passes up my street while we're talking, I ask, "Where are you taking me, exactly?"

"My house. I'll make you breakfast."

I've spent plenty of time at Conn's over the years without thinking twice about it, but now, with all sorts of inappropriate thoughts about him rattling around in my head and screwing up my innards, his kind invitation to get me fed after a sleepless night makes me simultaneously uncomfortable and strangely excited, like there's some sort of potential there. But that's *only in my head.* Where I have been spending way too much time. It's making my thoughts all warped and delusional and unhealthy. Conn, on the other hand, has no idea what I'm thinking. To him everything between us is exactly the same as it's always been.

He parks the car in his driveway, jumps out, and opens my door. After a moment or two he prompts, "You coming?"

I realize I've been sitting here, motionless and weak, for a little too long. "Sorry. Can you just…give me a minute?"

"Sure." He's worried about me—I can see it on his face—but all he says is, "What do you need?"

"I don't know."

Then I'm out of the car and heading for the steps down to the beach. Conn is beside me in an instant. "Want company?"

"No. Thanks."

"Okay. I'll call you when breakfast is ready."

I leave him behind, continuing down the weathered steps, kicking off my flats when I get to the cool sand. The tide is in, so there isn't far to go. The desire to go for a run that I had a while ago has evaporated. I don't even have enough energy left for a leisurely stroll up the shore. After trudging a few yards, past the smoldering remains of one of last night's bonfires, I plop down and rest my forehead on my knees, completely drained.

CHAPTER TWENTY-TWO

———

The sun has burned off the morning haze and warms the back of my neck. The beach is deserted. Everyone is probably still sleeping off the effects of the festival. The ocean is calm, and the shushing of the waves quiets my mind. Maybe I can stay here until it's time to pick up my dad from the hospital, turtled up like this so I don't have to talk to anyone I know who might happen by.

Unless someone knows the back of my neck. Like now.

"Here."

Conn stands above me holding out a speckled beige mug with a green owl on it. He's got a matching one in his other hand. I recognize them. We used to drink hot chocolate out of them when we were kids.

"Everything all right?"

"Everything's ducky," I answer, accepting the mug and taking a sip of coffee.

"Your sarcasm betrays you." I watch him lift his own mug to his lips as he stares out at the horizon. "How about if you just relax and enjoy the view?"

I know he means the morning sunlight on the ocean, yet I'm looking at him, and it still applies. Even so, I obey and turn to the magnificent display of nature in front of me instead of the one settling onto the sand beside me. Suddenly the seascape is as blurry as an Impressionistic painting. Before I even know what's happening, I'm sobbing uncontrollably and Conn's arm is around me.

"Hey," he murmurs, "it's okay. Everything's okay."

It is, I know. My tears are simply a release of tension from the stressful events of last night. My father's fine, which is the most important thing. And no matter what might happen in the near future, Conn's still beside me now.

"I'm sorry," I blubber, quite unattractively, wiping my eyes on my sleeve. "This whole thing with my dad scared me to death."

"Of course it did." Conn's grip tightens, and he rests his temple against mine. "We all worry about losing our parents when they get older."

"He's all I've got." The thought triggers a fresh round of sobbing.

"Well, that's not true. You've got me."

I just nod. I'm too tired to argue, and I certainly don't want to think about our conversation last night.

"You don't like it when people leave, do you?" His voice is soft and sympathetic, drawing even more tears out of me.

Don't like it? That's an understatement. I could be the poster child for abandonment issues. My mom's swift departure after my parents' divorce and clear lack of interest in maintaining a relationship with her only child did a number on me, so much so I ended up clinging to Taylor, despite her wild ways. It was a poor substitute, but it was *something*. Even as a fully functional adult, I was devastated at being abandoned again when Taylor moved to Provincetown. Maybe Conn was right when he implied I had ulterior motives for taking Hannah under my wing. Not to feed my ego though. Maybe I was more lonely than I let myself believe.

I stay silent for a few minutes, long enough to make sure I'm not sobbing or hiccupping when I ask, "What about you?"

"Am I planning on kicking it from a toxic appendix?"

I pull back a little to be able to see his expression when I ask, "Do you ever think about leaving Abbott's Bay?"

"Nah."

He doesn't even hesitate. It's reassuring, and I want to believe him, but I'm not sure I do. "Not even with the new restaurant?"

"Chain," he corrects me with a sheepish grin. "The big plan is to open up a lot of locations."

It's news to me, although I can't say I'm surprised. Why should he stop at two? "Wow. Those are big plans. Too big for Abbott's Bay."

"I still need a base of operations. I think the compound for Garvey Incorporated would work great here."

"Compound, huh?" Only Conn could make me laugh so soon after a mini nervous breakdown, even if my laughter is diluted by a few lingering tears and an ache in my gut. "You're right. Why not?"

"All right, now what about us?"

My breath catches at his sudden change of subject. "Us?"

"Are we, you know...are we good? You never really answered me before."

We should be, if I can manage to get out of my own head and not act like a lovestruck idiot around him. "Sure," I answer, telling myself to stop there. But when do I ever listen to my own advice? "Only..."

"Uh-oh."

"About you and Sasha..."

"Oh, honey, not that again. Please."

"But—"

"Just wait a minute. What I was going to explain last night, before we were interrupted—"

"By Sasha."

"Not intentionally."

"You believe what you need to, pal."

"Can I finish, please?" I clamp my lips shut and gesture for him to go ahead. "When I said I invited Sasha here—and Jack too, by the way—it wasn't for my birthday or any other social reason. I'm looking for angels. Investors. I need some backing—to help finance the Provincetown location now and the rest of the chain in the near future. I hope. Which requires a lot of cash. If I have to have partners, I'd rather have people I know and trust. So I asked Sasha—*and* Jack—to come up for a day or two to talk it over."

I think about this for a minute. It would explain the "business" Jack said he had in the area. And they *are* both loaded. Normally I'd have plenty to say about the word *trust* in relation to Sasha, but I leave that alone as something else pings in me, a tiny stab in the vicinity of my heart.

"First the Provincetown location, and now investors?

Conn, why didn't you tell me any of this sooner?"

"I'm sorry. You know I tend to keep my business plans to myself. And finding investors...it's a delicate thing."

My voice is hollow and weak when I say, "You didn't ask me."

"Ask you what?"

"To be an investor. Why didn't you? I have money."

A small smile steals across his lips. "I wouldn't dream of asking you. What if there was a problem? Jack and Sasha can afford to take the hit if it doesn't work out. I wouldn't want you to run that kind of risk."

He's protecting me? I don't want protection. I don't want him to humor me, or watch over me, or...still see me as a teenager, cute and harmless.

Less than.

"Okay," I say slowly, trying to keep my voice strong and businesslike. "But when I told you I was going to give you all the money from Your New Best Friend—"

"M..." he sighs in protest, but I cut him off.

"I still want you to have it."

"I told you, I don't—"

"—Need it. I know. This isn't charity. I want to be one of your investors."

He gives me an assessing look. "You do, huh?"

I fire back my best steely glare. That's right. I'm an adult, buddy, with my own money and decision-making ability, in case you haven't noticed.

"Okay," Conn says quietly, sounding a touch amused.

"Okay?"

"Fine. You can be one of my angels for DBC."

After a moment's hesitation I murmur, "All right then." I finish the last of my lukewarm coffee. That's one victory. Let's try for another. I take a deep breath. "Now promise me you won't let Sasha suck you back in."

"Melanie, for God's sake—"

"I don't care if you think she's only here about the restaurant. If you can't see she wants you back, you're an idiot." Conn's jaw clenches as he glowers at the horizon. "And I...I couldn't handle watching her ruin you again. Not after the last time. It broke my heart."

"Don't get confused," he bites out, suddenly prickly. "That was *my* heart."

"Hey, I had to stand by and watch you fall apart. What do you think that did to me?"

Now he's staring at me—hard. "Tell me why you're making this about you."

"I-I'm not," I stammer, although he's right—I absolutely am.

"So you're just dying to dole out your advice for altruistic purposes. Like I'm one of your clients."

"Sort of like that." *Nothing like that.*

Conn pauses, and I can tell he's working on containing his irritation. "All right, go ahead. Lay it on me. I'm one of your New Best Friends. Advise me."

"You're not one of my New Best Friends. You're my oldest best friend."

"Pretend I hired you. Tell me what you'd tell one of your clients. Be your usual blunt self. What you're known for."

"Thanks a lot."

"Go on."

"Fine." I take a breath, set aside my empty mug, and wrap my arms around my knees. "I'll give you a picture of what's going on now, and you can tell me how right I am." Conn snorts at this. "Let's see…" I start slowly, as though I actually have to think about this, as though I hadn't figured it out days ago, as soon as I spotted Conn and Sasha through Vernon's telescope. "Sasha has loved her fabulous life, but she's gotten tired of traveling all over the world, poor thing, and she's seriously thinking about settling down in one place, marrying again, starting a family. She's missed you, and she thinks the divorce was a huge mistake. She wants to try again, right here, close to home. She's always loved Abbott's Bay. Or hey, Provincetown is always great. You two could get a new start there. She could open a practice—you could oversee the new restaurant. Beebs or Tommy would be a great manager for the Abbott's Bay DBC. It practically runs itself."

"Very…inventive."

"You mean accurate."

"Not so much. But go on."

"I would advise you—as my client, you understand—not to fall for it. She's going to wreck you just like last time, because Sasha doesn't change. Do you really want to put yourself through that again?"

With a growl, Conn surges to his feet. "Ms. Abbott sounds like she's letting her personal opinions cloud her judgment."

"I could say the same about you."

He doesn't answer, just starts marching back toward his house. It feels like we're continuing our argument from last night. Apparently, we're *not* okay, despite my assurances to the contrary. Are we going to keep going around and around like this forever?

"Conn!" I shout, standing as well. To my surprise, he stops. I reach him in a few strides. Looks like I have to play my last card and tell him about Jack and Sasha. "There's something else—"

"You know," he says as he squints at me and rubs his earlobe, the casual gesture a sharp contrast to his harsh tone, "all that stuff you just said? Every last thing was completely wrong. You were wrong. But hey, don't let that stop you."

My stomach flips, partly from embarrassment that I made any sort of mistake in my assessment, partly with hope that Sasha isn't angling to get Conn back. "What was wrong about it?" I challenge him.

"Sasha's always hated this place. It played a big part in our breakup, in fact."

I hold my breath, stunned at his words. Conn has never shared any intimate details about his divorce before now. I've always been curious, but I've respected his privacy too much. Well, also because every time I ask too invasive a question, his barricades go up, his face becomes a mask, and he makes it all too clear the subject is out of bounds. Is he finally going to open up?

He doesn't continue, however, so I prompt him timidly, "You wanted to live here? And she didn't?"

"I swear she decided to take the residency in Seattle because it was as far as we could get from Abbott's Bay and still be within the continental forty-eight," he says, still sounding bitter.

Huh. I always thought it was because she wanted to pretend she was a regular on *Grey's Anatomy*. Insert meow.

"But the Pacific Northwest didn't make her happy either. What she really wanted was to travel, like we did after college, but permanently. She never suggested it, because she knew I was ready to settle down and start a family, ideally in Abbott's Bay. I missed living here. But *I* buried *that*. Nice, right?"

"You compromised. It's what married people do."

"But it has to be done willingly. With us there was so much...resentment underlying everything, spoiling everything, and we couldn't overcome it. We were...well, incompatible doesn't begin to describe it. She was always so..."

"Perfect?"

Conn grimaces. "Sasha is most definitely *not* perfect."

"I want to hear everything."

"I'll bet you do." After a pause he says, agitated again, "More important, has it ever occurred to you that no matter what Sasha wants for the future, I wouldn't be interested? I mean, what do you take me for? Why would I ever, *ever* think being with Sasha again would be a good idea? Especially when..."

He doesn't complete his thought, and I'm stuck hanging on his words, waiting. "Especially when" what? Does he know about her and Jack? I sincerely hope so, because I don't want to be the one to tell him if I can help it.

"You're so sure you know what's going on in everybody's head, don't you?" he marvels. "But you really don't. Not that it ever stops you from believing your own imagination. I've gotta ask...do you do this for all your clients, or is this VIP package just for me?"

"I—"

"Thought you knew everything, as usual."

"Conn, please don't lecture me. I'm in no mood for it."

"And I'm in no mood for you to mess with my life. So just stop, okay?"

He's right. Friendships have boundaries, and I've pretty much crossed all of ours...most of them within the past twelve hours. No wonder he's fed up with me. I can't look him in the eye. Instead I'm captivated by the empty coffee mug dangling from his fingers. I've left mine near the water, and I don't care—not even if his mother comes down hard on me someday when she finds out one is missing. (She's absolutely the type of person who would take inventory of the items in her old house.)

Conn and I have been around one another for decades, in varying degrees of closeness. But just because I probably drank out of one of those mugs twenty years ago as we kicked one another under the dining room table doesn't mean I have the right to think I know what's best for him now. I've gotten overconfident lately, thinking I know everything about him, and it's wrong. I'm wrong.

"I'm sorry," I whisper, my eyes brimming with tears again. I'm apologizing and crying more today than I normally do in a month. But it's warranted. "I…want what's best for you. And I worry about you." My intentions are good, but I don't own him. I've got to stop acting like I do. Starting now. "Do whatever makes you happy."

"M—"

He stops when I step closer and put a hand to his cheek. I take a moment to study the face I, yes, love. It's a marvelous face—so handsome, with those eyes that can be playful one minute, thoughtful the next. He's thoughtful now. I regret making this so heavy. That's not what we're about. Someday we'll get back to the fun, teasing relationship we've always had. It might take a while though, considering how gutted I feel as I brace myself to walk away from this man who truly is my best friend.

"Are you okay?" he asks.

Not in the least.

"Yeah. Fine. I'm going to go. Thanks for the coffee."

Then I do it. The thing I've wanted to do—forever, if I'm going to be honest with myself—but told myself I couldn't. I give him a little kiss. It's not passionate. It's not an invitation. It's simply an acknowledgment of everything we've been to each other over the years. The tingle that goes through me when my lips brush against his is bittersweet, because I know I'll never be able to do it again. If I were a different person—Taylor comes to mind—I would really go for it to see what would happen. But I'm not Taylor. And I'm not Sasha either. I'm just Melanie, in love with the wrong guy.

I pat his chest, give him a small smile, and turn to go. I don't even check his expression because I don't want to know how he's taking this.

Doesn't matter—I find out immediately. I'm yanked back, his grip hot on my arm.

"Hey," he snaps. "What the hell was that?"

Dammit. I've pissed him off, and now he's going to deny me my melancholy, noble exit.

"I expect better from you."

Here comes the lecture. About what? A little nothing kiss between friends? He's got to be kidding. It was a tiny peck! I start to argue when he cuts me off, his breathing shallow.

"At least do it like you mean it."

Wh...what, now? The words go into my ears, but my brain refuses to accept them. Stops them right at the border, in fact, and sends them packing. But my heart understands, and it starts hammering away in my chest like it's trying to make a break for it.

Now I know what people mean when they say time stands still. But it's not quite like that. Everything freezes, yes, but everything's moving at top speed at the same time. It's a surreal feeling, exacerbated by the rush of blood in my veins, by the lurching of my stomach, by the way every single nerve ending becomes hyperaware of every sensation—the cool breeze on my flushed cheeks, the rasp of my clothes on my skin, the way I can't seem to take a deep enough breath. One thought rises above the chaos in my head: is he *daring* me?

I force myself to look into Conn's eyes. In today's palette of pale bluish-green, I see that dare, that defiance. I also see frustration and agitation and something else that looks suspiciously like...need. Hunger. And a little bit of trepidation and vulnerability. It makes my rabbiting heart pick up the pace even more.

Part of me is afraid it's a joke, a prank. I'll reach for him and he'll back away, slap my hands down, and laugh as he says, "Don't be ridiculous!" My confusion must be showing on my face, because Conn has one more thing to say on the subject.

"Go on, Abbott," he says, and there's the tiniest quaver in

his voice. "Take your shot."

This can't be real. This is Conn, after all. It doesn't matter what I think I just heard. And yet I'm taking a step toward him, my hand reaching out...then I stop before I make a complete fool out of myself. I can't—

The next thing I know, Conn pulls me into a tight embrace, fusing us together along the entire length of our bodies.

"Do I have to do everything myself?" he growls.

"Shut up," I whisper.

I wrap my arms around his neck and my lips find his...his find mine...we find each other.

Connacht Garvey is actually kissing me, and I'm drowning. My head is buzzing. My knees weaken, and I hold him tighter just to stay upright. The kiss is gentle and easy and hard and urgent all at the same time. His lips are soft, his stubbly beard rough on my chin. Those huge arms of his are even tighter around me. One hand splayed on my back and the other in my hair, he presses closer yet.

This is beyond anything I...anything. At all. In the entire world.

My lips part without any coaxing from him. I couldn't resist if I tried. He kisses me deeply then pulls back slightly, peppering me with a few smaller kisses. But when I sigh against his mouth, he's back full force—pressing, always pressing, as though he can't get close enough. My breath is gone, stolen by the moment, the feel of his body—even the warmth of his cheeks and the gentle bump of our noses, a necessary clumsiness that's not in the least bit embarrassing but instead sexy as hell. When he groans against my mouth, "God, Melanie," I'm lost, flung sideways into a parallel universe I thought I could only imagine. But my imagination was nothing like this.

I pull back a little, and he stares at my mouth, eyes half-lidded, his breathing as heavy as mine. The sight of him makes me land with a bump, back in the reality I've known for thirty years. This is Conn. *Conn. Connacht Garvey.* Mister Untouchable. Always on the fringes of my life, yet always in it at the same time. But never...

Don't say a word, I warn myself. *Not one word, if you know what's good for*— "Is...is this weird?"

Dammit.

His eyes start to focus. "Weird?"

"Is it? It is. Weird, I mean. Isn't it?"

I feel him tense up, and suddenly I'm keenly aware of my arms still wrapped around him.

"Melanie Abbott. Don't you dare freak out on me."

"I'm not!"

I am. I mean, come on—I've known this guy my entire life, and no matter what fantasies I've entertained about him off and on over the years, I've always thought deep down he was completely out of reach, and now…this. It's messing with my head something fierce, not to mention my heart and…other zones.

"I…I should go."

"M—"

"No, it's…I'm fine. This was…" Unbelievable. Sensational. Mind blowing. Literally breathtaking. "…Nice." *Oh, for God's sake!* "But I have to stop home before I, you know, go back and pick up my dad. And it's a half-hour drive at least. More, if I wait too long and end up in rush-hour traffic. So…"

During my rambling, I've managed to extricate myself from Conn's embrace. I move back one more step, stumbling over something in the sand. It's the owl mug. Conn must have dropped it when we…yeah. For some reason I keep staring at it until Conn puts a heavy hand on each of my shoulders. Normally I love when he does that—his touch grounds me, calms me. But this time it feels like I'm going to sink into the sand from the weight.

"Hey. Don't do this."

"Do what? I'm not doing anything. I really have to go. I might stop at the office to let everybody know what's going on with Dad, and…"

I really need to stop babbling, is what I really need to do. So I duck out from under him, smile bravely, and trip across the sand, up the steps, along the side of his house. I force myself to look back and wave before climbing the stairs to the road. Conn is staring at me from the beach, hands on his hips, but he makes no move to come after me. Once I'm four or five houses away, I lean against a brick pillar at the end of someone's driveway,

knees shaking violently, and bury my face in my hands.
I am so dead.

CHAPTER TWENTY-THREE

How I get through the rest of the day, I have no idea. I mean that literally—I barely recall the drive to the hospital to pick up my dad, the procedure we go through to get him discharged, or what we talk about on the way home. In my head I'm still on the beach, locked in an embrace with Conn.

One thing that does cut through my mental fog is realizing how well my father's doing already. He seems almost back to normal, even joking with the nurses and eating the hospital lunch with gusto while we wait for his discharge papers. By the time I get him settled at home with his housekeeper Magda, I'm no longer worried about the state of his health or any complications from the surgery. There isn't even any point in my sitting with him for the rest of the day, which I'd planned on doing. When he shoos me away, I make sure he's comfortable on the sofa, admonish him to take it easy like the doctors and nurses advised, give him a kiss and a hug, and retreat to my apartment. I should stop by the real estate office. I should check in with my New Best Friend clients. But I can't. My brain is on overload, and all I can do is hide out until it reboots.

I trudge upstairs, my bones aching like I've aged decades in only a day, to find a cellophane monster blocking my door. The entire landing smells like a greenhouse. I creep up on the monster sideways, slowly, so as not to startle it, and poke it with my key. The giant fan shape tips sideways. I catch it before it can do a giant face-plant (plant-plant?) then drag it into my apartment.

I'm not sure how I feel about this. I've never been much of a flowers person—ply me with food and I'm all yours, but I could always take or leave posies. However, this giant bouquet is stunning. And intimidating. Is this a declaration of—okay, if not love, serious feelings on Conn's part? Or is it an apology for what happened? I almost don't want to read the card to find out.

I spend way too much time struggling with the ribbon, the paper, the cellophane, the rubber bands, the individual water reservoir nipples on each stem, as a way of avoiding the moment of truth when I have to open the small envelope tucked inside and see what Conn has to say about what happened this morning. I ball up the wrapping and throw it away. I trim the stems. I find a couple of vases. I share a bit of my carefully hoarded vodka with the flowers to prolong their lives.

I allow myself one swig to steady my nerves, because my heart beats triple time whenever I glance at the envelope on the counter, now puckered from stray droplets of water. I don't even know what I want it to say. If it's a declaration of love, will I handle it as poorly as I did this morning? I got what I wanted and promptly ran away. Who *does* that? I do, apparently. But if it's an apology and a request to go back to being friends, I'll be devastated.

I never said my brain was ready to make sense of the situation yet.

Instead of ripping the note open and finding out the truth as soon as possible, I take a long shower then wrap myself in my security blanket, a plush robe stolen from a spa Taylor and I went to a couple of years ago. It was Taylor's idea to boost the robes. Even though I know the place just added the cost to our bill, I felt so guilty afterward that I pushed it to the back of the closet and only wear it when I need to wrap myself in senses-deadening fluff. Like now, for instance.

After that I do a little standing in the middle of my living room. Nothing else. Just standing and staring like a drugged-up lunatic in an asylum. I'm exhausted, I remind myself. So I try to nap…and end up staring at my bedroom ceiling…decamp to the sofa and stare at the living room ceiling instead…stop myself from lying on the kitchen floor to stare at what's overhead by reminding myself it's an extension of the living room ceiling.

I give up on a nap and raid the fridge.

Meanwhile, the little white envelope catches my eye repeatedly, until I lunge for it. There's no genteel loosening of the flap here. Instead, I wrench it open, almost mangling the card inside as well, and force myself to read it while my stomach does nonstop backflips.

> *Sorry I didn't see you before I left, Miss Melanie—had to go on a business trip. Think about my offer. Hope you say yes. Love, Jack*

What...what? I read the message again. *Jack?*

Jack, not Conn? Sent me flowers? When did he ever do that before? Never. Why would he now? And what offer? Say yes to wh—?

Then everything stops. Is he referring to what he said on the beach? About us spending some "alone time" together? Was he serious? *Is* he serious?

I start to fidget as another thought comes to me. If Jack's offering, does that mean I'm wrong about him and Sasha? If that's the case, I'm glad I never said anything to Conn. I don't think I could stand being wrong about his personal life *again*.

Jack, huh?

I scoop up my phone and dial the number on the card. "Well, aren't you the romantic."

Jack laughs softly in my ear. I can imagine his tanned face lighting up as he stretches in his office chair. Or maybe he's on a chaise at a hotel pool. I really have no idea where he is or what he does when he goes on business trips. "Like 'em?"

"What's not to like? They're exotic, impressive, and expensive."

"Exactly what I was going for. So are you thinking about it?"

"I'm honestly not sure what to think."

"Ah, Miss Melanie, you're always playing hard to get. Okay, picture this: a few days in New York..."

What? A few *days*? Most people would start with dinner.

"VIP treatment all the way. I'd personally introduce you to the network's president and pitch the guest spot on one of our highest-rated news shows. There's no way they'd be able to turn us down. Literally no way—National Network News is a Rossiter-owned company."

"Er..." My sleep-deprived brain has to work overtime to catch up to what he's saying. What *is* he saying? If this is a date, it's the weirdest one I've ever heard of.

"So what do you think? Want to be on television?"

Television? And then I remember his offer on the golf course, to promote Your New Best Friend on national TV. "Jack…"

"Come on! Say yes! It'll be the best thing ever. National attention! Your business would be huge! Plus I'd make it worth your while."

I know he's talking about money, but he makes it sound sexual. It's unnerving. I have no idea how to answer. Then I'm snapped out of my daze by the sound of banging on my door. It's startling, not only because it's loud and sudden, but because the number of people who come to my apartment is small: Hannah, Taylor, my father once in a blue moon, and the UPS guy. Three of those four aren't around, and I'm not expecting—

"Melanie? Open up."

My God.

"I know you're in there. Open the door."

Conn has never, *ever* come here voluntarily. The last time he was at my apartment was a year ago, when I shamelessly complimented him on his muscle definition until he agreed to carry a really heavy chair up the stairs after the deliverymen dumped it in the entryway while I was out. Even then, he barely stayed long enough to accept a bottle of water in payment.

"Miss Melanie?" Jack prompts in my ear.

While I'd like to pretend I'm torn between these two men, there really is only one option for me. "Jack, I'll have to call you another time."

"I'll be back in New York next week. I can get something set up then, so don't take too long to think about it. Okay?"

I may agree and say goodbye politely, but I'm not sure. In a daze, I drop the phone onto my coffee table, cross the room, and lean my forehead against the door as I try to get my breathing under control.

"M? You there?" A pause, then, "I have ice cream."

He gets me. Damn him.

I press my eye to the peephole, even though there's no way that voice could belong to anyone but Conn. The entire sightline is filled with the MooMoo's logo stamped on a white paper bag.

"It's a sundae with caramel sauce, and everything's melting."

Well, we can't have that. MooMoo's should never go to waste. I open the door.

As slowly as I move, to brace myself for the sight of the man I love holding the ice cream I love, seeing Conn on my doorstep still sends me reeling. It's like gazing into the sun; I can't look directly at him.

I decide to focus on his gift instead. "Chocolate or vanilla soft serve?" I ask brusquely as I unceremoniously relieve him of the bag and peek inside.

"Yes."

I need to marry this man.

Nope, those kinds of thoughts have had me so immobilized I already lost an entire day. I can't go back to that again. Noticing they forgot to include a spoon, I hurry into the kitchen and pull one out of the drawer. After a moment's hesitation, I get another. Manners dictate I share my ice cream, and the thought of using one spoon gives rise to dangerous notions, like feeding each other. Or drizzling—

Stop.

Conn blocks the way out of the kitchen. It doesn't take much. In fact, his presence makes my entire apartment seem incredibly small all of a sudden. He fills the space, a large, rough-hewn, masculine contrast to my mostly pastel, decidedly girly surroundings. He's entirely out of place.

It makes me dangerously tingly.

What's worse, he's staring down at me, studying me intently, and not budging from his position in the doorway. Not speaking, not moving. Just staring. Damn, if the ice cream wasn't melted yet, it is now, from the heat that's suddenly coming off me in waves.

I need room. I need air. I need to get rid of this fifteen-pound robe. Er, wait—bad idea, considering I'm not wearing much of anything underneath it. Or maybe it would be a really good idea, come to think of it.

While I work to keep myself from hyperventilating, Conn's eyes flick over to the two vases of flowers on the counter but still says nothing.

The heat waves intensify. I expect the paper bag I'm holding to ignite and disappear into thin air like a magician's flash paper. My robe might be about to do the same.

"Are you going to stand there, or are you going to sit down with me and eat this ice cream?" I sound bossy enough that he backs up a step. I squeeze past him, reeling when my breasts brush up against his arm. Well, not my breasts, exactly—there's all this foot-thick fabric in the way. Stupid robe.

While I'm distracted by filthy thoughts, Conn saunters over to the sofa and sits there, settling in and gesturing me over. I had planned on herding him toward my small table by the window. Now it's too late. I sit. Perch, actually. Every muscle in my body is seized up tight. Conn, on the other hand, has relaxed into my couch entirely, even going so far as to do a touch of manspreading. Not enough to be obnoxious, just enough to make my eyes drop to…

"Have some? Ice cream, I mean." Did that shrill voice come out of me?

I plop the spoons and the bag onto the coffee table, swipe off a jumble of magazines, rip the bag down the side, take the plastic dome off the bowl. I hand one of the spoons to Conn. We eat in silence. Well, he takes some every once in a while, but mostly he stays out of my way and lets me go at it. I don't worry about how this looks. He's seen me eat a vat of ice cream on many occasions. I do glance over once though, thinking how weird it is that he hasn't said a word since he walked in, and he smiles knowingly around a spoonful of chocolate and caramel.

"What?" Yes, I even talk with my mouth full. This is what years of constantly being around one another will do.

"Nothing," he finally says, placing his spoon carefully on one of the napkins instead of gumming up my coffee table. I notice these kinds of things. I appreciate these kinds of things. He looks me up and down, assessing. "Better now?"

"Better than what?"

"Earlier. You're stressed. You're tired. I figure you haven't eaten all day. And you know how you get on an empty stomach."

It's pointless to argue. I am indeed a wreck when I'm off

my sleeping and eating schedule. "So this was, what, intended to placate the beast?"

"Of course. And a way to get you to sit still and talk to me for five minutes."

"So it was a trap."

"You took the bait."

"You suck."

"I know what I have to do to get the job done."

His last statement hangs there, filled with all sorts of innuendo, and I'm hot all over once again. I lick some caramel off my thumb and stare into the now empty bowl.

"And what job is that?"

"To get you to stop freaking out."

"I'm not—"

"Stop it. I know a Melanie freak-out when I see one. And may I say you've outdone yourself this time."

"I—"

"I mean, it was really impressive. You couldn't get away from me fast enough this morning."

I'm offended and want to argue, but I stop short, shocked when I realize he's laughing. A lot. At me. "Oh *really*?"

"Little..." He can barely get the words out. "Little cartoon puffs of smoke shooting out behind you..." He wiggles his fingers to imitate my apparently scooting feet as I ran from him.

He doesn't sober up. In fact, he actually laughs harder. It's a rare sight, Conn roaring, tears of mirth in the corners of his eyes. When it does happen, it's pretty glorious.

"Well, can you blame me?" I exclaim indignantly, giving him an exasperated shove. "It *was* weird. All the...I mean...you and me and..." I can't describe it, so I start making exaggerated kissing noises like I'm nine years old again. Now he's got me laughing.

"Yeah, okay. I'll give you that." He dries his eyes with the heel of his hand as his laughter finally winds down. "It was...*unusual*."

"Unusual? Seriously? It was downright surreal."

"Good surreal or bad surreal?" he asks evenly.

"There's a difference?"

"Yes. And I'm going to take a chance and bet on 'good surreal,' because I didn't catch you wiping your mouth with the back of your hand as you sprinted off."

"Maybe I hid that from you."

"I doubt it."

"Ego!"

"I dunno," he says slowly, "for a while there you weren't exactly fighting to get away from me."

His voice has dropped into that sexy register with a frequency that seems to have the ability to dissolve things. Like my resolve. And, I'd bet, my underwear. He's leaning in, and so am I. Neither of us is laughing now.

"So which is it, Abbott?" he rumbles. "Are you going to stay freaked out about what happened, or are we going to discuss this like rational adults?"

"That depends," I say, my voice suddenly hoarse. I clear my throat.

"On what?"

"What you're thinking about our little…incident this morning."

"Incident?" he repeats, incredulous. "That's what you're going to call it?"

Development? No, that sounds too hopeful, like there's a future attached to it. Adventure? It certainly was, although I can't tell if it was a good one or a bad one yet. Encounter? Awfully sexual. A connotation I approve of, mind.

When I don't answer, Conn rests his elbow on the back of the sofa and his temple on the heel of his hand. "Yes or no." He means it as a question, but it comes out as a demand.

"Yes or no what?"

"Did you want it to happen? Or not?"

Oh God, more than anything. "I—" My voice catches, and it feels like my vocal cords have seized up. Nothing more comes out. I feel my cheeks flush. "Did you?"

"Yes."

That single syllable lands like a punch. There's no equivocating, no waffling, no skirting the issue. He's looking at me steadily, and if I weren't sitting already, I'd collapse from shock.

"Oh." My answer is barely more than an exhaled breath. "But it's—"

"Weird, I know. You've said that already. A lot. Too weird to even think about though? *Do* you ever think about the possibility of...us?"

"Sometimes," I whisper. Every waking moment. To the exclusion of all else lately. I think I walked into a tree a few hours ago because I was thinking about it. Us.

"In a good way or a bad way?"

So, so good. Since this morning's kiss, however, deliciously..."Define *bad*."

Conn smiles broadly, and damned if he doesn't look outright relieved. A glimmer of hope ignites in my chest.

"And you?" I dare to ask.

"Do I think about..."

"Us. Yes."

"I wouldn't have let you kiss me if I didn't."

"*Let* me—? You told me to!"

"Like you ever do anything because I tell you to."

I roll my eyes. I really can't argue, and he knows it. All our lives, I've tended to do the exact opposite of anything he ever advised.

But before we can fall back into one of our usual fake arguments, Conn tucks his hand under my hair, caressing the back of my neck with his strong fingers. I melt at his touch. "The truth is," he murmurs, leaning in and drawing me closer, "I'm crazy about you, Melanie Abbott. And I have been for a long...long...time."

I don't even have the chance to take a breath before his lips are on mine again. This time I freeze for only a moment before I kiss him back, first tentatively then as hard and deep as he's kissing me. His arms go around me again. I can't believe this feeling, or that I've managed to live without it till now. I'm flushed, but I'm shaking at the same time. The feel of him is something I never expected. When I imagined kissing him, before I actually did, I couldn't quite conjure up the physical sensations, only the emotions. But this...soft lips, tickly beard, shoulders like granite...I could get used to this.

He says something against my mouth, so softly I can

barely hear him. "So sweet."

"I'm not sweet, mister."

"I'm talking about the ice cream."

"Shut up and kiss me again."

Instead, he pulls back, entirely out of breath. "Well?"

"Well what?"

"How are you doing? Are you freaking out yet?"

Trust Conn to have the presence of mind to check on me at a moment like this. I want to reassure him, but it's more fun to shock him. So I say, with a wicked grin, "Yes."

"Uh-oh."

He starts to pull away even more, but I keep him where he is by tightening my arms around his neck.

"In a good way."

Now I know. I've wasted a whole day in shock, but I've recovered, possibly thanks to the ice cream, but more likely thanks to the man who brought me the ice cream. I want this. I want Conn. It may feel a little odd, switching from friends to…well, more than friends, but I'm ready to make the leap. I'm even more convinced when he starts kissing my neck in the perfect place, as though he's known all along what will drive me crazy.

"Really?" he asks, and I nod, breathless. "What's that like?"

"A little like this."

Time to show him I'm serious. I push him against the back cushions of the sofa and climb onto his lap, my knees on either side of his thighs. I rise above him and kiss him the way I really want to. The way I've always wanted to. Passionately. With abandon. With more confidence than I'm actually feeling. I'm glad he's looking out for me, but I don't want caution now. I need him to lose himself in me the way I can lose myself in him. I need to know he means this, he wants this.

A groan from Conn morphs into a growl. "Jesus, Abbott, you're killing me."

"Want me to stop?"

"Not on your life."

I kiss him deeply one more time then take the biggest risk so far. Our foreheads nearly touching, my hair a curtain on either side of our faces, I whisper, "So. No more Sasha?"

He looks puzzled for a second then, to my relief, smiles. "Sasha who?"

"Come on!"

"There is no Sasha," he says evenly. "She's never said anything to me about wanting to get back together—I swear. Everything you speculated about this morning?" He taps my temple gently. "It was all in there. You have a very vivid imagination."

"Oh, you have no idea."

The color rises in his cheeks and his eyes sharpen. "I don't want to talk about Sasha anymore."

"You don't, huh? Well, what do you want to talk about?"

"How about what's going on under this robe of yours?"

Good lord, Connacht Garvey is trying to feel me up. I never thought I'd see the day. The last thing I want to do is slap his hands away, but I do it all the same. "Hey, now. We haven't even had a real date yet."

"You want a real date?" He finds this pretty darn funny. "Like going out to dinner and getting to know one another?"

Well, when he puts it that way…"You're right. Never mind. How about you kiss me instead?"

CHAPTER TWENTY-FOUR

———

A sunny morning, some chirping birds, a flippy skirt, bouncing curls, a skip into town. I'm behaving like a damn Disney princess, and I don't even care. My heart's too big for my chest today, and all the extra happy is leaking out of me in odd ways.

I'm heading for Deep Brew C because Conn asked me to. "Come for breakfast. I want to see you first thing in the morning," he said last night. A sweet sentiment made incredibly hot. Because he was saying it with his lips against my neck. Punctuating his words with sexy little swipes of his tongue. How could I refuse?

My pulse starts fluttering the closer I get to the commercial district and DBC. I've only been away from Conn for several hours, but I'm desperate to see him again. Yes, I managed to kick him out of my apartment late last night before any under-the-robe exploring took place—well, not much, anyway—and we established some ground rules so we don't mess up this delicate operation: we agreed to set a modest pace when it comes to anything physical, and we decided to keep our new status quiet for now. This is going to be a shock for our friends and relatives. If they don't approve, it might derail us completely before we get a chance to even get comfortable with each other.

The one exception is Hannah, whom I called before Conn was even out of sight down the sidewalk. Yes, I stood at the window and watched him go. One should never miss an opportunity to watch that man's backside in motion. I forgot it was the middle of the night, but when I told her the news she was so excited it didn't matter what time it was—she insisted on getting all the details. I had plenty for her, like his answer when I demanded to know how he came to this sudden conclusion we should be more than friends.

"Sudden?" he repeated, looking at me like I had two heads. "It wasn't sudden. Do you think I just *decided* I was hot for you, like, last week? I told you, I've felt this way for a long time."

"Which is so weird to me. Why didn't you tell me you've been carrying a torch for me for a while?"

"Who says 'carrying a torch' anymore?"

"Don't mock. It's a perfectly legitimate expression."

"If you're a time traveler from 1894."

"Stop avoiding the question."

Conn looked at me steadily, which stirred up a butterfly colony in my stomach, then said, "I didn't think you felt the same way. So I kept it to myself."

"For how long?"

"Ages."

"Ages?" What constituted an age, let alone more than one? I didn't know. "You'd better not mean when we were kids. Because, you know—ew."

"No, of course not. You were a pain in the ass when we were kids. And I was only interested in football anyway."

"And not when I was a teenager, because to you I was jailbait. Double ew."

"Definitely not," he agreed emphatically. "You were still a pain in the ass then—just a bigger one."

"You're running out of years," I cautioned him.

That familiar grin spread across his face, and he reached out to curl a lock of my hair around his index finger. "Later," he murmured. "When I moved back to town after my divorce."

"I find that hard to believe. You were in such a dark place then, you despised every individual with two X chromosomes."

"You're right, I did. Well, not despised, but I was perfectly happy avoiding the female half of the species for a while. I couldn't avoid you though. You wouldn't let me."

"Hey!"

"Admit it—you showed up whether I wanted you to or not. Repeatedly."

"Of course I did! I couldn't let you waste away by yourself."

"I was grateful. You were there for me, and I let you in because you were my friend. You were safe...I *thought*. But when I got my head straight, opened the restaurant, started over...there you were, in a *really* different way."

I felt my cheeks flush at his simple words that said so much, at the shrug of one shoulder that told me he realized we were an inevitability, coupled with a hungry look in his eye making it quite clear he welcomed the inevitability.

"I didn't appear in a puff of smoke," I demurred.

"It felt like you did. Suddenly you were a grown-up, self-possessed *woman*. At the same time the old Melanie I'd always known was still in there. That was a dangerous mix. Look what it did to me."

"I'm not sure I'm buying this. You bitched at me constantly!"

"Smokescreen. Deep down, I wanted you around. I *needed* you around. You were a light at the end of the tunnel. One I always looked for, because you made me happy. It's...you're..."

"What?" I whispered, thrumming from head to toe as he leaned forward to kiss me once again.

"Perfect," he whispered back before giving me the gentlest of pecks on my lips.

Which, of course, didn't stay gentle for long.

Needless to say, last night was pretty much everything I always dreamed of. Why, then, am I hesitating on the sidewalk across the street from DBC? Maybe I'm afraid it was all an ice-cream-induced hallucination, and when I walk into Conn's place, I'll be facing His Royal Grumpiness, as usual.

However, the pull of wanting to see Conn is stronger than any worries I can conjure up, so I force my feet off the curb and across the cobbles. I fling open the front door with my usual flair, even though my knees feel like they're made of Jell-O. There's no sign of Conn, which ratchets up my panic level. He could pop out at me from anywhere, at any moment. Or he's not even here though he said he would be.

This is ridiculous. I'm being ridiculous. Summoning the

old Melanie—and holding her by her collar to keep her here—I march up to the counter.

"Beebs, my love, how are you?"

"'Morning, Melanie. You look nice today."

"Aren't you sweet."

"Triple espresso?"

I do *not* need that much caffeine. My nerves are already practically piercing my skin. "How about a latte instead? I feel rested today."

"You sure seem happy about something."

I smile coyly at him and move over a few steps to wait for my drink. Some movement in the kitchen, which I can see through the pickup window, makes me jump. It's not Conn though. It's Ornette, the cook. He waves me over.

"How's my favorite chef today?"

He smiles brightly—when he does that, the skinny man seems to be all teeth, brilliant white against his rich, dark skin—and rests the heels of his hands on the open ledge. "You got a minute, Melanie?"

"For you? Always."

"Meet you in the back hallway?"

When he joins me, his smile turns self-conscious. "I, uh, was wondering if you had some time to help me out. Professionally. I..."

"Need a friend?" I try to focus on him, but I'm also on high alert for any sign of Conn. It's hard not to be distracted.

"Yeah. Do you...find dates for people?"

Now he has my full attention. I have done a few matchmaking jobs, but they've been fewer and farther between than I expected. Petey Fagle is probably my greatest success, although because he already had someone in mind, I didn't have to find him a date. If Vernon and Zoë become a couple, they'll be another success story, albeit accidental. Still, I think I'm pretty good at putting people together, and the way I'm feeling right now about my own love life makes me want to find someone special for everyone.

"I don't even know where to start," Ornette confesses.

Fortunately, I do. "Ornette. Buddy. Don't tell me you can't see the obvious."

"What?"

I glance around—still no sign of Conn, but that's not who I'm looking out for this time—before I lean in and whisper, "Beebs has had a crush on you forever."

Ornette draws his head back in surprise, but he's smiling again. "You think so?"

"Oh, I know so. You should go for it. You won't be turned down. I guarantee it."

"Wow, just like that? I mean, I didn't think you'd have an answer for me this fast."

"Just like that." I don't tell him I've had this gut feeling about him and Beebs for ages.

"Thanks!"

"My pleasure."

"Do you bill me, or—?"

"If you two get together, it's all the payment I need." I pat his arm reassuringly. "I want to see you both happy."

"Thanks," he says again then hesitates. "Wait. What does Conn think of—"

"Coworkers dating? I'll bet you anything he'll be okay with it."

"Are you sure?"

"If he has any doubts, I'll convince him." I have skills. And recently acquired special influence. "In fact, I'll talk to Conn about it right now. Do you happen to know where—?"

"Melanie?" I whip around to find Conn leaning out of his office. "Hey. Can I talk to you a second?"

I'm not sure if I should be happy or alarmed. His face is a blank. I gulp and nod. He opens the door wider. I walk into the office, head high, giving no sign I'm suddenly grappling with my deepest fear: what if he's going to tell me last night was all a mistake and we should go back to being just friends?

The minute he slams the door and sandwiches me between it and his body, so tightly I can barely move, that fear vanishes. He kisses me hungrily, like I have the only supply of the air he needs to breathe.

"Where have you been?" he demands, teeth grazing my skin.

I shiver. "Did you miss me?"

Nodding, he says, "Maybe my leaving last night wasn't the best idea."

"You know it was," I say, even though I don't believe it.

"I almost called you when I got home."

"So why didn't you?"

"I was busy."

"Doing what?"

"Thinking about you."

The way he says "thinking" implies something quite different. I give him a shove. "Pervert."

"Your fault. All your fault. You left me with too much to…think about."

"Wait a minute. You definitely should have called me." He swings me around effortlessly, leaning me against the edge of his desk. I laugh, but it's more breathlessness than anything else. "Oh my God, stop."

"Stop what? Talking? Or this?" He slips a hand under my skirt, runs his palm over my ass, and I'm pretty sure I'm going to faint.

"Never mind. Carry on."

Moving his hand down the back of my thigh, he tickles the inside of my knee and lifts my leg, wrapping it around him. I don't fight this either. It all feels too damn good.

"So. Talk to me about what?" he asks.

"Mm?" I'm too distracted by the line of soft kisses he's placing on my skin, one after the other, from my neck to my shoulder, to comprehend what he's saying.

"I heard you tell Ornette you were going to talk to me about something."

"Oh. Right." I let out a huge sigh as he moves the fabric of my sleeveless shirt and bra strap aside to continue the line of kisses. "Ornette wants to…oh God." Conn has reversed direction. His kisses are coming back along my collarbone and heading down the V of my shirt, turning my brain to mush.

"To what?"

"He wants…to ask Beebs out, but he's afraid you have some rule against employee…um…" I've actually lost my ability to form words.

"Fraternization?"

"Yeah, that."

He tickles my sensitive skin with another light kiss. "Did you have anything to do with it?"

"S-sort of. I told him to go for it."

As a particularly shaky breath escapes from me, Conn looks up from under devilishly arched eyebrows, but he doesn't lift his head from the top edge of my breast. He's got to quit. He can't go any lower.

I *need* him to go lower.

"Good. It's about time those two got together."

I start to say, "I'll tell him—" And Conn goes lower. I cut off my own comment with a rather loud, involuntary yelp.

He's back at my lips immediately. "Shh." His whisper flutters over my cheek. "People are going to wonder what's going on in here." And to make sure I don't raise the alarm, he covers my mouth with a captivating, all-consuming kiss.

When I can catch my breath again, I pummel his shoulder. "Quit it. I've got to go to work."

"You're going to leave me like this?"

"Lock yourself in here and…do some thinking."

"You're cruel."

But he does step back. I can barely stand as I make a business of straightening my clothes and smoothing my hair.

Conn brushes a few stray strands back from my eyes and, hands on the sides of my face, kisses me one more time. "Can I see you tonight?"

"Can't. I'm teaching Aurelia Hoffstader proper social media etiquette and how to take a selfie. She wants to start internet dating."

"Seriously?"

"Hey, no disrespecting my clients. All their needs are important."

"Yes, ma'am."

"I'll call you after I'm done."

When I present myself for review, turning to one side then the other, he looks me up and down and nods. "Squared away," he says, opening the door.

He reaches for me one more time, but I hold him off with a hand to his chest. It has the opposite effect. He yanks me back inside, completely messes up what I just straightened, then pushes me out into the hallway…right into Beebs, who's standing there, fist raised to knock, his mouth open in shock. I blush violently. He smiles. Delightedly.

I doubt Conn and I are going to be able to keep this a secret for very long.

*   *   *

Beebs catching us doesn't dampen my mood in the least, however. If I thought I was floaty and stupid earlier this morning, I'm even more so as I make my way to the real estate office. The bell over the door sounds like the sweetest church chimes, Eric the Red doesn't look as coked up as he usually does, and even Maude's pinched expression doesn't bother me. Is this place cheerier, or is it me? I suspect it's the latter.

Then I have the biggest surprise of the morning: my father is in his office.

"Daddy, what in God's name are you doing at work?"

"I brought donuts!"

"That explains Laura's white mustache. Maybe. Anyway, this isn't like you. Have you had a stroke?" Maybe a fever has set in and he's delirious. I toss my things onto the leather sofa and round the end of his desk to put my hand on his forehead. "What's wrong?"

He pushes my hand away, but gently. "Nothing's wrong. Can't your old man come into his own place of business? And bearing donuts, no less?"

"Why are you not following the advice of a doctor for once and taking it easy for a couple of weeks?"

"I'm sitting at my desk. It's just like sitting at home but less infuriating. Have you *seen* the state of daytime TV lately?"

"Don't change the subject."

"It is the same subject. You asked why I'm here. I'm answering you. It's because *Maury* drives me up a wall."

"Dressing, driving, and sitting here are all stressful. Aren't your incisions hurting?"

"Magda dropped me off, and I have wonderful painkillers. Now, I want to talk to you."

He sounds almost serious. I wonder if he's had some complications. Or maybe the pre-op tests found something wrong, something more serious than his appendix. "What is it?"

"You think I should take it easy," he begins.

I nod. I did do some thinking about this while he was in surgery. "Absolutely. You're not getting any younger, and—"

"I beg your pardon!"

"What I mean is, maybe you should take a look at how you're living your life. All the unneeded stress. Like running for office. Maybe you should consider withdrawing from—"

"Not on your life."

"Okay." I'm prepared for this. I have a backup plan. "Then how about letting me take care of your appearances from now till November?"

"No."

"Charles, you're pissing me off."

"That's not very ladylike."

"Look, old man—"

"Let me talk, offspring," he commands. "I have done a bit of soul searching lately, but not about backing off or taking it easy. Quite the contrary, in fact."

"Dad—"

"Listen. Please. Before I found out all this was just my appendix, I came up with at least a dozen different deadly diseases and conditions that could be causing me all that pain."

"Of course you did." No need to wonder where I get my overactive imagination from. It runs in the family.

"Anyway, I realized I've spent half my life trying to find something wrong with me. Physically. You know."

"I do know. Very well."

"But once something *actually* turned out to be wrong with me, I realized what a waste it's been, worrying about nothing all these years. It's kind of a sick hobby, isn't it?"

"I'd go with 'weird pathological behavior.'"

"I'm sixty-five years old. I have decades ahead of me if I play my cards right. Why should I spend any of it looking for illnesses I don't have? I know this is a cliché, but life is short, isn't it? We should be living it instead of spending our entire time on earth afraid of it."

"I agree."

"Good."

"Does this mean you're turning the real estate office over to me now?"

"Nice try."

Oh well.

"This goes for you too," he continues. "You've got that lovely new business of yours. Make the most of it. It could really be something."

"Oh, I don't know," I demur. It started off as an accidental opportunity to get paid for doing what I usually do: be too free and easy with my advice. Without a practical business plan, I can't see this thing having a very long shelf life. The summer people will be leaving in a few short weeks, and I'll be back to helping out the locals, which I've always done anyway, as part of my noblesse oblige.

"Keep your options open, is all I'm saying."

"I will. I promise. So how are you going to live your best life then?"

"Enjoy it. Not take it for granted. Not try to hasten my trip to the burying ground. Stay healthy enough to enjoy my grandchildren."

"Hey. Don't go thinking too far ahead, mister."

"I suppose not, considering you haven't even dated anyone in…how long has it been? Months? Years?"

"Okay, you can stop right there."

"Don't make me wait too much longer, that's all."

I kiss my father on the top of his white head and say nothing, absolutely nothing, about Conn, even though I want to. For the first time in my life, I can actually envision that sort of a future. I don't want to jinx it.

CHAPTER TWENTY-FIVE

You awake yet?

I am awake, but barely. I squint at the text. It's from Conn. Yesterday, after eight days of ridiculous, if secret, bliss, he actually asked me out on a date. I was ready to turn him down flat because the concept of drinks and dinner still feels pointless. But hey, we wouldn't be us if we didn't fall into this thing completely backward, right? Then he supplied the details: he needs to check out some properties in Provincetown, and he asked me to go along, not only for the company, but because he values my opinion. How could a girl say no?

I pictured a nice drive out to the Cape, a lunch stop, investigating his real estate options, and maybe a little stroll around Provincetown before driving back. Plus I'd get to see Taylor again. But Conn is contacting me so early, I'm certain something's come up and he's canceling.

What's going on? I text back.

Change of plans.

Arg. I knew it. Then another text comes in.

Picking you up now.

Wha—*now*? I'm not showered, not dressed, not primped and primed. I can't go *now*. I start to text back, when he anticipates me.

Don't worry about doing yourself up. You're perfect the way you are. And it's too late anyway—I'm outside your apartment.

Damn him. *Cool your jets*, I answer. *Be out in five.*

I'm planning on ten, but he doesn't need to know that.

Seven minutes have gone by when he starts banging on my door. I'm mostly ready, just stuffing random items into my purse, so I grab my shoes with one hand while I open the door with the other.

"Let's go! Time's a-wasting!"

"Don't you clap your hands at me, mister. You can't change plans and expect me to jump. You haven't even come bearing coffee." I give him a rude view of my backside as I slip on my sneakers.

"It's in the car. We need to go *now*."

"Why the rush? Has Godzilla risen from the waves and is stomping toward Abbott's Bay this very minute?"

"Because the conditions are perfect to go to the Cape by boat. There isn't a ripple out there, and the forecast is clear all day. I figured we could take the old tub for a farewell journey."

There's so much packed into his statement I don't know where to start. First of all, traveling from the North Shore to the tip of the Cape can be dicey, even in summer, depending on the winds and the currents. Conn's a responsible boater, so I trust he checked the marine forecast repeatedly before considering it, but it still comes as a surprise. And…"Farewell journey? You sold her?"

"Frank Comey is a very happy guy."

"I heard him say he was going to fleece you!"

"I know it. He's completely predictable. I jacked up the price, so when he chewed me down, it was the exact amount I wanted in the first place. You're not hanging with a dummy, I'll have you know."

"Oh, I do know."

"So? You up for it?"

Of course I say yes immediately and quickly dig my beach bag out of the closet, stuff a sweater into it, and make sure my sunscreen is in there.

Taylor meets us at the marina in Provincetown, where she's finagled a docking spot for the day from a friend. From the look on her face when we walk up to her in the parking lot, it's clear she isn't expecting me.

"Oh my Goooood!" After some squealing and hugging, she pushes me away from her abruptly and looks me over. "You're different."

"I'm exactly the same."

"Nope. Something's different. Did you get laid?"

I can't tell if she's actually expecting an answer.

Fortunately, she bounces to another subject immediately. "Hey, how's your dad?"

"He's doing well."

"So you had some free time to come along and keep an eye on me, make sure I don't cheat Garvey, here?"

"Something like that."

"Well, you don't scare me. I've got some hot properties you're going to love."

On the way to the first place, Taylor starts spouting statistics about the locations she's selected, frequently glancing in the rearview mirror at Conn to gauge his interest. He sits forward, elbows on his knees, and asks a ton of intelligent questions. The guy is shrewd, smart, and hot as hell when he's speaking my language of real estate. He doesn't need my advice, or Taylor's. He knows what's up all on his own.

Still, as we finish touring the first space, he takes my elbow, sending electric currents up my arm, and murmurs in my ear, "Professional opinion, please?"

"It's a dump."

"I concur."

Really, the place should be torn down and the land sold as a building lot, but I'm not sure it'd be worth it even then, as the location is terrible. Conn's new place needs to be in the heart of Provincetown where there's a lot of foot traffic. This is not that place.

"Taylor's just getting the crap out of the way first, so you'll fall for the most expensive property. Whatever you see last will be the one that sticks with you."

"I don't know. This place is pretty sticky."

It's true. When I lift my foot off the kitchen linoleum, the floor doesn't quite want to let go. "Can we get out of here before we carry Eau de Grease with us for the rest of the day?"

"Hey."

I've started to walk away, but Conn pulls me into his arms. I glance over my shoulder to see if Taylor's around. I hear her voice in the distance—she's busy on her phone—so I relax into his embrace. "Yes?"

"Thanks for doing this. I know it's a pain."

"Not at all. As a real estate agent and an investor in this venture, I reserve the right to make sure you're making the correct choice of venue. Plus I could never say no to you."

"Oh really?" he says slyly as he nuzzles my nose. "I'm filing that away for later."

"Are you, now?"

I let him kiss me, only a little nervous about Taylor walking in on us. Then, the more forward he gets, the less I care about what she sees, what she thinks or, really, anything at all concerning…what's her name, again?

When that person we're with—oh, right, Taylor—calls from the dining area, "Let's move, people! More to see!" Conn releases me with one final small peck, and I walk ahead of him feeling like I could take on the world with one hand behind my back. Which is where one hand needs to be, to bat away someone else's hand that keeps reaching for my ass. Naturally we degenerate into one of our usual slap-fests, but this one is so very different. There's a lot of giggling on my part, for one thing, and the wrestling portion is much more intimate. It culminates in Conn grabbing me around the waist from behind and lifting my feet off the floor. He carries me over to Taylor and deposits me there, where my old friend stands in stunned silence, one eyebrow raised suspiciously. I merely pat down my clothes and continue out the door under my own power.

By the time we check out the third property, Taylor has gone nearly silent. She's too busy watching our every move to make small talk. I know her. She's waiting for the right moment to pounce, and pounce she does, as soon as she gets rid of Conn by sending him out back to look at a small patch of dirt that could be this location's herb garden.

When she rounds on me, I play dumb. "I like this one," I comment, looking out the window at the other shops on the street. "This location is perfect. So many successful businesses nearby."

"All right, how long has this been going on?"

"How long has—?"

"Oh, cut it out. You and Conn."

"What? Friends help friends look at real estate."

"Oh, you are so far beyond friends now it's not even

funny. And it's about time, if you ask me." She crosses her arms and studies me intently. "So how is it?"

"How's—"

"Do *not* say 'how's what?' Cut to the chase. Tell me about the sex."

I know better than to keep denying Conn and I are together. Taylor always could get the truth out of me with one look. And if her patented glare doesn't work, she resorts to noogies.

I can feel myself blushing as I admit, "Okay, you've got me. But it's new, all right? Really new. So don't jinx it."

"You didn't answer my question."

"I am *not* telling you how the sex is." Because we haven't had any yet. I'm not telling her *that*. "This is…special."

Taylor tilts her head and smiles. "Okay."

"Are you happy for me anyway? I want a hug, bitch."

"Of course," she says, throwing her arms around me. "Congrats. You finally got what you wanted."

"What are you talking about? I never expected this."

"Sure. Whatever."

She releases me without another word, but I know what that smirk on her face means: *I knew you liked him when even you didn't know…this has been coming for a long time…*pretty much everything I've already heard from Hannah. Maybe they're right. Maybe they could pick up on my true feelings for Conn even when I couldn't. Or wouldn't. I don't care about the past though. What matters now is the future. Which is why I decide it's time to clear the air completely.

"One more thing: I want to apologize."

"What did you do?"

"It's silly."

"All the more reason to tell me."

"When you came back to Abbott's Bay to have your oh-so-secret meeting with Conn, I thought you were, you know…after him."

"*After* him?"

"I thought you were plotting to get into his shorts that day."

She laughs and flips her gorgeous hair. "Oh, believe me,

if Connacht Garvey had *ever* expressed even the remotest interest, I absolutely would have nailed him."

"You're kidding."

"Honey, I would never kid about an ass like that." Taylor's phone rings, and she turns her attention to it while she tosses off, "Oh, hey—if it doesn't work out between you and Conn, I want to be the third to know. I want a shot at him."

"You're so nasty."

"Proud of it," she whispers with a wink as she answers her call.

Taylor is nasty, but I know we've gotten her stamp of approval.

* * *

That night Conn and I finally get our dinner date. Maybe being buffeted by the stiff breeze off the ocean on the home-bound journey wore down my resolve...or maybe it was the sight of Conn as captain, squinting fiercely at the horizon as he piloted us home. All I know is when we get back to dry land at sunset, I hear myself suggest we go to the Bay Inn for dinner, just so I can spend a little more time with him.

Dinner turns out to be really nice, like any pleasant get-together with an old friend, but even better because that old friend—that handsome, hot, charming, and funny old friend—spends the evening staring hungrily at me across the table like he wants to have me for dinner instead of his steak.

Despite the fact that Conn and I agree none of the properties are what he's looking for, meaning Taylor has to come up with a new round of options, it's been the perfect day. I'm happy.

Until Conn pulls up to my apartment and helps me out of his car. I've been digging in my purse and beach bag but can't find my keys.

"They didn't slide off the deck into the Atlantic, did they?"

"Very funny. I stowed my belongings properly, like a smart boater." I delve deeper and come up with only a half-eaten granola bar, a used tissue, and some ATM slips. I stop fumbling and try to recall what I did this morning. Conn hustled me out of my place so quickly, I...crap. "I think they're up there," I say, lifting my eyes to the dark windows of my apartment. I can almost picture them in the straw basket on the table next to the door.

"That's okay—"

"Ugh, I don't want to call my dad. He promised me he'd go to bed early while he's recovering. And the key to *his* house is on the same key ring—"

Conn does his familiar move of putting his hands on my shoulders and locking eyes with me till I focus. "M, it doesn't matter."

"You're not going to break my door down, are you?"

He laughs a little and shakes his head. "No. And I'm not handy with a lock pick either. But you can stay at my place."

"I...uh..."

"Melanie, it's not a big deal."

It absolutely is. This is huge. This is loaded.

"Relax," he says. "You can have my bed, and I'll sleep in my old bedroom."

"The one with the twin bed you can't get to unless you climb over all the boxes of Christmas decorations and the dusty Bowflex?"

"Hey, I use the thing. Occasionally. Anyway, the couch is also comfortable, no matter what you think of it. Does. Not. Matter. I will give you whatever you want."

If I'm going to be honest with myself, sharing a bed with Conn is what I want. But I'm not going to be the horndog who violates our pact first. With a sigh I wave him back toward his car and drop into the passenger seat again.

CHAPTER TWENTY-SIX

"See? Big house. Plenty of room."

"I know what your house looks like, Garvey."

I walk past him as he holds the door open. Shadowed and silent, the setting makes my skin prickle. It's not that I'm *afraid* something might happen. It's that our decision to delay sex has built it up into a really big deal. Not to mention the thought of sex, in relation to this house, which has remained unchanged since I hula-hooped in the living room, raided the fridge for Kool-Aid, played—and argued—with Conn and other neighborhood kids while playing *Tomb Raider* on the family PlayStation, is—once again—downright weird.

Not weird enough to stop me from entertaining the idea, however. I can't ignore the waves of heat washing over me every few seconds at the thought. I want it—I want Conn—there's no denying it, but I also want to make sure it's *good*. Great. Incredible. Memorable. Magical. This cannot be done impulsively. Good, great, incredible, memorable, magical requires time and preparation. Wax and razors must be employed beforehand. At the very least.

As I stand in the kitchen, not sure what to do next, a pissed-off Harvey stomps in and starts his loud where-have-you-been-feed-me yowling.

"Eat your dry food," Conn admonishes his cat.

As usual, the place looks nothing like a bachelor pad. Besides the fact that it still has all the trappings of a family home, it's clean and neat—no newspapers on the floor by the sofa, no crumb-laden plates on the table. In fact, the only incongruous item is a small white paper bag, top crisply folded over a couple of times, sitting on the end of the kitchen counter.

"I didn't know you liked sweets."

"What?"

I reach for the bag. "This. From Macomb's, right? I can't remember the last time I saw you eat candy. I'll bet you're a gummy worms kind of guy though."

Conn's between me and the counter in an instant. His arm flies out, and he backhands the bag, sending it sailing into the air. It lands on the floor and slides halfway to the fridge, startling Harvey away from his food bowl. "No. Nothing. Never mind. What?"

Okay, that wasn't weird at all.

"Do you want something to drink? Or eat? Not candy. I mean, that's not...or are you tired? Do you just want to go to sleep? I can get you a T-shirt."

Is he *nervous*? I've never seen Conn nervous before. Not before a big football game in high school, not before he took his GMAT, not even on the day of his wedding. But here he is now, standing in front of me, digging his right thumb into the palm of his left hand. Nervous. That's so hot it's broken down the last of my resolve. Pact schmact. What are we waiting for, again?

I close the distance between us. "I want to go to bed."

"Okay. Sure."

He gestures toward his bedroom and follows me down the narrow hall. I pause in the doorway because it's so dark. He puts a gentle hand on my back as he squeezes past me to turn on the lamp next to the bed.

"I'll find you a clean shirt and then get out of your way."

He rummages in his dresser drawer and comes up with a battered Red Sox T-shirt. He holds it out to me. I toss it onto the end of the bed. His nerves have eradicated mine. Entirely. I wrap my arms around his waist and go up on my toes for a kiss.

"I don't think you understood me," I whisper, pecking his jawline. "I said I want to go to bed."

"Right. That's what...oh. *Oh*."

The way the light dawns over his handsome face makes me laugh.

"Melanie, are you sure? I thought we agreed—"

We can either get into a protracted discussion about this, or I can communicate my decision using shorthand. I go with the latter. I kiss him as passionately, as earnestly as I'm able, to let him know I don't want to wait another minute. I don't care that my makeup washed off in the sea spray earlier today or that I'm not wearing fancy matching lingerie. My underpants might even have a hole by the elastic. Doesn't matter. All I care about is this wonderful man in front of me. I've never wanted anyone more.

"That's a yes?" he asks with a smile.

"That's the biggest yes in the history of yeses, mister."

Within seconds he's got me out of breath and weak in the knees. It's the way his tongue dances with mine, the way his hands push my hair back from my face, the way he kisses me hungrily, everywhere—under my ear, down my neck…

"You taste like salt," he murmurs as he touches the tip of his tongue to the hollow of my throat.

"Too much for your blood pressure?"

"That's not the salt doing that."

Oh, he's smooth. I'm surprised my panties haven't left the building all on their own already.

"Should I shower?" I offer, only half serious. Anyone who's grown up on the coast has kissed many salty lips in their day. It shouldn't be a big deal.

Conn groans loudly. "Keep talking like that and we're going to have a problem."

"Problem?"

Before my imagination can go to a dozen dark places, he says, "Look, it's…been a while. For me. Plus it's…this is…with *you*. So I'm doing my best not to make this brief. Not high-school-era brief, but…"

A problem? That's not a problem. That's an opportunity. "I see," I answer, mock serious. "Well then. It appears we'll have to do this more than once. As many times as possible, in fact, until we've balanced you out."

He looks at me in surprise and laughs out loud. God, I love to hear him laugh, watch his eyes crinkle up. Cupping his hands at the back of my neck, under my hair, he says warmly, "You're perfect. Have I mentioned you're perfect?"

"You may have, but it bears repeating as often as possible."

"Noted."

"So this stretch of time you're talking about…don't tell

me it's been the whole five years you've been newly single."

"No. I'm not a hermit, just discerning."

"I never saw you with anyone—"

"Of course you didn't, nosy. I keep that sort of thing private. Yes, even when it comes to you. It was just a summer person here and there. But not this summer. Not for quite a while, to be honest. And never anything serious."

"Why not?"

"Why didn't I get serious with anybody?" He shrugs. "I didn't want to."

"What about now?"

Looking into my eyes steadily, he runs the back of his curled fingers along my cheek. His touch makes me shiver. "I wouldn't be here with you if I weren't completely serious. You mean so much to me, Melanie. You always have."

And my insides have now melted and are oozing all over the floor. "Oh, keep saying things like that and you can consider your drought over, buddy."

"Works for me."

Conn scoops me up into his arms and throws me into the center of his large bed. I land with a thud, sinking into the soft mattress, as Conn lowers himself over me and kisses me slowly. He slides one hand under my shirt and runs his thumb under the bottom edge of my bra. It's nowhere near enough contact. I push up into a sitting position against the headboard and nearly clock him in the chin with my elbow in my rush to get my sleeveless polo off.

"You're not even going to let me undress you."

"Not this time, Garvey. You're telling me we could have been doing this years ago. I'm not wasting another minute. Let's go. You can get creative another time."

"You're adorable. Anybody ever tell you that?"

"Lose the shirt."

He's not fast enough, so the minute he's up on his knees, I start tugging at the hem. Once it's over his head and flung onto the floor, however, I have to stop and stare. The sight of that broad expanse of bare chest, muscles shifting under his smooth skin, brings me up short every time.

A little light-headed, I run my hands over his solid

shoulders and down his chest, fluttering my fingers over his abs as he sucks in a breath, then tucking them into the waistband of his shorts. I start fumbling with the button, but suddenly my fingers no longer work, because now *he's* staring at *me*. Really staring.

"What?" I demand, resisting the sudden urge to cross my arms over my breasts. I'm not usually this modest, but that raw look of his is doing things to me.

Conn reaches out and draws his fingers along my skin, following the swells and curves at the top of my bra, so lightly his touch raises goose bumps.

"These are new," he finally says, in an awed whisper.

Not what I was expecting. "Are you implying I *bought* them?" I realize I might be stalling, because it's quite possible I'm going to faint from his touch.

"Not at all. I mean they're new to me. I noticed when I moved back to town. And they're as magnificent as I suspected."

"You've been ogling my boobs for five years?"

"Maybe." He cocks an eyebrow at me, still slowly caressing the anatomy in question, which makes it hard for me to follow the conversation.

I want to sink down onto the mattress again and let him keep doing what he's doing for eternity—or the next few minutes at least—but I can't let this go. "So you never noticed I had boobs until five years ago?"

Realizing we're about to press the pause button on the action, he sighs heavily and settles next to me, propping his head on one hand. The other is still lazily exploring my bare skin. "Melanie, let's put this into perspective, okay? I've always known you were a girl—we've established that, right?"

I punch his shoulder. He removes his hand. I put it back. He goes back to making slow circles with his fingertips, and I melt a little more.

"Okay. Later on, when you were older, like in college, I thought you were cute—you know, in the abstract—and some guy was going to be lucky to have you. I never dreamed, back then, that the gap between our ages would…compress to a point where it doesn't even exist anymore. I never dreamed *I'd* be the guy lucky enough to have you."

I actually feel tears pricking the corners of my eyes. Wanting Conn is intense enough. When he says things like that, I feel myself tumbling into an abyss, the plummet thrilling and terrifying at the same time. "We can stop talking now."

"Thank God."

He pulls me down and I'm under him again, the contact of his skin on mine almost too much to take. His kisses become more aggressive, and I can barely keep up. They drift downward, along my throat and breastbone. He slips my shorts off then slides back up to kiss my lips again, knowing full well how to make me crazy. I need to level the playing field, so I have another go at his shorts. This time I manage to undo the button, drop the zipper, and push the waistband down low enough that he can kick them off.

"Condoms." I can barely form words, but I have the wherewithal to get that one out.

"I have some."

I can't help it—a nervous laugh escapes me. "How old *are* they, if you haven't done this in a while?"

"I, uh, bought them last night."

I gape at him. "Oh my God, that's what's in the bag, isn't it? Were you plotting? Did you hide my apartment keys too?"

"What? No!"

His shocked look makes me laugh again, and he joins in, but grows somber after a moment. "Melanie, you realize this changes everything."

"It's already changed. You've seen me mostly naked."

"I'm serious."

"I know. You're right—everything has changed. But for the better."

"I want you to know, if you're still not sure—"

"I've been sure for a long time now."

"But—"

"Good grief!" I exclaim, pushing at him. "Who's the Chatty Cathy now? Get out of my way! I'll get those condoms myself, dammit!"

I jump up and run for the kitchen, but Conn's faster and his legs are longer. He catches up to me in the hall, grabs me around the waist from behind, and lifts me into the air, making me shriek with laughter. He spins around and puts me behind him then dashes the rest of the way into the living room. Giddy, I'm coming after him full tilt, so I have no idea why I've just smacked right into his back as he stands, stock still, at the end of the hall.

He spins on his heel to face me. "M," he whispers ominously. I still don't get it. He puts his hands on my shoulders and gently but persistently pushes me backward.

"Conn?" comes an unexpected voice.

"Just a minute, Mom!"

CHAPTER TWENTY-SEVEN

———

"Your *mother*?" I exclaim in a frenzied whisper, frantically scrambling for my clothes. "Your *mother's* here?"

"Dad too," Conn answers grimly, doing up his shorts. "I knew I should have moved the spare key."

"We didn't hear them come in."

"We were distracted." He stills, his eyes drifting to my breasts.

"Conn?" comes the familiar—and entirely unwelcome—voice from the living room.

"Dammit."

He snaps out of his daze, scoops up whatever fabric is closest, and tosses it at me. It's the T-shirt he was wearing earlier. I pull it on before the Garveys decide to follow their son down the hall. I wouldn't put it past them—they're a little short on formalities in their own former home. His shirt smells like his deodorant and soap and ocean. I only allow it to distract me for a moment.

"Now what?"

Conn shakes his head slowly in a hell-if-I-know kind of way. "Want to come out and say hi?" I start giggling at the ridiculousness of it all, and he flashes his sideways grin. "Stay here, okay? I'll see what they want and then send them on their way."

He steals a small kiss then comes back for a better one. Another reassuring smile and, with a martyred sigh, he's gone.

I can't hide in the bedroom, waiting for him. It's ridiculous. I should walk out the sliding door and around the deck then text him when I get home…the home I can't get into. Crap. I can't call someone for help either—I left my bag, with my phone in it, by the front door.

But the truth is, I don't want to leave. I'd rather outlast them. All optimism, I'm sure Conn will get rid of them soon enough. To amuse myself in the meantime, I can eavesdrop. I figure Bruce and Constance owe me, considering they may very well have glimpsed more of me a minute ago than they've seen since I was a toddler.

"What are you doing here?" Conn's voice is low and a bit heated but controlled. I don't recall a single time he's blown up at his parents, not even during his volatile teenage years, so of course he wouldn't now, even though they just walked right into his house. It's not in his nature.

"We can't have coffee with our son? We were at Rose Perdue's," his mother explains. "Such a lovely dinner party. We thought we'd stop by on the way back to the Davises'. We didn't think you'd be...*busy*."

Conn ignores her pointed comment. "Are you all right? The stairs..."

"I'm fine. Sasha said—we had brunch while she was in town, did I mention that? We had a lovely time. She said I needed to start using my hip more and do my therapy exercises regularly. Move it or lose it, she said, and she's right."

I'm so busy rolling my eyes at Constance's ham-handed name-dropping that I almost miss Conn's exasperated response.

"I've been telling you that all along. Dad's been telling you that. And your surgeon, *and* your internist, *and* your physical therapist back in Phoenix."

"Yes, but I trust *Sasha*," Constance insists. She pauses as if she's going to change the subject, but the next minute she asks bluntly, "Are you going to make your *friend* stay in the bedroom all night?" I know the segue's intentional. She sounds hopeful. Why...?

"It's not Sasha," Conn answers, just as bluntly.

Oh. Interesting. They may have seen some skin, but they didn't see my face, thanks to Conn's quick thinking, blocking me from their view.

He adds, "And I'm not going to say anything more about it."

"You're seeing someone? What about Sasha?"

"What did I just say, Mom?"

"Then why did you ask her here for a visit?"

"Strictly business, the same reason I invited Jack."

It's not surprising he hasn't told them about his plans for the new restaurant. He's always been fiercely independent, never accepting much from his parents, even in college and business school. They practically had to force this house on him, and I suspect he agreed to it only because they were moving to Arizona. If he talked about his business plans too soon, his father would try to give him money, and worse, his mother would waste no time planting a seed of doubt by moaning it could never work.

Bruce defends his son with a classic dad line: "Leave the boy alone, Constance."

Of course that line never works.

"I mean," Conn's mother persists, "she's saying the nicest things about you. Can't you two work things out? You were so wonderful together."

"No, we weren't, Mom. Sasha and I are over, we've *been* over, and I'm more than fine with that."

"You were so heartbroken—"

"And now I'm not."

"Because you're cozying up to some tramp? I hardly think that's the solution."

What! I mouth silently, my hands in fists at my sides. Conn doesn't sound too happy either. In fact, he's so agitated he almost slips when he defends me. "Mel—*she's* not a tramp. Not at all."

"And yet you haven't introduced her to us," Constance sniffs.

"It's early yet."

No, no! You've given her an opening! Aaaaannnd his mom pounces on it.

"But you're sleeping with her already."

All right, that's it. Conn's squirmed long enough.

"Mrs. Garvey. Mr. Garvey. Nice to see you." I'm amazed my voice is calm and even, considering Conn's shirt is barely covering my ass cheeks, and my underwear isn't doing much more. I nod at them with a little smile as I cross the room, heading for the kitchen.

There's complete silence behind me, although I think I hear a muffled dismayed groan from Conn. I yank open the fridge, letting the cold air cool my flaming cheeks, and take out a bottle of water. I shut the door, take a breath, and turn to the Garveys with my placid smile intact.

Bless Bruce's heart, he breaks the silence with a cheery, "Little Melanie! It's good to see you, dear. Where have you been hiding yourself?" he asks innocently.

This elicits a derisive snort from his wife, which clearly translates into *Your son's bed, apparently.*

Conn's squirming, so I decide to take it down a notch. "I'm locked out of my apartment, and Conn was kind enough to offer me a bed tonight. I didn't want to disturb my father to get the spare key."

Of course this doesn't explain why I have no pants on, but perhaps we'll all be civilized enough to ignore this.

Constance's expression tightens even more—I didn't think it was possible—as she snaps, "We left Charles having a nightcap at Rose Perdue's a few minutes ago. You'd know that if you'd bothered to try to find him."

This bit of information takes me by surprise. "He's supposed to be resting. He promised me he'd take it easy a while longer."

"Mm," is all Mrs. Garvey deigns to say.

I don't appreciate the implication that I'm lying. I look at Conn a little desperately. He just widens his eyes at me. I know what this means: *never try to defend yourself to Constance Garvey when she's already determined you're guilty.* He doesn't have to remind me. After nearly thirty years of experience with her, I know when to retreat.

I make a very slight detour, grateful I have the kitchen counter between me and the Garveys to hide my...*assets* as I bend down to pet Harvey, who's meowing and rubbing against my ankles. "Have a good night," I say, straightening up and making a beeline for the bedroom.

Bruce cheerily returns my good wishes. Constance does not. I can feel her glare burning into my back.

I don't even get a chance to shut the bedroom door before Constance fires the first shot. "Well, this explains a lot."

"Mom…"

"How long has this been going on?"

"A *very* long time."

I pause in unscrewing the cap from my water bottle, confused. A very long time? It's been a little over a week.

"Well, I think it's wonderful."

Good ol' Bruce. Constance doesn't take his defection well and starts spluttering again, so loudly I almost don't hear what Conn says next. Almost.

"I love Melanie."

"Of course you do," his father agrees amiably. "We all do."

"You don't understand, Dad." Conn's voice drops, and I nearly tip over into the hallway trying to hear him. "I mean I love her. Very, very much. I have for a really long time."

"But…" I know what's coming from his mother next. I even mouth the word as she says it. "Sasha!"

"That's over with. I've moved on. You need to move on as well." He says it so kindly, but so firmly, it should convince Constance, but she's pretty darn stubborn, especially when it comes to her ex-daughter-in-law.

"You two were so in love once."

"And then we weren't. In fact, Melanie helped me get over all that. You have no idea what she's done for me. She helped me get my life back."

Constance snorts again, and I bristle. She thinks I convinced him to leave Sasha behind so I could get my hooks in him.

Bruce is far more accepting. "It's no wonder you love her then."

"Can we please stop using that word!"

Thanks, Constance. You're a peach.

"I mean really. Melanie Abbott? Don't get me wrong— Charles is a wonderful friend, but his daughter *sells real estate*." Her horrified tone puts my job in the same class as running drugs or cleaning up roadkill. "Sasha's a doctor!"

We *know*, Constance. But thanks for the reminder.

"Plus Sasha's so beautiful. And Melanie, she's so…*short*."

Hey, now—that's just mean. Constance says "short," I hear "dumpy." Conn has shown me countless times how attractive he finds me, but his mother's comment still stings.

When neither man answers her, she goes for the Hail Mary. "What will her father think?"

"I hope he'll be happy for us," Conn replies evenly. "I think he will be. But it's not your news to tell—not to him or anyone else. Please keep it to yourself."

His mother lets out a very unladylike grunt. "It'll pass."

"No. It won't." He says this so decisively I practically run out into the living room and throw myself in his lap. "You need to leave now. And give me the house key, please." I can picture him towering over his mother, holding out his hand expectantly.

That's about as angry as he gets at his parents, and I'm in awe. Naturally Constance doesn't give up the fight that easily. She circles back to the same nonsense but a little more desperately this time. It doesn't matter. Everything Conn has said about me went straight to my already full heart, and now it feels as though it could burst any second. Getting naked didn't change everything. This did.

* * *

I've just turned off the water in the bathroom when Conn knocks on the door. "M?"

"Just getting cleaned up."

"I'm so sorry about this."

"It's not your fault."

"I mean *really* sorry. Please…"

"What?"

"Don't leave."

Leave? I pause. "Conn?"

"Yeah?"

"…I heard what you said."

"Oh." He doesn't say anything else for a moment. Then, "Are you freaking out?"

"I'm definitely not freaking out."

"I'm not sure I believe you. You'll have to come out of

there so I can see for myself."

I take a deep breath and open the door. Conn looks me up and down, wide eyed, from my wet, now salt-free hair to the tips of my toes. He has such small bath towels, I'm not all that surprised at his reaction. I can barely keep the thing closed over my chest with one hand. I raise my other hand to show him the white bag I retrieved from the kitchen earlier.

With a delighted smile, Conn scoops me up and carries me into the bedroom. The towel doesn't make it that far.

Good? Try great.

Incredible.

Memorable.

Magical.

CHAPTER TWENTY-EIGHT

———

The next few weeks are perfect. I'm not exaggerating. *Perfect.* And not only because they're filled with lots of hot, naked sexytimes with Connacht Garvey. Which is beyond fabulous.

I should get a few points out of the way before I continue. First of all, I'd heard some, er, *things* about Conn Garvey back in the day, before he devoted himself to Sasha, and while I wasn't exactly sure what those older girls were talking about, their comments stuck with me, and a part of me always wondered. Now I know: he's amazing. He's clever. And affectionate. And a take-charge kind of guy. Attentive, inventive…let's just say the boy's a giver. He likes to give. He gives and gives. And gives some more.

And that's all I'm going to say about that.

Best of all, more important than anything else, he loves me. It's the thought that's with me when I wake up in the morning and when I go to sleep at night and all day long in between. It's not weird. It's not creepy. It doesn't freak me out. I'll admit, sometimes I'll look at Conn and feel some sort of…shift…a listing, like I'm still on the deck of his boat and it's hit a huge wave. It's then I realize my new reality is vastly different from the one I've known. Or is it? Sure, Conn and I stepped into this midstream, but with a few minor adjustments on my part once in a while, as I get my sea legs, it's the most natural thing in the world.

The other parts of my life are going great as well. My dad is practically back to normal. He's made a sincere effort not to go looking for health-related trouble, but he can't help complaining once in a while. That's okay. It's still progress.

Hannah came back from Ohio after three weeks away. If

she hadn't texted me once in a while, mostly demanding details about me and Conn, I'd have thought she'd fallen off the face of the earth. She doesn't talk much about what she did back home, but the glow in her cheeks gives her away. I think she's avoiding telling me she's been seeing Marty again because she's afraid I'll lecture her for not following my advice. I'm not sure I would though. Oh, I still think she's making a mistake, but the lingering sting of Mrs. Garvey's criticism makes me more inclined to keep my mouth shut about other people's relationships.

Speaking of the Garveys, they're actually honoring Conn's wishes and not talking about us. Constance still gives me the stink eye, of course, but Bruce is actually the one we have to watch out for. He's so thrilled his son and I are together, we're convinced he's going to slip first. Not that it much matters. Conn and I have gotten a bit sloppy about how we behave in public, which got us our own blind Bite on the Bottom in the latest Bugle Bites column. Something about some new/old lovebirds in town, often sharing the same nest. It wasn't the *Bugle*'s best work, and consequently it didn't raise much suspicion. We simply went about our lovebirdy business, unconcerned.

With the season in Abbott's Bay winding down, the summer people are disappearing a few at a time. The rest will get called back to Mother Ship Manhattan, Boston, or wherever else over Labor Day weekend, and the town will go quiet again. Your New Best Friend is slowing down at the same time, as I expected. And, like it does every year around this time, the real estate market has picked up, as a number of renting summer people look into buying properties to prolong their love affair with Abbott's Bay, so I'm spending more time working as a real estate agent than a New Best Friend.

I'm glad my schedule is flexible, because Conn's is packed, what with running the old DBC and planning the new one. I meet up with him whenever he has time. Sometimes our lifestyles dovetail perfectly: there's nothing more heavenly than lounging in Conn's bed, sipping his coffee and perusing the real estate database for newly listed Provincetown locations.

Then he makes one of those moments even better when he says, almost casually, "How about a quick trip to New York for an investors' meeting?"

On equal footing with Conn, Jack, and Sasha, talking about Conn's future, bringing his dream to fruition? Yes, please. I set my coffee aside and express my approval with a deep, prolonged kiss.

"We should stay overnight," I suggest. "You need a break from all this restauranting."

"I do," he agrees, stretching his arms over his head, and I'm momentarily distracted by the captivating sight of his flexing triceps. "But I can't right now. Once things settle down though, I would be happy to wine and dine you in New York."

I rest my chin on his chest. "If I'm in New York, I'm going to feel an irresistible need to go shopping."

"Shocker. Well, you could go earlier, and I could meet you there, or you could stay overnight and take the train back the next day. Far be it from me to keep you from the fall fashions."

"Aw, you do love me."

I stretch up for another kiss, and he meets me halfway, pulling me to him, and the scratch of his chest hair against my bare skin drives me so crazy I barely notice his laptop is making noise. Reluctantly breaking our kiss, Conn glances at it.

"Huh. Video call from Jack."

He doesn't think twice about answering, while I squeak in panic and roll off the bed, landing on the floor with an unladylike thud.

"Dude. What's up?"

"What's up? I think I need to ask *you* that. Are you dying or something? You look like you're in bed, and it's past 5 a.m."

"It's been known to happen."

"Maybe for the rest of the population. You're usually up to your eyeballs in coffee and food orders and paperwork by now."

Trying to stay out of the camera's view, I flail around, looking for my underwear. Conn and I haven't discussed revealing our relationship to Jack, but we're aware it's going to have to come up eventually. When I'm naked and freshly flipped out of Conn's bed, however, is not that time. Staying low, I reach out a hand and grab hold of my bra, which is pinned under Conn's torso. I give it a couple of tugs. Conn rocks to one side to let my bra loose. It promptly snaps back and smacks me in the face.

"Ow."

"Oh crap!" comes Jack's gleeful shout. "I'm sorry——why didn't you tell me you've got a...*guest*?"

I scuttle farther away from the bed like a crab. Conn looks over at me and starts laughing. Yeah, not one of my sexier moves.

"It's fine. Really. Not a big deal."

Thanks a lot, I mouth at Conn as I get to my feet. I know he doesn't mean it though, by the lustful look he's giving me as I back out of the room.

"I think I should leave you and your special friend alone." When Conn doesn't answer, Jack continues, "One quick thing—I need to move our investors' meeting to two o'clock. Is that okay?"

"Yeah, yeah—not a problem. Gotta go."

Conn slams the laptop shut, leaps off the bed, and chases me into the bathroom.

* * *

A few days later I'm checking my outfit in my full-length mirror. The mountain of rejected clothes on the bed behind me illustrates my desperation to impress the fashionistas in New York, but really I've just got Sasha in mind. I've settled on a tan linen pencil skirt with pale pink ribbon trim and a little flare at the knee, and a cream-colored crossover silk blouse. I could have gone with one of my business suits, but that would make me look like I'm trying too hard. This outfit, on the other hand, works perfectly—it's feminine, a little more casual, and quite honestly looks more like me. Plus, if the cut of the skirt puts a wiggle in my walk, so much the better for my sex life. Conn watching me move like that all day can only work to my advantage in the long run.

We settled on traveling separately so I could squeeze in a little shopping before the midafternoon meeting. That means I had to get up at the crack of OMG to catch the first train of the day—if I can get to the station on time, that is. I come out of the carriage house to find a black car in the driveway blocking mine.

And a man in a suit standing next to it.

"Miss Melanie Abbott?"

"Er...yes?"

"Courtesy of Mr. Rossiter," he says, smoothly opening the rear door of the luxury sedan.

Get outta town.

Which, apparently, is Jack's plan.

Of course I call him the minute I'm settled in the back seat and the driver, who introduces himself as Xavier, hands me a bottle of water from a refrigerated compartment. "You sent your *driver*?"

"I sent *a* driver."

"What do you want, Jack?"

"It's not what I want. It's what I need. And that's for you to arrive as soon as possible."

"Jack..."

"Oops, I've got another call. We'll talk when you get here."

That scam artist has me fretting the entire drive, which lasts several hours. Most women like it when Jack Rossiter turns on the charm, but it only makes me suspicious.

Xavier pulls the car over and opens the back door for me somewhere in the middle of Manhattan, at the front entrance of an impressive high-rise amid many more impressive high-rises. The Rossiter Building. Of course. A well-dressed gentleman meets me at the door, greets me by name like Xavier did, and leads me to the elevators. I'm dizzy by the time the elevator reaches its destination, and not just from the speed of the ascent. When the doors open, I see a huge sign on the opposite wall: *National News Network.*

Jack steps away from the reception desk where he's obviously been charming the knickers off the young woman seated there, judging by the high color in her cheeks, and approaches me, arms outstretched. "Miss Melanie! Now, wasn't that a nicer way to travel? I mean, I could have sent the helicopter, but I figured you might think it was a bit much."

"Jack." I don't give him the hug he's reaching for. "If this is what I think it is..."

"Like I'd have forgotten our little deal."

"We have no deal."

"There were flowers and a promise."

"I never said I'd take you up on it."

He puts a hand on my back and steers me toward a door. "Just come see what I'm talking about."

Down some narrow hallways, through some office areas, around some corners, and we're in an actual TV studio ensconced in the windowless center of the building. A tangle of taped-down cables all over the floor, hot overhead lights, cameras, a production booth, a set with a tall news desk.

"That could be you up there, behind the desk, next to the host of our noon show," Jack says in my ear. "A special segment, maybe weekly? Your New Best Friend goes national." He pauses but only for a moment. "Come on, Miss Melanie—it's a no-brainer! Say you'll do it, and I'll talk to the producers right now."

National exposure? Me on TV? Ludicrous. And completely unnecessary. More important..."Why?" I demand, looking Jack squarely in the eye.

"Why what?"

"Why are you doing this?"

"Because I want to make you happy, M." My shortened name sounds strange coming from him. It's too intimate. Usually only Conn calls me that. "Don't you want to be successful?"

I pull away from his encircling arm. "I am successful."

He laughs winningly and stuffs his hands into his pockets, bunching up his suit jacket in the most charming way. "Okay," he says. "I mean, of course you are. For Abbott's Bay."

"I was covered in the *Huffington Post*."

"And that's *great*." Ah, that patronizing tone. It makes me feel seventeen again. "But I'm talking *television*."

"Why didn't you talk to me about this after the meeting this afternoon? Why get me here early?"

"Well, now. There's nothing I like more than a little alone time with Miss Melanie."

Oh, he's definitely pulling out all the stops to charm me, but it's not going to convince me of anything. Then his cell phone goes off, and he answers it with a wink at me, his index finger up in a "just a minute" gesture. He goes out into the hallway, leaving me standing on the fringe of the set. I watch technicians and producers bustle about, preparing for today's show. It's interesting, but it doesn't pull me in. I decide to give Jack a solid no. If he ever comes back, that is. Five minutes, seven, ten. Still no Jack. I duck out of the studio before they go on the air so I won't be stuck there till the first commercial break.

The hallway's empty.

* * *

"There you are."

Conn's face lights up at the sight of me, and it looks like he's about to lean in to kiss me. While normally I'd be all for it, I have to stop him with a raised eyebrow, because Jack is in the conference room as well, on his phone again.

Conn settles for a subtle squeeze of my hand then pulls out one of the leather chairs and drops into it. "How was the train?"

"Funny story. I'll tell you later."

"And the shopping?"

I shrug. I wasn't exactly in the mood after Jack disappeared on me. I waited for him a while longer then somehow found my way out of the NNN labyrinth alone. I was a few blocks away when Jack called me, confused as to why I'd disappeared. The nerve. He convinced me to have lunch with him later, but I insisted we order in instead of going to a restaurant. We were just finishing up when Conn arrived.

Jack finishes his call, and he and Conn fall into their usual warm, jokey guy banter. Fifteen minutes later, Sasha sweeps in with kisses for everyone.

When she gets to me, she looks me up and down and exclaims, "Melanie! I love your outfit! It's so cute!"

"Cute"? My heart sinks. Now that I look at it from her point of view, it is "cute," especially compared to her sleek couture ensemble. She's managed to knock me down with one word. But she's smiling at me and the guys as she pulls her giant dove-gray cashmere shawl-wrap away from her neck.

"Goodness, it's warmer than I thought. Didn't need this old thing."

"This old thing" looks brand new and obscenely

expensive, but all right.

"This is exciting, isn't it?" she enthuses. "And Melanie, it's so wonderful to have you here too. Are you taking notes for us?"

What?

"No, of course not," Jack says. "One of the assistants is on her way in."

"Oh!" Sasha flashes a bewildered look around the table. "Well, it's nice that you came along with Conn. It must have been a lovely day for a drive."

"Sasha," Conn says patiently, but I detect an underlying note of irritation, "Melanie is one of my investors."

"Is she?"

Conn must be able to feel me tense up, because suddenly his hand is on my knee. One squeeze and my hips sink back onto the cushion. Two, and my rigid back relaxes a bit. Three, and I'm ready to take on Sasha with her own weapon of choice—sickeningly sweet disingenuousness.

"It's true," I say to her with my best smile. "I'm here to keep Garvey honest."

"Aren't we all!" She laughs then says, almost offhandedly, "It's very daring of you to dip into your trust fund for this."

"I don't have a trust fund, Sasha."

"Break your piggy bank then."

Oh, I swear…but Conn's hand is on my knee again, so I settle. Not before Sasha's eyes lock onto Conn's arm. She can't see under the table, but he's clearly reaching over to me.

Just then Conn's phone rings. He apologizes for the interruption, but Jack waves a lazy hand at him to take the call. He rises, walks over to the windows, and stares out at the view as he talks. Sasha excuses herself, murmuring something about a visit to the "little girls' room."

I use the free moment to lean over to Jack and say quietly, "Okay, fine. I'll do the TV spots. But it's going to cost you an obscene amount of money."

Without a moment's hesitation he shrugs and says, "Name your price."

My price? Enough to move me up into Jack and Sasha's

stratum of this venture. Enough to earn Sasha's respect. Enough to stop being Little Melanie pretending to be a grownup.

CHAPTER TWENTY-NINE

———

Once I agree to Jack's proposal, things move quickly. He and I hammer out the details in several conference calls over the following week: I'll be a guest on the noon news program with anchor Trudy Something-or-other. I've already checked out the show and come away with an impression of a lacquered helmet of hair, perky attitude, and way, *way* too many teeth, but not her last name. It doesn't seem to matter. Three spots to start, each on a Friday, then we'll reassess and come up with a more substantial contract. As a savvy young lifestyle advisor, I'll talk about the basics of my business then give advice on how to "live your best life" or something, maybe even take calls for one-on-one mini-counseling sessions.

I can do that.

Well, I'll figure it out.

When I tell Conn I'm going to the TV studio at the end of the week, he congratulates me and wishes me luck, which is better than what I feared: that he'd lecture me again. After all, this is the guy who wasn't in favor of Your New Best Friend in the first place. Instead, he's nothing but supportive. He does add a word of caution, however.

"Remember what I said about Jack, okay?"

"Again? Yet?"

He straightens from his squat behind the bar, where he's been stocking bottles, and studies me carefully. "I'm just saying if you're going to be spending any amount of time with him at all…"

"I doubt Jack is going to have any free time to babysit me. There are producers for that kind of thing."

"You're excited about this?"

"I am."

I'm also terrified, but he doesn't need to know that.

"Well, good."

"You sound surprised."

Leaning on the counter, he studies me thoughtfully. "I thought you were happy with your business the way it is."

His comment sounds a little wistful, and I don't know where that's coming from. "What, you're the only business owner in Abbott's Bay who might want to branch out?" I ask with a wink.

"Point taken." He smiles back and holds up his hands in surrender before collecting a cup and saucer to start a triple espresso for me.

I switch to a sultry voice and purr, "So Garvey, now that Your New Best Friend is an even bigger thing, who's a girl gotta sleep with around here to get a *Reserved* card for the spot by the fireplace?" To stack the deck I lean forward on my barstool, giving him a clear view down my shirt. His eyes flick downward. Score.

"Still not permanently reserving those chairs when you only use them once in a while," he growls, but with his eyes still locked on my cleavage, I suspect I have a better chance at persuading him than ever before.

"We'll see about that. Can you bring my coffee over there? I'm meeting with Laura."

"Don't tell me she's doing another article on you."

"No, she said she wants to hire me."

"That's sweet."

"Sweet? This could be a disaster." I have to raise my voice to be heard over the noise of the espresso maker. "What in the world is she going to hit me up for?"

"Don't question. Just help. You are not here to judge," Conn calls over his shoulder.

"Don't tell me my business, mister. I get paid to judge." The machine winds down, so I lower my volume as well. "But I do it in an uplifting, constructive way."

"You're a true artist."

"That's what I keep *saying*!"

He slides my coffee toward me. "Here you go. Take it yourself."

"The service here is terrible. Especially from the owner."

"That's not what you said last night."

I let him have the last word because the memory of last night's…service…and the way he stares at me, promising more of the same as soon as possible, leaves me weak in the knees. Needless to say, I have a little trouble shifting gears when Laura arrives. To buy some time to get my head straight, I suggest she order some coffee while I get settled in my usual spot.

Before she joins me there, my phone rings. "Melanie! *Quel horreur!*"

"Rose?"

"I need you right away, dear," she cries, frantic. "It's a matter of life and death!"

Or a crisis having to do with our Founder's Day celebration which, to Rose, amounts to the same thing. Every year on the third Saturday of October, the whole town honors my ancestor, the original real estate mogul who had the foresight to claim a giant chunk of land with a lovely ocean view on which to build his town. After a parade, penny carnival, and 5K and 10K runs, the day wraps up with a fancy-dress charity ball at the country club. Rose is in charge of the ball, and she's hired me to help her. We're supposed to meet later this afternoon.

"Hold on, Rose. Deep breath." She obeys, and a whooshing noise sounds in my ear. "Better?"

Out of the corner of my eye I see Laura hovering nearby. I wave her over as Rose chokes out, "Charity—disaster—mini-golf—ashes!"

It sounds like she's stringing random words together, but I get the gist. We'd talked about having an indoor miniature golf course as the night's fundraiser, but from what I can decipher after a few more of Rose's panicked exclamations, the barn in which the portable golf course components were being stored caught fire. Although it's a shame, it's not an insurmountable problem. I try to tell her this, but she's inconsolable.

"Melanie, you have to come now!"

"Can't it wait one more hour? I've got—"

"Melanie!" she wails.

Well, she is paying me double my usual rate. I assure her I'll be able to pitch five fundraisers we can do on short notice to replace the one we've lost, end the call, and turn to Laura.

"I'm so sorry. I have an emergency, and it can't wait." I stand up and hoist my bags on my shoulder. "We can reschedule. You have Hannah's number, right? Give her a call and set up a time. Okay?"

"Oh." Laura blinks at me from under her heavy bangs—I sure hope she wants a makeover—and I take it as some form of assent.

"Thanks so much. Sorry again. I'll see you another time!"

I try to sweep out of the restaurant, but Conn snags my elbow, bringing me up short.

"That's it?" he asks, with a significant look over at my coworker, who's still standing where I left her, looking lost.

"I've got to get going. Rose is having a crisis."

"Hm."

There's a whole world of commentary in that tiny syllable.

"I'll take care of Laura later, I promise." I look down at his hand on my arm. "Unhinge, darling. I'm losing daylight."

* * *

I'm not able to squeeze in a meeting with Laura before I travel to New York again two days later, and I feel bad about it, but then the television thing swallows me up. I arrive at the Rossiter Building midmorning, courtesy of Jack's car service once again, and I'm immediately shunted from room to room, signing forms, discussing flattering on-air outfits, and allowing myself to be primped, prepped, and coiffed to within an inch of my life. It's completely overwhelming.

It sounds wonderful to jump straight into the national spotlight, but believe me, it's not the best idea. The proper process would have been to start on local TV first. Baby steps, a learning curve. However, thanks to Jack, today I'm starting at the top.

Okay, it's not like I've got my own prime-time show on one of the Big Four networks or anything. Triple N isn't even in the same league as the most popular cable news channels. But it has a sizeable viewing audience—large enough to make me grateful for the dress shields that are probably going to be sorely taxed once I get on camera.

The one thing they don't tell you before you go on: how bright and blinding the lights are. I know there are cameras with people behind them at the edge of the surprisingly tiny set, and engineers in a booth beyond that, but darned if I can see any of it. Maybe it's better this way though. Maybe I'd be too intimidated if I could see all the inner workings of the broadcast while I'm trying to focus on answering Trudy Helmet-Head (really, her hair is alarmingly large and quite stiff) beside me as she makes small talk. I wish I'd asked Hannah to come along. Or Taylor, who'd have pumped me up with a lot of "suck it up, bitch" haranguing until I believed I could take on the world. Most of all, I wish Conn were here with me.

I'm snapped out of my reverie, but not my panic, when I hear my name mentioned. Trudy is talking rather urgently with the director, whose name I didn't catch, and they glance over at me every once in a while.

When they realize I'm tuning in, the director—Roger? Ralph? Ronaldo?—says, "So, um, we were thinking…*Melanie* is quite a mouthful, isn't it?"

I've never thought so. "It's just my name."

"Doesn't have to be."

What? "It'd be kind of weird to change it."

"You could shorten it."

"What…now? Right now?"

"Why not?"

"Well, sometimes my friends call me M."

"Nah." Roger/Ralph/Ronaldo states decisively. "Too short."

"How about Lanie?" Trudy suggests.

"Perfect." The director slaps the desk. "That's why you get the big bucks. Lanie it is. You okay with that?"

His last question is directed at me, but it's obvious my opinion doesn't matter. I'm already officially Lanie Abbott in their eyes. I nod and smile gamely.

In. Over. My. Head.

Once the lights go up, I lock eyes with Trudy and answer

all her questions in a pithy yet lively manner, making a few jokes along the way, as I was coached. Our chat is safe and reassuring. I talk about where the idea for the business came from, and I make sure to mention Hannah by name and express how grateful I am for her inspiration.

Trudy looks at me a little blankly. Although she seems interested and engaged, I detect a dead spot behind her eyes, and I feel a small urp of panic in my gut. Am I boring her? Is my business unexciting? I can't tell.

We go to a commercial break, during which Trudy barely acknowledges me. When we come back, she plugs my business, repeating all my social media accounts where I can be reached, and then says, "Our time is up, Lanie. One last question before we go: how would you sum up Your New Best Friend? Tell us your motto. Your words to live by."

"Er..." Motto? What motto? I have no motto! "I want to help you be the best you that you can be!" I make up on the spot.

Ew.

When the lights dim, I clamber out from behind the desk and head for the door. Jack's there, leaning against the wall, checking his phone.

"Fabulous, honey," he says, kissing me on the cheek. "I knew you'd be a natural."

I put on a smile for him. After all, he went to great lengths, throwing his weight around, to get me this gig. "You saw all that?"

He doesn't answer my question. "How about a late lunch?" When I hesitate, he amends it to, "It can be a liquid lunch."

"I can't. I've got to get back to Abbott's Bay."

Jack sighs. "I swear, I don't know what you see in that place. Fine. Next Friday. Be sure to set aside some time for me. I mean it!"

But the following Friday, Jack's nowhere to be found...on the day I really could use a friend. Richard the director (I finally heard someone call him by name) and Trudy aren't as obliging as they were the first time I showed up. In fact, after a sort of lackluster performance on my part, I catch them muttering to one another and shaking their heads as they glance in my direction a couple of times. Apparently the honeymoon's over. It isn't my fault. I may be exhausted and a little off my game from all this early rising and hours spent traveling, but the callers we took didn't exactly give me much to work with.

First there was Ted, who said, in a tight, anxious voice, "Uh...I wish I were taller?"

I stared out at nothing, staying perfectly still, like a puppy waiting for its master to say it's okay to flip the dog biscuit off its nose and into its mouth.

"Well, I'm afraid I don't have a medieval rack in my basement to stretch you, Ted," I began, while Trudy let out the type of hearty chuckle all newscasters seem to have learned in broadcast journalism school. "But you don't need stretching anyway."

"Lifts? Like the ones Tom Cruise is supposed to wear?"

"Not lifts either. If you want to be taller, Ted, you have to act taller."

The disbelieving pause went on so long, Trudy had to prompt him. "Are you still there, Ted?"   .

"I don't get it."

"You have to believe in yourself, buddy," I explain. "The minute you do, you'll start walking taller, and it can add inches to your height."

"It will?"

"Yup. And make a wise investment—get your clothes tailored so you don't look schlubby. Okay?"

"Okay," he said, sounding a little skeptical but mostly mollified.

The next person said I was beautiful and asked me for a date, which we laughed off as a producer ditched the caller at lightning speed.

"Would I look good as a blonde?"

I gently reminded this next caller she was on the phone and advised finding an app that lets you mess around with your hair color in a photo before taking the plunge.

I was still stinging from that lame exchange, wondering if every call was going to be about physical appearances, when a youngish-sounding woman named Whitney said, "I need a *real* best friend."

I jumped in immediately, glad someone brought this up. "You're absolutely right. Never let a friend for hire replace real friendships."

"So how do I get a real one?"

"Be one." Kind of glib, but hey, we didn't have a lot of time. "Get out there and do things you like, be around people who like the same things. Smile, be friendly, be helpful, and things will fall into place."

I thought it was a great exchange, but Richard and Trudy didn't seem to agree. That was when they started their muttering in the corner, pausing only to summarily dismiss me for the week.

As I hurry out of the studio, eager to scrape off my camera-ready layers of makeup before heading back home, I can't help but note the difference in the atmosphere between my first appearance and my second. Am I failing at this?

When I get back to Abbott's Bay, I beg off dinner with Conn, hunker down at home, and fire up the NNN noon show on my DVR to analyze the hell out of my segment. After the first viewing (I plan on several, with note taking), I call Hannah.

"I'm watching myself on TV," I whine.

"Don't do *that*! Are you crazy?"

"I need a new wardrobe. I need to go on a diet. I need to buy Spanx. Lots of Spanx. I need better highlights. Should I get a spray tan?"

The irony's not lost on me that I'm obsessing about my looks after spending today's segment allaying other people's fears about their looks.

"Do. Not. Move."

Hannah is at my door within minutes.

"Put the remote down. And the phone. Nobody orders Spanx today. Do you hear me? Not on my watch."

"But..." I'm still in whining mode as I shuffle back to the couch and unpause the recording. "Look. I'm pale and puffy—ooh, maybe a facial? But look how lumpy!"

"You are *not* lumpy."

"I have squishy bits."

"You're female. Plus you're sitting down."

"Trudy Helmet-Head doesn't have squishy bits, and she's

sitting down."

"You said Trudy Helmet-Head isn't human, and I think you're right."

I slump back against the cushions and close my eyes. I can't tell Hannah what I'm really worried about, which is I don't know what I'm doing and I'm not sure I want to be doing it anyway.

"I need help," I peep.

"The first step is admitting you have a problem." Hannah takes the remote out of my hand and turns off the TV. "I've called in reinforcements—"

At that moment, Conn lets himself into my apartment, extending a takeout container. "Cuban sandwich, extra fries."

"This is what true love looks like." I accept his offering, despite my conviction only moments ago that I have to lose weight.

He drops down on the other side of me, his elbows on his knees. "You're stressed, Abbott. You've been stressed ever since you started this TV nonsense. Is Jack pushing you too hard?"

"She's pushing herself too hard," Hannah says.

"Are you sure you want to do this?" Conn asks softly, and I become as melty as the cheese on my sandwich. It's like he can read my mind.

I want to say no, I'm not sure at all, but I'm a stubborn bitch. Giving up and walking away isn't what I do. I nod, but I can't get any words out, afraid they'll be pushed out on a sob. I'm still scared, but I have my friends with me.

Conn gathers me into his arms. "If this is what you want, we're all pulling for you. You've got the support of the whole town. In fact…I've reconnected DBC's cable so everyone can watch your show."

I pull back, gaping at him. Conn doesn't believe in having TVs in the restaurant. He tried it for a while, but he always says he'd rather the patrons talk to each other instead of staring at something overhead, so he pulled the plug. He got the cable switched back on just for me? That's huge.

Hannah stands up. "I'm going to go. Conn, worship her until she feels better. Melanie…" My friend studies me with a sharp eye for a moment, and suddenly I'm impressed with how much she's changed in the past few months. She's stronger, more confident, more put together, less hesitant, less timid. I did that. I *do* know what I'm doing. "You're allowed *one* pair of Spanx. One. No more. And don't get them in too small a size either. You don't want to be fainting on set, right?"

I jump up and give her a tight hug. "Thank you."

"Kick their asses."

CHAPTER THIRTY

———

If I expect Jack to show up and give my ego a boost—and protect me from the not-very-secret criticism of the NNN crew—I'm sorely mistaken. I text him the day before my next show to see if he's going to be there. Which, in itself, is kind of freaky. I'm looking to Jack for my peace of mind? It's so wrong.

He answers right away, but his message makes my stomach bottom out.

Aw, Miss Melanie, I'm sorry—I'm in London. What do you need?

Nothing urgent, I text back—a complete lie. *I was hoping you'd be able to give me some feedback, help me improve.*

You look like you're doing fine so far. Something wrong?

It feels like the producers want something I'm not giving them, but I'm not sure what I can do differently.

Are they not supporting you?

I think back to the frequent Richard and Trudy conclaves, and I want to share my fears, but I don't want to complain. I backpedal immediately. *Everyone's great. Having a great time!*

Jack signs off with more words of encouragement and a promise to watch from wherever he is. It makes me feel a little better, but when I get to the studio today, I still wish he were there.

I heave myself into my chair beside Trudy Helmet-Head, who gives me the briefest of smiles. It's hard to get comfortable, as I'm basically a lot of sausage in too tight a casing. I didn't listen to Hannah's advice and bought some too-small shapewear, and now it feels like any part of my body above my boobs and below my thighs is swelling up. Hey, all that cushioning has to go somewhere.

Even though I told myself I wouldn't, I catch myself looking for Jack lounging along the wall, as if by some miracle he could, let alone would, get back to New York in time for my guest spot. He's not there, of course. I look up at the booth, which I can see into for a few minutes before the set is hit with enough lumens to mimic the surface of the sun. All I see is the usual handful of techs and producers going about their pre-show business.

And speaking of producers, Richard appears as if from out of nowhere and does his usual soft slapping of the desk in front of me with his palms. "So, Lanie. Good to see you," he says, entirely unconvincingly, then charges ahead. "Let's chat a second. What you've been doing is great, don't get me wrong, but it's a *little* flat."

"Flat?"

"A little. So what say we punch it up some? Let's make it more interesting. Just follow Trudy's lead. Okay? Great."

Punch it up? More interesting? How…? Before I can ask, Rich slips back into the shadows at the edge of the set, the lights come up, someone counts down, and Trudy's introducing me, giving her usual brief summary of who I am and what I do for folks who haven't seen me on the show before. Then she swings around to face me.

"Lanie, we've heard about what services you provide. Give us some examples. Tell us about your clients back home in Boston."

"Abbott's Bay," I correct her, as politely as possible. "On the North Shore."

"Of course. Beautiful area. What sort of unusual requests have you had?"

Unusual? Reginald the ferret comes to mind, but I don't want America thinking I spend a lot of time harboring dead rodents. "Well…" I can't think of anything. Not a thing! You'd think with the many clients I've worked with already something would come to mind, but that mind of mine is a blank. Trudy watches me expectantly. A trickle of sweat makes its way down my spine. Her encouraging look starts to crumble around the edges. It feels like five minutes have passed, when really I know it's only been a few seconds. Still, a few seconds of dead air is a broadcaster's worst nightmare. Then something finally surfaces from the murk fogging my brain.

"I did help one particularly awkward friend win the woman of his dreams."

"How did you do that?"

And I'm off, telling the tale of Petey Fagle and his bait shop girl. I don't name names, of course, but I do ramble on about Petey's quirks and the details of his clumsy courtship, and how I used my expertise to turn him into the most romantic suitor possible, given the circumstances.

Once I finish his story, I think I'm off the hook, but Trudy immediately requests another.

"Er…" I laugh nervously, trying to run out the clock. The spots seem so short…until you've got Trudy bugging her eyes at you, silently demanding more.

So I launch into the tale of Zoë and her mom, again not naming names, culminating with, "The posture thing was just a side effect. It was so obvious. The girl might as well have had a sign hanging over her head: *Raised by Nannies*. Her mother is stuck with a kid she barely knows, and she's trying to force her to become perfect—well, her idea of perfect, anyway—when the poor thing is going through her standard teenage awkward phase. She needs to be allowed to be a kid. And she needs to get some unconditional love from that harpy who birthed her."

"Fascinating stuff. It seems like there isn't one person you don't try to help!"

"Of course, I'm never sure I *can* help everyone. After all, this started because I tried to tell my friend Hannah not to get back together with her ex, and she's *still* not listening to me."

Trudy laughs cheerily, and I feel absolutely elated at having given her what she and Richard were looking for.

Then her expression drops from mirthful to dead serious in a nanosecond. "Now, Lanie, I have to ask…isn't this, well, rather dangerous?"

I'm brought up short. Confused at the sudden change of subject and tone, I stammer, "I'm…not sure what you mean."

"You've said yourself you're not a licensed therapist. You're giving advice based on your own ideas about how people should live their lives. Wouldn't you call that irresponsible?"

My God, I'm being ambushed. How can this be happening? Haven't Trudy and I bonded? Aren't we buds now? I mean, I got her to laugh. That has to count for something, right? Apparently not, as she's still giving me her serious-journalist glare. Somehow I get the feeling she's been dying to hit me with this sort of accusation for the past three weeks. I can actually feel my blood pressure spike as I scramble to get on top of this.

"Of course not. I give very good advice. I get to know my clients before I advise them, if I don't know them already. And believe me, I know plenty of people who are...let's say anything I do for them can only be an improvement."

"Such as?"

And God help me, *now* I have an example ready. "A woman I work with, for one. Strange little thing, she's afraid of her own shadow. She's asked me to help her, and I don't know where to start. She'd be a lifelong project!"

With Trudy prompting me with nods and significant looks that demand more, I give up a detailed description of Laura—her eccentricities, her tics, her thick glasses and lank hair, her awkwardness. Lifelong project indeed, especially the way I sell her on air, solely to survive until my segment is over.

And I hate myself for it the minute the lights go down on the set, leaving me and Trudy in half-shadow.

CHAPTER THIRTY-ONE

───────

Late in the afternoon, I have Xavier drop me off in front of Deep Brew C. It's just rained, and a cool, fishy-smelling breeze gives me a little chill as the setting sun filters through the remaining clouds, dipping behind the hills and casting the downtown area in shadow.

DBC is quiet, with only a smattering of locals now that the vacationers have gone home. It gets even quieter when the patrons spot me—ominously so, like a saloon in an old Western when the mysterious stranger walks in. The lump in my stomach that appeared as soon as I finished today's TV spot grows bigger and heavier.

"Hi, all," I say, nodding at my friends and neighbors. Tommy's pulling beers and doesn't—or won't—catch my eye. "How's Abbott's Bay this evening?"

My friends and neighbors pointedly turn back to their drinks.

"Tommy." I'm surprised I manage to keep my voice steady as I lean on the bar. He finally glances over at me. "Is Conn in?"

After a moment's hesitation, he answers, "He's at home. Harvey's not doing too well."

That's all it takes for me to hurry to Conn's house, dodging puddles, my arms wrapped tightly around my torso to fend off the evening chill. I peek in the window before opening the door. He's in the leather recliner, staring out the picture window at the fading light. When I let myself in he looks over but doesn't get up.

"Hey," I say softly.

"You're back."

"Yep." Suddenly I feel awkward and out of place in his

house, in his presence. "I heard there's something wrong with Harvey. Is he going to be okay?"

The cat doesn't look unwell right now. He's splayed across his owner's thighs, twisting this way and that to get comfortable while trying to maximize the belly massage Conn's absently giving him.

"We had a little scare."

I want to get closer and see the cat for myself, but the vibe from Conn is keeping me halfway across the room. "What happened?"

"He'll be all right. I tried some new cat food because he's getting pickier, and it wreaked havoc with his stomach. The vet gave him an IV and said he needs to take it easy and eat 'senior' cat food."

"Oh, good. I mean, that the problem is only his food."

"Uh-huh."

More silence. The vibe gets heavier, and I know it's not only because Conn is worried about Harvey. I knew this was coming—I've just been trying to ignore it all day.

"Conn..." I start, but he cuts me off.

"We saw your interview." His words are conversational. His tone is not.

"We?"

"A lot of the town came to the restaurant on their lunch break to watch the show."

I swallow heavily and sit on the caved-in couch, nerves keeping me on the edge of the cushion. "Well, that was nice."

"Mm." He continues to pet Harvey, giving the cat his full attention. I get the feeling he doesn't want to look at me. "It was interesting."

"It's been...harder than I thought."

Finally he looks up. He must tense up as well, because Harvey shoots his owner a dirty look before slipping off his lap and stomping away. "You didn't seem to have a hard time telling stories about your clients."

Here we go. "I didn't name names."

"You didn't have to."

"Nobody outside of Abbott's Bay will know who I was talking about."

"But everyone *in* Abbott's Bay knows. You violated confidentiality."

"I don't have any promises of confidentiality!" That really stings. It reminds me of Trudy's attack, accusing me of being irresponsible because I'm not a licensed therapist.

Conn pushes to his feet and crosses to the kitchen to dish up some of Harvey's new cat food. "Yeah, well, maybe you should have thought of it sooner."

I know that look on his face—he's already judged me and found me lacking. Just like old times. My defenses go up immediately. Conn wasn't the one in a big corporate news setting, broiling under the set lights, surprise-attacked by the anchor I thought was starting to be my friend. Or at least a friendly acquaintance.

"Excuse me for helping people, *and* doing a decent job of it all summer, not to mention making the best of a stressful situation on live TV. It's *not* easy, you know."

"Why do you do it, then?" When I don't answer, he fills in the blanks for me. "Because it's too tempting, right? Melanie Abbott, TV star. The next rung on the ladder, never mind if you step on your friends to get to it?"

"You're overreacting, and you're being cruel."

"Seems you know from cruel."

Now I'm on my feet as well, trembling with adrenaline. "You know, I don't need this right now. I just got back, I'm exhausted, and this is unfair. Come find me when you have something reasonable to say."

I try to storm out, but Conn throws himself in front of me, blocking my path to the door. "Look, Melanie. You hurt a lot of people who like you and look up to you. Laura especially. You should have seen her face. It was…" He shakes his head. "I don't care what was going on in that TV studio. It doesn't mean you get to make your friends the butt of a joke."

"I didn't—!"

"You did! And I saw the looks on their faces that proved it. It's like you brought out some…exaggerated version of your worst self or something. *Lanie*," he spits.

"Hey, Lanie wasn't my idea."

"Not the point. Viewers all across the country saw some

heartless, catty woman getting some laughs at her clients' expense. And that's inexcusable."

"Whose side are you on?" I'm shouting now—something I never do. Well, if I do, it's usually when I'm arguing with Conn, and he's arguing back, but this isn't our usual bickering. This is mean. I'm furious that he'd condemn me like this.

"I'm on your side—more than anyone else in this town," he says. "But sometimes I have to tell you things you don't want to hear. This is one of those times. You *hurt* people today, all to make yourself look good." Then he gets very quiet. "Look...I love Melanie. But I don't even *like* Lanie."

Well. Welcome back to the world of Judgy Conn. It's been so long I'd almost forgotten what it was like. I should have known a month of heart-melting affection, hot sex, and bandying around the L-word wouldn't banish it for good.

He's wrong this time though, I tell myself as I march back up the road toward town. I did what I had to do, and I'll bet nobody thought anything of it, nobody was as hurt as badly as he says they were. I didn't say anything that wasn't true. The irony is Conn really hurt *my* feelings.

I need to see a friendly face, so I detour over to Hannah's instead of going straight home. She'll be able to give me a better perspective of people's reactions at the viewing party instead of Conn's gloom-and-doom reporting.

I knock, growing chilled again as I wait on her stoop. Nobody comes to the door. I try again. I think I can hear movement inside, but the door doesn't open. That's weird. After a third knock and calling Hannah's name, I lean over the railing and peek in her front window. It brings to mind my dad's potentially felonious behavior with the nude yoga tenant, but this is Hannah. She wouldn't call the police on me.

It might be a reflection on the glass as I move, but I could swear I see a flicker of light inside. A hint of dread trickles through me. What if I did hurt people, including Hannah, and she's avoiding me now? I accused her on air of not taking my advice to stop communicating with Marty, which was pretty mean, even though I credit her stubbornness with starting the business.

I pull out my cell phone and call hers. I can hear her

ringtone coming from inside. Then it stops. Her voicemail greeting sounds in my ear, and I do my best to sound cheerful and not at all suspicious as I leave her a message.

"Hey, Hannah! I'm back from New York! Dying for some MooMoo's—want to get some before it closes for the season? Call me!"

I click off and hurry home, keeping my head down so I don't catch anyone's eye on the way. I turn off my phone, turn off my brain, and try not to think about my last disastrous TV appearance. I don't, however, delete it from my DVR unwatched. I make it almost forty-eight hours before I cave on Sunday afternoon.

It's awful. It's worse than I thought. No wonder everyone's avoiding me. *I'd* avoid me if I could. Suddenly there's nothing I want more than to go back in time and reject Jack's offer. My first instinct had been the correct one—I never should have gone on TV. This whole experience has been miserable from beginning to end—which, I decide, is now.

I text Jack, informing him I won't be continuing my segments on the NNN noon show. I expect him to be on the phone in an instant, no matter what country he's in today, demanding to know why I'm quitting, encouraging me to sign a new, extended contract, but my phone stays silent.

After three days hiding in my apartment, I run out of food, so I have to leave my self-imposed prison. I decide to go to the office. Work is always my refuge when I've screwed up royally in all other aspects of my life. I can bury myself in paperwork, pretend everything's normal, and not have to think about anything else.

Except Laura's there. After a moment of hesitation in the doorway, I charge toward my desk. Everyone's looking at me. I can feel it. Jason, Maude, even Eric the Red, who of course today—of all days—is not only in the office, but able to focus on things, like me. And Laura...I sneak a furtive peek. She's *not* looking at me, and somehow that's worse.

I change my mind and change direction, making a beeline for my father's office instead. I slink in, shut the door, and curl up on his couch without a word. He acts like he doesn't see me, which makes me wonder if he's angry with me as well.

Then he says, while still staring at his computer, "So my little girl's famous."

"For all the wrong reasons," I groan.

"Now, now. I hear any publicity is good publicity."

"Tell that to the residents of Abbott's Bay."

"True. It didn't play in Peoria."

"I have no idea what that means."

"It means," he says, finally swiveling his chair around to face me, "while most of the audience probably enjoyed your anecdotes as much as your interviewer did…who was that, again?"

"Trudy Helmet-Head."

"Stage name?"

"Something like that."

"Anyway, while the rest of America may have been entertained, your neighbors didn't take kindly to being outed on live TV."

"I helped all the people I talked about."

"Not Laura. Not yet."

"How do you hear all these things, old man?"

"I have my finger on the pulse of this town and you know it," he says with a wink. "I know things, my daughter. Many things."

I sit up and brush back my hair. "I've probably ruined your chances for re-election with all this…this…notoriety, haven't I?"

Dad joins me on the couch. "Oh, don't be silly." He puts his arm around me, and I rest my head on his shoulder. "You're not *that* important."

"Charles!" I swat at his chest, but he just holds me to him.

"As you're so quick to remind me, I'm running unopposed, I'm the incumbent, and people love me. I'm a shoo-in. Don't worry about me."

"Well, I do."

"Just…get yourself straight, all right?"

I think about Hannah hiding from me, the glares from my neighbors, and, worst of all, Conn's flinty eyes when he blasted me about my TV appearance. What if there's no coming back from this?

"How about you start with Laura?" Dad suggests, nodding toward the outer office. I follow his gaze, only to see the woman in question look up from her work, lock eyes with me, and...grab her things and rush out of the office.

I deserve this. "All right," I sigh. "One makeover, coming up. She'll be my biggest challenge and my greatest success."

"She doesn't want a makeover."

"She should." My father waits for me to locate my manners. "Sorry. I mean...she doesn't?"

"No. She needs someone to go with her to visit her grandmother, who's in a nursing home in Lowell. She's not doing so well, and Laura is finding it difficult to go by herself. Her grandmother raised her, and she's really emotional about this. She, well, needs a friend. For support."

"Oh."

I do believe I've made it to the final round of the Worst Person in the World contest.

* * *

After a restless night, I get up bright and early and head to work, solely to find Laura. She's not there—Maude tells me she's taken a day off—and isn't at home either. I try her cell, but she's not answering. She's always a ghost at the best of times. Now, when she wants to avoid me, she's patently invisible. I decide to check her favorite places around town...but I don't know what they are. The tea shop? She seems like a tea drinker. The yarn store? I assume she was the one who knitted that god-awful doggie hat, but I could be entirely wrong. What if she likes fencing, or paintball, and I just don't know it? Confounded, I stand in the middle of the street, hands on my hips, as I realize I don't know much about Laura at all.

I wonder if I should dare to enter Deep Brew C. Would Conn be there? Most likely. Would he throw me out? Not bodily, but his laser glare might cut me off at the knees. I have to chance it though.

The place is fairly busy for late morning. One of the

local churches' prayer groups is taking up a pair of tables, exchanging pleasantries with a small but raucous knot of senior citizen ladies noshing on muffins, apparently fresh from their Zumba class, judging by their colorful workout gear. But no Laura. Then I notice a familiar face at a table in the back.

"Hey, Hannah." My voice is shaky.

She looks up, surprised, as does her companion—a pleasant-looking guy I recognize from the dozens of photos she's shown me over the past few months.

"You must be Marty."

He half rises from his chair and shakes the hand I hold out. "And you're Melanie. I've heard a lot about you."

"Likewise."

Average-looking, with a round face, overlong sideburns, and a shock of unruly brown hair, Marty Roberts would hardly stand out in a crowd. But Hannah looks at him like he's the most perfect man in the world, so I stop myself from writing him off as unremarkable. Superficial snap judgments have gotten me into a lot of trouble lately, after all.

"Hannah didn't tell me you were visiting. When did you get in?"

"Monday."

"May I sit?"

Hannah hesitates, but Marty gets up and brings over a chair from a nearby table. "Please join us. I'm really excited to finally be talking to the famous Melanie Abbott."

Marty realizes his poor choice of words but isn't sure how to recover.

"Famous, infamous," I demur with a smile. *It's all awful,* I want to add, but I don't.

"I got your message," Hannah says tentatively, turning to me with that deer-in-the-headlight look I haven't seen in a long time. "I was going to call you, but I've been a little—"

"Of course you've been busy, with Marty visiting. I understand. So, Marty," I venture gamely, feeling all-over awkward, "Are you going to take our Hannah back to Ohio with you now that the summer's over?"

"Well, that's the question. She really likes it here, and I can see why. It's a great town." He takes Hannah's hand again, rubbing his thumb along hers, gently. "But it's up to her." An entire conversation is exchanged in their looks, their smiles, and I start to understand what Hannah's been on about all summer.

"I'll go wherever Marty is," Hannah says.

Her bags are probably already packed, and it hurts my heart. People are always leaving. I thought I was used to it. I'm not.

Marty says to Hannah, "It doesn't have to be Ohio, you know. You can pick the place. There are jobs for me everywhere these days."

"What do you do?" I ask him, desperate to get out of my own head and make proper small talk.

"Organics. Right now I'm running a co-op, but I've done farm to table—"

"You're a farmer?"

"Distribution, mostly. I've got to admit, I'm really impressed with how many sustainable, zero-waste food places there are around here."

"This restaurant is one, did you know that?"

"This restaurant is what?"

I jump at the sound of Conn's voice behind me. It's not harsh, not cold—not like the last time I saw him, which is encouraging. I give him a wavering smile.

"Farm to table and sustainability," I tell him. "Marty here does…distribution of organic crops."

While Marty and Conn get acquainted, I look at Hannah and try to silently send her a message: *I'm so sorry.* I can't tell if she picks up on it or not. I interrupt the men's excited conversation about produce suppliers and co-ops and certified organic farms when I notice a duffel bag at Conn's feet.

"Going somewhere?"

"Yeah. I'm going back to Provincetown."

"More properties?"

"Taylor says a couple just came on the market I have to see. She's even got a meeting lined up with one seller's agent tomorrow. She's convinced this is the perfect place and I'm going to want to put in an offer right away."

God, our conversation sounds so stilted. It's excruciating. The only way out of this is through, but now is not the time to hash it out with him. So I say, "What about Harvey? Would you like me to check on him?"

"He's fine. I've got it covered." Belatedly, he adds, "Thanks anyway."

"Well then." I stand up, suddenly desperate for some air. "Drive safely." As I step away from the table, I kiss him on the cheek, and he lets me. So that's something. I even dare to make a joke. "Watch out for Taylor. She's got a thing for your ass." I wink at him, say goodbye to Marty and Hannah, and escape into the sunshine.

CHAPTER THIRTY-TWO

———————

I don't know how to fix this. Any of this. My fight with Conn, yes, but also all the other relationships I've damaged. My heart is aching. I don't even call Taylor for one of her what-do-they-know pep talks. I don't deserve one. Something is fundamentally wrong with me, with what I've been doing—namely, coasting through life. So far nothing's touched me. Sure, there were some rough times when my mother left, but since then I've had a pretty good life, one that's lulled me into a certain complacency that's given rise to a dangerous cockiness. At other people's expense sometimes. Okay, often. I can ignore it most of the time…until it comes back to bite me in the butt, like now.

I mean literally—or, rather, journalistically. I'm the featured Bite on the Bottom in this week's edition of the *Abbott's Bay Bugle*.

"Oh, just what I need," I mutter aloud, even though I'm alone in my apartment. "Go ahead. Kick a girl when she's down." I shake out the paper and fold it back. "'Abbott's Bay's golden child has a tarnished crown…' Nice and subtle. 'Tainted by her brush with fame and fortune…' Good lord. 'And taking her friends down with her.' Blah, blah, and blah."

I don't usually throw things, but this time I take some satisfaction in launching the newspaper across the room. Its pages unfurl and flutter all over, shrouding my furniture in crappy journalism and subpar photography. I want to leave it there, but I'm tidy by nature, so I immediately pick up all the loose pages. Unable to resist, I read my blind item again with disgust. Then I read the next one. It starts with yet another reference to "lovebirds," but this time I don't think it's about me and Conn, as it goes on to talk about "a hot couple cooking up something good" but the "soufflé collapsed almost as quickly as it had been made." Though the wording is ham-handed, as usual, the Bite sends a chill through me. What if...

I'm on the phone immediately. "Beebs? Tell me it's not true. About you and Ornette."

There's a heavy sigh on the other end of the line. "Melanie, it's kind of busy here—"

"Please. I have a vested interest in this. Are you and Ornette over already?"

Another sigh then silence. After a moment he says quietly, "It's no big deal. Sometimes things don't work out."

I groan. It *is* a big deal. I told Ornette he had nothing to worry about if he dated Beebs. I could have sworn they'd make the perfect couple. "It goes to show you...nobody should listen to me. Ever. Now or in the future. My advice is crap, my instinct blows—"

"Melanie."

"What?"

"It's not about you. Okay?"

Oh God, he's right. Beebs and Ornette are both probably hurting and embarrassed *and* they have to work together, and here I am, making it all about me.

"I'm sorry, Beebs. Really." At this point, I normally would have continued, "Let me fix it—trust me." But they shouldn't trust me. I sure don't. So I hang up and keep to myself.

By late afternoon I'm climbing the walls. I have nothing to do. I don't even have any New Best Friend clients to check in with, but I'm fine with that. The way I feel right now, I'm ready to let this thing die a quiet death, before I ruin anybody else's life.

As for people to talk to...I'm dry. Taylor and Conn are real estate shopping on the Cape. Hannah's with Marty. My father is in Boston for the day with the Garveys. I've got no one. Heart hollow, I bundle up against the new cooler weather and go for a walk. I can do one good thing without screwing it up: check on Harvey. No matter whom Conn employed to look in on the cat, it couldn't hurt to be a backup.

Trudging around the bend in the coastal road, I'm hit with a new sight that sends me reeling: an Abbott Realty "for sale" sign stuck in the strip of grass at the edge of the Garvey property. With Laura's name, photo, and contact information in the slot on top.

Serves me right.

When I let myself in with Conn's hidden key—now secreted on top of the doorframe instead of hidden in the ceramic frog—I can tell an agent has been here. The place is spruced up with new curtains, a slipcover hiding the sofa's worst sins, different artwork on the walls, new decorative items set out on the tables, family photos put away. The Picture Hook of Doom has been removed and the nail hole patched. It feels as though the house is already gone, no longer a part of the Garveys' history. And, by association, no longer a part of mine.

Well, there's still Harvey. I call for him, but he doesn't appear right away. When I tap on a can of cat food, however, he materializes behind me. I wonder where his hiding place is. If Laura's shown the house while Conn's been gone, strangers tromping through here may have upset him. They certainly would upset me. I dish out his food and pick the deposits out of his litter box. When he's done with his post-meal bathing, I scoop him up for a cuddle.

"Oh, Harvey, this is something, isn't it?" I sigh as I drop into Conn's recliner, putting the cat on my lap and scratching the spot he can't reach at the base of his tail. He sticks his butt up higher, encouraging me to continue. "We can't move you from this house. You're too set in your ways to get used to a new place now. You tell Conn this is unacceptable, all right?"

I'm so busy chatting with the cat, who's rewarding me with head butts to my chin, leaving a couple of fine gray hairs stuck to my lip gloss, that I don't hear the door open at first. I do, however, hear a surprised squeak in the kitchen.

"Laura?"

"H-hi, Melanie." She closes the door behind her, awkwardly, because she's carrying a couple of shopping bags, which she deposits on the counter. "What are you doing here?"

"Checking on Harvey," I say. "You know—so he won't be lonely." It's at this moment, of course, that the cat abandons me as if to prove he doesn't actually need me around. "Congratulations on getting the listing. It's…really great."

She nods, still not meeting my eyes. "It's a nice house."

"It is." And I mean it. For all the grief I give Conn about how ugly it is, deep down I don't think it's so bad. "I like what you've done with the staging."

"Thanks."

Laura puts apples and oranges in the fridge, leaving some spices on the counter. I know what they're there for.

"When's the open house?"

She'll simmer them in a pot on the stove to make the place smell nice—homier and more inviting—to entice total strangers to imagine living here.

"Pretty soon. Conn says he wants to sell fast, even at a loss."

Well, that would be stupid. He could get top dollar. It's not up to me though. I gave up the right to express my opinion when I refused to take the listing. I cross the room and lean on the counter dividing the kitchen from the living room. Toying with the ribbon tying the bundle of cinnamon sticks together, I mumble, "Hey, Laura?"

"Yep?"

"I want to say I'm sorry. About what I said on TV." I want to add that I didn't mean it, but the problem is...I did.

She turns to me, pushing her glasses up her nose and blowing her bangs out of the way. I force myself to look straight into her eyes. I've never really done that before. They're large and very dark brown. Pretty, really. Her hair is thick and shiny as well. She's nowhere near as hopeless, style wise, as I make her out to be. And if she wants to be...eccentric...who am I to decide she shouldn't be? At least she's unique. Unapologetically so.

She's also nice enough to say, "It's okay. I understand."

"Let me make it up to you. My dad told me what you need a friend for, and I'd be honored to visit your grandmother with you. If you still want me to."

"You don't have to."

"I wouldn't dream of making you go alone. I wish we'd known each other better before this, so you would have felt comfortable asking me to go as a real friend, instead of hiring me. When are you going next?"

"I...I don't know."

I realize I'm pushing a little too hard, so I table the discussion and offer to help her place the additional art prints, scented candles, and antique candy dishes she's brought around the living room. We talk shop a little bit, and by the time we're done I feel lighter, almost hopeful.

And then I run into Petey and his girlfriend at Henry's market. He spots me first, although I try to hide behind a display of tall, gorgeous bottles of gourmet infused oils. Petey makes sure I get a good look at his furrowed brow and narrowed eyes, even if they are distorted by cut glass and truffle oil. Then he puts his arm around Bait Shop Girl defiantly. *Hey, buddy,* I think, *you wouldn't have your Bait Shop Girl if you hadn't come to me in the first place.*

I understand where he's coming from though. I helped him achieve his goal, but I had no right to make fun of him afterward. Gathering what's left of my confidence, I force myself to approach him.

"Petey, hey."

He starts to turn away, but Bait Shop Girl clutches at his shirt, keeping him there.

"Hi," I say to her. She seems more receptive than Petey. "I'm—"

"Melanie. I know. I'm Caroline."

I wonder if Petey told her I helped him woo her. I don't ask, just shake her hand, smile briefly, and say to Petey, "Um, look…what I said on TV the other day? It was…wrong. I want to apologize."

He shrugs. "It doesn't matter," he says blankly.

"It doesn't?" Finally, someone who understands me! And it's Petey Fagle, of all people! Relief washes over me.

Until he adds, "I'm used to it. You've been like this your whole life. You were like this back in school."

My eager smile fades in an instant. "Oh. Right." Conn can give me grief about my teenage reign of terror with Taylor, and I can refute it every time he brings it up, but Petey experienced it firsthand. I can't deny it in front of him. Which, of course, confirms that Conn was right. I'm starting to get used to his being right about pretty much everything. "Well, I still want to apologize. Although I don't expect you to forgive me or anything." He stares at me longer, and with an even blanker expression, if that's at all possible. I glance around the store and then desperately grab a bouquet of sunflowers and other colorful late-summer blossoms. "Anyway, I hope you'll accept these as part of my apology."

"What am I supposed to do with flowers?" he asks as I shove them at his chest.

"I don't know. Give them to Caroline."

"She likes vegetables."

Oh, Petey. But far be it from me to argue. I'm about to present him with a stalk of Brussels sprouts when Caroline takes the bouquet out of his hands.

"I like flowers, Petey," she says with a shy smile.

"You do?" He sounds completely confounded.

That's my cue to leave and let Caroline take it from here. I pat Petey on the arm as I move away. "Make a note of it for later," I can't resist whispering to him.

He nods at me, still blank-faced. I realize that's the best I'm going to get. I'll take it.

* * *

"What are you doing here on a Saturday?" my father barks at me when I stick my head into his office. "Are you feverish?"

"I work on Saturdays all the time, Charles, and you know it."

He grunts and says, "Well, do me a favor then. I need you to contact a couple of Laura's clients. They're interested in the Garvey house."

Ignoring the jolt that shoots through me, I ask, "Why? Where's Laura?" I've been feeling almost protective of her ever since I found out what's going on in her personal life.

My father puts down the contract he's been reading. "She was in early today. Then she got a call from her grandmother's nursing home. It didn't sound good."

"I'm so sorry. Where can I find her?"

"You?"

"Don't sound so surprised. She wanted to hire me for this

and I avoided her for too long. The least I can do is help her out now."

"Are you sure she wants you there?"

"I'll let her decide when I get there. Now, where's her grandmother? What home?"

"I don't know."

Dammit. How can we know so little about one of our employees? Well, my dad knew about her grandmother when I didn't, so I'm worse off here, but we should be more sensitive to their personal issues. Then I have an idea.

I call Randall, Laura's other boss at the *Abbott's Bay Bugle*, and get the name of her grandmother's nursing home in a matter of minutes…for a price. All I have to give him in return is an exclusive about the latest developments with Your New Best Friend. My one stipulation: that I write the article myself. I have a lot to say.

But that's not important right now. I drive to Lowell as fast as I can, find the nursing home, check in at the front desk, and quietly slip into the hospice room.

"Laura?" I whisper.

I don't know how she'll react when she sees me. I don't know how I'm going to explain myself to a room full of teary relatives. But it's only Laura, sitting quietly at her grandmother's bedside. She looks up at me, shocked, and I'm already regretting my impulsive decision.

I stammer, "I…I was worried. My dad said your grandmother…never mind. I can go."

She says nothing for a minute—just stares, as only Laura can, light glinting on her glasses, her pale face even more peaked than usual. Then she turns back to her grandmother without a word. I'm trying to determine if this means I should leave when she reaches over and pulls a second chair alongside hers. I sit and slip my hand into hers.

CHAPTER THIRTY-THREE

———

"Oh my God, chica! Where have you been? I've called you like five times. Did you turn your phone off? There's only one reason you'd be turning your phone off, and I know he's not back in Abbott's Bay yet!"

Taylor's overly chipper voice is phenomenally jarring and makes my throbbing headache worse.

"I had some stuff to take care of," I say as I wipe tears away with the heel of my hand.

I'm sitting in my car, still in the nursing home parking lot. Laura's grandmother is gone. I wasn't with Laura for that, of course. She and I sat in silence for several hours, waiting as the old woman's breath became more labored then quieted, alternately. When a nurse came in to check on her and said, with the matter-of-fact nature of a caregiver who's seen this process countless times, that it wouldn't be long, I gave Laura a hug and waited in the hallway. Another hour passed before she came out, bleary but resigned and, it seemed, at peace—as much as she could be, that is.

I stayed with her until she announced she was ready to take care of the rest of her duties—talking with the funeral director, gathering her grandmother's things—on her own. Then I gave her another hug and left the building. I haven't been able to see well enough to get back on the road quite yet though.

"What's the matter with you?" Taylor demands, her voice muffled as she shifts the phone. She's probably multitasking, cleaning her kitchen sink, or sending emails while she waits for me to pull myself together.

"Nothing."

"Like I believe that. I don't suppose it'd have anything to do with a certain six-foot-two specimen of manhood, would it?"

My stomach clenches. "Why? What did he tell you?"

"Not a word. You know how he is. But I figured you guys had a fight or something. The entire time he was here, he was hanging his head, looking like a basset hound stepping on his own ears. He wasn't even excited about the place I found him."

"You found him something?"

"You'd better believe it. It's *perfect*. Right on Commercial Street, in the thick of things, *and* it's an entire building with rooms upstairs. He can expand, or he can rent it out, or hell, he can even live in it."

I swallow around a new lump in my throat. "He said that?"

"Said what?"

"That he'd live there?"

"Well, he's got to have a place to stay when he comes here to check on the renovations, right?"

"Did he say anything about being there…" The word *permanently* won't come out.

"What?"

What if Conn moves to Provincetown? He said he wouldn't, but what if he's changed his mind? What if this isn't a fight we've had but something more serious? Did I offend him so much that he'd move to the Cape to get away from me?

"Never mind. It's nothing."

"Girl, what's going on between the two of you?"

"Trying to find out if your turn is coming up?"

"Shut up. I mean it. He's moping, you're crying—again, shut up. I know when my bestie's been crying. You sound like somebody punched you in the nose. I'm starting to worry."

I'm not about to tell Taylor I'm crying about Laura and her grandmother, not Conn. Or maybe there are some Conn-related tears in there as well. I don't even know anymore. "Let's say I've been experiencing some fallout from my TV appearance."

"Oh, that was *righteous*," she crows. "If anybody has a problem with it, you tell 'em where to get off. I mean it."

Exactly what I expect from Taylor and exactly what I don't want to hear. Not anymore. "No. That…it was like the adult version of our reign of terror. And that's not a good thing."

"Oh, whatever. You're being way too dramatic. Hey, make up with Conn so you can come along next time he has to come out here, okay?"

Obviously Taylor doesn't grasp the gravity of the situation and isn't interested in having a serious conversation. Which is just about what I can expect from her, and always has been. I'm in no mood for a shallow chat, so I make my excuses and end the call. I have some work to do.

* * *

Taylor's right about one thing: I should be making up with Conn. It would be at the top of my list of things to do, but he hasn't come home yet. I know—I keep checking. Fortunately I'm busy enough that I don't text him every five minutes like I want to. Okay, I *might* check my phone every five minutes in case I missed a call or a text from him, but that's it.

The Founder's Day Ball is in exactly one week, but I can't even think about it yet, because I'm focusing entirely on my article for the *Bugle*. I don't rest until it's finished, and I even manage to turn it in early. Although a stab of fear hits me right before I email it to Randall, once I force myself to click *Send* I feel nothing but relief. I hope this brings closure. I've spent too many days up my own butt with the whole TV thing. It's time to move on.

Digging in at work is my next priority. I've let my actual profession slide for too long. I go in early and stay late, catching up with the endless paperwork I usually put off. I feel like I've gotten in touch with my inner Mary Poppins. Suddenly nothing's more important than clearing out the cobwebs and setting everything to rights.

That includes facing the music with Hannah. Again, I'm wracked with nerves, but I force myself to go to her house and knock with a confidence I'm not really feeling. I may have destroyed the easy relationship I've had with her. Now is when I find out. When she answers her door, I stay on her doorstep instead of pushing my way inside without a second thought, the way I used to.

"Okay," I say, a little breathlessly, as I hold up a sheet of paper. "I know you're not sure where you're moving, or when, or anything. But in the meantime, I want—" I stop, close my eyes, shake my head, and start again. "I mean…you can stay here as long as you like. I've drawn up a month-to-month lease for you now that your summer lease is up. I hope you'll stay. Please stay." I wait only a split second, taking in the startled look on my friend's face, then rush to add, "With Marty. By all means, with Marty. You two are perfect together, and I gave you terrible advice when I told you to walk away from him instead of working it out. I'm so sorry." Still she says nothing, just stares, wide-eyed, so I hand her the paper. "Anyway…do what you think is best. And call me sometime. If you want."

Hannah's fingers finally grasp the corner of the lease. I let go. Then her other arm flies out and pulls me into a hug, and I nearly drown in the wash of relief.

Once Hannah and I gleefully make up, I turn my attention to the Founder's Day celebration. I spend most of my time with Rose Perdue, finalizing the details for the ball, including the replacement charity event for the indoor miniature golf tournament that literally went up in smoke. I had come up with a bunch of different options, as promised, and she zeroed in on one that made her giggle like a schoolgirl—one that's also easy to pull off on short notice, if you've got the know-how and the focus. And I do. I don't mind putting in the extra hours either—it helps me keep my mind off the fact that my article will appear in this week's *Abbott's Bay Bugle*.

When the *Bugle* comes out on Friday, I'm shocked to find my story on the front page. Above the fold. I didn't ask Randall for that, but he said this was hot news everyone would want to read—so much so that he made sure, for the first time in ages, to have someone at the *Bugle* update the paper's website, solely to put my article online as well.

Soon after the paper hits people's mailboxes, my phone blows up, but in a good way. Everyone wants to talk about the article. I'm fine with that, but not to soak up their praise. I have a lot of apologies to make. When I do, and when my neighbors accept those apologies without a second thought, I'm humbled. My friends in Abbott's Bay are generous and understanding, and

I've never appreciated those traits more than I do right now. Conn said Sasha used to make fun of this town and couldn't get away fast enough. I feel sorry for her; she doesn't know what she's missing.

Best of all, I receive a lovely message from Zoë, my accidental first client.

> *Hi Ms. Abbott! I hope you don't mind getting an email from me. I got your info from Vern. I saw you on NNN. So did my mom. You can guess how that turned out. But you were right about everything. I WAS raised by nannies! Anyway, my mom was talking about suing you for a while, but she got over it. She's changed lately—she's been trying to be a lot nicer. Sometimes it works—sometimes it doesn't, but what matters is she's trying. You help people so much, Ms. Abbott. I've always felt bad I never thanked you for everything you did for me, so here it is now: thank you! I had a wonderful summer in Abbott's Bay, and I'm so happy I met Vern. Who says hi, by the way!*

Now *that's* an endorsement. Zoë sounds like she's becoming quite the confident young lady. I wouldn't draw a direct line from my straightening her posture to her future as President of the United States, but anything's possible. In any case, her message means the world to me. It shows I wasn't a complete failure. I didn't run around destroying people's lives. I *did* do some good, even if the bad overshadowed it for a while. I decide to remember my successes instead of focusing on my failures, but rectify the failures if I can.

Like Beebs and Ornette. They're next.

"Beebs, my love, a gloppy mocha, if you please," I say, bellying up to the bar. "And an egg and cheese sandwich too."

The barista looks at me funny. "Melanie, you never order that."

"Well, maybe I like trying new things." Or maybe I like sending Beebs to the kitchen with an order so he can talk to Ornette.

"I got it." Conn appears from out of nowhere and starts to head to the kitchen window to save Beebs a few steps.

My brain stutters. Conn. He's back. *Conn's back.*

The sight of him sends fireworks careening around my insides, destroying my stomach and making my hands, feet, and scalp tingle. I'm not sure, however, if those are good nerves or bad ones. Maybe both. After all, he's been gone more than a week, and I didn't get a call or a text the entire time. If Beebs hadn't told me he'd checked in from time to time, I'd have gone into a cold, hard panic. It's the longest we've gone without talking every day, the longest he's been away from Abbott's Bay…and me…since he moved back to town. I'm relieved he's okay. I want to throw myself into his arms even at the risk of him pushing me away. I want to pummel him for not letting me know where he was or what he was doing. Yet none of that matters more than my urgent need to keep him from scuppering the scheme I've got working at the moment.

"Wait!" I yelp, and Conn turns to me, puzzled. "I—I've changed my mind. Conn, I've missed your triple espressos. Will you make me one instead of the mocha? Please?"

He gives me a look, but complies, while Beebs takes my order to Ornette.

Once Beebs is far enough away, I lean over the counter and hiss, "What is the *matter* with you?"

"Why? I just…"

I hitch my head toward the kitchen, where Beebs and Ornette are talking, and glare at him until he catches on.

"Ohhhh."

"God, you're crappy at this."

Yes, it's the completely wrong way to talk to him now that he's right in front of me for the first time in eight days, but I feel a certain thrill that we're still able to fall back into our usual verbal sparring with no effort at all.

I'm rewarded with a hint of his familiar warm smile when he says, "That's why I leave the manipulation of innocents to you. Me, I just make the coffee. Nice to see you, by the way."

I stand at the counter, fidgeting as I watch the familiar choreography as he makes my espresso. God, I've missed him. I'm terrified to finally deal with what happened between us before he left, but I'm more terrified not to.

"Conn," I start hesitantly when he hands me my coffee.

Eyes alight, he's poised, attentive. God, I hope he wants

to talk—

"Melanie...?"

What timing. Maude, my hateful coworker, shows up out of nowhere? And she wants to talk to me *now*, when she usually does everything in her power *not* to talk to me, ever? I want to put her off, but it doesn't matter—Conn is approached by another customer, and the moment's lost. *Dammit.*

Tamping down my disappointment, I put on a smile that's probably more of a grimace. "Can I help you with something, Maude?"

She fidgets, glances around, and then finally mutters, "I need help. Socially."

Ain't that the truth. Too bad she's a little late to the party. "Maude, didn't you see the article in today's paper?"

As if she doesn't hear me, she charges ahead with the rest of her pitch. "My high school reunion is coming up, and I want to...you know. Impress people. Show them I'm doing okay. High school wasn't my best four years, if you know what I mean."

I can imagine. I don't say that. Instead, I try to figure out what to do to get her to understand the word *no.*

"Laura said you were...a good friend. Helpful. And I need help." She hesitates then adds, "Please."

Wow. "But...you hate me."

"Yeah, I do."

At least she's honest. "Why, Maude? I mean, I'm curious. What did I ever do to you?"

"Do? Nothing. It's the way you *are.* That...air of superiority, like your feet don't touch the ground. It's irritating."

"I do that?"

"Well, you've been different lately. Still acting superior, but at least now you don't look through everyone. Apparently you're still pretty self-centered though, since we just ended up talking about your issues instead of mine. Nice work," she grumbles. Then she hitches her shoulders defensively. "You know what? Forget it."

She turns to go, but I stop her. "Wait. I do want to help. But not as a client. As a friend."

"You mean I won't have to pay you?"

Good grief. "I will not send you a bill. I promise."

"Maude."

Conn's voice doesn't come from across the counter, but at my side. When his hand cradles my elbow, I jump. But I don't move away.

He continues, "Would you mind if I steal Melanie for a minute? I'll have Beebs make you a cappuccino while you wait. On the house."

She nods, even smiles. Of course. Not even the sourest of crabapples can resist Conn's charms.

He ushers me into his office and shuts the door. I can't help remembering what happened in this office nearly two months ago. Judging by the color creeping up Conn's neck, neither can he. This time, however, instead of pressing me up against the desk, he reaches past me and around his computer monitor.

"So what's all this about?" He's holding a copy of the *Bugle*.

Funny how my words have deserted me, like I spent all of them on the article and have none left. "You read it?"

He nods and glances over the piece again while I watch him, trying to gauge his mood. "It was impressive."

"I always did get good grades in English."

Looking at me from under his eyebrows, he murmurs, "You know that's not what I mean. It took a lot of nerve to write all this."

I guess it did. It's not easy composing the world's biggest apology to all of Abbott's Bay in general, and to my New Best Friend clients in particular, for everything: the missteps I've made with my business…taking advantage of my friends and neighbors…the on-air insults…hell, I even copped to my part in the Whitfield-Abbott Reign of Terror fifteen years ago. I got it all out there. Then I announced Your New Best Friend is ending its run. I've done enough damage. I'm taking myself off the market, so to speak. As I said to Maude, if people want my help, I'll be happy to offer my services—as a friend, not a friend-for-hire. Because the latter is just tacky.

That's the last line of my article, in fact. I thought it was pretty good.

I shrug. "It had to be said."

"Why didn't you tell me you were doing this?"

"You weren't exactly available."

He scrubs his scalp with his fingertips and sighs. "I know. I'm sorry. I needed time to think."

My stomach clenches. "About..." My voice sticks in my throat. "About what?"

"Lots of things." He sounds agitated but weary at the same time, and I'm terrified he means he needed time to rethink our relationship. His eyes meet mine but only for a split second. I'm the one who looks away. "I wanted to spend some time at the Cape by myself, without Taylor doing her hard sell in my face."

"I hope you're talking about real estate."

That gets a laugh out of him.

"She pinched your ass at least once. Admit it."

"She did not," he insists. "I wanted to get a better feel for the property before I signed on the dotted line. It's great, by the way."

"I'm sure it is."

"And most important...you. Us. How we left everything. I want to apologize. I was too hard on you."

That was *not* what I was expecting. "No, you weren't. I said some terrible, unforgivable things."

"You were pushed into it. I saw it. I was watching that show right along with everyone else in the restaurant."

"That's TV, baby. Conflict plus drama equals ratings."

"Jack was supposed to be looking out for you."

There's a hard edge to his voice when he mentions his friend. Obviously he's holding Jack responsible. But he's wrong. Jack threw me in there, but after that it was all me. I'm the one who has to shoulder the blame.

"I didn't need to be babied."

"You didn't need to be ambushed either."

"So you don't hate me?"

"Hate you?" Conn's eyes widen. "Never."

I want to wrap my arms around his broad chest and bury my face in his shirt, feel him hold me tight. But although he's got a smile on his face, it's uncertain. It makes me stay put, a foot away.

"So," he says, and it sounds awkward as hell. "The Founder's Day Ball."

"Yep."

"How's the planning going?"

"Really well."

"Got a date?"

Now it's my turn to fidget awkwardly. "I...do, actually."

"Oh."

The genuine smile that had been on his face only a moment ago falls away. He's shocked. I'm uncomfortable. It makes me babble.

"Jack called the other day. He apologized for what happened at Triple N, in fact. It was surprising. I think he really means it. We got to talking about other things, I told him I was helping with the Founder's Day Ball, and he asked if he could escort me. We're going as friends," I rush to add. That's the most important thing, as far as I'm concerned. "You were gone, and I wasn't sure when you were coming back, or even if you...if we were..."

"I understand." Conn's words are kind, but his expression is grim. "When did he call?"

"Two days ago. Why?"

"No reason," he mutters, shaking his head. Then he takes a breath. "He'll be the perfect escort. You'll look great together. Have fun."

"Conn—"

But he turns away and opens his office door, essentially ushering me out. "I've got to get back to work. I'll talk to you later, okay?"

CHAPTER THIRTY-FOUR

————

"Absolutely beautiful."

Jack has come up next to me as I stand in the doorway of the country club ballroom, surveying my handiwork. The room is festively but tastefully decorated (if I do say so myself, as I was responsible for most of the decorating) and warmly lit. The sun has nearly set over the golf course on this chilly late-October evening, and there's a pleasant feeling of camaraderie among the Abbott's Bay residents. It's the perfect setting for the Founder's Day Ball.

I let myself gloat. Just a little. "It is, isn't it?"

"I was talking about you."

"Stop." I elbow him in his expensive Armani tuxedo then take a breath, square my shoulders, and smooth down my dress. It's a stunner—midnight blue (my best color) sleeveless chiffon with a flirty keyhole cutout, not much of a back, and a bit of rhinestone trim around the neck, armholes, and waist. I'm flattered he noticed, but I'm looking around for Conn. I'd rather hear something like that from him.

I don't even know for sure if he's coming to the ball— just hoping.

His parents are already here. Is that a good sign? Wait. What am I saying? He's a good son and loves his mom and dad, but it certainly doesn't mean he's going to go to parties with them.

When the Garveys come up to greet us, I kiss Bruce on the cheek and compliment Constance on how well she's getting around without her cane. She thanks me politely, but she's distracted, surveying the crowd. Then her face lights up, and she reaches out a hand to Sasha.

Good lord.

"I'm so glad you could come, dear."

"I wouldn't miss it for the world, Constance."

Sasha? At the Founder's Day Ball? For a fleeting moment I think Conn brought her as his date, and stabs of jealousy and fear nearly double me over.

Then Sasha adds, "Thank you for inviting me."

Good old Constance, about as subtle as a sledgehammer upside the head. So she believes if she puts Sasha in front of Conn frequently enough, he'll fall for her again? Well, that means Conn will be here, anyway.

I have to admit Sasha's looking lovely—elegant as usual, in a chic dove-gray strapless wide-leg jumpsuit trimmed with satin, again accented with minimal jewelry, her hair in its usual super-tight bun. I can't argue with her fashion choices, but she could change it up once in a while. In my opinion. Which, in keeping with my new life philosophy, I will keep to myself.

"Well, this should be fun."

Conn has come up on my other side. I don't even have to look to know it's him. His height, his build, the heat of his body against my arm—it's all so familiar. And wonderful. I glance over anyway and wish I hadn't. Jack might look rich and dapper and perfect, but Conn in a fitted tux is a sight to behold, triggering about half a dozen lust-filled fantasies of mine in the space of a moment.

Before I dare to act on any of them, Rose Perdue sticks her face between our shoulders then forces her body into the gap she's created. "Melanie! Why haven't we got this one on our list yet?" she demands, grasping Conn's arm.

"List? What list?" Conn looks a bit alarmed. As he should be.

Rose is only too happy to fill him in. "You're being drafted for our bachelor auction! All proceeds go to charity!"

Yep, Rose went for the bachelor auction I pitched to her. Nothing else would do. From the first moment guests began arriving tonight, she's been cornering the most desirable gentlemen, from young hotties to silver foxes, convincing them to join in.

Conn colors and laughs nervously, shaking his head as she tugs on his arm, trying to drag him over to the signup sheet.

"Do it, Garvey! It's for charity!" Jack crows.

"Well Jack, if Conn signs up, I think you should too," I say cheerfully.

The frozen smile Jack turns my way is worth everything in the world. "You bet. Anything for you, Melanie." To prove it, he crosses to Conn and gives him a shove, putting the bachelor train in motion behind an elated Rose.

Hannah and Marty arrive, saving me from having to make small talk with the Garveys and Sasha. Marty's cleaned up nicely in a dark blue suit, white shirt, and narrow understated tie. I'm impressed. Hannah is breathtaking in a flattering column dress I found for her. She balked at the bold pattern of peach and lemon yellow swirls at first, but I talked her into it, and she looks amazing.

My father turns up last after glad-handing in the foyer, and we all drift over to our reserved table. Conn and Jack meet us there, neither of them looking thrilled that they probably just signed up to spend several hours with some rich old biddy, making cocktails (likely shirtless), then being chased around a solarium by said biddy. But hey, it's for charity.

The dinner is lovely of course—our town goes all-out for Founder's Day—even though I've got Jack on my right instead of Conn. Actually, the seating arrangement comes in handy, because Conn is across from me, and I can stare at him all I want under the guise of paying attention to conversations going on all around the table. More often than I expect, he catches my eye, and we give each other significant looks. I prefer to think we're sending messages along the lines of *I'm sorry...No,* I'm *sorry...Why aren't we here together?* I hope it's not wishful thinking on my part.

As the dinner starts winding down, my father gets up to make his speech. It's warm and friendly and personal. He mentions many of the people in the room by name, cracks jokes, and infuses the gathering with pride in our town. Even if he weren't running unopposed, he'd win his assembly seat, not only because he's charismatic and politically savvy, but because he really loves and believes in Abbott's Bay. Thanks to the wonderful messages I've received from my neighbors recently, so do I.

When everyone is free to disperse and visit the bar or investigate the dessert buffet, Jack wanders off for a little while then announces his return by touching a cold glass of chardonnay to my shoulder.

"I still can't believe it," he says, handing it to me and slipping back into his seat with his own cocktail. "You're really done with Triple N? Say it isn't so." His voice is so neutral and congenial I can't tell if he's mocking me or not. I *can* tell he's been enjoying multiple drinks—his face is slightly flushed and his eyes glitter.

"Television wasn't for me, I'm afraid."

"You shouldn't let one little setback get to you."

"You mean my incurable case of foot-in-mouth? Not to mention Trudy Helmet-Head throwing me under the bus on camera without any warning? You know," I venture congenially, "I get the feeling if you weren't the one who wanted me on the show, I might not have lasted even as long as I did."

Jack doesn't deny it. "It always helps to have someone in your corner. Especially if that person owns the network."

"I don't want to succeed like that, Jack. It's icky."

"Ah, grow up, Miss Melanie. It's the way the world works. Do you think everyone who's at the top of their game got there through talent and willpower alone? Please."

"Mm. True." I rest my chin on the heel of my hand and study him. "Old family money and influence go a long way...don't they, Rossiter heir?"

The corners of his lips tighten as his smile becomes forced. "I was trying to help you, M."

"I don't want that kind of help."

"Then it looks like you'll be stuck in this backwater burg with your two-bit dog-walking business for the rest of your life. Is that what you want?"

I look over at Conn, who's deep in conversation with his parents, and warmly study his handsome profile. "It's exactly what I want." And I mean it.

Jack starts to retort, but he's interrupted by Crystal and Floyd Phelps, who stop by the table to compliment me on my *Bugle* article. I give Jack a smug little smile. Crystal and Floyd prove my point better than this slow-burn fake-polite argument we're having. Jewel Loftus also comes by to chat. She's left Reginald the ferret at home tonight, but he's doing well, she informs me.

While I talk with my former clients, Jack ignores them and instead fidgets in his chair, glancing around the room as he drains his drink. When the music starts, he pulls me away from my friends.

"Come on. Let's show off that gorgeous dress of yours."

Without much choice in the matter, I let him lead me onto the dance floor and steer me around for a while. Despite his occasional compliments, he doesn't really seem all that captivated by me. He doesn't look at me or engage me in conversation. Instead, he scans the room the entire time. I know what—or, rather, whom—he's looking for.

Tired of this, I decide to end this decade-long charade. "Jack..." I begin in my strongest, brook-no-nonsense voice.

When he looks me in the eye, I think I've finally got his attention, but instead he breaks out his perfect smile and cries, "Dip!"

I only get part of one word out—"Wha—?"—before I'm flipped over backward for a second or two. Even worse, when he pulls me back upright, he's looking at me a little *too* attentively, if you know what I mean. It's too sudden a change, and I'm immediately suspicious, especially when he draws me even closer.

His lips right against my ear, Jack murmurs, "I said it before, and I'll say it again—absolutely smokin'," then plants a kiss in the hollow under my earlobe.

Ew.

I pull away. I don't want Jack kissing me. He doesn't seem to care. The song ends, he's stepping back, and I'm already forgotten. Without a word I veer away from him, fully intending to spend the rest of the evening with Hannah and Marty, when my dad scoops me up for a fox-trot.

"Lovely speech, Charles," I say once we're back on the parquet. "Not too long, not too political, not too self-absorbed. I'll bet you've got this one in the bag."

"Very funny," he mutters, but he's smiling down at me. "You look very pretty tonight."

"Thanks, Dad."

"Everything all right?"

This song's not long enough for me to relate the sorry state of my love life, so I just say, "Everything's great."

"Your article is the talk of the town. Are you going to take up journalism part time?"

"I think I'll leave that to Aurelia. And Laura. How's she doing lately?"

"She'll be fine."

I don't doubt it. Everyone in the office attended her grandmother's funeral, and Laura held up magnificently. She's stronger than I ever thought she was.

"We're having lunch next week," I tell my dad.

"Good." He pauses then says, "I'm proud of you, by the way. Not only for helping Laura, but for rising above everything lately."

"Did you ever have any doubts? I *am* your daughter, after all. Besides, you were the one who told me to go out and do that whole 'living life' thing, which happened to be a pretty timely message." When he squints at me dubiously, I protest, "Hey, I listen to you!"

"Mm. I think you can do more."

"More what?"

"That whole 'living life' thing," he quotes me as the music stops. He leads me off the floor, straight to Conn, leaving me there with a wink and a kiss on the cheek…and a significant look in Conn's direction.

"You should listen to your father," Conn says with a smile.

"This is a conspiracy, isn't it?"

"I know nothing. How's your date going?"

I roll my eyes. "It's not a date."

"Mm, you're right. Or it's a bad one. I mean, if you were *my* date, I wouldn't leave you alone like this. Someone else could come up and sweep you off your feet."

"Really? What have you heard? Who's interested?"

I'm pretending to look around the room for a likely candidate when Conn puts his warm hand on my bare back, and it makes me jump.

"Care to dance?"

"Thought you'd never ask."

But as he turns me toward an open spot on the floor, the music ends abruptly. Rose climbs the steps to the stage and taps the microphone, drawing three thumps out of it. Looks like she's starting up the bachelor auction a little early. She probably can't wait any longer. After an enthusiastic introduction relating the rules and that this year's charity recipient will be the Abbott's Bay food pantry, she cycles through the volunteers pretty quickly, employing her vast experience separating the wealthy from their money to rack up lots of donations.

When Jack's name comes up, I look around, realizing I haven't seen him since our dance. He doesn't come to the stage. Rose calls his name repeatedly, but there's no sign of him. I scan the crowd for Sasha and don't see her either. Fancy that.

I have to help Rose out—she's starting to sound a little frantic. Thinking Jack might be outside on the terrace having a cigarette, which he's been known to indulge in once in a while, I head for the bank of French doors overlooking the golf course. I shove aside the heavy brocade draperies, and my arm smacks into something solid. I absently wonder what idiot tucked away a piece of furniture or display pedestal where someone could walk right into it. Then I realize the pedestal just swore.

I pull away the fabric to find Jack. And Sasha.

I groan. "Oh, not *again*."

Sasha gasps, flustered. Jack grins and brushes down his hair. "Miss Melanie. This is awkward."

"We were just—" Sasha begins, but her words die out as she focuses her startled gaze past me.

"Oh, hey, man," Conn says, coming up next to me. "You're going to miss your auction slot. Don't chicken out on me, now."

"Uh…"

As Jack stumbles over his words, I feel Conn's whole body stiffen beside me. "Something going on?"

"Don't ask," I snarl before Sasha or Jack can start making excuses. Never one to know when to quit, Jack opens his mouth to speak, and I can't stop myself from lashing out. "Don't even bother. Nobody wants to hear it." I start to turn away, disgusted, but can't resist asking, "One thing though: has this been going on since the last decade, or do you two get together every couple of years just to keep things interesting?"

Again, Sasha's eyes flick to Conn. "Really, Melanie! What are you imply—"

"You're going to need a stepladder to climb down off that high horse, Sasha." That stops her. I look from her to Jack and sigh, exasperated. "Why can't you keep all...this..." I gesture at them helplessly, "to yourselves for once?"

Jack actually laughs. "Okay, okay, confession time." He puts his hands in his pockets, takes a breath, trots out his best game-show-host smile, and says, "It's true that Sasha and I...we were...look, we've been spending a lot of time together lately, and...hey, I don't think I need to explain." He pauses, waiting for someone to let him off the hook.

But Conn says in a raspy voice, "Oh, I think you do."

"Well, you know...sometimes we get...carried away. Can't seem to help it." He takes Sasha's hand and looks at her lovingly. Sasha's expression, however, is one of pure panic at Jack's sudden confession. He doesn't notice or doesn't care. "You get it, right?" Jack grins at Conn, implying some sort of "bro" understanding about Sasha, which is unbelievably repugnant.

When Conn doesn't agree or fist bump him or whatever Jack's expecting, just stands there staring at the couple, Jack takes it as a sign that Conn is cool with everything. It's certainly not the case. The air seems to crackle between the men. It feels like Jack's admission made things more tense, not less.

"Really glad you're okay with this, man," Jack says, oblivious. "It could have been ugly, right? And hey, M? You were a great cover." He salutes me cockily. "You are relieved of your duties. Carry on." Then Jack lets out a huge, relieved breath and claps his hands together. "Phew, it feels so good to get it out in the open, doesn't it? I think it's time for another drink. Let's hit the bar."

He barely takes two steps before Conn's blocked him. He shoves Jack roughly then grabs his lapels and pulls him up on his toes. Party guests nearby, startled by the sudden commotion, freeze in their tracks and stare at the men.

"What did I tell you, Rossiter?" Conn growls, expression

coldly livid.

Jack laughs again, but this time it's pretty shaky. "Hey, don't bend the suit. Tell me what? You know, you tell me a lot of things—"

"I made a special detour to the Hamptons last week for this very reason. I *thought* I'd gotten my point across, but apparently you don't get it. How many times do I have to say it? Don't—mess—with—her."

"Conn," Sasha breathes, blushing delicately, "that's so sweet—"

"I was talking about Melanie," Conn snaps at her, letting go of Jack. Then he says, almost conversationally, as he casually unbuttons his jacket, "Hey, M? I apologize in advance, but I'm going to have to disrupt your beautiful party."

He looks over at me and flashes a ghost of a smile. Then there's a sudden, startling blur of motion—Conn lunges forward, his arm flies out, and his fist connects with Jack's face.

CHAPTER THIRTY-FIVE

―――――

"Don't ever make me hit you again," Conn snaps at Jack, who's on the floor, his hands to his face, Sasha kneeling over him. Then he turns his attention to his knuckles and mutters a calm, understated, "Ow."

Among the gasps and shrieks—I'm certain I can hear Constance exclaiming in the crowd—I demand, "Conn, what the *hell*?"

"Sorry, but he's had it coming for a long time."

"Of course he did. I'm not arguing that. I mean, what detour to the Hamptons?"

"It's why I was late getting back. I wanted to have a little *talk* with Jack," he says, glaring at his (former?) friend. "I didn't like the way he treated you at Triple N. I didn't like the way he was flirting with you over the summer. But apparently talking doesn't work with him. And now this, tonight…I got tired of talking." He turns to me with a sheepish look on his face. "Too caveman?"

I have to be honest. "Just caveman enough."

Jack says something, but it's muffled behind his hands.

"That had better be an apology," Conn snarls over his shoulder.

"I *said*," Jack emphasizes, sitting up and blinking, "I'm pulling my investment."

"Good. I don't want your money."

"Conn…no," I whisper. He can't lose his funding because of this…because of me.

"It'll be okay," he murmurs to me with a reassuring smile. "I'll figure something else out. I'm sorry about all this. You're his date, and he's off with Sasha…I couldn't stand to see him hurt you."

"Hurt me? He didn't hurt me. I'd have to care about him first."

Conn stares at me, a new light in his eye.

Before he can reply though, a nervous-sounding Rose Perdue says loudly into her mic, "Let's continue, shall we?"

"I agree," Conn calls to her. He shakes out his hand as if to get rid of the pain in his knuckles, squares his shoulders, and rebuttons his tux. All eyes are on him as he marches across the room and leaps up onto the stage. His words are picked up by Rose's microphone: "I'm sorry about the disturbance, Rose. I believe it's my turn next?"

Never underestimate an act of chivalry, even if it arrives wearing a caveman's loincloth. The hostess beams with relief, and suddenly the space at the foot of the stage is swarming with women poised to bid. I hate to break it to them, but they don't stand a chance.

Rose barely gets a word out before my hand is in the air and I'm shouting, "Five thousand dollars. Sold. Next bachelor."

There's a dramatic pause, and I freeze for a moment. Then I climb the three steps to the stage, take hold of a highly amused Conn, and pull him down into the crowd. The women I've skunked give me dirty looks even as they clap politely, but I don't care. Everyone else is laughing. I don't care about that either.

Conn seems pleased, which is all that matters. "Very...uh...decisive on your part, Abbott. Pretty hot, in fact."

He's standing there, looking a little stunned and more handsome than I've ever seen him. I don't know what we are to each other at this point, whether we've sufficiently buried the hatchet, but I'm determined to find out. Ignoring the surge of fear in my belly at the thought that he might reject me, my arms go around his neck, and I pull him close. He lets me.

"It's been a rough month."

"It has."

"Forgive me?" I whisper.

"Already done," he whispers back. "And not just because you own me now."

Then I kiss him—and not chastely—in front of everyone we know.

"Did I say pretty hot? I meant *very* hot," he amends then goes back to kissing me in the middle of the crowd.

I practically faint with relief.

* * *

"I can't believe you punched Jack," I marvel as I gingerly place a cloth napkin with some ice in it on his hand resting on the bar. "It was pretty much exactly the way I pictured a fight with Jack would go too—one pop in the nose and it's over. Except…did he ever say 'Not the face'? I always figured he'd say that."

"Hey, I talked myself out of it for years. I couldn't anymore."

"Years? How many years?"

"About fifteen."

Keeping my eyes on the makeshift ice pack, I ask carefully, "So…you knew?"

"About him and Sasha? First I suspected; later I knew for sure."

"I…I…" I can't believe I'm about to tell him this. Suddenly, though, it's clear that I need to get this out in the open. "I knew."

"Sometimes I think everybody did."

"No, I mean…I knew before the wedding. And…and…I should have told you," I whisper. "I've always felt terrible about it. Instead, I talked her into going through with it, even though she was having doubts. Conn, I'm so sorry—"

"Hey. Don't. I figured it out before the wedding too."

I stare at him, horrified.

"I know. And I married her anyway. Naïve? Optimistic? Stupid? Maybe all three at once. She swore she only wanted me, and I chose to believe her. I thought we deserved a shot at making it work." He looks down at his hand as he flexes his fingers under the ice, and he's silent so long I start to worry. Then he squints up at me and says, "God, the wedding though. That was a weird day, wasn't it?"

I don't know what to say, so I just wait.

"For instance, you," he continues, gazing at me warmly,

"you bled for me."

"That's a little exaggerated."

"No, you literally did. You fixed that…that weird twig on my lapel, remember?"

"Yes." Of course I do. I remember every moment.

"And you spent the rest of the day with a huge bandage on your thumb."

"I wanted to save the smaller ones for Sasha, in case she needed them."

"Every time I looked at you, all day, all I could see was that giant honkin' Band-Aid. It was a good look for you."

"I was trying to start a fashion trend. It didn't catch on."

"You were trying," he corrects me softly, "to make everything right. Like you always do." Conn abandons the ice pack, pulls me into his arms, and kisses me. "That's when I knew you'd grown up to become a good person, Melanie Abbott. And you have been ever since."

"Oh, I don't know about that—"

"I do. Want to get out of here?"

I'm all for that. "I'll get my purse."

Conn fills another napkin with ice and offers it to Jack, who's now in a chair, holding the bridge of his swelling nose. Jack takes it but shoots his friend a dark look. They don't exchange a word.

The minute Conn crosses the floor, folks from town converge on him, dying to know why Abbott's Bay's favorite son walloped someone in the middle of the country club. As if Conn wasn't enough of a legend already. A small smile steals across my lips as I scoop up my bag. Then there's a hand on my arm, holding me back. Sasha.

"Melanie. It seems congratulations are in order. You and Conn…that's *amazing*."

Good grief, she doesn't need to make it sound so unbelievable.

"Look, Sasha…"

"Oh, don't apologize."

"I wasn't going to."

"I'm happy for you. Really."

"Wasn't asking for your approval either."

"You finally got what you wanted," she says softly. "It's commendable."

"And you got yours."

"I admire your fortitude," she continues as though I haven't spoken. "And your patience. It just goes to show, if you wait long enough, sometimes you get your chance. This time it really paid off." She tilts her head gracefully, studying me like a specimen in a lab. "It makes sense though. Both of you tied to Abbott's Bay for the rest of your lives. You might as well be tied to each other at the same time."

"You make Abbott's Bay sound like a death sentence."

"No, no, it's fine. Some people prefer being big fish in small ponds."

"You can't mean Conn," I say, stunned. "He's meant for big things, whether or not you and your boyfriend are backing him. I assume you're pulling your funds as well."

She shrugs. "He did punch Jack."

"Which was *fabulous*. But I thought you, of all people, would want to help him. After everything you put him through, don't you think you owe him at least that much?"

Two tiny spots of pink appear on her prominent cheekbones. "You know, when Conn and I were married, I kept encouraging him to dream bigger, do greater things. He rejected all my suggestions, all my plans. He doesn't want real success. It's what ended our marriage."

"Funny, I thought your obsession with Jack Rossiter ended your marriage."

"Jack chooses success—real success, not little nickel-and-dime ideas. Conn doesn't. I had to give up on him."

"Apparently you didn't give up completely, considering you were trying to get him back over the summer."

"Oh, Melanie." She's got that infernal condescending tone in her voice, implying I don't understand how grownups think. It makes me hate her—completely—for the first time in my life. "I wasn't trying to get him back. When Conn invited me to Abbott's Bay to talk about the restaurant, I thought it was the perfect time to try to make amends between us. To smooth the way between Jack and Conn…for the future." She puts her hand on her belly and gives me a superior little smile. "I want us all to act like mature adults."

"You're…?"

"Due in January. A boy, we hope. We're finding out next week. We'll get married after that. When I'm less of a *whale*."

Do I need to point out at this moment that there isn't even the slightest hint of a bump? No, I do not.

I hide my fingers behind my purse and count quickly. Due in January means conceived in April. She might not have known she was pregnant right away, but as a doctor, she probably figured it out earlier than the rest of us would. By the end of July, when she and Jack visited Abbott's Bay? She had to know then.

"But you haven't told Conn yet."

"There never seems to be the right moment. Oh, I tried. Believe me. I had him alone, the night of the festival, on the beach, and then there you were, dropping your cell phone and looking adorably disheveled in the moonlight. I tried to get him up to the house, but he stayed behind, because he'd always rather be arguing with you about God knows what. I tried to get him away from the hospital, but he wanted to stay and be a hero for you to lean on. You're just…always in the *way*, Melanie."

I ignore her jabs. It never had anything to do with me. I know she could have found a time to tell him if she really wanted to. No, there never seemed to be a "right moment" because, even though Sasha's acting pretty happy with the way her life has turned out, it's obvious that in addition to the future Rossiter in her belly, she's also carrying a hefty dose of guilt that's keeping her from confessing everything to Conn. And there's a tight set to her mouth that makes me think she's not entirely over the moon about this turn of events.

But all I say is, "You'll want to see to your fiancé. Don't let me keep you."

I disengage from Sasha and catch up with Conn. When I reach him, he draws me to his side.

"What was all that about?"

"I found someone else besides your mom who doesn't approve of us," I murmur, taking his arm.

"Who cares what she thinks?"

"She's sure got a mean streak."

"I *told* you she wasn't perfect. So can you get that out of your head, finally?"

"Done and done. But...there's something else." If Sasha isn't going to tell him, I have to. I refuse to repeat my mistakes from a dozen years ago and keep any more secrets. "About her and Jack."

"Well, if they're together—again, yet, whatever—I'd assume they're planning on getting married?"

"Yes. And sometimes things happen in a different order."

"Oh." Conn goes very still, and my stomach twists. "Baby?"

"Right."

Then he shrugs. Not in an uncaring way, but as a gesture of acceptance. "She did say she was ready to settle down. You got that part right when you speculated about what she said to me this summer."

"Somehow I get the feeling she might be having second thoughts about who she settles down *with*."

"If they haven't been able to stay away from each other all these years, maybe they're inevitable."

I laugh a little. "They can be together to protect two other people from their...*imperfections*."

"They sure can leave scars on us unsuspecting folk."

"Oh, I don't know. I think you've recovered pretty well."

"Thanks to you."

Conn smiles down at me, and I swear, the rest of the world really does go away. My heart blooms in my chest and a warmth fills me from head to toe. I've never been happier.

My dad passes us on his way back into the ballroom. "There's my little girl."

"Honestly, Dad..."

"Take good care of this one, all right?" he says to Conn.

"Yes, sir—don't have to tell me twice."

Charles kisses me on the cheek, claps Conn on the back, and says to him, "Don't forget—call me Monday," before moving past us.

"What are you two plotting?" I ask Conn.

He sighs—happily—and kisses the top of my head.

"Who needs Jack's money anyway? Looks like I have new investors."

"My dad?"

"Your dad…and, when your dad told them about the Deep Brew C franchise, about a dozen more of our neighbors."

I glance over my shoulder at the full ballroom, which is finally back to normal after Conn and Jack's little dustup. The band has even started playing again. "Gotta love Abbott's Bay."

"Oh, I do. Now…how about giving me some orders, since you paid for me fair and square?"

I pretend to think for a moment. "You can make me some coffee."

CHAPTER THIRTY-SIX

————

Deep Brew C is dark and chilly this late at night. Despite the restaurant's generous space, it feels intimate, especially when Conn closes the door soundly behind us. A single lamp burns beside the cash register, along with some subdued track lighting highlighting some new decorative additions to the place: Hannah's paintings. When Conn found out she'd been painting dreamy watercolors of Abbott's Bay landmarks, he invited her to display them at DBC. It turns out the restaurant is the perfect gallery space for them. She's sold quite a few to the natives, and she'll definitely sell even more when the tourists return.

Conn also added Hannah's boyfriend to the DBC family. A regular bromance has sprung up between Conn and Marty based on their common interests of compost, heirloom vegetables, and free-range chickens, so when Hannah and Marty decided to stay in town, Conn happily gave him a part-time job. It's been working out fabulously—Marty's a natural, and he and Conn are of the same mind regarding the mission of the place.

"Sit down. I'll be back in a minute."

Conn disappears into the back hallway, and I sit at the bar. When he comes back, he says nothing, just slips behind the bar and falls into his usual rhythm, setting cups in saucers, leaning down to get the milk jug out of the mini fridge under the counter, grinding the beans. I don't think I'll ever get tired of watching him work.

He makes me a cappuccino then goes back into the fridge, fussing with something behind his back so I can't see. I sip my coffee and wait. In a moment or two he turns around with a small plate in his hand, the other shielding the flicker of a candle flame from random drafts. It's a cupcake. Chocolate cake, white frosting, with curlicue chocolate shavings.

"Happy birthday."

"That's two weeks from now," I chide him, trying to hide my smile. I fail.

"I was planning on waiting, but suddenly I don't feel like it."

"I'm not going to argue when there's a cupcake involved."

He slips a rectangular, flat gift-wrapped box onto the bar next to it. "And a present."

"Well, now you're talking." I tear off the wrapping. The box contains a plain key, one I recognize, and I'm puzzled.

"I already know where to find a key to your place."

"This is the one I hid outside. I'm not leaving it out for anyone to let themselves in anymore. It's now yours. Plus, it's symbolic: I'm taking the house off the market for a while."

I'm more than a little surprised. "Why?" It's true he hasn't had any offers yet, but it hasn't been on the market that long. "It'll sell. Let it sit for a while longer—"

"Hang on. I'm taking it off the market for now so you can have free rein with it. Go ahead—renovate it the way you've always wanted. I mean top to bottom, not just spruce it up. You were right," he shrugs. "It's too tired looking, and nobody wants to take on that challenge. So do your thing. Then we'll turn it back over to Laura to sell."

"Wait a minute. Back up. When you asked me to list it—"

"And you *refused*—"

"Can't guilt me."

"You thought I needed the money because DBC was in trouble. It wasn't—which you would have found out if you'd just *asked* me—"

"Yeah, yeah. So why are you selling it?"

"Well, let me tell you a little story." With a sigh, he rounds the bar and sits on the stool beside me. "But blow out your candle and make a wish first, before you have a puddle of wax in the middle of your frosting."

I do as he suggests, sneaking a finger full of frosting as I turn back to Conn. "Okay, tell me a story."

"When I asked you to list the house last spring, I had

decided to sell because I was getting kind of...restless."

"You were bored with Abbott's Bay?" Unthinkable. "You told me you'd never leave here."

"I *wanted* to stay, but I didn't think I could anymore. I...couldn't take being around you."

I'm horrified. "Did I annoy you that much? You told me it was an act, a smokescreen."

"It was. I figured if I stayed annoyed, I wouldn't act like an idiot around you. There I was, crushing on you so hard, while you looked right through me."

God, that was what Maude said when she asked me for help—she accused me of never noticing other people around me. And it may have been true. But never with Conn. I take his hands in mine and say earnestly, "I always saw you. Always."

"But not the way I wanted you to. You didn't feel the same way."

I'm so stunned I don't know what to do. So I shove his shoulder. "Why didn't you ask me out, you doofus? You could have convinced me. Easily."

He grins. "Sure, I know that *now*."

"So you were going to sell everything you owned and leave?"

"I thought maybe I could get you out of my head if I didn't see you every day."

"Thank goodness you stuck around." I give him a long, reassuring kiss. "So why did you end up listing it with Laura anyway? God, when I saw that *For Sale* sign, I thought you were going to dump me and move to Provincetown."

"What? Never!" Conn takes a breath and says in a rush, "I still want to sell it because you hate it. I want you to be happy. I figured I'd sell the ugly house so you and I can have a fresh start...in a house you like."

You and I? Conn is asking me to move in with him? I lean forward and interlace my fingers at the back of his neck. "No." Then, before Conn can get worried, I add quickly, "You love the house. And I...*like* it. We should live in it."

"Really?"

"*If* you really meant it when you said I could renovate it."

"Oh, I meant it."

He looks so happy I can't resist kissing him again. "There's just one small problem."

"What's that?"

"Us living in sin. Your mother's head would explode."

"Hm. You're right. We can't have that."

Well, damn. I don't expect him to backpedal so quickly.

I'm scrambling to come up with a way to invoke a no-backsies rule when he says evenly, "Maybe we should get married then."

A buzz starts in the back of my head and my brain switches off. My breathing grows shallow, and I vaguely wonder if I'm hyperventilating. Especially when Conn brings out a ring. The man. Has. A ring. A gorgeous one. I look from the diamond to his anxious but hopeful handsome face to the diamond to Conn to the cupcake (don't judge—I said my brain has switched off) and back to Conn.

"Wh-where did you get this?" I breathe, awed.

"Oh, I've had it for a while. Tonight…it seemed like the right time."

A while? How long is a while? "So you didn't…because…the other day, when you found out Jack asked me to the ball…"

He laughs softly. "No, I didn't rush out and buy a ring out of jealousy. In fact, if you really want to try to get Jack away from Sasha, just say the word…"

"And what? You'd support me?"

"Well, no. I'd question your sanity, to be honest."

"So would I." My eyes are drawn to the ring again. "And you're serious?"

"Completely."

"I mean…*me*?"

He puts on an exaggerated puzzled expression and glances around the empty restaurant, pointedly indicating he hasn't confused me with anyone else. It's amazing how he can still get a laugh out of me even when I'm a stunned wreck.

Then he grows serious, saying earnestly, "Melanie, I love you. I've loved you for a long time, in so many ways over the years I don't even know exactly when I fell in love with you, but I did. Completely. Wholeheartedly. And permanently. Do you need convincing? Because I've got ammo for that. We've known each other forever. You know me better than anyone in the world."

"And you know *me* better than anyone in the world. That's the problem."

"How is it a problem?"

My insides surge as I brace myself to reveal my deepest fear. "A while back, you said I was perfect. We both know I'm not."

"M, come on."

"I'm a spoiled brat."

"You're not."

I just raise an eyebrow at him.

"You grew out of it," he amends.

"I waged a reign of terror."

"You grew out of that too. I'm not so sure Taylor did, but..."

God, he's got me laughing again. But I still need to get this out. "And the whole TV thing...you accused me of doing it because it was a boost to my ego, but that wasn't the reason. I wanted to be..." I hesitate, because saying it out loud might make it seem as ludicrous as I suspect it is.

"What?"

"Worthy of you."

"What in the world are you talking about?"

"You and Jack and Sasha all have your 'big things' that you do, the things that make you special. Being on TV gave me a chance to...I don't know...*be* somebody, get to that level."

"Are you kidding? You already are somebody. You're Melanie Abbott, totally unique and irreplaceable. Empress of Abbott's Bay. Own it. There's nothing better."

"Be serious."

"Look, whatever you thought you were trying to achieve, that level you were trying to reach...it's not real. There is no *next level*. And you're *definitely* not beneath Jack or Sasha. I mean, look at them. All the money in the world can't fix that hot mess."

"You're making it really hard to be serious right now."

"Do you want to go back to Triple N and try again? Be

the next Trudy Helmet-Head?"

"No," I say emphatically. "Lanie was a horrible person, and I'm glad she's dead. Good riddance."

"So you don't regret quitting? You could have been famous."

"Famous for all the wrong reasons. No, no regrets. Besides, I can't go back now. You punched my boss."

Conn laughs then takes my hand. Softly and seriously, he says, "M, you have nothing to worry about. You think I don't know you're not perfect? I've seen you at your worst for years."

"Hey!"

"*And* at your best. Believe me—your best far outweighs your worst." I'm still dubious, and my expression must show it, because he adds, "Of course you're not perfect. Nobody is. When I said you were perfect, I meant perfect for *me*. I love you, Melanie Abbott. You say you love me—do you mean it?"

"I do. I love you with all my heart."

"Okay then. I want to spend the rest of my life with you. If you'll have me." I'm back to being speechless. This is really happening. I must be quiet longer than I think, because Conn asks worriedly, "Melanie? Are you freaking out?"

Yes. Yes, I am freaking out. But not for the reason he thinks. I'm observing our entire lives collapsing in on our present reality. My head is flooded with memories of Conn and me, at all stages of our lives together—when we were kids, playing on the beach…okay, he was playing football and I was running up and down the sidelines, in awe of him…when I was a teenager and almost shy around the cocky collegiate who seemed so much more mature than I was, Conn at his wedding, our close friendship over the past several years. I've known and loved a dozen different versions of Conn, and now they've all converged into the wonderful man in front of me. The one who's waiting for my answer.

As if there's ever been more than one option.

"Yes," I whisper.

"You *are* freaking out?"

"No! I mean yes, I'll marry you."

"You will?"

His bewildered squeak makes me laugh even as I start

crying—happy tears. "Don't sound so shocked, will you please? Yes. I'll marry you." My voice is shaky, but my decision isn't. Not at all.

Finally his face lights up, and he grabs me, holds me tight, kisses me over and over. "I promise," he whispers into my hair, "I will do everything I can to make you happy for the rest of your life."

"You've got a pretty good head start already." As he rests his forehead against mine and brushes my tears away with his thumb, I murmur, "Melanie Garvey," for the first time. Well, the first time out loud, anyway. "That'll work."

"Oh, no. You can't change your name."

"Why not?"

"Because you're Melanie Abbott first, last, and always. Don't ever change."

EPILOGUE

———

Two and a half weeks later, my dad wins his assembly seat, and quite handily too. He's so excited, he calls his erstwhile boyfriend Jerome to tell him, and they have a lovely, long conversation. I'm hopeful for a reconciliation.

Election Day also happens to be my birthday this year. My mother calls—an interesting, unique twist on our birthday phone tag. I let it go to voicemail. I call her back eventually.

Two months later, Sasha and Jack have a baby girl. Conn and I send a card. It's a nice card.

Four months after that, a party of DBC loyalists travels from Abbott's Bay to the Cape to celebrate the opening of DBC II in Provincetown. It's a stunner of a place, which Tommy will be managing. Conn hates to lose him, but he knows the new restaurant will be in good hands. Besides, he fills Tommy's old job instantly, bumping Marty up to full-time manager. There's much happy-dancing by me and Hannah about this.

Three months after *that*, Conn and I have a glorious August wedding on the beach. Bare feet, picnic food, dancing till dawn—everything that makes us happy. (And everything that's the complete opposite of Conn and Sasha's dignified, traditional nuptials. Yes, I planned it that way on purpose.) We get top billing in the *Abbott's Bay Bugle*'s Bugle Bites column. All our friends are there, including Beebs and Ornette (as a couple—I was right all along—it just took them a little more time to get there), Hannah and Marty, Vernon and Zoë (who are so happy to spend another summer together in Abbott's Bay), Taylor and some new guy she's dating, and as many of the residents of Abbott's Bay who want to attend. Dad is thrilled, as is Bruce Garvey. Constance is another matter, but I'll win her over eventually. Never underestimate Melanie Abbott. Sasha and Jack politely send their regrets, claiming their daughter isn't quite up to traveling yet. They send a card. It's a nice card. Ours was better.

Then, in the dim, dove gray light of a new morning, Conn pulls me away from the party, which is finally winding down, and takes me to Deep Brew C.

"Making me coffee?" I ask, as he leads me inside, the train of my lace dress swishing on the oak floorboards.

"I will if you want. But I have a wedding present for you."

"It can be coffee."

He doesn't turn the lights on, just leads me through the shadowy restaurant to my favorite wingback chair, and whispers against my ear, "You might start Your New Best Friend up again, or you might not. But no matter what, this is always, always your spot."

Standing on the cushion of the chair is an engraved brass place card that reads, *Reserved—M.A.*

My breath catches, and suddenly I'm crying and laughing at the same time. I've got what I've always wanted. And the *Reserved* sign too.

ABOUT THE AUTHOR

Jayne Denker divides her time between working hard to bring the funny into her romantic comedies (six and counting) and raising a young son who's way too clever for his own good. She lives in a small village in western New York that is in no way, shape, or form related to the small village that's the setting for her Marsden novels, *Down on Love, Picture This,* and *Lucky for You.* When she's not hard at work on another romcom, the social media addict can usually be found frittering away startling amounts of time on Facebook (Jayne Denker Author) and Twitter (@JDenkerAuthor). She has an Instagram account (@JayneDenkerAuthor), but she's not sure why. Stop by her blog, http://jaynedenker.com, and say hi.

Enjoyed this book? Check out these other romantic reads available in print now from Gemma Halliday Publishing:

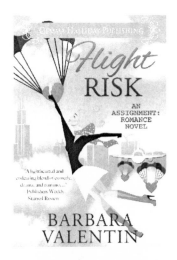

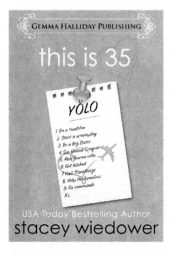

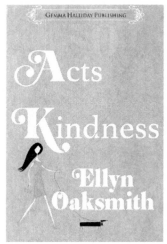

www.GemmaHallidayPublishing.com

CPSIA information can be obtained
at www.ICGtesting.com
Printed in the USA
LVOW12s0020240118
563793LV00001B/17/P